Imaginary Journeys I

Unabridged Translation of
Original Karl May Manuscripts Published under various Titles
as listed below each story heading

**Travel and Adventure Tales
by
Karl May**

**Translated by
Herbert Windolf**

Original German text by Karl May [1842 – 1912]
First published in various magazines and papers
as noted under each story heading

English translation by Herbert Windolf

ISBN: 978-0-9794855-6-5

This book is printed on acid free paper.

Nemsi Books - rev. 02/23/2008

Acknowledgements

The following original stories were downloaded from the Karl-May-Gesellschaft web site.

I am very much indebted to the following friends and relative who kindly edited my translation of Karl May's adventure stories. They are in alphabetical order: Mavis Brauer (An Adventure on Ceylon), Jim Conley (In Mistake Canyon), Peter Dickinson (An Oil Fire), Jon Haupt (The Fire in the Oil Valley), Kathee & Vern Johnson (The First Elk & The Tornado), Zene Krogh (The Revenge of the Ehri & The Ehri), Matt Lukaszewski (Inn-nu-woh & Winnetou), Felipe Morales (The Stakeman), Keith Powers (A Prairie Fire), and Anne Schwerdt (The Revenge of the Mormon) and, finally, Manfred Wenner (The Hamaïl & Ibn al-'Amm), who, in particular, verified the Arabic terms Karl May used and transcribed them into contemporary Arabic and English.

Gratefully acknowledged are also Michael Michalak's elucidations on the 'Stune' scent in the 13th story, The Fire in the Oil Valley, as well as his contributions to the individual Forewords to the stories.

Herb Windolf, Prescott, Arizona

Karl May – translated by Herbert Windolf

Foreword

Karl May's travelogues and adventure novels cover the globe. While the reader may be familiar with his novels, many of his short stories are unknown. Following is a sampler of the writer's shorter works, many of which take place in the Wild West, while others happen on islands in the Pacific Ocean, on Ceylon (Sri Lanka), North Africa and the Sudan. Some of these narratives feature May's well-known heroes, Old Shatterhand, Winnetou and Sam Hawkens, some are told by May's persona, while others are accounts of different characters.

From several of the narratives the reader may learn, if not already known, how Karl May modified his story lines to incorporate aspects of them into later ones, or, how he used entire sections in subsequent novels.

Enjoy!

Herb Windolf, Prescott, Arizona

Karl May – translated by Herbert Windolf

Contents:

Karl May – translated by Herbert Windolf

Imaginary Journeys I

Karl May – translated by Herbert Windolf

1. Inn-nu-woh

The Indian Chief

In this early 1875 travelogue, Karl May created the outline of his greatest hero, who was to become the famous Apache Chief Winnetou. One can find in this story about Inn-nu-woh some of the noble characteristics that were to become the hallmark of Winnetou. However, Inn-nu-woh, although noble, is in many ways still the savage, a far cry from the almost saintly Winnetou who died in Winnetou III.

This story appeared in 'Deutsches Familienblatt' (German Family Newspaper) in 1875 titled 'Aus der Mappe eines Vielgereisten' (From the Portfolio of a Much Traveled).

As you read the following story, called 'Winnetou', notice the way it differs from Inn-nu-woh, and you will gain a glimpse of the evolution of Karl May's stories and characters.

It was that time of year when Yellow and Black Fever made it hazardous for Whites in New Orleans. Strong justification was needed to live in the miasmic atmosphere of the lower Mississippi. Those who could afford it exchanged the swampy river delta for the cleaner air found at higher elevations.

The cautious aristocracy of the city had long since made itself invisible. Those who had been held back for business reasons, tried to get away. Already there was talk of several sudden deaths. Thus, I too, had gathered my few belongings and stood waiting for the steamer at the pier to travel to St. Louis, where relatives were expecting me.

Ned, the old gray-haired Negro, the hotel's factotum, who had shown me particular affection, had carried my luggage to the pier. While standing next to me, he leaned against a crane that heaved the enormously heavy loads on and off board ship. Baring his teeth in broad grins, he made droll remarks about the various characters busily wending their way around us.

Suddenly, he grabbed my arm and, with a strong jerk, turned me around to look behind me.

"Do Master see Indian over there?"

"Which one? Do you mean the sinister looking fellow coming towards us?"

"Yes, yes, Master. Does Master know Indian?"

"No."

"Indian is great Chief of Sioux. Name is Inn-nu-woh. Is best swimmer in United States."

"Really? That would take a lot."

"Well, sir. But it be so, really so."

I did not respond but looked the man over closely, who was just then passing us with a proud bearing. I knew his name. I had heard much about him but had always doubted the truth of the wonderful stories told about his expertise and endurance in swimming. He was not very tall but the built of his compact body, in particular the breadth of his chest, caused my previous doubts to resurface now.

Now an open coach appeared carrying an elderly gentleman and a young, veiled lady. The amply dressed coachman directed the chariot through the crowd with obvious lack of consideration, snapping his whip about the ears of those in his path. Alarmed, people scattered. Only the Indian kept on walking quietly, not budging a hair's width from his original direction. There was room enough on the side of the carriage to pass on smooth, wide pavement stones, just as there was right across on the small pavement.

"Make room up front, redskin! Are you deaf?" the coachman shouted. Despite the loud and rude call, Inn-nu-woh continued on his way without turning. The driver went on, brandishing his whip, "Get off to the side, Nigger, or my whip will show you the way!"

Although the term 'Nigger' is the greatest verbal insult to an Indian, Inn-nu-woh did not seem to pay attention to it but slowly continued in his stride. That's when the whip cracked once more. The strap sliced across the red man's face, where the trace of the strike was instantly visible. The next moment the Indian stood on the box and, with a strike from below, tore the rude coachman's lip and nose open. He lifted the coachman from his seat and dumped him forcefully onto the pavement, where he remained silent, his arms and legs akimbo.

All had happened so quickly that the gentleman in the carriage could not come to the aid of his employee. He now pulled a revolver from his pocket and pointing it at the Indian, shouted:

"Damnation, canaille, that will be for you, if my man does not return to the coach within a minute."

Without any change of his features or batting an eyelash, the threatened Indian took his rifle from his shoulder and aimed it at the Yankee. Surely, a serious action between the two would have happened, had not several policemen hurried up to intercede, asking the owner of the carriage to pocket his weapon again.

"Please, drive on, sir," warned one of them. "Your coachman is up again and, aside from his torn face, will not experience any lasting damage. Your incautious man ought to know that, according to Indian law, a strike like this can only be expiated by death."

Following American custom in which one never engages in the disputes of others, people often display their interest in a quarrel only by making room to fight it out. In this manner, the bystanders had formed a circle around the carriage to see the outcome of the event. However, when the shrill whistle of the approaching steamer sounded, the risen coachman, upon his master's urgent call, directed the coach towards the landing bridge. The circle of people quickly dissolved and everyone hurried off to gain a good place on the boat.

It wasn't one of the usual, very comfortably equipped passenger boats, but one of the giant packet ships, which serve only occasionally for the transport of a large number of people who need to travel at the beginning of the fever season. This is why this ship was missing in the comforts by which the Yankee makes travel less cumbersome. On a packet ship like this the passengers had to find accommodation where they could find it.

After my Negro had bid his farewell, I climbed onto a pile of merchandise balls flanking a row of square boxes that stretched almost along the entire deck. From up there, I had a more open view. A cool breeze also fanned my forehead pleasantly. Furthermore, I could unceremoniously stretch out up here, which made my spot a rather splendid one.

Looking around, I noticed that the owner of the carriage with his lady, as well as the Indian, had also come on board. In any case, the owner was a member of the upper class and took the packet boat only to escape the dangerous grounds as quickly as possible. The Indian might have sold a bale of furs in the city and was now returning to the prairie, where he might lead his tribe in new hunts and adventures. He also seemed to find it too hot and uncomfortable in the crowd below and climbed up but, so as not to invade my space, stretched out on the first crate.

As he sat down, a sound shattered the air, so deep and rumbling, so roaring and terrible, that every single passenger jumped up frightened, looking about for the cause of this frightful noise. Only Inn nu woh remained totally at ease, although the angry, thunder-like rumble had come precisely from below his seat. Not a feature of his brown, immobile face displayed even the least expression of surprise or consternation, like the alarm displayed by the other people on the deck.

A hatch then opened from which a man climbed out. Seeing him, I immediately had the explanation for the roar. I had seen him in Boston, in New York and in Charleston and had established a close acquaintanceship with him. It was Fred Forster, the famous tamer of wild beasts who, at the time, was visiting the major cities of the United States with his menagerie and, wherever he came, caused a justified sensation by the power he exercised even over the wildest of beasts.

The crates were his and contained the cages of his zoological collection. The Indian had taken his place on the travel lodgment of the lion and had disturbed the animal in its siesta, causing it to produce the angry roar. Forster had heard it and, of course, hurried up to check on its cause.

In Europe, where people are more cautious, one would beware very much of transporting an entire menagerie on a ship that also carries passengers. But

3

Americans are less cautious in this respect. On the American frontier, danger is ever present. People are familiar with it and know it in its various permutations. One respects it, but is not afraid of it. They are used meeting the four-legged denizens of forest and prairie courageously and fearlessly, thus they are not shy when meeting animals in a tame condition outside the wilderness. Only the unexpected had alarmed the travelers. When the content of the numerous crates became known, people laughed about the fear they had displayed. The owner of the animals was urged by everyone to open the covers of the cages.

"Well, I don't mind if you'll enjoy it, ladies and gentlemen. A bit of fresh air will do the creatures good. But ask the captain first. I can't do it on my own," he told them. Turning to the Indian he said:

"Won't you be good enough to descent from your throne, man? The lion is king and doesn't care to have anyone on top of it!"

The Indian, without moving his lips and with only a slight movement of his hand, indicated that he found it quite pleasant up there and that he had no intention of vacating his spot.

"Well, it's fine by me. But don't complain if something unpleasant happens to you."

The captain was brought over who, after a moment's hesitation, gave permission to open the crates on one side. With the help of the handlers, this was quickly accomplished. Since Forster could use the opportunity to feed the animals, the spectators were soon offered a highly interesting and entertaining spectacle.

The collection consisted mostly of truly gorgeous specimens. Particularly, a Bengal tigress drew much attention. The animal had only recently been captured. It was brought from India to America, where his current owner had purchased it. Grown up in the wilderness and as yet not fully tamed, it offered an imposing sight, and by the build of its mighty limbs, the innate suppleness of its movements, and the marrow-jarring sound of its voice, elicited loud exclamations of admiration.

"Do you also enter the cage, sir?" one of the bystanders asked the tamer.

"Why not? The beast can't be tamed from the outside. One needs to enter to get its respect."

"But you risk your life every time."

"That I've done already a thousand times and am quite used to it. I carry a weapon. A single strike with this blackjack will stun the animal. If the strike is made hard and proper, it subdues even the strongest animal. But I rarely need it. The power of a true and right tamer lies somewhere else. At times, I enter a cage without any weapon."

"But you wouldn't dare enter this one like that!"

"Who says so?"

"No, you wouldn't dare!" challenged the carriage owner who, until now, apart from everyone else, had not looked at the cages. His companion, who was afraid of their occupants, had walked to the front of the ship where she gazed across the railing into the waters rushing up to the bow.

"I wager a thousand dollars for my assertion!"

The American has a passion for betting, and where he finds a spicy opportunity for one, he will not let it pass.

"You are not being cautious, sir!" Forster replied. "Look how quiet and fearlessly the Indian sits on the cage of the Namibian lion. Do you really think that I, the owner of these animals, have less courage?"

"Pshaw!" the Yankee responded with a disdainful move of his hand. "It's not courage this kind of people has, but ignorance and stupidity. Had he an understanding of the danger of his position, he would soon be standing down here with us and crawl in some corner to hide. He doesn't even know what a lion is. These red scoundrels know only how to cowardly approach an enemy by night to attack him from behind. But to face a danger openly, they fall short."

Inn-nu-woh understood every single word but the features of his finely chiseled face remained immobile. Not a limb of his body moved even the slightest.

The tamer said:

"You are mistaken in the Indian as well as myself. Whoever gets to know the peoples of the prairies like I have, has learned to respect them."

"Don't be ridiculous in the midst of these honorable people! Just let the very first of your small animals, maybe the porcupine over there come out, and I'm convinced that, as soon as the Indian sees it free, he will jump into the river from pure fear. These canailles are as cowardly as they are cruel. But we are getting away from our bet."

"Let's proceed then. Captain, you are the witness."

"That I am, but I can't permit you to join the tigress. I am responsible if an accident happens on board."

"But you can't forbid any free American to do with his property as he pleases. And concerning an accident, it could only happen to me. I'm man enough, sir, I can carry the responsibility myself. Don't you think so?"

The captain, like any good Yankee, was just as much interested in a good bet. Having given his warning and thus thinking to have discharged his duty, he answered:

"If you are responsible for the consequences, I don't mind you doing it. Do as you please!"

"All right then! Step back, you people!" Forster commanded and handed the captain the whip with the black jack. He then approached the cage with firm, sure steps and, with his eyes wide open facing the animal, moved the bolt.

The tigress had crouched down in the back of the narrow cage with her broad but short head resting on the outstretched front paws. Her tail had risen against the back wall and her eyes were blinking up from the bottom. When the tamer approached the gate, her eyes opened wide focusing on him. Then, her pupils narrowed more and more, her paws curved back and were pulled closer to her body. The rear of the carnivore rose silently and almost unnoticeably. The instant the bolt made its noise, a brief shiver flew over the soft, beautifully marked fur. Then, a horror causing sound thundered from between the iron bars. Forster lay prone on the floor with one of his arms torn bloodily from his shoulder. The now freed animal crossed the deck in mighty leaps.

A general scream of horror filled the air with everyone trying to save themselves. It was a moment of the greatest confusion and fear for life. People rushed, tumbling over each other, towards hatches, corners, masts and rope ladders, with the animals erupting in such a howl that even the noise of the engine became inaudible.

I had jumped back up onto the merchandise balls that I had left earlier. Now, I stood up there immobilized by horror, for there, just ahead of me, I saw the poor girl standing by the railing, impossible to be saved. The tigress leaped directly towards her and now crouched down for her ruinous leap, barely eight or nine paces away from the girl. The face of the poor child was deathly white and rigid. She stood with arms outstretched, as if calling for help, not able to make any move. In a second, she would be lost.

That's when, with catlike agility a figure leaped past me, down from the cargo balls, vaulting with long, carnivore-like leaps across the ship's central open space past the tigress. He grabbed the girl with his left hand and supported himself on the railing's upper rung with his right hand. An instant later, the two disappeared in the deep, dirty-yellow flow of the Mississippi. It was Inn-nu-woh.

A single shout filled the air emanating from all on board. Was it a shout of joy or one of new concern? No one knew, for the tigress had also launched herself over the railing in pursuit of the two people. She then disappeared in the waves. Everyone dashed to the ship's railing to look down.

The captain commanded loudly:

"Man at the wheel: Heave to! Machinist, stop!"

A short time passed when no one dared to breathe. The escaped carnivore lay on the water with its four legs stretched out from its body and with glowing eyes was watching every ripple of the water. Then, barely twenty yards away, the Indian came suddenly shooting from the water. He rose to almost half his height above the surface. One could clearly see that the nearly unconscious girl had instinctively grasped both her arms around his neck.

Inn-nu-woh had hardly time to catch his breath. He noticed the tigress had spotted him and was now rushing towards him. Again, he dove into the water to surface a distance away. He took a breath but was immediately pursued by the animal and driven down again. This terrible pursuit continued for around five minutes, which, under the conditions, became five eternities.

Many ropes had been tossed over board and the ladder had been lowered, but the smart Indian knew very well that these measures were of no help to him. Before he would be able to get up the ladder by a few feet, the tigress would have reached him. There was only one way to save himself and the girl. He had to dive underneath the ship. This was quite possible since the ship's engine was at rest. If he swam around the ship, he would have been noticed by the pursuing animal. Climbing up the ladder at port side would have been just as impossible as at starboard.

He therefore tried to remain as long as possible on the water's surface to fill his lungs with sufficient air. Gesturing with his hand, he signaled his intention and then disappeared once more.

"Ropes down at port!" the captain commanded.

Everyone hurried to this side where Inn-nu-woh quickly appeared on the surface. He headed towards the next rope.

"Come on, come on, hurry up!" the captain urged. Because his voice clearly expressed great concern and fear, everyone turned to him.

Without another word, the captain pointed to the yellow waves. All eyes followed his arm's direction and immediately, everyone shouted the same message the captain had just hollered.

Not too far away, three furrows could be seen in the water rapidly closing on the ship.

"For God's sake, hurry, hurry, the crocs are coming!" was shouted by everyone along the ship's railing.

"My child, my child, my poor child!" lamented the girl's father, bending far over the railing with wide-open eyes and fear-distorted features.

Inn-nu-woh had heard the shouts. Looking back, he realized the closeness of the new danger. He reached for the rope and with almost Herculean strength, catapulted himself up. Since he was unable to hold the girl, it was fortunate that she clung semiconsciously but tightly to his neck. He had barely reached a third of the way up to the deck, when he heard below him a dull sound as if two timbers had been banged together. The first alligator had reached the ship and had snapped at him. But he was safe now. Gripping firmly, he reached the top of the rope and climbed the railing onto the deck.

Everyone wanted to rush towards him but were prevented by a call.

"The tigress, the tigress. Look people!"

The tigress had searched for her disappeared prey and was now swimming around the stern of the ship towards the port side. Quickly, everyone rushed to the railing once more. Only the father remained with his unconscious daughter.

It was a beautiful sight to watch the quiet and strong movements of the animal.

But now three furrows moved lightning-fast towards the tigress. She tried to turn but it was already too late. There arose a roar, so terrible, so frightening that it caused the listeners' hair to stand on end. The waters were whipped up into a spray and foam, some of it splashing high. A deep, hollow gurgle sounded followed by a rattle. A funnel opened in the water whose color turned from yellow to blood-red. Then, it was quiet. The alligators had pulled the tigress into the depths.

A sigh of relief was felt by all the spectators. They looked at the two people who stood hugging each other next to the ship's funnel.

"She's alive. She's conscious again!" shouts rang out from all sides. The captain came over to offer the exhausted girl his cabin.

While everyone else had been focused on the Indian's rescue, the menagerie handlers had prepared a resting place for their master and put a makeshift bandage on him. It would be necessary to take him off the ship at the next stop for proper medical help.

Finally, the people asked for Inn-nu-woh, the girl's father not being the last.

The Indian hung way up in the shroud rungs and seemed to be giving a signal with the fur that he had taken off his shoulder. From the opposite bank, a canoe appeared, paddled strongly by two Indians who were heading towards the steamer. They came to pick up their chief. The son of the prairie does not know fixed places. He leaves civilization as he pleases and where he will find his people again.

Inn-nu-woh had climbed down. That's when a hand touched his shoulder and a trembling voice spoke:

"You must not go. You saved my daughter for which I want to show you my gratitude."

The Indian slowly turned and, while straightening up, looked intensely at the father. Then his eyes flashed over the bystanders and his voice sounded sharp and clear, as he spoke the first words to be heard from him.

"The white man is mistaken. I did not intend to save your daughter. I only jumped into the waters of the holy Father of Rivers because I feared the porcupine you let loose."

With a proud nod of his head, he turned away and stepped down the lowered ladder to paddle off with his two people. For some time one could see his rich, mane-like hair waving in the wind. The sound of his voice reverberated for a long time in the ears of the listeners. Today, I still think of Inn-nu-woh when people call someone a 'Hero'.

2. Winnetou

In 1878, Karl May rewrote his narrative, Inn-nu-woh, and had it published under the title 'Winnetou, A Travelogue' in the newspaper 'Omnibus'. Most of the elements and characteristics of his greatest hero, the 'Noble Indian', were now in place, except that Winnetou, at fifty years of age, was much too old in this short story!

When May wrote Winnetou I, years later, using various earlier stories to assemble the Winnetou series, he made Winnetou much younger, about twenty years of age, like the friend he was to find in the young railroad surveyor, the later Old Shatterhand, Karl May's alter ego.

The rest is history.

I had come to the United States to get to know the country and her people. After having crisscrossed the civilized East sufficiently, I found myself in New Orleans. From here, my plans were to first steamboat up to St. Louis, where I thought I could cross the prairies to reach the Rocky Mountains.

My arrival in the Metropolis of the South happened to fall at that time of year when Yellow Fever made it hazardous for Whites in the lower Mississippi area. Strong justification was needed to live in the miasmic atmosphere of the swampy river delta. Most would exchange it for the cleaner air found at higher elevations. The cautious aristocracy of the city had long since made itself invisible. Those who had been held back for business reasons tried to get away. There was already talk of several sudden deaths. Thus, I too, in due course decided to cut my visit short and use the next opportunity to travel to the capital of Missouri.

I now stood at the pier waiting for the steamboat. Ned, the old gray-haired Negro, the hotel's factotum, who had shown me particular affection, had carried my luggage here. While standing next to me, he leaned against a crane that heaved the enormously heavy loads on and off board ships. Baring his teeth in broad grins, he made droll remarks about the various characters busily wending their way around us or were waiting, like us, by the riverside.

Suddenly, he grabbed my arm and, with a strong jerk, turned me around. He then lifted his arm pointing into the agitated throng of people in front of us.

"You see Indian over there?" he asked in his poor English.

"Which one? Do you mean the sinister-looking fellow coming towards us?"

"Yes, yes, Master. Does Master know Indian?"

"No."

"Indian is great Chief of Pimo. Name is Winnetou. Is best swimmer in United States."

"Really? That would take a lot."

"Well, sir. But it be so, really so. Or does master think Ned is lying?"

I did not respond but looked the proud man over closely, who was just then passing us, looking straight ahead. His name was known to me. I had heard much about him but had always doubted the truth of the wonderful stories told about his expertise and endurance in swimming.

Winnetou was the most famous Chief of the Apache. Among their enemies, their cowardice and cunning had resulted in the abusive name of 'Pimo'. However, since Winnetou had been elected leader of his tribe the cowards had slowly transformed themselves into astute hunters and daring warriors. Their name was feared across the ridge of the Rockies and their endeavors were always successful. With little manpower they undertook daring raids through enemy territory. There was a time when at every camp fire, in the smallest bars, as well as in the saloons of the finest hotels, Winnetou and his tricks were the frequent subject of conversation.

Now, suddenly, he was here at the Mississippi to see, as he himself supposedly had said, the 'Huts of the Palefaces' and to speak with the 'Father of the White Men', the President. He had sent his few companions back across the river into the western forests to travel by himself to Washington. This had taken place several months ago. He had now returned to once more cross the enormous distance from the 'Father of Rivers' to the shores of the Pacific, a task exposing him to thousands of dangers.

He seemed to be in his early fifties. His not very tall figure was of an unusual sturdy and compact build. Especially, his chest displayed a width that a tall and long-necked Yankee could only have admired. His sojourn to the civilized East had obliged him to dress in a less conspicuous outfit. However, his full, dark hair hung in long open strands far down below his shoulders. He carried a Bowie knife in his belt and a bullet and powder bag. From a rain cover that he had picturesquely draped across one shoulder, peered the rusty barrel of a rifle that might have sent many a frontiersman the last 'valet'.

An open coach now appeared carrying an elderly gentleman and a young, veiled lady. The amply dressed coachman directed the chariot through the crowd with obvious lack of consideration, snapping his whip about the ears of those in his path. Alarmed, people scattered. Only the Indian kept on walking quietly, unconcerned of the rising noise behind him and not budging a hair's width from his original direction. There was room enough on the side for the carriage to pass on smooth, wide paving stones, just as there was right across on the small pavement.

"Make room up there, redskin! Are you deaf?" the coachman shouted. Despite the loud and rude call, Winnetou continued on his way without turning. The driver went on, brandishing his whip, "Get off to the side, Nigger, or my whip will show you the way!"

Although the term 'Nigger' is the greatest verbal insult to an Indian, Winnetou did not seem to pay attention to it but slowly continued in his stride. That's when the whip cracked once more. Its sharp strap sliced across the red man's face where the trace of the strike was instantly visible. In the blink of an eye the Indian stood on the box and with a strike of his fist from below, tore the rude coachman's lip and nose open. Winnetou then lifted the man from his seat and dumped him forcefully onto the pavement where he remained silent and motionless, his arms and legs akimbo.

The horses stood still. All had happened so quickly that the gentleman in the carriage could not come to the aid of his employee. He now pulled a revolver from his pocket and pointing it at the Indian, shouted:

"Damnation, canaille, that will be for you, if my man does not return to the coach within a minute."

Without any change of his features or batting an eyelash, the threatened Indian quickly pulled his rifle from below his serape and pointed it at the Yankee. Its hammer cracked. Surely, some serious action between the two would have happened, had not several policemen hurried up, asking the owner of the carriage to pocket his weapon again.

"Please, drive on, sir," warned one of them. "Your coachman is up again and, aside from his torn face, will not experience any lasting damage. He ought to know that, according to Indian law, at strike like this can only be expiated by death!"

"Well, well! But don't get involved in my affairs, you people. What you say here about the laws of the red fellows may be quite true, but doesn't matter to me the slightest bit. I am Colonel Webster from Lindsfort and know very well how a free American must deal with such fellows. Step back from the carriage, I'll finish with this scalper without your help."

The situation appeared to become more dangerous but also more interesting. Following American custom in which one rarely engages in the disputes of others, people often display their interest in a quarrel only by making room to fight it out. In this manner the bystanders had formed a circle around the carriage to see the outcome of the event. However, when the shrill whistle of the approaching steamer sounded, the situation immediately turned peaceful.

"Climb up again, Jim!" the colonel called. "The boat's arriving."

Winnetou withdrew his rifle, put the cock at rest and jumped off the box. The carriage rolled towards the landing bridge. The circle of the curious broke up with everyone hurrying off, intent on acquiring the best place on the boat.

It wasn't one of the usual, very comfortably equipped passenger boats, but one of the giant packet ships, which serve only occasionally for the transport of a large number of people who need to travel at the beginning of the fever season. This is why this ship was missing in the comforts by which the practical

American makes travel less cumbersome. On a packet ship like this the passengers had to find accommodation where they could find it.

After my Negro had bid his farewell, I climbed onto a pile of merchandise balls flanking a row of square boxes that stretched almost along the entire deck. From up there, I had a more open view. A cool breeze also fanned my forehead pleasantly. Furthermore, I could unceremoniously stretch out up here, which made my spot a rather splendid one.

Looking around from my raised position, I noticed that the owner of the carriage with his lady, as well as Winnetou, had also come on board. The Colonel together with his lady companion had settled down beside the railing. The Indian, who had found it too hot and uncomfortable in the disorderly press of people, also climbed up on the balls of merchandise, but so as not to invade my space, he stretched out on the first crate.

As he sat down, a sound shattered the air, so deep and rumbling and so terrible, that every single passenger jumped up frightened, looking about for the cause of this frightful noise. Only Winnetou remained totally at ease, although the angry, thunder-like rumble had come precisely from inside the crate he was resting on. Not a feature of his brown, immobile face, now disfigured by a thick wale, displayed even the least expression of surprise or consternation, like the alarm displayed by the other people on the deck.

A hatch opened then from which a man climbed out. Seeing him, I immediately had the explanation for the roar. I had seen him in Boston, in New York, in Philadelphia and Charleston and had established a close acquaintanceship with him. It was Fred Forster, the famous tamer of wild beasts who, at the time, visited the major cities of the United States with his menagerie, and wherever he came, caused a justified sensation by the power he exercised even over the wildest of beasts.

The crates were his and contained the cages of his zoological collection. Winnetou had taken his place on the traveling lodgment of the lion. The Indian had disturbed the creature in its siesta, causing it to produce the angry roar. Forster had heard it and, of course, hurried up to check on its cause.

In Europe, where people are more cautious, one would beware very much of transporting an entire menagerie without the utmost care and comprehensive security. But Americans are less cautious in this respect. On the American frontier, danger is ever present. People are familiar with it and know it in its various permutations. One respects it, but is not afraid of it. Being used to meeting the untamed denizens of the wilderness, it is thus the same to them when they are found in a tame condition.

Only the unexpected had alarmed the travelers. When the content of the numerous crates became known, people laughed about the fear they had displayed. The owner of the animals was urged by everyone to open the covers of the cages.

"Well, I don't mind it much if you'll enjoy it, ladies and gentlemen. A bit of fresh air will do the creatures good. But ask the captain first. I can't do anything on my own," he told them. Turning to the Indian he said:

"Won't you be good enough to descent from your throne, man? The lion is king and doesn't care to have anyone on top of him!"

Without moving his lips and with only a slight movement of his hand, the Indian indicated that he found it quite pleasant up there and that he had no intention of vacating his spot.

"Well, Mister Buffalo Kid, it's fine by me. But don't complain if something unpleasant happens to you."

The captain was brought over who, after a moment's hesitation, gave permission to open the crates on one side. With the help of the handlers, this was quickly accomplished. Since Forster could use the opportunity to feed the animals, the spectators were soon offered a highly interesting and entertaining spectacle.

The collection consisted mostly of truly gorgeous specimens. Particularly, a Bengal tigress drew much attention. The animal had only recently been captured. It was brought from India to America, where its current owner had purchased it. Grown up in open wilderness and as yet not fully tamed, it offered an imposing sight and by the build of its mighty limbs, the innate suppleness of its movements and the marrow-jarring sound of its voice, elicited loud exclamations of admiration.

"Do you also enter the cage?" one of the bystanders asked the tamer.

"Why not? The beast can't be tamed from the outside. One needs to enter to got its respect."

"But then you risk your life every time."

"That I've done already a thousand times and am quite used to it. I also prepare myself. I never enter without a weapon when I approach an animal that I'm not entirely sure of. A single strike with this blackjack stuns even the strongest lion, if the strike is made strongly and properly. But I rarely need it. The power of a true and right tamer lies somewhere else. At times, I enter a cage without any weapon."

"But you likely wouldn't dare enter this one like that!"

"Who says so? I'd dare it any time, also now. While the tigress has smelled her food already, she hasn't seen the meat yet. And as long as her eyes haven't seen blood, I have no reason to fear her."

"No, you wouldn't dare get in with her!" suggested the Colonel, stepping closer, who, until now, apart from everyone else, had not looked at the cages. His lady, who was afraid of their occupants, had stayed at the front of the ship, from where she gazed across the railing into the waters rushing up to the proud bow.

"I would wager a hundred dollars for my assertion, against anyone matching this sum."

The Yankee has a passion for betting, and where he finds a spicy opportunity to indulge this passion, he will not let it pass.

"You are not being cautious, sir!" Forster replied. "Look how quiet and fearlessly the Indian sits on the cage of the Numidian lion. Do you really think that I, the owner and Master of these animals, have less courage?"

"Pshaw!" the Colonel responded with a disdainful move of his hand. "It's not courage with this fellow, but ignorance and stupidity. Had he an understanding of the danger of his position, he would soon be standing down here with us and hide in some corner. He doesn't even know what a lion is. These red scoundrels know only how to cowardly approach an enemy by night and to attack him with superior force from behind. But to face a danger openly, they fall short."

Winnetou understood every single word but the features of his finely chiseled face remained immobile. And, as he had done before, he kept watching the forest standing close to the water on the right bank of the river. For whatever was happening and was spoken nearby, he did not appear to pay the least attention.

"You are mistaken in the Indian as well as myself. Whoever gets to know the peoples of the prairies like I have, has acquired a less disdainful opinion of their abilities and characteristics. I'm a White, but I've seen many a Red who would have given the best Kentucky man his worth."

"Don't be ridiculous in the midst of these honorable people, master! Just let the very first of your small animals, maybe the porcupine there come out, and I'm convinced the Indian, as soon as he sees it free, will jump into the river from fear and anxiety. These canailles are as cowardly as they know to be cruel. I know them better than you. One can make twenty redskins from a good trapper, but never from a thousand Indians a single, sturdy trapper. They neither possess spirit nor feeling, neither intellect nor heart. They are just redskins, not human beings. But we are getting away from our bet."

"I hold it. Captain, you are the witness."

"That I am," the ship's commander answered. "But I can't permit you to join the tigress in the agreed-upon manner. I am responsible for everything happening here on board."

"No one is disputing this. But you can't forbid any free citizen of the United States to do with his property as he pleases. It is my animal and I can enter the cage now or later, today or tomorrow, armed or unarmed, for training or for a wager, entirely according to my discretion and pleasure. Or do you think differently? And concerning an accident, it could only happen to me. Being man enough, I can carry the responsibility myself. Is it so or not?"

The captain was Yankee enough to be interested in the outcome of such a rare bet. Having given his warning and being of the opinion to have thus discharged his responsibility, he answered agreeably:

14

"If you carry the consequences, I don't mind you doing it. Do as you please!"

"Thanks, sir! Now step back, you people!" Forster commanded and handed the Captain the whip with the blackjack. He then approached the cage with a few firm, sure steps and, with eyes wide open facing the animal, moved the bolt.

The tigress had crouched down in the back of the narrow cage with her broad but short head resting on the outstretched front paws, her tail risen against the back wall. Her eyes were blinking up from the bottom. When the tamer approached the gate, her eyes opened wide, focusing on him with a sinister and threatening look. The bloodthirsty denizen of the Indian jungle had been disturbed from her dream of her distant homeland by the presence of the many people and been reminded of her captivity. The greenish flickering pupils narrowed more and more, her paws curved back to be pulled closer to her body. The rear of the carnivore rose silently and almost unnoticeably. The instant the bolt made its noise, a brief shiver flew over the soft, beautifully marked fur. And then, a horror-causing sound thundered from between the iron bars. With irresistible force, the tigress had launched herself against the gate and while Forster was tossed far away by the impact, the animal crossed the deck in mighty leaps.

A general scream of fear arose with everyone trying to save themselves as quickly as possible. It was a minute of most terrible dismay and confusion. All the animals of the menagerie arose in howling, roaring, screaming and raging voices. People rushed, tumbling over each other, towards hatches, corners, masts and rope ladders. Some called for help, others looked for any kind of weapon, all causing such a ruckus that even the noise of the engine became inaudible.

I had jumped back up onto the merchandise balls that I had left earlier to say hello to Forster. Now, I stood there immobilized by horror, for there, just ahead of me, I saw the poor girl standing by the railing, impossible to be saved. The escaped animal leaped directly towards her. It was now crouched down for its ruinous leap, barely eight or nine paces away from her. The face of the poor child was deathly white and rigid like that of a corpse. She stood with arms outstretched, as if calling for help, not able to make the smallest move. If not something impossible was going to happen, she was, in the next second, likely to be torn to pieces on the deck.

That's when, with catlike agility, a figure leaped past me, down from the cargo balls, vaulting in long, carnivore-like leaps across the ship's central open space past the tigress. He grabbed the girl with his left hand, while supporting himself on the railing's upper rung with his right. An instant later, the two disappeared in the deep, muddy-yellow flow of the Mississippi. It was Winnetou.

A single shout emanated from all on board. Was it a shout of joy or one of a new concern? It was difficult to answer, for the tigress had also launched herself over the railing in pursuit of the two. Everyone dashed to the railing to look down. The captain quickly commanded loudly:

"Man at the wheel: Heave to! Machinist, stop, stop!"

A short time passed when no one dared to breathe. The carnivore lay on the water with its four legs stretched away from its body and with its glowing eyes, watched every ripple of the water. Then, barely a few man's lengths from it, the Indian came shooting from the water. He rose to almost half his height from the water. One could clearly see that the nearly unconscious girl had instinctively grasped both her arms around his neck.

He had hardly any time to catch his breath, since he noticed that the tigress had spotted him and was now rushing towards him. Again, he dove into the water to surface a distance away. He took a breath, but was immediately pursued by the animal and driven down again. This terrible chase continued for a while, which, under the conditions, became an eternity.

Many ropes had been tossed over board and the ladder had been lowered but the smart Indian knew very well that these measures were of no help to him. Before he would have been able to get up a few feet on the ladder, the tigress would have reached him. There was only one way to save himself. He had to dive underneath the ship. This was quite possible with the ship's engine being at rest. If he swam around the ship, he would have been noticed by the pursuing animal. Climbing up the ladder at port side would have been just as impossible as here at starboard.

He therefore tried to remain as long as possible on the water's surface to fill his lungs with sufficient air. Gesturing with his hand, he signaled his intention and then disappeared once more.

"Ropes down at port!" the captain commanded.

Everyone hurried to the other side. Winnetou quickly appeared on the surface to strive for the next rope hanging down.

"Come on, come on, hurry up!" the captain urged. Because his voice clearly expressed great fear, everyone turned questioningly to him.

Without another word, the captain pointed to the yellow waves. All eyes followed his arm's direction, and immediately, everyone shouted the same message that the captain had just hollered.

Not too far away, three furrows could be seen in the water rapidly closing on the ship.

"For God's sake, hurry, hurry, the crocs are coming!" was shouted by everyone along the ship's railing.

"My child, my poor child!" lamented the girl's father.

He had already seen her saved but now saw his daughter and her courageous savior exposed to a new and even greater danger. With wide open eyes and fear-torn features, he leaned far over the railing, stretching his trembling arms towards them as if to grasp both before they could be reached by the alligators.

Winnetou heard the shout. Looking back, he realized the closeness of his new foes. He reached for the rope and with a supreme effort, he did not climb but literally sprung up on it using both his hands. Since he was unable to hold the girl, it was fortunate that she clung semiconsciously but tightly from his neck. He had barely reached a third of the way up to the deck, when he heard below him a dull sound as if two timbers had been banged together. The first alligator had reached the ship, its jaws snapping together. But both were safe now. Gripping firmly, he reached the top of the rope and climbed the railing onto the deck. Everyone wanted to rush towards him but was prevented by a loud call.

"Look people, the tigress! The tigress is coming."

The tigress had looked for her disappeared prey and was now swimming around the stern of the ship towards the port side. Quickly, everyone rushed to the railing once more. Only the father remained with his unconscious daughter.

The deliberate and sure moves of the beautiful and strong animal presented a truly wonderful sight. She paddle easily and playfully across the waves and her mighty muscles and supply body were even more obvious than before. Now, she looked in the direction where Winnetou had climbed up and where the alligators still were. She made an effort to turn, to flee. But it was already too late. Now, the three furrows moved lightning-fast towards the tigress. There arose a roar, so terrible, so frightening, that it caused the listeners' hair to stand on end. The waters were whipped up into a spray and foam, some of it splashing high. A deep, hollow gurgle sounded followed by a rattle. A funnel opened in the water, whose color turned from yellow to blood-red. Then, it was quiet. The alligators had pulled the tigress into the depths.

A sigh of relief was felt by all the spectators. They looked at the two people who stood hugging each other next to the ship's roof.

"She's alive. She's already conscious again!" shouts rang out from all sides.

The captain walked over to offer the exhausted girl and her upset father his cabin.

Now the ship resumed its run upriver. Aggrievedly, Forster looked towards the spot where he had lost his most beautiful animal. The others were now also asking for Winnetou. His rifle across his shoulder and his rain cover on his arm, the Indian hung way up in the shroud rungs. His eyes were penetrating the darkling forest thicket on the opposite bank. He refused to come down and did not respond to the plea of the colonel, who had come up from the cabin. It was obvious the Indian was looking for something.

When the general attention had already turned away from him for a quarter of an hour, he gave an easily recognizable signal by waving his rain cloth. From the bulrushes along the bank, a canoe appeared, paddled strongly by two Indians heading towards the steamer. They came to pick up their chief. The son of the wilderness does not know fixed places. He leaves civilization as he pleases and where he will find his people again. He climbed down, and with a brief move of his hand, signaled the captain his intention to leave.

Then a hand touched his shoulder, and a trembling voice spoke:

"You must not go. You did save my daughter for which I want to show you my gratitude."

It was the colonel. Immediately a circle formed around the two. The Indian slowly turned and, while straightening up, looked intensely at the colonel. His eyes flashed over the bystanders and his voice sounded strong and clear as he spoke the first words to be heard from him:

"The white man is mistaken. Red men have no courage and no heart. They are not human beings. Winnetou did not intend to save the young squaw but jumped into the waters of the holy Father of Rivers only because of the porcupine the palefaces let loose. Howgh!"

With a proud nod of his head, he turned away, threw the cloth over his shoulder and stepped down the lowered ladder to paddle off with his two people. He had just completed another heroic deed that would be spoken about for a long time.

For a while one could see his rich, mane-like hair fluttering in the wind. The sound of his voice reverberated for a long time in the ears of the listeners. But for the longest time, people would talk about his noble-mindedness. Had he not repaid the colonel's evil with kindness?

At the time, I wasn't aware that I would soon see him again. By his side, I was to cross the prairie in its entire breadth and width, became indebted to him more than ten times for my life, and could tell of many adventures during which I might have been lost without him. I call him the best, most faithful and most noble of my friends. And when people talk of who deserves the name 'Hero', then I think of Winnetou, the Chief of the Apache.

3. The Revenge of the Ehri

Three versions of this story exist, the first having been published in serial format in the magazine 'Frohe Stunden' – Happy Hours – in 1878 under the pseudonym of Emma Pollmer, Karl May's first wife.

Its locale is the South Seas without featuring Karl May's persona. However, in this account the good characters portrayed are heathen, whereas Christians, that is missionaries, are the bad people. Karl May may have been hiding behind Emma's name in this, for him, atypical portrayal of Christians.

For a comparison, read on to the following story, 'The Ehri', taken from May's 'Am Stillen Ocean' – At the Pacific Ocean. In it he reverses the names of some characters, but more so, their ideological stance. Even Charlie, his persona, plays a major role in it, together with the Henry Rifle.

Near the 16th degree of southern latitude and the 22nd degree of eastern longitude from Ferro, or the 216th from Paris, lies an island archipelago which was discovered by Quiros in the year 1606. It was thoroughly explored for the first time by the famous Captain Cook in 1769. To honor the Royal Society for the Sciences in London, he named the archipelago the Society Islands.

Separated by a broad strait, the islands are divided into two parts: the windward and the leeward group. To the first belong Tahiti or Otaheiti, the most important island of the archipelago. Then, there is Maitea, also called Osnabruc, and Eimeo or Moorea. The leeward islands go by the names Huahine, Raiatea, Taha, Bora Bora and Maurua or Maupiti.

The entire group of islands is of volcanic origin, however, the small, almost microscopic architects of the sea, little polyps, work incessantly on their enlargement. They surround every single isle with sharp-pointed coral reefs from which new land arises. This makes navigating the waterways between the islands highly dangerous.

The islands' soil is generally rich and fertile. The mountains are covered by dense forest, and the shores are well watered by creeks. For this reason, the vegetation is luxuriant and produces an abundance of sugar cane and bamboo, breadfruit, palms, bananas, pisang, plane trees, sweet potato, grains, yams and arum root, together with other tropical plants.

The inhabitants are of Malay-Polynesian origin and are a dark copper color, with women usually being of a somewhat lighter complexion, well and sturdily built, social, hospitable and good-natured. They live by monogamy, keep their women rather withdrawn, and love music, dancing, fencing and race their fast boats passionately.

The inhabitants of the Society Islands originally adhered to a polytheistic form of religion in which even human sacrifice was not unusual. Their priests, who were simultaneously healers and soothsayers, exercised extraordinary influence. Counter to this influence, however, were the missions founded by the British up until the end of the eighteenth century. Later, France also sent her emissaries to save the poor heathen from eternal damnation and to win them for heaven, although they led a totally contented and happy life. This meant that the former heathen had been turned into Christians. Whether this was to their advantage and benediction is, perhaps, a question, which the adherent to Christianity should best leave unanswered.

Civilization has its barbarism, light its shadow, love its egoism and, from the place of eternal bliss, one can, as the parable Lazarus, of the rich man and poor man teaches, look down into hell. Christ's love, and his lessons for mildness and compassion, have been hoisted on the tips of swords by intolerant zealotry and by a cunningly calculating lust for conquest. Despite that, Christianity has spread across the larger part of the globe. Entire races and peoples disappeared and even today, writhe in their final terrible death throws. Through such destruction, our future has lost important cultural forces and impulses. The faithful missionary who hunts with self-sacrifice after lost sheep, who never before were part of his flock, turns his back on the numerous and evil illnesses which find their victims in the stable at home.

When the Society Islands were discovered, their residents were found to be a childlike-naive, happy people, living in paradisiacal innocence. A rich environment supplied everything lavishly to fulfill all needs for a contented, worry-free life. The arriving strangers were received with friendly hospitality, honored almost like gods, and received everything their hearts desired. They brought the message about this home, where the desire arose for like pleasures. Thoughts also stirred to lift the islanders' happiness to a higher level through the preaching of God's word, while also making them politically dependent. Ships were outfitted which brought weapons, bibles, clergymen and – all kinds of immoral rabble to the islands. The conversions began; the weapons and the introduced illnesses began their work. While human sacrifice was prohibited, one after another hecatomb was built in honor of Mister Bacchus and Miss Venus. Quickly, the 'poor heathen' became studying sheep, among which rarely a refractory ram surfaced who had to be eliminated, if he did not go on his own to where there is howling and the shattering of teeth. The good, sympathizing human being is never so odious as when he becomes importune trying to make his brother happy. This friendly striving has caused the spilling of uncounted rivers of warm blood and cost millions – who is able to count them – character, home, life and property. –

Tahiti, the Pearl of the South Seas, lay under a magnificent, blue sky. The sun shone hotly onto the shimmering waves of the sea and the forested peaks of the Orohena Mountain, and sparkled in the creeks and narrow cascades tumbling from the picturesquely rising cliffs. However, its glow did not reach the friendly settlements lying in the shadows of palm trees and the numerous fruit trees, thus receiving pleasant cooling fanned by the fresh ocean breeze.

In the soft, mild breeze the long-feathered fans of the coconut palms and the broad, wind-torn leaves of banana trees rustled. The faded blossoms of orange trees dropped to the ground spreading heavenly scents. However, their branches were already covered with golden fruit. It was one of these magically beautiful and wonderful days as can only be found in such rich splendor and glory in the tropics.

And, while the land presented itself so young and fresh in all its paradisiacal beauty as if it had just emerged from the hand of the creator, out on the corral reef the surf thundered its deep, eternal song. Times have changed and with them the people. Today, infinite, ever changing and yet ever constant, the sea still tosses its crystalline waves against the sharp-edged reef, as it has done for thousands of years. The white, flashing crowns of the waves rise and sink as if thousands of Naiads were looking across them, to where ever green tree tops rise. Below, a people destined to gradual ruin counted the final heartbeats of its existence.

There, on the beach, lay Papeete, the capital of Tahiti. A colorful, stirring throng of people waved back and forth in their white, blue, red, yellow and striped or flowery long dresses. How splendidly had the young, beautiful girls adorned their black, curly and silky-soft hair with flowers and the artfully woven, snow-white waiting fiber of the arrow root! Strutting among the beauties, their movements adroit and proud, were the native dandies, their colorful pareau or folded marra coquettishly slung around their loins, with the tebuta decorously thrown across the shoulder! Their long, fatty shining curls were interwoven with strips of white tapa cloth and red flannel, which went, not at all badly, with the complexion of their bronze-colored faces.

Then, suddenly, everyone rushed towards the beach. A canoe was approaching the island, in whose white sail the breeze was fully engaged, so that its occupant needed his paddle only to steer the craft on a steady course.

The canoe was the here common, round-bottomed boat, hewn from a tree trunk. Due to this design such a craft is capable of fast sailing, but would also quickly capsize if it were not protected by its outrigger.

The outrigger consists of two wooden supports, which are firmly attached sideways and hold a lightweight runner parallel to the craft. This wooden runner floats about four feet to the right of the boat and is securely tied with fiber to the two supports. This makes capsizing, even rocking the craft, impossible. The boat cannot tip to the left, since this would require lifting the weight of the runner from the water, nor to the right, because the distance of the runner makes it impossible to push it and its supports under water. Of course, without this outrigger one would have to move very carefully in the boat. The round bottom would follow even the slightest tilting of one's body. One would not only run the danger of capsizing upon the least sway and take an involuntary bath, but might pay for this small accident with one's life. The bays and waters of these islands swarm with sharks of the most voracious kind!

Like all islanders, the young man steering the canoe knew very well how to handle it. He cut diagonally across the waves and, when he was close to land, dropped his sail, so as not to be driven by the wind onto the rough coast. Using his paddle, he then worked his way through the corral reefs towards land. However, his labor seemed to be affected by the attention he paid to the unusually large number of decorated boats that were anchored side by side next to shore seemingly ready for departure. One in their midst was distinguished from the others by colorful pennants and a variety of flowers and leaf wreaths. He knew it very well. It had carried him, when Potomba, the father of his magnificent young wife, had taken him home from Eimeo, the closest island to the west of Tahiti, to his palm tree-surrounded house on Papeete.

He also recognized old, shriveled Potai who sat waiting in the boat. He squatted in the canoe just like he had done years ago. Did this all not look like a cheerful wedding party? And why did Potomba's boat excel beyond the others when he had only one daughter?

His paddle dug in faster and, a few minutes later, his canoe creaked onto the sand of the beach. He tied it to one of the rammed-in poles and jumped across to the old servant.

"Potai," he asked, "what are you doing here on Tahiti's beach?"

The old one looked up. His eyes glanced at the questioner with an indescribable look.

"Atua, the god of all-good be with you, Anoui! Go home and ask there what I am doing here!"

"Why don't you want to tell me?"

"I cannot, Anoui! My heart did think of you during the many weeks you spent on the Tabuai Islands. Oro, the god of evil, has come to Eimeo and bestowed his influence on Potomba, the great prince, who has thrown off the faith of the fathers and now prays to the God the old, pale mitonare proclaims."

Mitonare means missionary and, with this term, the simple island folks designate everything connected with the Christian religion, such as church, preacher, altar, sermon, blessed, holy, pious, and so on. All is called mitonare.

"Is it possible, Potai?" the young man asked so frightened that one noticed, despite his bronze-colored face, that the blood had drained from his cheeks. "Oh, had I only stayed home! I knew that this sneaky foreigner was entering Potomba's house to steal from him the belief of our fathers. But rich gain drew me to the lands of Tabuai, and the trade that kept me there for so long, did bring me wealth. I shall talk with him; I shall lead him back to the truth of our priests and Manina will gladly help me!"

"Manina, your wife?"

"Yes. She loves me more than her life. Leaving her father, she followed me from Eimeo to Papeete. She cried when I left, a whole ocean of tears. Oh, my sweet Manina. Today, you will see me again and we shall tear Potomba away from the hands of the mitonare! But, tell me, what are you doing here?"

"My mouth will remain closed. Words are too heavy for it!"

"Potai, your mind is dark and your eyes are wet! You love me. Your face tells me even without words that bad fortune is threatening me. It is about Manina. What's the matter with my wife?"

"I will not tell you, but remember Mahori, your rival!"

"Mahori?"

Anoui uttered only this word, then, with a single leap, he crossed between the canoes and dashed inland. He did not pay attention to the crowd whose looks of compassion rested on him. He even ran past those who stepped out to have a word with him. He run right through Papeete until he reached a building distinguished by its size and the extent of the attached plantation.

In this house, he had spent the golden years of his youth. Here, he had observed the reverence which had been extended to his father, Tahiti's greatest chief. Here, too, he had experienced the destruction of all conventional and, therefore, sacred rules which had cost his father his power, his respect and, finally, his life. Nobility had become worthless. Together with his brother, Anoui had started a trading business with the nearby island archipelagoes and had gained the riches which he had lost in influence as an Ehri, a prince. Then, he had been very fortunate to win the most beautiful and best girl of the island group as his wife, even though Mahori, the powerful priest's son, who had become a Christian and local mitonare, had asked for her hand in order to gain for himself her father's influence.

What had happened to her now? He entered the house to find his brother sitting glumly in a corner.

"Ombi, what happened?" he demanded breathlessly.

"Anoui, you are here? Atua, who has sent you, be praised. Now, my soul is relieved of the pain weighing it down! Are you strong enough to listen to what I have to say?"

"I am strong. What's the matter with Manina? Why does she not come to greet me?"

"She's no longer here."

"No – longer – here?" He stammered the loaded words only with difficulty. "Where did she go?"

"Potomba fetched her and is giving her to Mahori as his wife. Today is the wedding. The canoes are waiting to take the groom to Eimeo."

Anoui did not reply but stepped to the open window breathing in air, so that he would not suffocate. His chest heaved convulsively and his breath came rattling from between his deathly pale lips.

He stood there for a long time until, finally, he turned around slowly.

"Ombi, did she follow him gladly?"

"No. He fetched her when I wasn't here and lured her away. She is now with him, and he has complete power over her."

Relieved, Anoui breathed easier.

"The foreign teachings bring hate, discord and falseness to our hearts. They will grow over our beliefs like weeds over good plants. I shall leave the land of our fathers and will never return."

"Leave? The voice of desperation speaks from your mouth!"

"No, Ombi. Manina still loves me. I am at peace. But can I stay if . . .?"

He stopped in mid-sentence, but his brother understood the look of anger and the quick move of the speaker's hand.

"Anoui, you are an Ehri, princely blood courses in your veins. You have been robbed of your wife. The two mitonares are guilty of it. Do as your heart commands you. Ombi, your brother, will stand faithfully by your side!"

"I do not require your help, but I will have to leave immediately – tonight. Get everything I need and do not tell anyone where I'm going to."

"I shall keep silent and follow you. Atua has left the Pearl of the Southern Ocean. I shall go where I know I will find you."

"Then I say to you '*Joranna*' (goodbye, farewell). Have the big canoe with provisions ready behind Loga Point by midnight. I leave now!"

From the wall he took a sharp, two-sided *kris* (dagger), putting it into his belt.

"*Joranna*, Ombi. I am an Ehri and Manina remains mine!"

"*Joranna*, Anoui, the god of all good be with you. May he let his sun shine on you during the day and his stars in the night, so that your path may remain lit and will never be obscured by darkness!"

Anoui left. He avoided people and walked to a place on the beach where he was not seen by anyone.

The wedding flotilla, which had picked up the groom, had set sail for its way to Eimeo. Anoui lay on the ground covered by the broad leaves of the banana trees, and waited.

Only after the canoes had disappeared and the crowd had dispersed, did he rise again to walk to his canoe. He entered it, rowed through the coral reefs, and then set sail.

His direction took him to and around the island of Eimeo to the village of Tamai, located not far from Opoauho Bay. There, Potomba lived, the one who had broken his word and robbed him of his wife. There, the wedding was to take place with great splendor, since the bride's father was a prince and the groom a local man and the first mitonare to have such a ceremony performed.

In the rearmost room of the house Manina waited for the festivities to begin. On her request, her servants had left her. Now, that she felt alone, her held-back tears flowed down her pale cheeks. Once before, she had sat here as a bride, but how happy she had been then. And how unhappy, how utterly unhappy she was today. And her finery, what did it consist of? She had a slender, noble figure, still full of youthful freshness, as one could see, despite the heart-wrenching sorrow that now wracked her body. Her beautiful, dark eyes were dimmed, her sharply cut eyebrows firmly drawn together and her delicate lips pinched. Not a single flower or any other bauble decorated her hair or anywhere else on her body. Yes, she even seemed to have disdained the garments and the cloth that had been brought to her by the Whites, these hated foreigners. A pareau of soft, yellow-brown tapa cloth, reaching just below her knees, enclosed her hips and showed the faultlessly beautiful shapes of her lower legs. A *Tehei*, a brief wrap of the same material covered her shoulders and torso. Her raven-black hair hung long, full and curly down her neck, neither decorated with a single flower nor being held by wafting fiber of arrow root. She was herself a flower, who had been torn from the place where she would have blossomed most beautifully and could have spread her scent most pleasantly.

Now, she heard a noise outside bamboo wall.

"Manina!" it sounded softly.

She knew this voice. Was it possible he could be here? She had been told that he had not returned yet.

"Anoui!" she called jubilantly.

"Do not speak loudly, Manina!" it came from outside. "Oro, the god of evil, together with his spirits, watches outside this house, which is why you must be quiet and cautious."

"But, if you are seen, Anoui?" she asked anxiously.

"The *pisang* (banana tree) covers me, sun of my heart. Tell me: Do you still love me?"

"More than a thousand lives!"

"And yet you went with the disloyal?"

"No, never! I carry a dagger below my dress. It would find my heart the moment Mahori would touch me. Believe me, Anoui!"

"I know you and believe you! Do you wish to remain my wife?"

"So very gladly, but it will not be possible!"

"It is! Walk with Mahori before the foreign priest. I shall come and speak. And if my words won't help, then you must remember to jump into my canoe when he brings you back to Papeete. Will you do this?"

"Yes."

"Don't be afraid of the words and ways of the pale mitonare. He cannot let our union remain valid, because our priest did pronounce it and so, also his benediction will disappear like nothing in the sea. Farewell, Manina. *Joranna, Joranna*, my magnificent wife!"

The pisang rustled outside; Anoui had withdrawn.

The flotilla arrived at Tomai. The groom stepped onto shore and was welcomed by Potomba. The guests settled down under the palm trees, enjoyed pleasant coconut milk, roasted plantains and other tasty fruit, all presented in great quantity.

Then, the sound of a drum and a flute arose. The ceremony was to begin. Under evergreen leaf trees an altar, decorated with flowers, had been erected, where the pale mitonare, the English missionary, waited for the bride. Mahori went to the house to bring her forth.

That's when a young man pushed his way through the circle of guests to step up to Potomba who stood next to the altar.

"Be greeted, oh Potomba, you father of my wife! She was made to come to you while I was gone, and I have come to take her back."

"Be gone, you heathen!" was the response. "I have nothing to do with you any longer!"

Anoui remained calm. He only put his hand onto his wife's shoulder and turned to the English missionary:

"Mitonare, this woman has sworn to be faithful to me upon the skulls of our forefathers. The priest of our people asked me:

"*Etia anei oe a faarue i ta oe vatrina*? Will you never leave this woman?" and I replied: "*Eita* – no! Potomba gave us his blessing. Do you have the right to separate us?"

The missionary raised his eyes to the heaven.

"The Holy Christian Church can, as the almighty mother, take her daughters and give them to whomever she decides. Go away, heathen, so that the anger of the children of God will not strike you!"

"Then come, Manina!" Anoui said, taking her hand.

That's when Mahori struck him to the face with his fist, and Anoui was grabbed and dragged away. Not speaking a word, he let it happen. But near the beach he tore free and jumped into his canoe.

"Tell Mahori that I will fetch my wife!" he called to them, then paddled out to sea. Sailing around the island, he arrived at Alfareaita, a village just opposite Papeete, where he went ashore to purchase a quantity of large and small fish.

When he thought the proper time had arrived, he returned to his craft and rowed out a distance from where he could overlook the strait between the two islands. It became darker, and night fell. The waves surrounded the canoe like liquid, transparent crystal. He tied one of the fish to a piece of bast and hung it into the water. Very soon a sharp pull yanked his line. A shark had taken the lure.

A little while later, the young man threw another tied-up fish overboard, and so he continued, until half a dozen sharks swam about his boat.

"Be welcome, you servants of the Ehri. I will take my revenge and you will get your food!"

He continued to bait and lure the ravenous monsters until flickering fires on the approaching boats convinced him that the flotilla, carrying the newlyweds, was close. Slowly, he paddled towards it, followed by the sharks.

Far ahead, alone, paddled Mahori. While he sat in the back steering, Manina sat up front in the bow. Suddenly, he saw a canoe ahead of him, blocking his way. He rose.

"Who is it?" he inquired.

"Anoui, to repay you for today's strike!" a voice came back.

At the same time, Anoui's boat moved broadside with Mahori's. Two quick cuts with the sharp kris through the fiber strings of the outrigger, and the cross-braces fell into the water. Now, with the least move of his, Mahori was utterly lost .

"Manina, jump!" Anoui called.

With a quick leap, his wife was with him. Mahori's canoe, now without outrigger, capsized. With a loud scream, he tumbled into the sea and was immediately devoured by the sharks.

Before the other craft arrived, Anoui had raised his sail and, in his sharp-hulled, well-built canoe 'flew' towards Loga. Never again was anything heard of him, nor of Manina. Ombi, his brother, also left Tahiti after some time and went, as it was told, to the Tubuai Islands. Some time later Potomba died. He had loved his only child and with his last word, it is said, he cursed the pale mitonare, whom he had to thank for the loss of his daughter.

Karl May – translated by Herbert Windolf

4. The Ehri

This is a two-part narrative Karl May wrote in 1893/94 for his collection of adventure stories 'Am Stillen Ozean' – 'At the Pacific Ocean'. Utilizing parts of an earlier short story, "The Revenge of the Ehri", he expanded it greatly, and introduced himself into the picture, while changing the narrative substantially by reversing the names of major characters and inventing new names for previous characters.

The above use of a previous publication is typical for Karl May, who incorporated many other such earlier accounts into later stories while sometimes changing the story line.

The second version of this story – the first was published in serial format in 1878 – appears to have been created in 1879, and was published in the years 1879/80 in the magazine 'Deutscher Hausschatz in Wort und Bild' – 'German Home Treasures in Word and Picture'. This version formed the basis for his collection of travel stories in 'Am Stillen Ozean'.

A third version appeared in 1880 under May's pseudonym Prince Muhamel Latréaumont.

I. Potomba

A pleasant, cloudless sky spread above us. However, the bright light of the sun was unable to banish the dark shadows from the features of the brave seamen I was sitting with. We sat around the blazing fire on which we were preparing our midday meal. In front of us lay the low beach, surrounded by sharp-edged, dangerous coral rings. Beyond them, the ocean's glistening waves tumbled. Between the reef and the shore, the waters were utterly calm as if never a storm had raged in these sun-drenched latitudes. From behind, the land rose, and here and there stood green eucalyptus bushes, densely grown *Melaleucees* (tea trees), and groups of *Callitris* conifers. Interspersed were numerous acacia and other fine-stemmed leguminosa types forming a dense ground cover. On the highest point of the island stood Bob, the carpenter. It was his turn to incessantly search the horizon with telescope in hand for any kind of sail, which might bring us deliverance from our less than comfortable situation.

Six weeks ago, we had left Valparaiso on our good three-master Poseidon to sail for Hong Kong. We had quickly passed the much-traveled areas of Callao, Guayaquil, Panama and Acapulco and, in a fast and happy passage driven by a stiff southeast trade-wind, had sailed straight west. At about the height of Ducir and Elizabeth, the trade-wind suddenly turned into a hurricane with a strength and fury I had never before experienced on my many journeys.

We were forced to take in all canvas, except for the storm sail. Nevertheless, the Poseidon remained a toy of the furious waves, not to be controlled by human insight, strength or skill. Now, our three-master lay stranded on the treacherous coral crags. Our cutter had been torn off, our sloop had acquired an irreparable leak, and our longboat was stuck on a pointed, needle-sharp reef, which had penetrated its bow like a Malay dagger. The surf was tearing plank by plank off our ship, which was beyond recovery. Using all our strength, we had worked for two days to salvage as much as possible of the cargo and provisions as we were able to snatch from the greedy sea.

This hard work finished, we now sat among the large cargo bales and barrels around the fire intent on surpassing each other with our gloomy spirit.

Beside us stood Captain Roberts, endeavoring to establish our latitude and longitude. Since this morning we finally had a clear sky, so it would not to be too difficult to solve this task since all our astronomical and nautical instruments had been salvaged.

"Well, Captain, are you finished?" asked the helmsman, while he pulled a mighty piece of salt pork from the fire to test how well it was done.

"Aye, aye, mate, I am," came the reply.

"Where are we?"

"We are sitting one and one half degrees north of the Capricorn at the two hundred thirty ninth degree east of Ferro."

"I wish we were sitting at home in Hoboken with mother Grys and had a firm chair or stool underneath and a glass of hard liquor before our nose. What do you make of this island, Captain? Can its name be determined?"

The captain lowered his head doubtfully.

"There are more islands here than pock marks on your face, and that's saying a bit, as you're aware, Mate. Do you have the proper name for each scar on hand?"

The helmsman made an effort to respond to the compliment entailed in this comparison with a sour smile.

"I've never yet thought to name the contours of my face, Captain. But if this unfortunate piece of coral doesn't have a name yet, we will truly be forced to give it one. I suggest we name it Mate Pocks Island!"

He seemed to consider his joke to be exceptionally witty, for his sour expression vanished and, next to the giant piece of chewing tobacco he had in his mouth, a laugh erupted, which couldn't have been heartier.

Ship's discipline is very strict, and even the least experienced ship's novice knows that everyone must join when captain or mate are so gracious as to laugh. However, one must participate more softly while another must do so the louder, depending on the rank he occupies on the ship's listing. That's why now all the men, from the boatsman down to the cabin boy, opened their mouths while dutifully employing their laughing muscles. Even the captain twisted his mouth as if he wanted to display an agreeable smile. He then said:

"I figure we are somewhere between Holt and Miloradowitch on a place far to the west. What do you think, Charlie?"

I had been the sole passenger on the ship with whom the otherwise taciturn captain had conversed. It had occurred to me that I might boast of his affection, for he had truly assumed the habit of asking my advice more often than is common for a seaman towards a layman. This is why the crew had a certain respect for me which, in some cases, was to my advantage and very often resulted in small favors.

"My earlier calculations quite agree with yours, sir," I replied. "Although I've never been in this area, I know a great deal about it. It is certain that we are on one of the Pomatu Islands, although this island has a different characteristic than its sister islands."

"I, too, haven't been here yet," the captain admitted. "Could you tell me about the make-up of the Pomatu Islands?"

"They are all of coral origin, mostly circular, and not much higher than the ocean's level. Most have a lagoon inside the surrounding coral reef and, usually, carry some fertile ground on top of the coral. The archipelago was first discovered by the Spaniard Quiros in 1606 and is part of over sixty island groups."

"How far do you think it is from here to the Society Islands?"

"As you know, they are located in the direction from southeast to northwest between the tenth and eighteenth degree of southern latitude and the twenty second to two hundredth degree of eastern longitude. We, therefore, need to first travel sixteen degrees going exactly west, then turn straight north fourteen degrees, cutting a diagonal through the meridians and longitudes towards northwest."

During this conversation, Roberts looked at me somewhat askance. While the good captain was, you know, a good seaman on the courses known to him, he appeared to be a bit insecure outside those.

"Fourteen degrees. That's a good distance, particularly if one is stuck and doesn't have a ship below one's feet!" he growled.

"Hmm! I suggested we salvage as much wood as possible to built a boat. We've got the carpenter and could all have chipped in. From the sloop and the cutter we might have also been able to build something, had we not let them go. But you decided to salvage the cargo, and now we are stuck, as you said yourself."

"Well, sir, that's your opinion," he replied annoyed. "But you know, that in such circumstances the captain's view governs. The cargo has been entrusted to me, which is why I must make every attempt to save it."

However, the ship and the lives of his men had also been entrusted to him, and he had had the obligation to consider that we would be as much as lost here if no ship showed up. Human life weighs heavier than money and goods. Yet I kept silent, since my reminder had made him sullen. It was not my intention to make him seriously angry and forfeit his goodwill, or to even incur his enmity.

"Come eat!" the mate now commanded, and everyone came closer to delight in the peas with salt pork. I had no appetite for this robust seaman's fare and picked up my rifle for a stroll along the beach. I had noticed large flocks of seabirds which are numerous on the Pomatu Islands, also called Flat Islands, Dangerous Islands, Low Islands and Pearl Islands.

After only a quarter of an hour, I returned with a good bag and was received with a happy halloo. The birds were unused to being hunted, which is why my buckshot had taken a great toll amongst them. They were quickly plucked and roasted and made a dessert whose tastiness returned the captain to his good mood.

"You are a good fellow, Charlie," he suggested. "You can aim shooting gear at whatever, whereas if I tried, I am convinced that I would not hit anything. To keep a steady rudder, that's more my task, but to shoot a roast, hmm, that's something totally different. Tell me, Charlie. Do you think there might be people here towards port or starboard?"

"I think so!"

"Of what kind?"

"Malays, of course. You are aware that many of the Pomatu Islands are inhabited."

"I know that. But whether there are people nearby is most important for us."

"It's possible. I think, that at least Holt and Miloradowitch, islands between which we probably find ourselves, will be populated"

"Are these dangerous folk?"

"Most of them are still savages, and it is said that some are still cannibals."

"Very comforting, Charlie! Of course, we don't need to fear these people, but I believe we couldn't even deal with them, since I know no one among us who understands their language."

The helmsman stuffed a colossal piece of salt pork between his teeth and suggested cold-bloodedly:

"I'm the one who understands them, Captain."

"You? How so? Where would you have learned that?"

"To cannibals you speak only with this here!"

He raised his knife, made the most terrible grimace possible, and moved with his arm as if wanting to stab someone.

"Do you understand Malay, Charlie?" the captain asked.

I had to smile. 'Charlie' was always the man the good captain believed to understand everything.

"The truth is, Captain, that I picked up a bit of Malay during my stay on Sumatra and Malacca. It is the *lingua franca* across the entire Austral archipelago. *Kawi*, the Malay priesthood's and written language, I do not understand. But I believe that I can make myself understood to the inhabitants of the Tahiti and Marquesa Islands in their respective dialects."

"Then you aren't a real German any more but a Polynesian!"

"It's simply that one finds easier entry to a foreign language, if one has laid a good philological foundation during one's student times. In the course of the conversion of the Malay tribes to Islam, their language adopted many Arab terms and is even today written with many Arabic letters. Since I understand Arabic, it can easily be seen that I won't have much difficulty in orienting myself in Malay."

"Then you must be our translator should we meet Polynesians."

"Ahoy - iiiiih!" it sounded from above.

"Ahoy - iiiiih!" the captain answered. "What is it, carpenter?"

"I'm sighting a sail!"

"Where?"

"South, close to east!"

"What kind?"

"Not a ship, but some kind of craft!"

A seaman is used to calling only three masters a ship. Bob once more lifted the telescope to his eyes and viewed the object closely. He then reported turning back to us:

"It is a boat, or something like it, like I've never seen before!"

"It must be a Malay pram," I suggested. "Let's climb up the hill to assure us of it, Captain!"

The others had to stay back while the two of us hurried up. When we arrived at the top, the sail could already be identified by the bare eye. I took the telescope from Bob, looked through it, then handed it to the captain.

"Look at it, Captain! It is a boat of the kind you find on the Society Islands. Do you see the outrigger on its side? It is to prevent capsizing, which could otherwise happen easily, since these long, narrow-hulled crafts are only wide enough for a single man and have a rounded cross section."

"I agree, Charlie! But look: there's one, two, four, five, seven, eight, ten, twelve, thirteen, fourteen sails following it!" Roberts counted. "They are still way out near the horizon and aren't larger than a dollar to the eye. Here, take the telescope!"

I convinced myself that he had seen correctly. Most of the dots became larger. There were a total of fifteen boats, each manned by a single individual, as one could assume from their construction.

"Step behind this rise!" I ordered. "We don't know their intentions, and I see no reason to have us spotted right away."

"Isn't it likely that the man in the closer boat has seen us already?" the carpenter asked.

"No," Roberts replied. "Although, to him, we stand tall against the horizon, if we can't exactly make him out, he can't identify us either. By the way, he must be a very adroit and strong fellow. Look, Charlie, how cleverly he's using the wind and every wave with his paddles! He's truly approaching as if he were on steam power and labors – trust me – as if he's being pursued."

"This truly seems to be the reason, Captain. I can clearly make him out in the spy glass and can see that he rises at times to look back."

"What are we going to do, Charlie?"

"We must investigate the situation prior to the others coming into eyesight. They may be pursuing him or not, they may be friendly or hostile towards us. But we must prepare as if we were expecting an attack."

"Hmm, yes, you're quite right. But, hmm! If I'm attacked on sea, I know what I've got to do, but here, on land – hmm! Wouldn't it be best if we post all our people up here? We would be protected and could cover the entire terrain down there."

"Quite right! But wouldn't it be better to take them between two fires?"

"How so?"

"We split up. Of course, we leave a guard with our goods. One half of us takes up position on the hill, the other half walks along the beach by the row of cliffs over there to gain the coral outcrop. Once arrived there, they lie down flat, so that they can't be seen. Should it really come to a fight, they can advance upon our signal along the coral ring to the point right in front of us. Where the reef opens to the lagoon is, in all likelihood, where the Malays will enter. That way they will be surrounded and must surrender if they chose not to die."

"Right on, that looks like the best solution, Charlie! But how do we learn what brings these people here and what their intentions are?"

"I shall receive the first man and talk to him."

"Really. You want to do that? But if he kills you?"

"He won't do that, Captain, rest assured of it. These people are either equipped with catapults, clubs, bow and arrows, lances or spears, and are therefore, totally harmless against a good rifle. If they own guns, then these are surely only old muskets and flintlocks from ages ago which can't do a thing against our equipment. If you wish, you can remain here with Bob, and I shall arrange what's necessary."

I hurried down.

"What did you see, sir?" the helmsman asked when I arrived.

"Fifteen savages with just as many boats, who are headed into the south lagoon."

"Well, that's good. Then, we can learn right away the name of this cursed island. You must be here to tell us to arm ourselves?"

"Indeed. Jim and Classen ought to stay here with our goods. You, mate, walk out onto the coral ring with half the men, moving carefully along it until you have the lagoon's opening in sight. There, you lie down flat, so that you aren't noticed by the enemy. If it comes to a fight, you rise upon the first shot or upon my signal, or that of the captain, and run forward to encircle the lagoon. Do you understand me?"

"Aye, aye, sir!"

"Ahead then! There's no time to lose!"

The helmsman quickly distributed weapons and munition among the men, after which they hurried off.

"You others go up to the captain. Take his saber and rifle along and another rifle for the carpenter."

They had already taken up arms and walked up the rise. I picked up my knife, the revolver and my Henry Rifle and then hurried alongside the base of the hill to meet the owner of the first boat upon his arrival. The island wasn't large, so it was only ten minutes before I saw him. He was approaching the coral reef, which left a passage just wide enough that one could cross it in a good rush. His sail had been reefed by now, and he was using only his paddle to overcome the quite difficult narrows.

He succeeded. The surf pushed him through the narrow canal into the calm waters of the lagoon. Having arrived behind the reef, he rose, put the paddle aside and reached for bow and arrow. Turning towards the island he aimed and let the arrow fly. It reached land about twenty paces inward from the beach.

I now was sure that he was being pursued by the others. He obviously intended to defend the passage and, by shooting the arrow, had tested it to see if that was possible. He now reached once more for the paddle and came closer.

This side of the island had a denser vegetation than the northern one where we had set up camp. Here grew a broad-leaved fern which made it easy to stalk unnoticed. I crept closer as quickly as I could.

Presently, his boat made landfall. He pulled it halfway out of the water, hung the quiver across one shoulder, took his bow in hand, then reached also for a musket he hung by its strap over his other shoulder. Then he walked to the spot where his arrow had fallen, picked it up, and walked in large, equal-sized paces straight inland. Obviously, he wanted to measure the distance, in case his pursuers succeeded in entering the lagoon and tried to land. His actions were like those of a daring yet cautious man who did not disregard any circumstance useful to him. He came so close to me that I could clearly hear him counting his paces.

"*Satu, dua, tiga, ampat, lima, anam, tudshuh, dalapan, sambilan, sapuluh,*" he counted from one to ten, then continued, "sapuluh-satu, sapuluh-dua, sapuluh, tiga, – "

"*Rorri* – stop!" I demanded, rising from the ferns and putting my hand on his shoulder. "What are you doing here?"

While he was startled by my sudden appearance, he caught himself in the blink of an eye, pulling his knife from the belt.

"*Inglo?*"

"No, I'm no Englishman."

"*Franko?*"

"Yes," I replied, thinking that he did not mean a Frenchman by this word, but was using it in a broader sense designating all Europeans.

"Oh, this is good! Are you alone, Sahib?"

Had he been in India that he used this honorific title? I preferred not to answer his question as yet, and asked:

"What are you doing here?"

"Escape!"

He turned and pointed to the boats, which were now so close that one could clearly make out the men's bodies.

"They are pursuing me and want to kill me."

"Why?"

"I am rich and am a Christian."

"And they are heathen?"

He nodded in the affirmative.

"Some are still heathen, although several had themselves baptized by the Inglo *mitonare*."

Mitonare means missionary. This word is used by these simple islanders to designate everything connected with the Christian religion, such as church, preacher, altar, cross, sermon, bible, blessed, holy, pious, etc. Everything is simply '*mitonare*'. In any case, he must be referring here to an English protestant missionary.

"Then these Inglo-mitonare-baptized men are Christians after all?"

"*Eita* – no. They still believe in Atua, the good god, and Oro, the god of evil. But they had themselves baptized so that they can trade with the Ingli and get nice things."

"What is your name?"

"*Potomba.*"

"From which island are you?"

"I live on Papeete, the capital city of Tahiti. I am an Ehri, a prince of the land, and shall kill all my enemies!"

He looked back. Just then the first boat of his pursuers attempted to cross the entry passage. He leaped back to where his arrow had fallen, picked it up and inserted it on his bow and aimed. The arrow flew off the string and would surely have hit the man, had not an advancing wave lifted the boat, causing the arrow to hit the boat's body. Involuntarily, the boatman had ducked down, fearing the arrow, and had lost control of his paddle. The same wave that had pushed him in on its trough, took hold of his craft and pulled it back out of the passage.

"Halloo - o - oh!" suddenly sounded from the corral enclosure, and when I turned sideways, I saw the helmsman with his men jump forward.

Falsely, the mate had thought the arrow to be the signal and was now wrecking my plan. Although the pursuers had seen me, they had not abandoned their intentions. But when they realized that the island was occupied by a great number of men in European dress, they decided to retreat. They immediately set sail again and took off.

I now walked to the beach where Potomba had sunk to his knees.

"*Bapa kami iang ada de surga, kuduslah kiranja namamu,*"[1] I heard him pray in the words of those converted by the mission. Now he joyfully jumped up and exclaimed:

"I have been saved! They flee, and I need not kill any one of them. My arrow could almost have killed Anoui, the false priest, who is after all, the father of my wife!"

Only his need had compelled him to oppose his pursuers. By his exclamation, and from his earlier thanksgiving prayer, I recognized in him a pious, truly Christian conviction which, among the converted, is not often found with such heartfelt sincerity. Right away, it gained the young man my goodwill. In any case, he had not become a Christian by calculation, but from true conviction.

"Who is Anoui?" I asked him.

"He is the priest of Tamai."

I pondered this reply.

"Is Tamai not located on Eimeo, an island adjacent to Tahiti?"

"Yes, Sahib. Tamai is not far from the Day of Opoauho. Pareyma, my wife, is the daughter of the priest. I am an Ehri, and an Ehri takes only the daughter of a sovereign or a priest for a wife. As long as Tahiti exists, no Ehri has ever taken the daughter of a *Meduah*, a vassal, or that of a *Towha* and *Rattirha* (common folk) into his house. And he does not know the daughters of the *Mahanunen*, the peasants and Tautau, the servants and slaves."

"And why is Anoui now your enemy?"

"Because I became a Christian. He asked me to return Pareyma, the pearl of my life, but I did not comply. That is when he accused me to the Ingli, who do not believe in the mitonare, the holy virgin Marrya. I, however, went to the Franki who have many mitonare men and women in the heaven of the good Bapa, and they helped me. I was allowed to keep Pareyma in my house, although she had not been given to me by the mitonare, but by our priest, when I was still a heathen. Then I had to leave for the Tubai Islands to trade for clothes, weapons and pearls. Since the Europeans have come to us, everything has changed and become worse. Even those who were earlier princes, must now earn money

---

[1] Our Father who dwelleth in heaven, holy be His name.

37

through work and trade. Anoui knew where I was going and followed me with his men. When I left the island of Tubai, he lay in wait to kill me and to take the riches I was carrying."

"He hasn't killed you, I notice. But how about your goods? Are they in your boat?"

"No. He did not get either, not my life nor my property, for my hand is stronger than his, and his mind is darker than the mind of an Ehri. When I saw him approach with his boats, I sailed towards him, but sent my servants with the boats carrying my goods by a detour to Papeete. Then I lured him here where I would have had to kill him, had he not fled."

His eyes shone and his dark cheeks burned from excitement. He was still very young and truly handsome as he stood so threateningly before me. On his black tresses he wore a feather-adorned turban, and two precious pearls adorned each of his ears. A yellow silk *Marra* served as a belt wrapped around the red and white striped *Tebuta*, which fell in rich folds from his shoulders to the knees, emphasizing the symmetry of his slender but sturdy figure.

"What are you going to do now?" I asked him.

"Ask first what you are going to do with me, Sahib!" he replied, pointing up the hill from where the captain with his men was descending.

"I am your friend and you need not fear anything from them. You can do as you wish. But I ask you that you will also be our friend! We ask for your help."

He looked at me somewhat surprised. I, myself, could not help suppressing a little smile. Totally different in built, I was a full head taller than he. The turban and veil I wore, the dense, full beard framing my cheeks and chin, my weapons, my adventurous-looking clothing, comprised of the fashions from different climatic zones which, down below, ended in a pair of giant seaman's boots. All that might have given the impression that I was used to relying on my own strength, and would, therefore, not easily require another's help or support.

"Who are you, and what are you doing here?" he asked.

"I am of the Germani people, and the others are members of the Yanki people."

"The Germani are good folks. I have seen their ships on the islands of Samoa. What they sell are honest goods, and what they say is like an oath for them. But the Yanki are different. Their tongues are slippery and unfaithful. Their wares are shiny and carry deceit inside. How come you are with them, and how did you get onto this island which does not even have a name?"

"I travel with them since I wanted to get to the land of the Chinese. But weather has driven us onto this island, causing our ship and our boats to break up. We now cannot leave and must wait for another ship to come to pick us up. Will you return to Papeete?"

"Yes. I long to return to Pareyma, to my wife, who is more dear to me than all my goods and my life. The voice of my heart tells me that she is in danger from Anoui, my enemy."

"There are always ships of the Ingli, Franki, Yanki and Hollandi on Tahiti, maybe even one of the Hispani or even Germani. When you get to Papeete, would you ask one of them to come here to save us?"

"I will do that, Sahib! But they may not believe me, and it would be better, if you send one of your men along who, himself, can speak for you."

"Can your boat take two men?"

"Without another to paddle: no. But if you select a brave man who is not afraid of the water, I will happily get him to Tahiti, for no one will be a match in sailing to Potomba, the Ehri."

At that moment the captain arrived.

"Now, Charlie. Who's this man?"

"He's an Ehri from Tahiti."

"An Ehri? What's that?"

"A prince, Captain."

"Pshaw! We know this kind of prince! The fellow must let us have his boat so that one of us can get help from one of the neighboring islands."

"He won't agree to that."

"No? Ah! And if I demand it?"

"Not then either, sir."

'Why not, if I may ask, eh?"

"Because I advised him already of the opposite, Captain."

"You? Oh, that's something different! I suppose you had with it our advantage in mind?"

"Of course! None of us is able to control such a boat and –"

"Well, Charlie, isn't that saying a bit too much? Should I, Captain Roberts from New York, not be able to manage such a craft with everyone knowing that I am quite the fellow to command even the strongest Orlog ship?"

"Can you shoot an ox, Captain?"

"What a question! Of course I can, despite what I said earlier when you came back with your game and provided the situation is such that the critter can't get to me, and I am allowed to shoot until it is dead!"

"Fine! But can you also shoot down a swallow?"

"By all means: no. That's impossible to do by a man, Charlie. You are a fine marksman, as you've proved often enough, but a swallow, no, even you wouldn't be able to shoot it in the air!"

"Yet, I've done it and not just once. I've seen fifteen year old Indian boys on the North American prairies do it."

"Ahoy, Charlie! Isn't that a canard the size of a sea monster?"

"No, it's the truth! But my comparison serves to demonstrate that the big is often easier that the small. You know quite well how to command a three-master. Yet, if you dare venture in one of your longboats, you are familiar with, onto the open seas, you'll find an enormous difference between the two. I have traveled the Missouri and Red River in fragile Indian bark canoes, rode the skin canoes of the Brazilians on the Orinoco and Marannon, and with the terrible catamaran of the East Indians the Indus and Ganges. These were the crafts of others on which life was dependent with every beat of the paddles, as you can imagine. But I will tell you frankly, Captain, that I don't dare do a discovery trip in this boat among the Pomatu Islands. If the least damage happens to the outrigger, then, in ninety-nine of a hundred instances, one is lost since the ocean here teems with sharks."

"By the devil. That's true! The shark is the most miserable creature I know, and whoever comes between its teeth, his time is ended without mercy and charity. But we need to look for a ship. You must admit to that, Charlie!"

"Of course! But not here among the Pomatu Islands, which we don't know at all, and to where larger ships rarely come. The Ehri, here, will sail for Tahiti. Have him take a reliable man along who will get us a ship. That will take care of us!"

"Hmm, it sounds all right! How long will it take the fellow to reach Tahiti?"

I turned to Potomba:

"How long will it take you to reach Tahiti?"

"If you give me a man who is a good paddle-man, I will need two days," was his answer.

I translated this to the captain.

"Listen, Charlie. What's the name of the fellow?"

"Potomba."

"I don't believe this. His name must be Muenchhausen. In two days from here to Tahiti! The man's lying like mad! I figure on a full five days. And for that, one would have to have a sleek-built ship with schooner rigging. Two days! That's humbug. It's impossible!"

"Look at his boat and this man, Captain! He doesn't look like a boaster. I'm inclined to believe that, with such a long, narrow wave cutter one can cover fifteen to sixteen miles per hour with a good southeastern trade wind."

"You really think so? Hmm! Then I must also believe that it is possible. But it's a feat, nevertheless! Hmm, yes, look at the fourteen sails out there! Not even ten minutes have passed since they turned from here, and I bet that they have traveled more than two miles already. You might be right, Charlie. It's now also obvious to me, which so far, I didn't believe, that even a well-equipped battle ship with a well-trained crew must beware of a flotilla of Malay prams. But look, here comes our mate! He carries a happy face for his success in putting these fellows to flight."

And, truly, the helmsman approached with such a self-satisfied and triumphant expression as if he had won a major sea battle.

"Well, sir. How did I do?" he asked me.

"Badly, very badly, mate!"

"Wha-wa-wat?" he asked totally surprised. "They didn't hurt us one bit and, when they saw me and my men, they sailed away as if the devil were on their heels!"

"But it's precisely that I didn't want them to sail away. They were to be captured inside the lagoon! You came much too early. They hadn't crossed through the passage yet. No shot had yet been fired by us, nor had you received from me or the captain the agreed-upon signal. I don't want to reproof you, mate, for your only mistake was to be a bit too brave. Maybe it was better for them to escape unharmed. But consider that we would have acquired fourteen boats, had my plan succeeded!"

The honest mate gaped at me with mouth open, then clapped his forehead with his hand.

"You know what I am, sir?"

"Well? A brave seaman and mate!"

"No! I am an ass, an ass with ears so long that one could build a three-master of them! We had them almost in our pocket, but I chased them off. One can't believe the giant folly an old seaman like me can commit."

"That's a noble insight for which you rise substantially in my respect, mate! But don't you want to return to our camp? We can leave a guard here in case those fleeing get the idea to return."

"You're right again, Charlie!" the captain nodded. "We've won big. I'll express my appreciation by permitting to fix a grog as stiff as the bowsprit of a Dutch coal bark!"

This 'military' command was received with a general jubilation. The men, holding arms in pairs like on parade, returned to our camp.

While the grog was prepared, I talked with Potomba. It turned out that he had truly been in India and that he had traveled through most of the island groups of the Australian archipelago. Being very clear and modest in his expressions, I soon took a liking to him.

"Now, Charlie, shall we choose the man to accompany your prince to Tahiti," the captain suggested. "I must stay here, of course, but the mate could do the job. What do you think?"

"I've nothing to say to such matters since you are the Captain. But I approve of your choice. The helmsman is an authority and will make himself better heard than a mere seaman, if you were to send one of them."

"I?" the mate asked. "What are you thinking, Captain! A good seaman ought not to leave his ship, and if that has sunk, not his people!"

"Only if the captain were missing and the mate had assumed his position," replied Roberts. "But I'm still around, following which you can readily sail for Tahiti, it not being against your duties and neglect of your responsibility. You know that my command counts. Whoever I delegate must follow orders."

"Do you really expect me, Captain, to entrust myself to such a floating piece of wood like the man's boat? And I can't exchange a single word in the fellow's language. How likely will it be for me to meet more people whose language I don't speak!"

"Hmm, that's true! Charlie, how about it? I'd rather keep you here with me, but you are the only one who understands Malay, even the dialect of the Society Islands. Would you care to accompany the man?"

"If you wish, I'll do it, Captain!"

"Fine. Then I ask you to do it! But – by the devil – what's that?" he suddenly said, pointing to the lagoon, which extended almost to our feet.

"A shark, truly, a shark, who's found his way in here through the passage!" the mate called. "Quickly, men, grab your harpoons!"

The shark's fin was visible on the surface. Maybe it had been attracted by our presence. The sight of a shark excites every seaman, he who knows no greater enemy than this ravenous monster. He makes every effort to kill it, even when he knows himself safe from it, and its death brings him no more than the satisfaction of knowing it is dead.

The men had all jumped up and got hold of various kinds of weapons. I, too, reached for my rifle to see if a bullet would suffice to kill the animal. That's when Potomba put his hand onto my arm and said:

"Don't shoot, Sahib. Potomba is master of all sharks and will command this one too to die!"

He threw off his tebuta and marra, to be left only with his loin cloth, grabbed his knife and launched himself from the beach far out into the water which closed above him with a splash.

A general shout of dismay arose.

"What is he doing?" the captain shouted. "He'll be lost!"

"Look for the fin!" the mate screamed, standing with a harpoon close by the water. "The shark has noticed him and is moving towards him. It will swallow him in a couple of seconds!"

I, too, was shocked but outwardly remained quiet.

"What's going to happen now to your trip to Tahiti, Charlie?" the captain asked. "This fellow isn't going to come out of the water again!"

"Let's wait, Captain! I've known divers in the West Indies who weren't afraid to attack a shark armed with only a knife. To bite, the fish must turn on its back. This allows the daring swimmer the time required to ram his knife into the animal's body and, with a forceful lunge, to cut open the belly of the creature. Look, Captain, the fight's started!"

At the spot where the fish was, the water erupted in a foaming swirl. Then, at some distance, first the head, then the chest of Potomba appeared. The man swung his knife high into the air and shouted a loud expression of victory.

"In the name of all cross and topgallant sails, he truly killed the creature!" the captain hollered. "Look, Charlie, the monster is drifting over there. Its body has been slit open from head to tail!"

Everyone around rose in shouts of joy not really suited to express recognition of the victor. Potomba stepped out of the water without paying attention to the men's praise surrounding him and came to me.

"The shark is dead, Sahib!" he simply and quietly reported.

"I knew it already when you leaped into the water," I told him, offering him my hand.

He took it, and I saw that this kind of appreciation delighted him more than the raucous and to him, incomprehensible praise of the others.

"Then you knew already that Potomba has a strong arm and a brave heart?"

"I noticed it already when you landed your boat. You weren't afraid of fourteen enemies. I am very fond of you, Potomba!"

"And I am your friend, Sahib! Tell this Yanki here that I will not take any one of them onto my boat to Papeete. You alone are to sail with Potomba!"

"I've told them already. When shall we sail?"

"Whenever you command it."

"Then get ready as soon as possible. I'm ready now. We will have to take a detour to avoid the flotilla of your foes. Right?"

"Yes, Sahib. I did not fear them here, for they would have fallen before stepping on land. But, on the open sea, they would encircle us, and we would be lost. Do you want the fish, Sahib?"

"Yes."

"Then give me a rope!"

It was fetched. He tied it to one of his arrows, placed the rope carefully on the ground and then shot it. The arrow deeply penetrated the shark's body, which could now be pulled in. While this happened, the Ehri put on his clothing, which he had dropped earlier.

"Are you ready, Sahib? Potomba is prepared to take you to Tahiti and will rather die than let anything happen to you!"

II. Pareyma

Between the previously mentioned longitude and latitude lies the group of islands, discovered by Quiros in the year 1606, subsequently explored more thoroughly by the famous Captain Cook in 1769. In honor of the Royal Society for the Sciences in London, they were named the Society Islands.

They fall into two parts: the windward and the leeward group, separated by a broad strait. To the first belong Tahiti or Otaheiti, the most important island of the archipelago. Then, there is Maitea, also called Osnabruc, and Eimeo or Moorea. The leeward islands go by the names Huahine, Raiatea, Taha, Bora Bora and Maurua or Maupiti.

The entire group of islands is of volcanic origin, however, the small, almost microscopic architects of the sea, little polyps, work incessantly on their enlargement. They surround every single isle with sharp-pointed coral reefs from which new land arises. This makes navigating the waterways between the islands highly dangerous.

The entire area of the Society Islands is no more than thirty-four square miles. There are many beautiful harbors, which, due to the coral barriers and the resulting heavy surf, are difficult to access. The islands' soil is generally rich and fertile. The mountains are covered by dense forest, and the shores are well watered by creeks. For this reason, the vegetation is luxuriant and produces an abundance of sugar cane, bamboo, breadfruit, palms, bananas, pisang, plane trees, sweet potato, grains, yams and arum root, together with other tropical plants.

The inhabitants are of Malay-Polynesian origin, dark copper colored, with the women being usually of a somewhat lighter complexion. They are sturdy and well built, social, hospitable and good-natured. Monogamous, they keep their women rather withdrawn, and love music, dancing, fencing and race their fast boats passionately.

In earlier times, they adhered to a polytheistic form of religion in which even human sacrifice was nothing unusual. Their priests, who were simultaneously healers and soothsayers, exercised extraordinary influence. Against this influence, however, there existed the missions founded by the British towards the end of the eighteenth century. Later, Catholic France send its emissaries who, with great difficulty, had to deal with the prejudices idolatry had injected into and otherwise, highly gifted race of men.

The holy religion of Christ is often unjustifiably accused. It is said: Civilization has its barbarism, light its shadow, love its egoism, and from the place of eternal bliss, one can, as the parable of the rich man and poor Lazarus teaches, look down into hell and observe the agony of the condemned. Christ's love and his lessons of mildness and compassion, have been hoisted onto the tips of swords by intolerant zealotry and, by a cunningly calculating lust for conquest depicted on its banner. With that, it has spread across the larger part of the globe. Entire races and peoples disappeared or, even today writhe in their terrible final death throws. By such events, history has lost an entire series of important cultural forces and impulses. The missionary, venturing into the wild abroad to convert the heathen, does not pay attention to the fact that these people are happier than us according to their needs. He does not take into account that his work might be more effective among the corrupt strata of his native nations than among those of different faith who often live in conditions resembling paradise!

This is a powerful reproach, yet it would be more than deplorable if it were based on truth. But isn't the race, the nation, the people, just as much an individual like a single human being, who is born, develops, then steps out of life again, once he has done his task? Already, the newborn carries within him the preconditions for his future death in every part of his constitution and organism. And so it follows that the society's totality is called to its demise by its own internal workings.

It is not the Bible's fault that man must die, nor is it the fault of the Koran or the Indians' Vedda. Nor can Christianity prevent the dissolution of nations. The holy teachings of love and forgiveness were given us to overcome death through our preparation and assurance for a better, higher and eternal future. And precisely because death and dissolution await all of us who dwell on this Earth, these teachings have the great and justified task 'to go out into the world', and redeem the entire Earth from the fear of the end which does not know a new beginning. Religion has not hoisted itself onto the tips of swords, but rather it is the politics of the conquerors, which sowed blood only to harvest blood again. The church counts among its faithful the strong peoples who providence has destined to stride victoriously across the globe But the church does not cause this triumphal venture, but follows it with its consolation to turn hate into love, pain into joy, and to reverse the curse the vanquished carries on his lips into a blessing.

Much has been spoken and written in this respect about the Society Islands. When this archipelago was discovered, its people were found to be childlike, naive and nearly without need. A rich, lush environment delivered to its people everything necessary for a contented and worry-free life. The strangers were received with friendly hospitality, were honored as gods and given everything their hearts desired. They carried this message home, awakening among other adventurers the wish for like enjoyment.

Ships were outfitted, and trade politics began to spin its plans. For their hospitality, the Tahitians received the vices and illnesses of the Occident and adopted more of the bad than the good characteristics of those calling themselves Christians, while not being true Christians in their hearts. This last fact is well worth remembering. To be sure, it must be sadly admitted that the virtues of the Tahitians, since their acquaintance with the Europeans, have suffered severely. But to blame Christianity for this fact is a major mistake. It is incorrect to identify the Holy Church with those calling themselves Christians. Christianity includes in its midst some of its greatest enemies. It must be deeply deplored that the missions, in addition to their real purpose, had to undertake the sad task of working against the immoral inheritance left behind by the mere Christians-in-name. –

Tahiti, the Pearl of the South Seas, lay under a magnificent, blue sky. The sun shone brightly on the shimmering waves of the sea and the wooded peaks of the Orohena Mountain and sparkled in the creeks and narrow cascades tumbling from the picturesque rising cliffs. However, its glow did not reach the friendly settlements lying in the shadows of palm trees and numerous fruit trees, which received pleasant cooling fanned by the fresh ocean breeze.

With this soft, mild breeze, the long-feathered fans of the coconut palms rustled, and the wind-torn leaves of banana trees dropped leisurely to the ground. The faded blossoms of orange trees dropped their petals from the weaving branches, spreading a delightful scent. However, their branches were already covered with golden fruit. It was one of these magically beautiful and wonderful days as can only be found in such rich splendor and glory in the tropics.

And, while the land presented itself so young and fresh in all its paradisiacal beauty as if it had just emerged from the hand of the creator, out on the coral reef the surf thundered its never ending and changing song. Times have changed and with them the people. The infinite, ever changing and yet constant sea is still the same and tosses still today, as it has done for thousands of years. Its crystalline, darkly-threatening and white-crowned spray continues to be driven against the sharp-edged reef. The waters, shot through by glistening reflexes, rise and sink as if thousands of Naiads were looking to where, above the waves' foam, green, waving tree tops rise. Below them a small people, destined to gradual ruin, are counting the final heart beats of their individual lives, not having the power of resistance. The same is true of the Amerindian race, making its death throws so terrible and dangerous for the white man.

There, on the beach, one could see Papeete, the capital of Tahiti. A colorful, stirring throng of people waved back and forth in their white, red, blue, striped, checkered or flowery long dresses. How splendidly had the young, beautiful girls adorned their black, curly and silky-soft hair with flowers and the artfully woven, snow-white wafting bast of the arrow root. Strutting among the beauties, their movements adroit and proud, were the native dandies. Their colorful *pareau* or folded *marra* was coquettishly slung around their loins and thrown across their shoulders was the decorous *tebuta*. They had their long, shining curls interwoven with strips of white tapa cloth and red flannel which went, not at all badly, with the complexion of their bronze-colored faces.

Then, suddenly, everyone rushed towards the beach. A canoe was approaching the island into whose white sail the breeze was fully engaged, so that its two occupants needed their paddles only to keep the craft on a steady course.

The canoe was one of the common round-bottomed boats, carved from a tree trunk. Due to this design, such a craft is capable of fast sailing, but would also quickly capsize were it not protected by its outrigger. The outrigger consists of two firmly attached wooden supports which are attached at right angles to the boat hull and hold a lightweight runner parallel to the craft. This wooden runner floats about four feet to the right of the boat and is firmly tied with bast to the two supports. This makes capsizing, or even rocking of the craft, impossible. The boat cannot tip to the left, since this would require lifting the runner from the water. Likewise, it cannot tip to the right since, because of the distance of the runner, it is impossible to push it under water, together with its supports. Of course, without these outriggers, one would have to move very carefully, since the round bottom would follow even a small inclination of one's body. One would not only run the danger of capsizing upon the least sway and thereby take an involuntary bath, but might pay for this small accident with one's life, since the bays and waters of these islands swarm with sharks of the most voracious kind.

The two men in the boat were Potomba and me.

The Ehri had been correct. After only two days, we arrived in Tahiti, although we had been forced to take a substantial detour. The steadily blowing trade wind had provided good assistance. Potomba knew very well how to use every single wave. Since we could take turns paddling and thus did not tire, our trip had been unusually quick.

Now, the magnificent isle lay ahead of us, about which I had read so many truthful things and many injudicious stories as well. Papeete rose ever higher the closer we came, and, at last, we could make out individuals in the crowd of people who were running to the beach to observe our craft.

I found it odd that such attention was given to our little, unimportant boat when there were many more important objects of interest in the harbor. I reefed the sails so that the breeze would not drive us onto the coral, which we were fast approaching, and asked:

"Do you see the people, Potomba?"

"Yes, Sahib," he nodded.

"How come it is our boat which is observed when there are so many others which could draw their attention?"

"These men and women know my boat, and Potomba is an Ehri, famous among his people. Sit still and hold on, Sahib, we are now entering the surf!"

We were approaching a small side passage through the reef, enabling only such small and narrow craft like ours to enter. A beat of paddles drove us into the surf. Its roiling wall tore us up, held us for a moment so that it seemed we were floating in the air, then shot us into the calm waters of the inner harbor.

To our right were anchored a number of sailing ships which had come in through the harbor's wider entry. The construction of one of them looked familiar. Only the hull could be seen since all sails were reefed in. Up in the shrouds hung a man, who seemed to have chosen this high point to get a better look at the town. He wore a Mexican sombrero. This reed fiber hat had an exceptionally broad brim, providing enough space for a sprawling family of peccaries to find protection underneath. Such an enormous brim had surely been made to special order, and such an order only a single fellow would be able to give, that is the very gallant and honorable mister Frick Turnerstick, on whose bark I had traveled from Galveston to Buenos Aires some time ago.

"Head for this ship over there, Potomba!"

"Why, Sahib?"

"Its captain appears to be an acquaintance of mine."

"Then you will leave me now in order to see him?"

"Only if I'm not mistaken about the man over there."

"Sahib, this ship belongs to a Yanki. Rather look for a ship of the Franki or Germani!"

"The man is my friend!"

"But I will not take you to him right now."

"Why not?"

"Did you not say to Potomba: 'I am fond of you!' Did you speak the truth?"

"I do not tell lies."

"Then I ask you to come to Papeete to my house to rest there until tomorrow. You should stay with me for a long time, many days, many weeks. But, since you promised your people to return quickly, I will keep you only until tomorrow morning."

"I would stay with you as long as my time permits, Potomba, however, if the captain over there is willing to pick up my people and can sail immediately, I must leave with him."

"He cannot leave earlier than tomorrow. The tide is coming in, and he must await the outgoing tide, which will come only at evening when it is too dark to dare passage through the reef."

"This is correct. Then he must wait for the second outgoing tide. But he could also have himself pulled out by a steamer during an incoming tide."

"You forget that such a big ship requires quite a bit of work and some time to get ready to leave."

"And you are not aware how fast the Yanki can get this job done!"

"Yet there ought to be enough time to come with me for at least one hour!"

"That is very true."

"Then promise me not to let me enter Papeete alone!"

"I promise!"

"I thank you, Sahib! Potai, my brother, will be glad that I have found a friend who is Germani."

We kept sideways to approach the stern of the bark, and once we came closer, I knew that I had not been mistaken. I recognized the ship's name written there in large lettering: 'The Wind'. The man in the shroud had turned his back to us and, therefore, did not notice our approach. When we had almost reached the starboard of the ship I put my hands to my mouth calling:

"Ship ahoi-ih!"

The man turned to peer at us.

"Ahoi-ih! Who's that? Lay to. There, at the rope!"

He climbed down to the deck with a speed which led me to think that he had recognized me. We fastened the boat to the rope that hung on the ship's side. I grabbed it and swung myself up. Barely had I climbed over the railing when the captain threw both arms around me, pressing me with such a force to his tar-scented jacket, that I came close to losing my breath.

"Charlie, old friend. You, here, among these island blots? What's bringing you to Australia? How do you come to Tahiti and Papeete? I thought you were still over there in America."

"By ship, by ship, I've come here," I laughed. There's no other way, my dear Mister Turnerstick. But, please, could you let me out of your clutches if it's not your intention to squeeze my soul out of my skin!"

"Well, as you like, Charlie! The trade wind would carry it along to China or Japan, where they wouldn't know what to do with it. Keep it then and tell me, finally, what you are doing in these latitudes!"

"To get to know land and people, as usual!"

"As usual? Hmm. To me it looks rather unusual! Here, this fellow steams, drives, rides, runs, hurries and jumps all over the globe, only because he's intent on getting to know land and people! Land and people! A free and open sea is preferable to me than all the land you get to see, and the people, well, my boys here are worth more than all the rascals you care to call 'people'. Stay on with me and sail on my 'Wind' over to Hong Kong or Canton!"

"You are headed for Hong Kong? That's wonderful! I'll come along!"

"Truly? Shake hands with me on it!"

"Right on! But I've one condition!"

"Oho! There are no conditions on my ship as you very well know!"

"Then I will climb back in my boat, Captain."

"That would be the silliest joke you ever committed in your life from which I must keep you. Tell me your condition then! I hope I can fulfill it."

"You must take my comrades along."

"What comrades?"

"Captain Roberts of the Poseidon and his men."

"Roberts? Poseidon? Isn't that ship and the man from New York?"

"Yes. We were headed from Valparaiso to Hong Kong, but were shipwrecked on one of the 'Dangerous Islands'. Roberts sent me to Tahiti to find a captain who's prepared to take us all on."

"Every good captain will do that, Charlie, and I'm glad that you came to me first! I know Roberts. He's a decent fellow, but doesn't appear to me to be experienced enough for these difficult waters. A storm hereabouts means something different from other areas. Had he tied his steering wheel firmly down with a strong rope, and would have kept a bit farther north of the Nukahowa Islands, there wouldn't have been a shipwreck. Where did you run ashore?"

"The island is unknown to us. It's located on the two hundred ninety third longitude east of Ferro and the twenty second degree of southern latitude."

"All right. That could be found! Is the ship badly wrecked?"

"It can't be pulled off the reef. When you arrive, the surf may very well have swallowed it already."

"Did you have many passengers?"

"I was the only one."

"How many sailors made it?"

"All of them."

"Hmm, that makes it necessary to take more provisions on. How much of the cargo was salvaged?"

"Most of it. It's mostly woolens and cotton cloth and a good supply of steel and other iron works."

"Then it's fortunate that I unloaded here without having taken on new cargo yet. Captain Roberts will be, of course, in a hurry, but we can't leave before the morning low tide. Who's this fellow?"

He pointed at Potomba, who had followed me on deck and had watched our conversation from a distance."

"He's an Ehri from Tahiti. He lives in Papeete. His name is Potomba."

"By the devil, a prince! How did you get to meet the man?"

"He arrived at our island, pursued by an entire flotilla of enemies and provided space for me on his boat."

"A literal adventure that! Who were his foes?"

"Their leader is a heathen priest from Eimeo. Potomba married his daughter and had himself married by a Catholic missionary."

"Ah! I hope you took good care of these rascals? You know how to do this well, Charlie!"

"They all escaped. My plan was wrecked through the clumsiness of the helmsman. Then you are willing to make your 'Wind' available to us?"

"Of course! Tomorrow morning, at low tide, we'll put to sea. But now come to my cabin. We've got to find out how well my bottles' contents kept south of the equator!"

"I can't deny you a drink of welcome, of course, but I cannot yet tie myself down. I promised Potomba to go on land with him, and he's impatient to see his wife and brother again."

"Then he can join us for a drink, and you'll permit me to accompany you. I have some business to conduct on land."

Potomba had to come along to the cabin where the good mister Frick Turnerstick treated us to one of his best. Then the three of us took one of the bark's boats, and with the Ehri's boat in tow, we rowed for land.

The closer we came, the more intense Potomba's look became. He seemed to notice something which totally absorbed his attention. He saw my questioning look and pointed ahead.

"Do you see the boats there, Sahib?"

On shore, ahead of us, were a large number of decorated boats, one next to the other. One in its midst was distinguished from the others by colorful pennants and a variety of flowers and leaf wreaths.

"Yes," I responded. "What's the matter with them?"

"Do you also see the boat with the pennants and garlands?"

"Of course. Why do you ask?"

"On both sides of its sharp bow, the words *Mata Ori* (Eye of the Sun) are inscribed. That's what I called Pareyma when I began to love her. And this, I also named the boat which I had built for her at Tamai on Eimeo for Anoui to fetch me on the day I was going to wed her and to take her to my palm-thatched house. I know that boat very well. Its outrigger is not attached with bast but with pegs. Today, the boat is decorated just like before when I paddled it as the groom. There must be a wedding on Eimeo, and Anoui must have lent it to the girl's father to fetch the groom with."

While he said this, his handsome, open features displayed a disquiet I could not understand. The memory should have pleased him, not disturbed him.

"And do you see the man in the boat?" he continued. "It is Ombi."

"Who is Ombi?"

"The servant of the priest, but he loves me more than him. He carried Pareyma in his arms when she was still a child, and has cared for her ever since her mother died."

The servant who was watching us seemed to recognize Potomba and, with a happy face, stood up. But he quickly sat down again putting his hands in front of his face.

Beach sand grated below our boat's keel, and we jumped on land. Potomba stepped over to *Mata Ori*.

"Ombi!" he addressed the servant.

The man made no move.

"Ombi!"

When again there was no response, he jumped into the boat and grasped the old Polynesian by his shoulder.

"Ombi, why don't you answer me?"

The servant removed his hands from his face and looked up. A couple of tears shone in his eyes.

"Does pain have words, Potomba?" he asked.

"What pain?"

"You abandoned Atua, the god of all good, and went to the mitonare."

"That pains you now? Did you not often admit to me, when I told you secretly about the messiah, the lamb of God, that the great Sahib, Jesu, is more dear to you than Atua, the god of Tahiti, who never came to cure the sick, to revive the dead and to die for our sins?"

"I did say this, Potomba, and say it still today. But I am the servant of a priest I must obey, and may not say what I think."

"You can say what you think and believe. Leave the priest of the false god and come to me! You love Jesu, the Nazari. You also love me and Pareyma. Why don't you want to be with us? Why do you cry when you see me? You never did it before!"

"I cry because I would love to be with you and yet cannot."

"Why can you not?"

"Because I cannot leave Pareyma, who needs me."

"Pareyma? If you come to me, you will also be with her!"

"No!"

I noticed the fright which suddenly paled Potomba's dark features. He faltered and let his fearful look sweep the surroundings. The people strolling the beach had come closer, observing him with sympathy but from a distance. He had to notice this and guessed more than I could – that something problematic had happened during his absence. Involuntarily, his hand reached for his sharp *Kris* (dagger) sticking from his sash. From his gnashing teeth, he hissed:

"Where is Pareyma?"

"Go home and ask. I am not allowed to tell you!"

Potomba took a step back. His eyes flashed and his lips twitched while he asked again:

"Ombi, where is Pareyma? Do you listen? I am asking you!"

The servant lowered his head and repeated:

"Go home and ask!"

"Ombi, you are still silent. Well, I shall go, but whoever has harmed Pareyma will have to pay for it!"

He left and the two of us followed him. The crowd, which had gathered, respectfully and sympathetically made room for him. He did not utter a word, turned only once to see if we were still with him. The path took us quite a distance through Papeete until we reached a building distinguished by its size and the extent of the breadfruit plantation belonging to it.

"Come!" he said briefly and entered.

In the first room, a young man sat on a mat who we recognized at once as Potomba's brother because of his likeness.

"Potai!"

"Potomba!"

The seated man jumped up and reached out with his arms as if to embrace the arrival but then stepped back and dropped his arms.

"What is the matter with you, Potai? Am I not your brother?"

Potai pointed down where a dagger was stuck in the earth.

"I sunk the kris into the soil until you would return, Potomba. I did swear not to touch you until the death of our mother has been avenged!"

"The death of mother? Speak, Potai, speak quickly, quickly! Where is Pareyma?"

"Away."

"Away to where?"

"To Eimeo, to her father, the priest of the heathen."

"Of her free will?"

"Of her free will! I traveled over to Maitea, and when I returned, she was gone. Your mother wanted to hold her back and fought with her. Potomba, your wife returned to the heathen idols and killed your mother."

"What with?"

"With her kris. I pulled it from our mother's heart. It was still bloody. Here it is, stuck in the earth!"

The Ehri bent down and pulled out the dagger.

"This is not Pareyma's knife. It is the priest Anoui's dagger!" he exclaimed.

"He did capture her, and so it is he who is the murderer."

"And she truly went with him of her free will?"

"I did not see any trace of a fight between her and her father. Did you see the boats and your *Mata Ori*?"

"Yes. What is the meaning of the flotilla?"

"Do you also know Matemba, your deadly enemy?"

"You ask as if I were a little boy!"

"You return at the right time. Anoui, the priest and father of your unfaithful wife, has come to fetch Matemba. There is a wedding in Tamai, and Matemba is going to be your wife's husband!"

Potomba stepped to the opening which served as a window.

He needed some air if he wasn't to suffocate. So far, the two brothers had ignored our presence. The captain whispered to me:

"You seem to understand these people's language. What's happening here? It does not look like anything good."

"It is terrible!" I replied. "Someone killed the Ehri's mother, and his wife is going to be wedded today to a heathen man."

"By the devil! That means murder and manslaughter!"

"These two men are Christians!"

"Pshaw! Vendetta persists even among the Christian Polynesians. You will see!"

Potomba now turned back. His features looked like stone, and in his eyes glowed a somber fire.

"Potai, what have you done so far?"

"I have sold everything."

The Ehri nodded in agreement. He seemed to have guessed his brother's plan at once.

"Also the boats I sent you from the Tubuai Islands when Anoui pursued me?"

"Yes. We shall go to Samoa."

"You did right. Are you ready?"

"I am only waiting for you!"

Potomba turned to me and asked, "is the ship of this sahib going to pick up your friends?"

"Yes."

"Where does it sail then?"

"To the country of the Chinesi."

"Then your way takes you past the islands of Samoa, which you call the Navigator Islands. That is where my brother and I want to go. May we travel with you?"

I translated this question to the captain.

"I'm willing to take them along. Then they did sell everything?" he asked. "It seems, after all, that Christianity has made lambs of tigers who take flight instead of revenge!"

"Oh, Captain, look at these people! Do they look like lambs?" I gave Potomba the desired information: "You can come along."

"When will the ship leave port?"

"At the beginning of low tide, this coming evening."

"Is my brother allowed to bring our personal belongings?"

This, too, the captain permitted.

"Potai, you are the younger one. You will obey me?" the Ehri asked.

The brother nodded.

"You will bring all that is ours to the ship I am going to point out to you!"

"Our possessions are in three mats."

"You stay on until I return!"

"No, Potomba. Do I not also have a kris?"

"First comes my kris, and only should I die, will come yours. Then you can avenge me instead of dying with me."

"I will obey you!"

"Then come, Sahib. I wanted to show you my hospitality, but I am now without a house."

We returned to the beach. Potomba pointed the bark out to his brother who then left without a word.

"What will you do, Potomba?" I asked.

"Do you believe that Pareyma is unfaithful to me?"

"I can't say, because I do not know her."

54

"But I know her. She has her dagger. She is brave and courageous. She will die, but will not go with Matemba. I shall rescue her from him and her death!"

"You intend to kill Anoui?"

"Yes."

"He is the father of your wife!"

"He is the murderer of my mother!"

"You are a Christian!"

"He is a heathen!"

"Do you know what the great Sahib, Christ, commands? Forgive, and you shall be forgiven!"

"I will obey him, for I shall forgive Anoui after I have killed him."

"That is not the right way, Potomba. I mean that –"

He interrupted me with an impetuous move of his hand.

"You are a Christian since birth, Sahib, but I am one only for a short time. Later, I will be also like you. Were you not going to kill my pursuers had they not fled but had attacked me?"

"I would have killed them, had there been no other help for you."

"Well then! They did earn death, and I do not have any help here in Papeete either. Or is an Ehri to beg for justice with the Ingli and Franki? Leave with your friend. I will come to the ship when it is ready to leave port. And should I not have returned by that time, then my brother may return to land and avenge me!"

"Don't you want to visit the grave of your mother before you go?" I asked, maybe to gain some time, maybe also from sympathy for his fate.

"Don't you know that the grave of a person is tabu? Am I to see her grave without being able to tell her spirit that her murderer has gone to Oro, you Christians call the devil? Pareyma is my wife. She was not going to have herself wed to me by a mitonare so as not to anger her father. For his sake, she remained heathen, although, in her heart she believes in the good *bapa* in heaven. This is why Anoui still has power over her. He came to her and she had to follow him. But I shall get her back again. *Joranna* (farewell), Sahib. *Joranna*!"

"I will not say Joranna, but will go with you!"

"You intend to stop me?"

"No, I want to share your danger!"

"Then you truly love me, Sahib! Come!"

I gave the captain the necessary explanation. Mister Frick Turnerstick, so careful and cautious in all adventures on land, seriously advised against my joining Potomba. But it was impossible for me to leave my friend; my presence might yet be of help to him. The captain went to town, while I walked with the Ehri to the beach. He searched among the moored boats until he had found one larger than his which might hold four people.

On the western horizon glistened the white sails of the wedding flotilla which carried his deadly enemy to Eimeo. When they had disappeared, he took the boat he had chosen, after having scratched a sign into the sand, probably for the boat's owner. I jumped in after him, then put my rifles away and grabbed a paddle. He raised the sail. The breeze filled it and we flew across the calm waters of the harbor, followed by the spectators' looks on shore.

We did not follow the flotilla but once we were beyond the reef, sailed instead along Tahiti's coast for some distance, and then headed directly for Eimeo. Of course, I had to leave the boat's steering to Potomba. He landed on a secluded spot where wild *pisang* scrub grew up to the water's edge. There, we took down the mast and, with some effort, pulled the boat into its leafy hiding place. Afterwards, Potomba scrambled through the brush with me following.

We came to a breadfruit plantation, which offered us good protection, and soon arrived at a rise from where we could overlook the entire island of Tamai. We noticed immediately that the place was exceptionally busy, particular on the beach where the boats of the flotilla that had arrived before us. In front of an exceptionally large house, its rear fronted by a bamboo grove, a large crowd of people was moving about. Just below the hillside where we hid, stood an altar decorated with palm leaves and flowers. Behind it stood the images of two idols, Atua and Oro, before which the ceremony was likely to be held.

"What do you intend to do, Potomba?" I asked the Ehri.

"I shall wait until they stand before the altar. Then I will get Pareyma."

"You won't succeed in that."

"Then I will fetch her from the boat when Matemba sails with her to his home."

"When is this to happen?"

"Today, at about midnight. This is what the teachings of the idols command."

"Whose is the big house over there?"

"It belongs to the priest."

"Which are the women's rooms?"

"Pareyma's was always the one towards the sea."

"Is her mother still about and does she have sisters?"

"No. Her mother is long dead, and she is the sole child of the priest."

"Isn't she going to be adorned for the wedding?"

"Yes. Afterwards, she is left alone to talk with the gods."

"The priest knows that you returned today!"

"Who tells you that?"

"Nobody. But don't you see the man who walks back and forth between the house and the bamboo grove? He carries a club to guard your wife. This is a sign that she was forced and did not go to Eimeo of her free will."

"I knew it! The Ehri of Tahiti does not fear the people of Eimeo. He will publicly demand the return of his wife!"

I did not know the local circumstances and, therefore, thought it best to let him make his own decisions. However, I decided to reconnoiter a bit. The prairie hunter was stirring in me. I put my rifles next to Potomba, informed him of my intentions, and then crept along the hillside to the bamboo grove. Dogs and other four-legged animals had trampled narrow pathways through it. Creeping along one of them, I arrived, unnoticed, very close to the house. That's when a lovely woman's voice arose in an undertone:

"Te uwa to te malema, te uwa to hinarro – the little cloud in the moon, the little cloud I love.

It was this touching love lament, which I had heard before sung by the women and girls of the Pele Islands, and I figured that the songstress was no other than Pareyma. Immediately I felt the need to speak with her. This venture could become unpleasant for me, but I carried my knife and revolvers with me, and for the good Ehri I could expose myself to a little danger.

I pushed myself, therefore, to the edge of the bamboo grove. The guard came and passed without noticing me, although it was broad daylight. Quickly, I rose behind him and hit him with my fist on his bare head. He collapsed, unconscious. I now stepped to the bamboo wall of the house from behind which the voice came. After searching for a few minutes, I found a small defective spot through which I could peer into the room.

If the young woman I now saw was truly Pareyma, I could understand the love Potomba entertained for her. Having finished her song, she now stood in the middle of the room, and an incessant stream of tears ran down her cheeks. She was a slim, noble figure, still fresh in her youth. One could still perceive her beauty despite her heart's suffering which wracked her body. Her lovely, dark eyes were dimmed, her sharply defined eyebrows were pinched and her fine lips closed. Not a single flower or any bauble was noticeable in her hair or on her figure. Yes, she seemed even to have disdained the dress and materials copied or traded from Europeans, which seemingly beautify the external appearance. A *pareau* of soft yellow-brown *tapa* cloth, reaching only a little below her knees, was wrapped around her hips, and a *tehei* of the same material covered her shoulders and her entire upper body. Her raven-black hair hung full, long and curly down her neck, neither adorned by a blossom nor any waving fiber of arrowroot. She was herself a flower, torn away from the place where she would have blossomed most beautifully.

Noticing that she had firmly closed the entrance with a strip of bast, I stepped a couple of paces away from the wall and called in a subdued voice:

"Pareyma!"

The sobbing stopped for she had heard me.

"Mata Ori, don't be afraid. Potomba is close!"

A barely suppressed shout of joy sounded inside.

"Who are you?" she asked.

"A friend of the Ehri. Do you wish to become Matemba's wife?"

"No. I still have my dagger and will kill myself if I find no rescue."

"Then you have remained faithful to Potomba?"

"Yes. My father came and forced me to follow him."

"Who killed the Ehri's mother?"

"My father. She fought him."

"Do you love your father?"

"No. I did love him, but no longer!"

"You will be rescued. Do everything your father demands. If we do not succeed soon, we will rescue you when you sail back to Tahiti."

That's when a tamtam sounded from the opposite side of the house. I returned to the unconscious man and put a stone near his head. Stones of this size lay on the roof to protect it from the wind. One of them could have rolled down and hit the guard. Then I returned to Potomba the way I had come.

He had been able to observe my moves from the height and greeted me with obvious desire. I gave an extensive report and was myself almost carried away by the delight my report raised in him.

Now we could hear the sound of numerous flutes mixed with the rhythm of the drums, as if the ceremony was to begin. Pareyma was led from the house followed by a long line of people.

"Do you see Matemba on her side, Sahib?" Potomba asked.

"I do see him."

"He was among my pursuers. Ori will devour him tonight. I shall not do any harm to anyone here. But while you spoke with my wife, I decided how I will get Pareyma back. I am a Christian. You are correct. And this kris is not to be reddened by any other blood than that of my mother's. Nevertheless, they are to die, but not from my hand!"

The procession arrived at the altar onto which Anoui, the priest, climbed to give his speech. That's when Potomba left me and disappeared into the bushes. I now pushed myself forward as far as possible, so that I could comfortably observe the slope below me. Matemba and Pareyma stood in front of the priest. The tamtams and pipes made an ear-shattering noise, which stopped at a sign from the priest. His speech consisted of invectives against Christianity, for which I would have liked to send a bullet through his head. Then came curses on the disloyal Ehri. Finally, the priest reached behind him to take several skull bones from the altar, which he held towards Matemba.

"Put your hands onto this skull which comes from the heads of your ancestors and swear: *Eita anet oe a faarue i ta oe vatrina?* – Will you never leave your wife? This is the heathen formula upon which the groom must answer with '*eita*' (no). This done, the marriage is concluded.

Matemba had not yet spoken his '*eita*' yet, when Potomba pushed through the crowd of listeners to step before the altar.

"Be greeted, Anoui, father of my wife!" he called. "She came to you, when I was gone, and I am here to take her back."

Dead silence ensued. In a gesture of dismissal the priest stretched both arms out and shouted:

"This place is sacred. Leave it and us, betrayer!"

Potomba remained quiet. He put his hand on Pareyma's shoulder and answered:

"Yes, this place is sacred because I, a Christian, have come here. I shall leave, but first, you will give me my wife!"

"Escape, or death will take you!"

"Death?" Potomba replied with a smile. "Did it take hold of me when you pursued me to take my life and property? You and hundreds of heathen, are not strong enough to send death to me, a single Christian. You can only kill women. Here, on this dagger rests the blood of my mother. You did kill her, Anoui, and I demand her life back today or yours for hers!"

"Then die yourself!" Anoui exclaimed reaching for him.

Potomba fell back a step and shouted loud enough to be heard far and wide:

"I am to die, I, the Ehri of Papeete? I am in the protection of my God, but you shall perish like I will now destroy your gods!"

With a quick step he leaped onto the altar. Grabbing first one, then the other of the heathen clay idols, he tossed them to the ground, where they burst into pieces. Then he swung his kris high into the air and shouted:

"And today, still, I shall take my wife from you!"

A single, terrible scream erupted from all throats. Everyone rushed for the altar to grab the daring man who had, however, jumped off before the first arrived and climbed up as quickly as possible, towards me. It was fortunate that not a single one of those present had carried a weapon to this usually peaceful ceremony, or the Ehri would have been lost. Not a single one? Did there not stand someone close to the altar who was just bending his bow, and there, under the banana tree, another? They were aiming at Potomba, and it could be seen that they would hit him. I had to prevent it. I leveled my carbine, aimed, and twice pulled the trigger. The two pagan bowmen dropped to the ground.

Now Potomba had reached me. Some of his pursuers came screaming up the hill, while others ran off trying to surround the rise on all sides.

"I thank you, Sahib, for your help. The arrows would have hit me. Let's get to the boat quickly! Can you run well?" he asked hurriedly.

I did not reply for there was no time. It actually did not suit me to run away from these people, but I knew that our rescue depended on our legs. Despite my heavy boots, I kept pace with the Ehri, who must have had respectable lungs and strong sinews, for our enemies remained a long way behind us. When we got to the boat, there was just enough time to push it into the water, leap in, and to gain a sufficient distance so that no arrow could reach us. Only then did the

Polynesians break through the thicket on the beach, throwing their arms into the air, and making malicious gestures.

We took the paddles and worked our way against the trade wind towards Tahiti. Without landing there, we let ourselves drift back with the current and wind to Eimeo and landed at Alfareaita, a small village, directly opposite Papeete.

There, we remained until dusk. Potomba did not tell me anything of what he intended to do. No doubt, his silence had good reason, so I did not bother him with any questions.

It must have been around eleven o'clock at night when we took off again. Earlier, the Ehri had purchased a rather large quantity of small fish and loaded them in the boat. I could not figure out what he intended to do with them, but was certain to find out soon. We rowed to about the middle between the two islands, Tahiti and Eimeo, where we stayed put.

Darkness lay on the water, but in the sky shone thousands of stars. The waves surrounded our canoe like liquid, transparent crystal. That's when the Ehri took one of the fish, tied it to a strip of bast, and hung it into the water. It did not take long for the line to be jerked sharply. After a while, Potomba tossed in a second, then a third fish, and continued until more than half a dozen sharks swarmed about our craft.

I had a faint hunch of his intentions. He was gathering the hyenas of the sea around his boat to serve him against his enemies. But exactly how this was to happen, was not clear to me. In any case, the nearness of these 'endearing' creatures was rather unpleasant to me. However, on our shipwrecked island he had referred to himself as the Lord of the Sharks. Although I can call myself a passable swimmer, I did not entertain particular sympathy for his man-eating creatures. In fact, I openly admit that I would have felt more comfortable on the 'Wind' of my good mister Frick Turnerstick, than on the little boat from whose low board one could have touched the sharks with a hand.

A spectacle, even as horrible as it was, presented itself. Despite the darkness of the night, the water seemed like liquid white gold descending to an ever darker bottom. In it, every movement was recognizable, and when the Ehri tossed in another fish, then six to eight terrible jaws approached the stern of the boat to fight for the prey. A battle ensued which could raise one's hair with the thought that only a thin layer of wood lay between these monsters and us humans.

Concerning the Ehri, he did not seem to be the least concerned about my unpleasant feelings. Tossing another fish out from time to time, his searching looks went into the direction from which the wedding flotilla with the bride and bridegroom was to come. I was quite certain that the wedding had not been consummated following our venture, he, however, seemed certain of it. When some faint lights appeared on the horizon he stood up in the boat for a better view.

The lights came closer and became brighter with every second. I soon saw that it was the flotilla with every boat carrying a torch at its bow.

"They are coming," Potomba said cold-bloodedly. "Now Pareyma will be mine once more!"

He tossed the red and white striped tebuta from his shoulders and got hold of his kris with his right hand, while simultaneously tossing one more fish over with his left hand.

"Serve me only for two minutes, Sahib, then I will obey you for as long as you wish!"

I got hold of the paddle. He did likewise, and with his direction, we sailed in an arc around the arriving boats, then steered towards them. Finally, when we were parallel to them, we rushed towards the first boat of the flotilla. This boat carried three people I could clearly recognize: Matemba, Anoui and Pareyma. Applying mighty paddle strokes along the right side of the flotilla, we reached the boat so that our left side forcefully hit the other's outrigger. The sharks had followed us. I held on to the paddles while Potomba now stood upright, kris in fist.

"Pareyma, come!" he called.

The woman rose and launched herself over the outrigger into our boat. The Ehri received her with his left arm and let her slide down. He then leaned over and, with two quick moves, cut the bast ropes connecting the wedding boat's outrigger to its supports.

A terrible scream arose from two throats. The boat capsized. Matemba and the priest tumbled into the water and were instantly devoured by the sharks.

Pareyma put her hands to her face. Potomba took hold of the other paddle and threw himself into a hard pull. As if launched from a bow we flew away while the flotilla wallowed in chaos from which only a single boat attempted to follow us. I reached for my rifle and said:

"I'm going to send this man a bullet!"

"Hold it, Sahib! It is no enemy following us but a friend. Only Ombi rows like this, the servant of my wife. No one else equals him and Potomba, the Ehri. Let him come close; he will join us!"

Behind us, the furious occupants of the flotilla howled, attempting to catch up with us. They did not succeed. Five minutes later, we had reached the 'Wind', from where they lowered the ladder-rope for us to climb up.

Ombi, the old gray-head, had jumped from his boat into ours.

Only now did Pareyma take her hands from her face.

"Potomba, you killed my father!" she groaned.

"Tell your heart to be quiet, Pareyma," he begged. "Your pain is also mine, and your fortune is my fortune. The idols have fallen and now, the good *bapa* with his son, who came to Earth, will be with us to change all misfortune into joy!"

We climbed up.

"Quickly, Charlie!" the captain shouted. "There come these fellows with their torch boats to get you. Up! Up! Turn the lights off, boys!" he commanded his men, "and quickly hoist the two boats on deck so that these rascals won't notice anything. They must think that everyone's asleep on our good 'Wind'. Pull up on the ropes boys! Pull, boys, pull! Now stop! In with these nutshells! Wonderful! That's good! Now pick up some clubs, and if anyone dares to stick his nose up here, give him a good whack!"

This measure proved to be unnecessary. The pursuers seemed to think that we had headed towards land and rowed for the shore from where we could see the torch light for some time.

Potai received his brother and his sister-in-law with joy. Of course, the captain had to be told everything in great detail. When I had finished, Pareyma offered me her tender brown hand.

"I thank you, Sahib! You saved me from death. I would have died by my knife before I would have left the house with Matemba."

By morning, we put to sea. Five days later, captain Roberts with his crew and salvaged cargo were on board with us. Then we sailed the 'Wind' north to west to reach the Samoa Archipelago.

There, on the island of Upolu, that is in Saluafata, lives, still today, a rich Polynesian trader who calls himself Potomba.

At times, when the sun bathes its burning vestment in the waters to go to rest, the old man Ombi rows out an outrigger canoe. In it sit Potomba and Pareyma, and if Ombi would care to eavesdrop, he would hear how the dark-skinned man whispers to his wife: *Mata ori*, you eye of my day, you light of my life!"

Maybe, in such solitary hours, the beautiful pair will remember the past, their fortune and the subsequent misery on Tahiti, the wedding day on Eimeo, the sail to the Pomotu and Samoa Islands, the old, neat mister Frick Turnerstick, and, maybe even the Germani with his big seaman's boots, to whom, still today, while he is writing this down, the grieving words resound in his ears:

"Te uwa to te malema, te uwa to hinarro."

5. A Prairie Fire

Penned in 1887, this brief story of a prairie fire is mostly taken verbatim from the account of an American hunter, J. T. Irving, who experienced such an event on the prairie.

The story was first published in "Der Gute Kamerad, Spemanns Illustrierte Knaben-Zeitung." – "The Good Comrade, Spemanns Illustrated Boys' Journal."

The translator has taken the liberty to correct two errors of Karl May's concerning the geographical placement of the State of Illinois, described as being Lake Wabash and Lake Superior, changing them to Lake Michigan and the State of Wisconsin, respectively.

Prairies, seemingly infinite, cover the northwestern part of the United States of America. These savannah-like plains resemble a dry ocean on which stiff grasses of dry mound-like growth form the waves. If a gust of wind sweeps across, this sea of grass billows in a lively dashing of waves, its surf dying away at the distant horizon.

The State of Illinois, located between the Mississippi and Ohio Rivers, and bordered by Lake Michigan and the State of Wisconsin, still maintains the most extensive prairies, making up two thirds of its entire territory. Farther west lies Iowa, a prairie state, situated between the Mississippi and Missouri Rivers. There, like in Minnesota, the grassy expanses are interspersed by woods and various creeks and lakes. Prairies also extend through the central and southern states of the Union. Missouri, in the north, is very fertile and is called the Garden of the West, its remainder being prairie. Louisiana, too, has its prairies as does Texas to an even greater extent.

Since 1869 the Pacific Railroad, this marvel of all railroad constructions, cuts through the North American prairies. The original residents of the endless grass savannah, the redskins or Indians, are being pushed ever further back by the advancing civilization. They also die off en masse by their contact with deceases carried by Whites.

In contrast to our German meadows, snugly bordered by hedges and woods, the prairies possess a sublime limitlessness, which, like the infinity of the ocean, fills the human mind with a reverential sense for the power of the Creator. Such an impression of the prairie is described by the writer Sealsfield through Colonel Morse's personal experience:

"I suppose I can say that I gained a living God, a God I did not know before, for the one I got to know on the prairie, is my very own God, my Creator, who manifests himself in the magnificence of his works. From this hour on, he stands before my eyes and will do so as long as I breathe."

As described before, prairie grasses are different from our German meadow grasses in that they are stiffer and are growing in mounds. And, likewise, the flowering plants growing amidst these grasses are different from our meadow flowers by their bushy height and denser grouping. The most important prairie grass is the buffalo grass, *Tripsacum* or *Sesleria distichoides*. "Where there is nothing growing anymore," says Karl Mueller in his 'Book of Botany', "where the soil becomes ever worse and sandier, this beneficial short-stemmed grass does not relinquish its rule and nourishes, together with peculiar types of clover, bison or buffalo who, in numerous herds, roam the infinite ocean of grass west of the Mississippi. This is the reason why this grass received its name: 'buffalo grass'. It would not be wrong to call it the actual plant for life on the prairies. Like the life of the wild oxen is tied to it, so is also the life of the manifold and fragmented tribes of the prairie Indians tied to these herds and this so strongly, that the extermination of the buffalo will also result in the extinction of these Indian tribes."

The paucity of trees and shrubbery in the western prairies is conspicuous. Some scientists find the cause of this paucity in the numerous herds of bison who trample all young tree growth, others in the frequent prairie fires which scorch all shrubbery.

Yes, these fires are the most terrible phenomenon of the prairie! The ocean has its storms, the prairie its fires. In the former cold waves devour everything. In the latter all is consumed by flames. In one, man finds a grave in the waves, in the other a grave in the flames. Either one is horrible, but the latter seems to me the most horrific. Whoever escapes this grave has, however, experienced a spectacle whose terrible magnificence is not attained by any other phenomenon.

Following is the report of an eyewitness.

In the pursuit of wild turkeys during a hunting expedition on the prairie, the American J. T. Irving, had been lured by the game into a small woods and became separated from his party. The sun, standing high in the sky, finally reminded him that it was close to noon and that it was time to join his companions.

"I now left the woods," Irving tells, "and walked across the open prairie towards the area where I thought to find the tracks of my traveling companions. But in vain did I look about, increased my pace, looked again, and used up my shooting powder. Nothing could be seen, not a sound was to be heard. The high grass wafted in the wind, but no living being could be seen. The prairie was a desert. Then I feared that I might have walked past the tracks of my party, yet it seemed impossible to me that I could have overlooked the imprints of such a large group. With hurried steps I climbed a hillock which provided a wider view. A wilderness of grassy plain, interspersed by small undulating knolls, spread before my searching looks, but nothing of my companions could be seen. Above me was the sky, below the grounds of the prairie, and I the only living being in this wilderness. It was time to look for a resting-place for the night, which is why I looked for a tree. But as far as I could see, none could be spied. Everywhere desiccated grass, some bushes, and again grass. I was like a mariner in the midst of an ocean without compass and map. Which direction was I to take? If I went west, I might come closer to my companions, but it was uncertain. I would have moved also farther from White settlements, I could surely reach to the east of me. Thus, I decided to head eastward as long as hunger did not sap my strength and until I would reach the banks of the Missouri.

"My pace became faster and more anxious. Foremost, I needed to find some shelter. It was towards the end of October. The wind was already noticeably cold and I had only my light hunting coat to protect me. Just when the sun was ready to sink below the horizon, I spotted, still several miles distant, a line of forest. This affected me like a horseman's spurs do a tired horse. With renewed courage I hurried up and down the knolls and trampled through the rough grass. But then the sun set and as soon as darkness fell, everything became indistinct. The forest, which could barely be two miles distant, was no longer visible. Again, I climbed a hillock to await at its top the moon's rise, since I feared to lose my direction in the darkness.

"A sad feeling overcame me as I sat there. There was nothing but the desolate desert around me, and the cold sky with its sparkling stars above. The wind changed to a blustery storm and whistling past me, occasionally carried the howling of a wolf. More than an hour did I sit, leaning on my rifle, peering to the eastern horizon, impatiently waiting fort the moon's appearance. Never before did I view its rise as happily than now, when it rose above the borderless plain.

"Right away, I continued my wandering and, after an hour's strenuous walk, I reached the forest. From Indians, I had learned to build a shelter from branches, and it did not take long, until I warmed myself by a happily flaming fire which I had started next to a fallen tree trunk. While my appetite was strong, my tiredness was greater, and I was soon asleep. However, the increasing force of the wind soon awoke me again. At times, the gusting wind sank to hollow tones, then swelled up again to rage howling and whistling through the crashing trees. For awhile I sat next to the dying fire, only to bury myself once more into my bed of leaves and twigs, but sleep had been banished. Something horrible was carried in the wind's sounds. At times it seemed to me as if voices were screaming through the forest, then, suddenly, every sound died. Eagerly, my ears took in every sound. A superstitious fear befell me, which I found difficult to fight. I took my rifle in hand, for my senses were so confused and impaired that, every moment, I expected an Indian to appear near me. Finally, I got up again and rekindled the fire. That's when a hard gust of wind blew through the forest blowing sparks and ashes in all directions. Instantly, fifty small fires shot their lapping tongues into the air, as if laughing triumphantly at me. Barely born, they rose quickly to a high pyramid of flames, hopping easily from one to the other of the spread-out tufts of dry grass. A moment later they had escaped onto the open prairie. Now a waving line of sparkling flames shone into the dark night.

"A new hurricane of wind was approaching. Nearby moaning and whimpering announced it in the distance. As it came closer, a cloud of swirling leaves filled the air, young trees bend to the ground with older trees crashing down. Then the gust arrived and rushed out onto the prairie. Myriads of glowing ash particles were tossed up high. Like meteors, burning bunches of grass flew through the air. The flames spread out into a giant sea of flames, a conflagration which, unstoppable, poured forth like a stream of lava across the expanse of grass, surrounding the forest into the farthest distance with a red ribbon. The glaring light made the gloomy darkness of the forest appear even blacker. The roaring and hissing of the flames was even stronger than the howling of the wind. There were uncountable pyramids of fire that danced and frantically leaped out there in the desert and awakened new dancers everywhere. Their dashing resembled the rush of a tossing ocean whose waves rear up against each other fighting in wild tumult. Right in the direction of their run stood a group of oak trees whose dry leaves still clung firmly to the branches. The blazing flood arrived illuminating the group. Now, black smoke enveloped the first tree – then the glowing fire rushed up to the branches and shot, leaping triumphantly, almost a hundred feet into the air. The effect was momentary, for in no time the fire had passed the trees. It once more sunk to the level of the prairie, and only a weak dark red glow played about the blackened branches. Greedily, the raging element streamed on, spying for nourishment through the dips and hollows. The fire raged for several hours with the entire horizon engulfed by a fiery belt. The more the circle expanded, the smaller the flames became until they, finally, wrapped themselves around the knolls like a thin golden thread. They must have traveled ten miles. At last, the glow abated, although the purplish shine, still reddening the night sky for hours, showed clearly that the indefatigable fiery element had yet to come to rest.

"The sun was rising when I abandoned my shelter and resumed my travel. What a change there was! The prairie had been transformed to an absolute desert. Not a single blade, not a leaf had been spared. The forest's trees stuck their naked, singed branches into the air – an image of attack survived. A thin layer of ash covered the ground, and some single trees whose twigs had nourished the flames, were still burning or were still sending high columns of smoke heavenward. Everywhere, the bare desert showed the run of the flames which, devouring the grass to its roots, had broken their way even against the wind's direction.

"The wind still blustered and whirled up the ashes so that, at times, it was impossible to see farther than one to two hundred yards.

"Overlooking the sad landscape I spotted a lean gray prairie wolf who slinked silently like a thief into one of the dips as if the scenery had made him afraid. He was the only visible living entity. He saw me, a fellow-wanderer, but did not flee. The roundabout destruction seemed, in the chain of beings, to have brought him closer to humans, since he had lost his fear of them. When he had reached the foot of a knoll, he stood still and sounded a deeply lamenting howl, upon which he received an answer from the woods. Soon, three more arrived to give him company.

"For a moment they stood still and looked at me with fiery eyes. Then one of them turned to approach me, his companions following him. Despite the solitude I did not care for this company of wolves. I aimed my rifle and sent a bullet towards them. A loud howl answered my shot and the limp of one, when the pack fled to the woods, convinced me that my bullet had reached its target."

Karl May – translated by Herbert Windolf

6. In Mistake Canyon

A gold digger story and erroneous killing in the Wild West, penned in 1889/90, sans Old Shatterhand and Winnetou.

First published in the "Illustrierte Welt. Deutsches Familienbuch. Blätter aus Natur und Leben, Wissenschaft und Kunst" - "Illustrated World. German Family Book. Pages from Nature and Life, Science and the Arts."

"Well, since we have now come to the right place, sit down, and let me tell you how the canyon got its name."

"Do you know it?" one of the gold diggers asked the old frontiersmen who had suggested this.

"I sure do! From this rock here, I'm sitting on, I fired the fateful shot. My eyes were thirty years younger then but still not sharp enough to tell the right one from the wrong one.

"I had a friend, a real, true one. He was an Apache by the name of *Tkhlish-lipa*, Rattlesnake. He owed me his life and for it, had promised to show me a place where a lot of nuggets could be found. I, therefore, found myself four upright fellows who were fit for the job. We had to be very careful since the place was located in Comanche' territory. This is why we Whites did not take any horses along, the Apache, however, refused to leave his mustang behind. To make my introduction short – we arrived up here at the canyon. Along the rim giant cacti grow individually, and farther back, there stood an entire forest of them. At its edge we built ourselves a hut for housekeeping, while our workplace was down below near the water.

"*Tkhlish-lipa* hadn't lied. Our yield was rich beyond expectation, although only four men were able to work, since one was needed to guard the hut while another had to hunt to provide us with meat. The hunt had to be done with utmost care since *Avat-kuts*, 'Great Buffalo', the chief of the local Comanche, was not only a bloodthirsty man, but also good in tracking. It was clear that each one of us not only had his shovel, but also his rifle at hand.

"We might have been about three weeks here, when the Apache had to stand watch at the hut, while our comrade, tall Winters, was out searching for meat. We others were working hard down here while the Red sat up there, bored stiff in the hot sun. He had taken off his upper cover, a new, valuable Saltillo blanket, and was rubbing bear fat, the Indian way, onto his body for protection from insects. That's when he heard a noise behind him. He turned around and recognized the feared Comanche chief about to club him with his rifle. Before he was able to move, the blow struck his head that he lost consciousness. His skull wasn't crushed because of his peculiar head cover, a kind of cap decorated with fox tails and rattlesnake skins.

"For the moment *Avat-kuts* left him lying there and stepped into the hut to see what was in there. He found our leather bags filled with nuggets and hung them on his belt. Stepping out, he tossed his old Calico jacket away and exchanged it for the Saltillo blanket. He also liked the cap of our unconscious red friend, which he put on his own head. He then whistled for his rawboned nag he had left behind some cacti, but found that the nearby grazing mustang of the Apache was a much better horse. He now thought of scalping the still living Apache. The Comanche stepped over the prone body; grabbed our friend's hair with his left hand to raise the victim's head. He then took his knife to cut around forehead and back above the ears to tear off the scalp with a strong jerk. However, he succeeded only partly. Rattlesnake awoke from the terrible pain and grabbed the Comanche's hands. A wrestling match ensued from which 'Great Buffalo' emerged the victor, since the other was half-blind from dripping blood.

"Meanwhile, tall Winters had had a successful hunt and was on his way home with his bag. He found the tracks of the Comanche, became alarmed and followed them. Stepping around the cactus forest's edge, he saw the two battling Indians and, because of the Saltillo blanket and cap, thought the Comanche to be the Apache. He fired his rifle, aiming at our bleeding friend but, fortunately, missed due to the great distance. The Comanche turned when he heard the shot, saw tall Winters, tore free, left his rifle, and leaped on the Apache's mustang and galloped off. Rattlesnake, almost crazy from anger and pain, wiped the blood from his eyes, and saw the Comanche riding off on his horse. In a split second he mounted the nag belonging to 'Great Buffalo' and chased after him, freeing his lasso from his waist. All the while tall Winters looking baffled after him, unable to understand what had been going on. Since Winters was blocking the path on the right, and the dense cactus stand blocked it on the left, the Comanche headed for the canyon. He knew of a trail, although dangerous, leading down the almost vertical wall to the bottom. He didn't know that four palefaces were down there.

"Over there, beyond the creek, you can see a projection, a narrow ledge sticking out from the rock wall, which leads up to the rim. This is the trail. It is difficult for a man on foot, but downright dangerous for a horseman.

"We were surprised when we heard the hoof beat of galloping horses coming from up there. Because they were high up, we, at first, could only make out the heads of the riders, but as they came closer, we were able to see their figures. Ahead ran the Apache's mustang, whose rider we thought to be Rattlesnake because he was wearing his cap and his Saltillo blanket. He was pursued by a horseman sitting on a strange horse. The man's bloody scalp hair was hanging from his head and, because of the rock wall, he couldn't get clear to throw his lasso around the pursued's head. We heard the Apache's voice calling incessantly: "*Hatatitla aguan, hatatitla aguan* - Shoot him, shoot him!" Of course, this was meant for us, which is why I reached for my rifle. The first reached the bottom of the canyon, over there, beyond the creek, and speeded on.

Then the other came. He could now handle his lasso more freely, and was swinging it through the air for his throw. I pressed the trigger – a scream, and he dropped off his horse. A few seconds later we stood next to him. Imagine our horror when we recognized him to be our scalped red friend! My bullet had hit him only too well. He pointed ahead and said, his voice breaking: '*Darteh litshane Avat-kuts* - this dog is 'Great Buffalo'. Then he was dead."

The narrator fell silent and stared sadly towards the spot where the Red had died. The others honored his silence by also remaining silent. After a long time he continued.

"His gift of gold was repaid by a bullet. We named the canyon Mistake Canyon, and this name has stuck to the present day. This story has often been told in my presence, but I never did say that I was its unfortunate 'hero'. I've tried to settle the issue inside myself in silence. However, today, while we are at the same location, it's got to come off my chest, and you may tell me, whether I should be called a murderer."

"No, no!" it sounded all around. "You are entirely innocent. But what happened to the Comanche? Did he get away?"

"No. We found him not very far away from here in some rock rubble where the horse had stumbled and had thrown him off. Imagine, there were now two corpses instead of one. That's the law of the Wild West. Let's no longer talk about it."

"And the gold, the nuggets?"

"Far less than we expected. It was as if an avenging angel had caused the gold to disappear deep into the Earth. After my bullet had hit the Apache, our yield became less day by day, until it finally stopped entirely. We dug and worked for quite a few weeks yet, but for naught. And what we took away, didn't last long; it soon disappeared – through drink and gambling. Only one thing remained for me, and will not leave me until my end: the memory of the moment when my lead tore the Red from his horse. I can still see him falling, and hear his scream. It rattles me. Come, let's go! I don't want to see this place any longer!"

7. The Tornado

An Experience in the Far West.

Karl May called this adventure "Unter der Windhose", which would translate "Under the Dust Devil". However, his description and the destruction wrought by the phenomenon, is not consistent with that of a Dust Devil, but is much more powerful. Yet, the characteristics also do not fully match those of a tornado. Karl May, who, himself, never experienced a tornado must have taken his descriptions, like he often did, from another report, whose writer may, or may not have experienced a tornado personally.

So, instead of calling it by its proper translation "Under the Dust Devil", to which the participants were actually not exposed, I have named it "The Tornado".

Karl May plays a role in this narrative, but is never called Old Shatterhand. He is known in this story only by the unexplained Apache term "Selki-lata', implying his status and being Winnetou's brother.

This story was first published in (1886) "Das Buch der Jugend - Ein Jahrbuch der Unterhaltung und Belehrung für unsere Knaben. 1. Band. K. Thienemann's Verlag - Gebrüder Hoffmann, Stuttgart." - "The Book of Youth - Annual for Entertainment and Education of our Boys. 1st Volume. K. Thienemann, Publishers - Hoffmann Brothers, Stuttgart."

It was a wonderfully pleasant June morning, a true rarity in this remote corner formed by the northwesterly edge of the Indian territory with the straight borders of Kansas, Colorado and New Mexico. There had been heavy dew during the night. Now, brilliant drops sparkled on grass blades and twigs, and the peculiar smell of the buffalo grass and that of the short and curly grama was so refreshing, that the lungs inhaled the balsamic scent of cumarin in long, deep measure.

A morning like this usually has a pleasant effect on man's disposition, yet I rode rather vexed into the magnificent day. The reason was simple: My horse was becoming lame. While galloping, it had tripped on a root yesterday. And to ride a lame horse on the prairie isn't just annoying, but can have even disastrous consequences. With daily threatening dangers on these plains life and safety of the hunter depend all too often on the health of his animal.

I had hunted with a few Colorado-men in the vicinity of the Spanish Peaks, then had come via Willow Springs to Nescutunga Creek to meet there with Will Salters at it's right bank. Months before I had hunted beaver with him in Nebraska, then, upon parting, had arranged the forthcoming rendezvous. We intended to cross the Indian Territory to its southeastern border, and from there to head straight west into the Llano Estacado to get to know this ill-famed desert.

This called very much for a good horse and mine was lame. It had carried me faithfully through many dangers. I did not want to exchange it for another, which forced me to allow it some rest until its foot had recovered. The loss of time this caused was highly disagreeable, which is why it wasn't quite unjustified that I found myself not in a good mood.

While my mustang limped across the prairie, I looked out for signs from which I could deduce the proximity of the river. Where I rode only isolated bushes grew. But to the north I spotted a dark line, which let me conclude that there was more profuse tree and brush growth. I, therefore, turned in this direction, for, where there is more vegetation, there must be also more water.

I was right. The dark line consisted of mesquite and wild cherry bushes, which grew along both riverbanks. The river wasn't very broad and, at least at the place I met it, not very deep either.

I slowly rode along the bank looking carefully for signs of Will Salters, who might have already arrived before me.

And right I was again! In the shallow water two large rocks lay right next to each other. A large branch had ben jammed between them so that a small twig on it pointed down-river.

This was our agreed-upon sign, which I found four more times at short intervals. Salters was here and had followed the river's course downstream. Since his tracks were no longer recognizable and the leaves of the signal-branches looked barely wilted, Salters could not have been here earlier than yesterday.

After a while the river turned more to the north, but seemed to make a bow. At this location the branch, Will had jammed into the beach sand, pointed out into the Prairie. This indicated that he had not followed the river's course, but had cut off its bow. Of course, I did the same.

Then I noticed straight ahead of me a single, not very high, but rugged mountain, which, due to its isolation, was well suited to serve a lonely frontiersman as a point of reference. In a bit more than half an hour I arrived there. Its peak was bare. Its base was covered only by brush, and that very poorly. Thus, after I had circumnavigated it, I was surprised to find on its eastern side several groups of sycamore. One of their biggest was almost comparable to the famous *Platano orientalis* I had seen in Bujukdereh near Constantinople. It was surely more than a thousand years old. I noticed that the earth was heavily dug up over a large area. There were holes of several yards depth, obviously dug with hoe and shovel. Might there be people here in this remote area? What had these holes been dug for?

I rode on, but stopped soon again, since I spotted tracks in the grass. I dismounted to inspect them more closely and found that they had been made by a female or not yet fully grown, male foot, shod in Indian, heel-less moccasins.

Could there be Indians here? Or was a White wearing Indian footgear? The impressions of both feet were equal. At the time, this detail did not strike me as peculiar, but I was reminded of it later on.

I should have actually followed these tracks, but they led north, towards the river, while my direction was eastward. I wanted to meet with Salters as soon as possible, which is why I mounted my horse again and rode on.

After some time, I thought, based on certain signs, that this area wasn't as poorly visited as I had pictured earlier. Nicked grass blades, little twigs broken on branches, and, here and there, a small stone ground to powder by a human foot, made me think that some offspring of the first human couple had passed by here. That's why I was only surprised, but not shocked, when later, arriving back at the river, I noticed a young tobacco and corn field right next to its bank. On the opposite side rose a low-slung log house, with a high but rather decrepit fence enclosing a rather large yard.

A farm, then, here at Nescutunga Creek! Who would have thought that? Inside the fence an old, worn nag rubbed its head on an empty fodder trough. Outside the fence I noticed a young fellow occupied with the repair of a break in the fence.

He seemed to be frightened by my appearance, but remained standing until I halted before him.

"Good morning, boy!" I greeted him. "May I ask the name of the owner of this house?"

Stroking his dense blond hair with one hand, he inspected me carefully with his bright Germanic eyes and replied:

"His name's Rollins, sir."

"Are you his son?"

He seemed to be barely more than sixteen years old, although his well-developed body made one believe him to be older. He answered:

"Yes, I'm his stepson."

"Is your father home?"

"Turn around. There he is."

He pointed to the narrow, low door, from which a man emerged, who had to bend down to avoid banging his head. He was very tall, lean and narrow-chested and under the few hairs of his thin beard, his skin looked like tanned leather. His Yankee physiognomy darkened when he saw me. He carried an old rifle and a hoe and didn't put either down when he slowly came towards me. His piercing, hostile look on me, he inquired with a hoarse-sounding voice:

"What do you want here?"

"Let me ask you first, Mister Rollins, whether a man stopped by here yesterday. His name's Salters and he may have left a message."

His son answered quickly:

"It was yesterday morning, sir. This Salters was . . ."

He was unable to continue. His father jabbed the rifle butt into his side so that the poor boy tumbled whimpering against the fence, and shouted angrily:

"Keep your mouth shut, toad! We don't care to serve every tramp!" And, turning to me, he continued: "Get lost, man! I live here neither for your Salters nor for you!"

This was simply rude. I had my own backwoods manners to treat such people, climbed slowly off my horse, tied it to the fence, and said:

"You need to make an exception this time, Mister Rollins. My horse is lame, and I shall stay here until it has healed."

Stepping back a pace, he looked me up and down with eyes blazing, and screamed:

"Are you mad? This is not a boarding house, and whoever intends to settle in here, I'll simply burn a load of buckshot on his hide. Damnation! There's also this miserable Indian again! Wait, fellow, I'll chase you off!"

My look quickly followed his which, upon his last words, was directed towards a not very distant group of bushes. A young Indian as approaching from there. Rollins raised his rifle and aimed for him. He pulled the trigger the moment I hit his barrel aside. The rifle sounded, but the shot missed.

"Dog! You lay hands on me!" Rollins roared at me. "Here, take this for it!"

He had quickly turned the rifle and reached out to strike me with its butt. Earlier, he had put the hoe down when he wanted to shoot. I rammed my fist under his raised arm and tossed him so hard against the fence that it broke from the impact. He dropped the rifle and I picked it up before he had risen again. Getting up, he pulled his knife from its sheath and rambled in a voice almost suffocating with anger:

"You did this to me! On my property! That calls for your blood and life!"

Just as quickly I had drawn my revolver, pointed it at him and told him:

"You must mean your blood and life? Put the knife away. My bullet is faster than your blade, man!"

He dropped the already raised arm, but looked away from me, towards the other corner of the log house. A horseman stood there, who had approached unnoticed and called to me now with a laugh:

"At work already, old chap? Right on! Bust the fellow down; he deserves it! But don't give him a bullet; he isn't worth the powder'"

The rider was Will Salters. He rode up, and we shook hands, while he continued:

"Welcome, friend! Had it gone by the will of this scurvy-ridden fellow, you'd not have seen me again. I guess he received you just like he did me, yesterday. I gave him a few nose punches for it, for which he sent a bullet after me which was, however, more courteous than he, since it went way past me. I had thought to wait for you here, but wasn't allowed. I told his son, however, that I would return today to find out if the man would be in a better mood. If it's all right with you, we can give him a lecture on how to treat people like us. In the meantime I'd like to make sure of him!"

He dismounted. That's when Rollins picked up the hoe and fled in long leaps. Surprised, we looked after him. His behavior was strange. First the inconsiderate coarseness and now cowardly escape! We did not get to comment on this further, for a woman stepped from the hut's door, behind which she had fearfully hidden until now. She had seen Rollins disappear in the bushes and now said, taking a deep, happy breath:

"God be thanked! I thought already some blood would be spilled. He is drunk. He fantasized the entire night, then finished the last bottle of brandy!"

"Are you his wife?" I asked.

"Yes, but I hope I won't have to suffer for it, gentlemen! It isn't my fault."

"Certainly not! One could almost think that your man is mentally disturbed."

"Unfortunately, that's the case. Oh God, you won't believe how unhappy I am! He imagines that a treasure is buried nearby. He wants to uncover it. No other is to find it, which is why he doesn't tolerate anyone else in this area. Over there, this young Indian is already here for four days. He can't go on, since he's sprained his foot. He wanted to stay until he can walk again properly, but Rollins chases him off every time. Now, the poor devil must camp in the open."

She pointed to the Indian who had come closer. All had happened so quickly that I had not yet had the time to pay attention to him.

He might have been eighteen years old. His outfit was made of brain-tanned deerskin and tasseled at the seams. These tassels were not of human hair, meaning, that he had not yet killed an enemy. His head was not covered. His weapons consisted of a knife and a bow with quiver. He might not be allowed yet to carry a rifle. On a brass chain around his neck he wore a peace pipe from which the head was missing. This was the sign that he was on the pilgrimage to the holy quarries were the Indians obtain the clay for their pipes. During this journey every one of them is inviolable. Even the most bloodthirsty enemy must let him travel on unharmed, yes, even protect him, if required.

The open, intelligent features of the youngster pleased me. His face had an almost Caucasian cut. His eyes were velvet-black and rested on me with an expression of gratefulness. He offered me his hand and said:

"You protected Isharshiutuha. I am your friend."

His assurance sounded very proud, which pleased me. But his name puzzled me. Isharshiutuha is an Apache word and means something like 'Little Stag', which is why I inquired:

"You are Apache?"

"Isharshiutuha is the son of the Chief of the Gila Apache, the bravest of all red men."

"They are my friends, and Winnetou, the greatest of their chiefs, is my brother."

His look went up and down my figure. Then he asked:

"Winnetou is the bravest hero. What does he call you?"

"Selki-lata."

That's when he stepped several paces sidewise, lowered his look, and said:

"The sons of the Apache know you. I am not yet a warrior and may not speak to you."

This was the Indian's humility, which recognizes another's rank openly, but doesn't lower the head by even a tenth of an inch.

"You may speak with me, for you will once become a famous warrior. In a short time you will no longer be called Isharshiutuha, 'Little Stag', but 'Pehnulte', 'Great Stag'. Your foot is injured?"

"Yes."

"And you left your wigwam without a horse?"

"I am on my way to obtain the holy clay of pipes. I walk."

"This sacrifice will please the Great Spirit. Come into the house!"

"You are warriors. Permit me to stay with my little white brother!"

He walked over to the handsome, blond and blue-eyed boy who had stood there sadly and silently, his hand on the spot where the rifle butt of his father had hit him. The two exchanged an unconscious look which I, however, noticed right away. They must not be standing next to each other for the first time. 'Little Stag' wasn't here without purpose. He hid a secret, maybe even one dangerous to the residents of the log house. I felt the desire to get behind it, but did not let on to it.

Thus, the boys remained outside. I followed Will Salters and the woman into the house, or rather the hut, whose interior consisted of only one room.

It looked extremely poor. I have been already in many a log house, whose residents had to make do with bare necessities, but this one was worse. The roof was defective and the chinking between the logs had disappeared. Through these crevices wretchedness crept in and out. In the fireplace hung a kettle. Their provisions seemed to consist only of a small number of corncobs, lying in a corner. The sole dress of the woman was a thin, faded cotton print. She went barefoot. Her only ornament was her cleanliness, which, despite her poverty, struck me pleasantly. Her son, too, had been insufficiently clothed, but every torn spot had been carefully mended.

When I gazed at the bed in the corner, which consisted only of leaves, and then looked at the worn face of this good woman the question crossed my lips, without actually wanting to ask it:

"You must be hungry, dear woman?"

She blushed almost as if insulted, but then tears broke suddenly from her eyes and she replied, her hand reaching for her heart:

"Oh God, I wouldn't want to complain if only Joseph could have his fill! Our field doesn't produce anything since my husband let it run wild. We are, therefore, dependent on hunting which doesn't bring anything either, since Rollins is deluded in wanting to always dig for the treasure."

I hurried out to my horse to fetch my supply of dried meat, which I gave her. Good Will Salters was, just as quickly, out to his horse and also brought in his supply.

"Oh, gentlemen, how kind you are!" she said. "One wouldn't think you to be Yankees."

"In that, at least concerning myself, you are very correct," I told her. "I am German. My friend, Salters, carries German blood only from his mother's side, but he's an even better fellow than myself. His mother was Austrian."

"My God! And I was born in Bruenn!" she called, clapping her hands happily.

"Then you speak German, too, and we can use our mother tongue."

"Oh yes, oh yes! I'm allowed to speak German only secretly with my son. Rollins won't permit it."

"A terrible fellow!" Salters opined. "I don't want to insult you, but I have the feeling to have met him years ago in not very savory circumstances. He has a great similarity with a chap, who was known only by his Indian name. I do not know the meaning of it. What was it actually? I believe something like Indano or Indansho."

"Inta-'ntsho!" it sounded from the door.

The young Indian stood there. Of course, he had not understood the German words, but had picked up the name. His eyes glowed hotly. When my looks fell inquiringly on him, he turned and disappeared from the entrance.

This name is taken from Apache, which you don't understand," I explained to my comrade. "It means something like 'Evil Eye'."

"'Evil Eye'?" the woman asked. "My husband utters these words frequently when he talks in his sleep or sits there drunk in the corner and quarrels with invisible people. From time to time he's gone for more than a week. Then he returns with brandy from Fort Dodge by the Arkansas; I don't know how he pays for it. Afterwards he drinks and drinks until he cannot think any more and speaks of blood and murder, of gold nuggets and of a treasure buried around here. For days and nights we don't dare leave the hut afraid he would kill us."

"You unfortunate woman! How come you dared to follow such a man into this corner of the wilderness?"

"Him? Oh, I would never have come here with him. I came to America with my first husband and his brother. We bought land and were cheated by the agent. The document we received for our purchase had been falsified. When we arrived in the West, the rightful owner was cultivating the place for many years already. Our money had run out and there was nothing else left to us but live from hunting. Doing this, we ventured ever-farther west. My husband wanted to go to California. He had heard of the gold that was found there. We made it to this place, then couldn't go on. I was ill and exhausted. We camped in the open but, fortunately, found this hut soon after. It had been abandoned. We do not know who its owner was. We got along as well as it was possible. But the thought of California didn't leave my husband at peace. He wanted to get there. I could not and his brother didn't want to. He was homesick. God alone knows, after how many struggles I gave permission to my husband to go by himself to the golden country to try his luck. My brother-in-law was to stay with me. My husband never returned. Half a year after he left I was made the gift of my Joseph. He never saw his father. He was three years old when, one morning, my brother-in-law went hunting and did not return. A few days later I found him lying by the river. There was a bullet wound in his head. He may have been murdered by an Indian."

"Had he been scalped?"

"No."

"Then his murderer was a White. But how did you manage to survive?"

"From the little store of corn we had harvested. Then, my current husband came here. He was going to hunt, then move on. But he stayed on and on and, finally, remained here forever. I was glad to have him. Without him my child and I would have starved. He went over to Dodge City and had my husband declared dead. I needed a protector and my son a father. Rollins became both. However, some time later he had a dream of a treasure supposedly buried here. Oddly enough, this dream repeated so often that Rollins not only believed firmly in its existence, but it literally became a delusion. During the night he fantasizes of the gold and in the day he digs for gold."

"It must be by the mountain where the old sycamores stand?"

"Yes. But I'm not allowed to accompany him there, and neither is my son. I cannot tell anyone how unhappy I am. I pray daily, even hourly, for deliverance. If God would only help!"

"He will, even if his help will cause you pain in the beginning. I have often experienced in life that . . ."

I was interrupted. Joseph had come in and asked us to step outside to look at the sky. We followed him, surprised by his request. 'Little Stag' stood there and looked attentively at a small cloud, which stood almost vertically above us. Otherwise, the sky was totally clear. Not a single other cloud could be seen.

"Joseph has told me that he thinks this little cloud is very dangerous to us."

'Little Stag' spoke decent English and could, therefore, make himself understood to the white boy. Will Salters shrugged his shoulders and said:

"This little cigar-like cloud dangerous? Pshaw!"

That's when the Indian turned to him and said a single word: "Iltshi."

"What does it mean!" Will asked me.

"Wind, storm!"

"Nonsense! A dangerous wind, a gust, comes only from a 'hole', when the entire sky has darkened and a round, clear hole appears in this black mantle. But this is different. Except for the little puff up there, the sky is totally cloudless."

"*Ke-eikhena-itlshi*", the India said.

Now I paid attention after all. The three words mean 'the hungry wind'. This Apache term means 'dust devil'. I asked the young man if he feared one to come. He replied:

"*Ke-eikhena-akh-iltshi.*"

It means 'the very hungry wind' and designated a tornado. How did the Apache arrive at this assumption? While I couldn't see anything suspicious in this little cloud, I also knew that these children of the wilderness possess a wonderful instinct for certain natural events.

"Nonsense!" Salters said to me. "Come inside! I have the feeling you begin to make a concerned face."

That's when the Indian put a finger to his forehead and told him:

"*Ka-a tshapeno!*"

He had noticed that Will spoke no Apache and used the Tonkawa dialect, in English meaning 'I am not sick', that is, in the head.

Salters understood him, but did not take his words wrongly and went back in the hut. I used the opportunity to show 'Little Stag' that I had not believed some of his previous claims. I asked him:

"Which foot of my friend is sick?"

"*Sintsh-kah* – the left foot," he replied.

"But why did my brother limp with his right foot when he came out of the bushes over there?"

A smile of embarrassment slid across his face but he quickly caught himself to reply:

"My brave brother is mistaken."

"My eyes are sharp. Why does 'Little Stag' limp only when he's seen? Why does he walk all-right when he is alone?"

He looked at me questioningly without answering, which is why I continued:

"My young friend did hear of me. He knows that I read the tracks, that no blade of grass, no grain of sand can deceive me. 'Little Stag' came this morning from the mountain and went to the river without limping. I read his tracks. Is he also brave enough to tell me that I am mistaken?"

He lowered his gaze and remained silent.

"Why does 'Little Stag' say that he is traveling on foot to the holy quarries?" I continued, "when he rode here from his wigwam?"

"Uff!" he exclaimed surprised. "How can you know that?"

"Has not the greatest chief of the Apache been my teacher. Would you think I would shame him by being deceived by a young Apache who isn't permitted yet to carry a rifle? Your animal is a *tshi-kayi-kle*, an appaloosa."

"Uff, uff!" he called twice with an expression of greatest surprise.

"Do you wish to lie to Winnetou's brother?" I asked him reproachingly.

That's when he put his hand on his heart and replied:

"*Shi-itkli takla ho-tli, tshi-kayi-kle* – I have a horse, an appaloosa."

"That is good! I even tell you that early this morning you practiced the entire Indian schooling."

"My brother is all-knowing like Manitou, the Great Spirit!" he exclaimed, literally perplexed.

"No I am not, but you galloped along with one foot hanging in the saddle and, with one arm hanging your body from the neck strap to the side of your horse. That is done in battle if one wants to protect oneself from the projectiles of the enemy, but in times of peace only if one practices the 'full school'. Only during such a ride is it possible for mane hair to get torn off and be caught on the blade of a knife. Such mane hair can only come from an appaloosa."

Both his hands went for his belt where his knife stuck in its sheath. On it hung several strands of hair. Despite his Indian skin color I observed that he blushed, thus added:

"The eyes of 'Little Stag' are bright, but not yet practiced enough for such trifles on which life often depends. My young brother has come here to see the owner of this house. Does he have a blood feud with him?"

"I have vowed silence," he answered. "But my white brother is the friend of the most famous Apache. I will show him something he will return to me again today. He can talk about it, because my hour has come."

He opened his hunting shirt and pulled out an envelope-like leather piece folded to a square. He handed it to me and walked off towards the cornfield were young Joseph stood presently. I saw that he took him by the arm pulling him along.

I unfolded the leather, which had been cut from tanned deer hide. Its content consisted of a second piece of leather, this one of buffalo hide, scraped clean of its hair, bated by lime and smoothened to parchment. It was folded twice. When I unfolded it I saw a series of figures in red color, drawn similar to the famous rock painting at Tsitsumovi in Arizona. I held a document in Indian writing in my hands, such a rarity, that I didn't immediately think of deciphering it, but hurried into the hut to show this treasure to Will Salters. He shook his head and suggested totally surprised:

"And this can be read?"

"Of course!"

"Well, then you read it! Even dealing with our own common writing I'd rather battle twenty redskins than three letters. I have never been a hero with writing. I rather write my letters to the addressee's body with my double-barreled rifle. That's quicker. The quill brakes between my fingers and the ink tastes badly. To decipher these figures, that's terrible! Here in the hut, which has only two small peep holes instead of windows, one cannot even identify the symbols."

"Then come outside with me!"

"Well, I'll come along, but you'll have to do the reading."

We went outside. The woman stayed back. She had lit a small fire in the fireplace to fry a few pieces of our meat.

Of course, my eyes were right away on the symbols, but Will Salters was looking at the sky. He grumbled thoughtfully:

"Hmm! A peculiar cloud! I've never seen one like that. What do you say?"

Made aware of this, I looked up, too. The little cloud hadn't become much larger, but had assumed a very different appearance. When it had earlier been bluish-gray, it now was of a bright red, transparent coloration, and it looked as if millions and millions of spidersilk-like, thin, faintly golden threads were spreading across and down the entire visual field. These barely visible threads did not twitch; they were totally unmoving, like being harnessed.

"Well?" Will asked.

"I've never seen anything like it."

"Should this young fellow, the redskin, be right with his whirlwind, versus us old, experienced prairie runners!"

"It looks serious. The Apache even spoke of a tornado. That would be worse."

"There may be what will. We cannot help but wait. I hope you'll find your way better around this Indian writing than with the incomprehensible tangle of threads up there. What do you think?"

"Hmm! Let's see. Up front I see a sun symbol painted with upward-directed rays. It must be the rising sun. Then come four horsemen. They wear hats, thus are likely Whites. The foremost has something hanging from his saddle, seemingly small bags. Behind those four two others come. They wear feathers on their bare heads and likely represent Indian chiefs.

"Well, that seems to be quite easy. Do you call this reading?"

"It's a beginning. One first needs to learn the letters before one can put them together as words. There are a few more small figures drawn above the larger ones. Above one of the Indians I recognize a buffalo opening its mouth from which come several small lines. From a mouth only a voice can come which likely means a roaring bull. Above the head of another Indian is a tobacco pipe. From its head come similar lines, which probably mean smoke. Therefore, the pipe is lit."

"Hey, I'm able to read!" Will said. "I remember there were two Apache chiefs, brothers. One was 'Roaring Bull', long dead now, the other's name was

'Burning Pipe', since he was of a peaceful disposition and loved to smoke the peace pipe with everybody. Supposedly, he's still alive."

"Then the two drawn here may be them! Let's see! Above the second White an eye is drawn with a line crossing it. Either, he has only one eye, or he's blind in one, or the eye is sick. Oh, that would be the name you mentioned earlier, 'Evil Eye'! Above the third White is a bag with a hand reaching for it. Could that mean theft?"

"Yes, yes, certainly!" Salters said quickly. "It's a stealing hand. I've got it, I've got it! Now I know where I've seen this Rollins! It was up in the Black Hills. His name was Haller then. He was a horse and beaver trap thief and was called 'Stealing Hand'."

"You could be mistaken!"

"No, no! 'Stealing Hand' and 'Evil Eye' were cousins or even brothers and kept together. It's them. Go on, go on!"

"Since the rising sun is up front, these horsemen rode towards sunrise, that is east. Here, on the second line the same figures are shown again, more frequently and in different groupings. In the first group the three Whites in the back shoot at the one up front. In the second group he lies dead on the ground and the three have his bags. In the third group Indians shoot at the Whites. In the forth group two Whites and 'Roaring Buffalo' are dead; 'Stealing Hand' flees. In the fifth group 'Burning Pipe' buries the bags. The sixth group shows 'Burning Pipe' carrying 'Roaring Buffalo' on a horse, following 'Stealing Hand', probably pursuing him. In the seventh group 'Burning Pipe' buries 'Roaring Buffalo'; 'Stealing Hand' has disappeared. This is followed by two smaller images. There are three trees. Below the middle one the bags are buried in the earth. Then, there is a large, single tree, below which one can see 'Roaring Buffalo' is interred. Now, the entire horrible event easily . . ."

"Stop!" Salters interrupted me. "Leave the story be for a moment and look up! Haven't you noticed that it's getting rather dark? For God's sake, look up at the sky!"

I followed his request and became alarmed. The faint-golden threads had disappeared. In their place I saw several dark lines, probably the result of their gathering. They connected the cloud, which had become very dark, with the northern horizon. The rest of the sky was bright and clear. As if by strong, tight ropes the cloud was pulled down and northward. It went ever faster. The further it was pulled towards the Earth, the clearer one saw rising from the ground an, at first, transparent, but ever more darker substance rising, broad at its base but thinning towards its top. It rotated and, with its upper, back and forth flapping tail, seemed to reach for the cloud above. The cloud sunk ever faster down, broadening above, but at its bottom was now sending out its own tail. The two tails sought and found each other. When they touched, it was as if the cloud was pulled down to Earth. But it remained airborne and formed a rapidly rotating double funnel. Its tips had connected at the center, while the two bases, the one down on Earth and the one up in the sky might have a diameter of over fifty yards.

Since there was only low brush in our area we were able to observe the scary phenomenon almost at shoulder-height. It developed and whirled rapidly forward, right for us. Around us the air was totally still, but suddenly sweltering heat set in, which quickly caused us to sweat from just about every pore.

'Little Stag' was right," I said. "We must fear for our lives. Quickly, Will, we must save ourselves and the woman!"

"How and where to!" he asked alarmed.

"On our horses."

"But we don't know which way to turn!"

"The movement of such a tornado cannot be deduced. We must change our direction of escape whenever it changes course. Maybe it will be stopped by the river and will not jump across to our side. Get Rollins' horse out from the fence. I'll hurry to get the woman!"

I found her by the fireplace, not having an inkling of the approaching threat outside. I grabbed her and quickly carried her outside, just when Will arrived with the horse.

"His animal is obstinate," he shouted. "I will mount it, but it isn't saddled. It would toss the lady off upon the first step. Put her onto my Sorrel! Hurry up, hurry up!"

He mounted Rollins' nag and galloped off.

"Can you ride?" I asked the woman.

"Not as it's needed here now," she wailed.

"Then I take you with me."

I jumped onto the Sorrel, who, likely, could carry two people easier than my lame Brown, pulled the trembling woman up so that she lay crosswise over my knees, took my lame Brown by the reins, and followed the speeding Salters ahead.

This had all happened so quickly that, from our first sighting of the tornado to now, not more than a minute had passed. My position wasn't very comfortable. With my right hand I had to hold the woman and with my left guided the Sorrel and led the Brown. But it worked. When we had covered a good distance I shouted to Will to halt. He did and we turned to look back.

The funnel had reached the river. The cloud was no longer visible. The tornado was a dark monster, exactly the shape of an hourglass or egg-timer, but of a giant size. Within it whirled torn-out bushes, stones, great sod pieces, and cart-loads of sand – a terrible, otherworldly monster.

Now it reached the river. Would it stop to travel along the opposite bank, up or downstream or, maybe, collapse? This was our question. Any person coming within the tornado's reach would surely be doomed. Whirled up and down and about he had to suffocate, if he wasn't smashed to earth or was squashed by the rotating debris.

The monster stopped as if considering what to do. The upper, downward thinning funnel leaned towards us as if it wanted to continue in the previous direction. It tore at the lower funnel and it almost looked, as if it wanted to tear itself off. Then there was a terrible crash; the dark, compact mass of sand, stones, brush, and sod disappeared, and a tall vortex of water rose. At first it assumed a cylindrical, even shape, but then narrowed at its middle, resuming the former shape of a double cone. The tornado had become a waterspout which, angry about the halt suffered by the river, now traveled at twice its former speed. It wrecked the log house and came right for us.

"Off now! There, to the right!" I hollered.

It had been difficult to keep the horses still for the moment. They recognized the danger and galloped away that we needn't drive them on at all. Looking back at the tornado, I happily noticed that it was taking a more westerly direction. It was moving away from us. We could halt once more and consider ourselves saved – if it wouldn't turn back towards us.

But this didn't happen. It continued traveling at the same speed, no longer transparent like by the water, but once more dark and obscure. It had torn up everything it had come across and had lifted it upward. We saw how it grew and became ever mightier. Everything it couldn't contain, it tossed far from itself. Thus it continued its path of destruction until, far away, a thundering noise erupted from which the Earth shook – and it disappeared.

However, almost at the same moment – we couldn't comprehend how – the entire sky had turned black and rain crashed down the size of peas.

"Our house, our livelihood! What happened to it?" the woman lamented, for the first time breaking her silence.

Instead of an answer we put our horses to a fast trot to return to the log house. To the log house? No – it no longer existed. It had been torn apart, tumbled about, like a thin, fragile straw weave. The heavy, man-size logs of which it had consisted, had been carried off, then tossed again to the ground. There was no trace left of the fence, not a single board, or pole – all tossed and tumbled through the air.

Dismayed, the woman sank into a condition of total insensitivity. That was fine with us. I thought of her husband, of her son, and the young Indian. Since I had the drawing, I knew where to find them – over there by the mountain, where the tornado had collapsed, it being an insurmountable obstacle in its path. But how did it end? In any case, like a dying giant, which, in his death throes, grinds apart everything he gets his hands on. A terrible scene might await us there which we hoped to spare her from. But when she heard that we were going to look for her son, she regained her energy. Neither begging nor anger helped; we could not leave her. She mounted up and rode along.

As suddenly as the rain had started, the sky cleared again. The clouds had disappeared like magic, and the sun once again laughed from the sky, as if nothing had happened.

But how badly the path looked the tornado had traveled! As drawn, its path was almost seventy yards wide. All plant growth looked like it had been shaved off. It had torn open holes and filled others with its debris. And far, far to the right and left beyond its path lay the rocks, bushes and other debris it had tossed about.

And at the mountain, what did it look like there? From afar we could see the devastation already. Brush had been torn from the earth, tossed and turned, and pushed together into bunches that could not be unraveled, then spit out to the left and right. For a long distance the tornado had searched for a way around the mountainside and, angered that it could not find one, had turned all life into death. The naked rocks looked like those in a deeply cut quarry. The sycamores I had liked so much when I rode past them, were barely recognizable. Man-size trunks, including their roots, lay torn from the ground. Branches, the size of a child, lay twisted like ropes. The tallest of the sycamores had suffered the loss of its top. With its deep and long cut injuries, it presented a pitiable sight. But where were – ah, over there stood an Indian-saddled horse, an appaloosa, by one of the mighty, chaotically twisted brush heaps, on whose leaves it was happily chewing. It was the horse belonging to 'Little Stag'. Where the animal was, there had to be its owner.

We rode over there to find a mighty sycamore torn out. In falling, its tough roots had opened up the surrounding ground. Below the giant root ball yawned a wide and deep, cave-like hole. In it sat blond Joseph and the young Apache, sheltered by the roots like by a rain-impenetrable roof. Happily, they laughed up to us. Quickly, the mother climbed down to hug her son to her heart. The Apache, however, jumped up and asked:

"Do my white brothers now believe that I know the signs of the 'Very Hungry Wind'?"

"We believe you," I replied. "But how did you save yourselves?"

"'Little Stag' had his horse hidden deeply in the bushes. He fetched it and mounted it together with the blue-eyed paleface to escape the wind. When the 'Hungry Wind' was satiated, Isharshiutuha rode here and found what he had been looking for with the little paleface for three days already."

"You secretly met with Joseph?"

"Yes. He is the son of the man with the bags who was murdered here. Come and see where 'Burning Pipe' buried the nuggets."

He led us to the opposite side of the root ball. There, the earth had burst near the trunk and we saw two mouldy-white little leather bags. When we opened them, they were filled with gold dust and gold kernels. Joseph already knew about it. When his mother now learned what I had guessed already – the murder of her first husband – she almost collapsed to her knees from sorrow. The unexpected ownership of the precious metal was, of course, a consolation, although she was barely able to believe it. Upon her questions the Indian told us:

"'Roaring Bull' was my father. He took off with his brother, 'Burning Pipe', to visit the Great White Father[2] to present to him the Apache wishes. The two chiefs rode off. They came across three palefaces murdering a White since he had found gold. Two of the murderers were 'Evil Eye' and 'Stealing Hand', the third they did not know. They punished and killed 'Evil Eye' and the third for the murder. 'Stealing Hand' escaped after they had shot and killed my father. 'Burning Pipe' pursued the remaining murderer, after he had buried the gold, and had placed the body of 'Roaring Bull' onto his horse, but could not catch up with him. 'Burning Pipe' buried his brother. Then he rode alone to Washington. The brother's murder calls for revenge. I must avenge him, for I am his son. But a long time passed because I was still little. But then I took off to get myself the murderer's scalp, because, I am now a warrior and may carry a rifle. The murderer lived in the hut of the murdered. He had made the wife of the victim his squaw. Through it the hut became his property and he could search for the treasure."

When the woman heard this disclosure, she shouted a scream of terror and fainted. Her second husband was the murderer of her first.

"Now you are going to see 'Stealing Hand'," the Apache said. "Follow me!"

Joseph remained with his unconscious mother. We did not begrudge her being out of it.

Salters and myself followed the Indian to the big sycamore. There, Rollins lay on the ground underneath an almost three foot thick main branch, which had dropped on him and had totally crushed his legs up to his torso.

"There he lies," the Apache said. "I wanted to get his scalp, but the Great Spirit has judged him. I only take the scalp of a man I conquer. This one was slain by the righteous anger of just Manitou, at the same place where he committed the murder. Do you now understand the images I gave you to read?"

"Completely," I responded.

"'Burning Pipe' does not know how to write. He had the images drawn by the great chief Winnetou whom he told everything. You are the brother of this famous warrior, which is why I will make the writing a gift to you. Look, the miserable one is opening his eyes. Maybe you can still talk to him. But I will go. He is the murderer of my father. I would have killed him but do not want to hear his whimpering. This red man also has heart, just like the paleface; he wishes to punish quickly, not slowly and painfully."

He returned to Joseph and his mother. But Will and I had to endure a terrible quarter of an hour, the dying minutes of the murderer. His consciousness

---

[2] President of the United States of America

returned; he felt death approaching and admitted everything. Although he was lacking the strength for coherent expression, he was able to answer our questions with yes and no. Thus we learned what we had already figured ourselves.

He had observed that 'Roaring Bull', who was pursuing him, did not carry the nuggets with him, thus must have buried them. He led the Indian astray and returned to the site of the attack. With great effort, he dug a hole for the bodies there, so that the murder would remain a secret. A few days later he also shot the brother of the murdered to insinuate himself to the woman as a welcome protector. Afterwards, he thought to be able to search comfortably for the gold. All succeeded, except for the main thing: he was unable to find the nuggets. His thirst for the gold and the pains troubling his conscience carried him towards madness. He tolerated no strangers so that nothing might be discovered by some fluke. This is why Will and I had been turned away, like he had also chased off 'Little Stag', who had played lame, to find access to him by this pretext.

God judged him by his everlasting justice. Right now, the murderer lay dying at the spot below which the bones of the murdered lay buried. And, in his final moments, he did learn from us that the gold, he had searched so long for in vain, had been found and handed to the boy he had hated so much.

And yet – the Merciful was kind to him: The crushed legs did not cause him any pain. He passed away without uttering a sigh.

We reported what had happened to his wife. She did not want to see him and rightly so. The two of us dug a grave for him and said a Lord's Prayer over it.

'Little Stag' soon rode off. We could not keep him any longer. And when the very tested woman offered him part of the gold, he proudly said:

"Keep your dust. The Apache knows where gold can be found in great quantity. But he despises it and does not tell others where to find it. The Great Spirit created man not to become rich but to become good. May he bring you now as much happiness as you have found suffering."

He mounted his horse and rode away.

The next morning we, too, left the area, taking Joseph and his mother along. The old nag carried the gold, the Sorrel the lady, and my Brown the boy; Will and I walked next to them. At the next settlement, where mother and son could await better transportation, we said our farewell. The tornado had brought these unfortunate people some terrible explanation, but also the means for a better existence.

And what did happen to Joseph and 'Little Stag'? The Apache became a famous warrior, and the blue-eyed Joseph, as young as he still is, has become an able government administrator who celebrated, not too long ago, a wonderful *Wiedersehen* with 'Great Stag' in the Rocky Mountains. But more of it – maybe next time.

8. The Oil Fire

In 1892/93 the following story was published in serial format in 'Das neue Universum', 'The New Universe'. Read on to the story 'The Fire in the Oil Valley', referred to in the below narrative.

Karl May appears to have had a fascination with precipitously steep basins, which, in this story being a crater, come up in many of his other narratives.

It is geologically doubtful that an oil well would be found inside a crater, but what does it really matter, if it provides for a good story.

Part 1: Killing Fire

Because of a somewhat problematic injury I had kept to bed for several weeks at Fort Cass at the confluence of the Bighorn with the Yellowstone. It had been a sad period.

I was not short of means to make the time of my forced stay as pleasant as possible – I had four full mule-loads of pelts along and received a nice little sum for it. But the locally offered pleasures amounted to the smoking of bad tobacco and drinking of bad brandy. The tobacco was half substitutes, and the brandy seemed more like diluted sulfuric acid.

In addition there were three or four decks of cards whose images one could barely make out any more, and a library of three volumes: namely, Shakespeare's Henry VIII, consisting of its covers and title page with the other pages used already as corks; then Voltaire's Charles XII, once dropped into a kettle with its pages now firmly glued together; and Volume IV of *Oeil de Boeuf*, which had once lain in the sugar box of the major and had been half-eaten by ants.

I could not go on any excursion due to the injury, and I rarely received any visitors since I don't possess any particular social talent. Also, I did not derive any great pleasure by the military gentlemen. The soldiers were assembled from all kinds of problematic elements, and the officer gentlemen weren't very convivial since my thoughts about the performance of their duties were very different from theirs. Thus I felt quite lonely during the time of my recuperation. When the doctor finally allowed me the first outing, I decided to use this liberty to a somewhat larger extent than he had intended.

Taking a good Indian bark canoe, I put my weapons in it, and paddled up the Bighorn River. I wanted to please myself once again by spending an entire night in the forest.

I took no provisions; there was water enough for drinking and roasts my rifle was to supply. Thus, since early morning, I had worked my way upriver with only brief breaks and, by evening, stopped at a place about fifteen miles from the Fort.

It was a silent, solitary place, right to my taste. The river broadened here, almost to a lake with several small coves. I put to the bank in one of them and tied up the canoe. While it darkened, I fried some fish which I had caught during the day. After I completed this simple meal, I put more wood onto the flames, wrapped myself with my blanket and settled down.

But there was no thought of falling asleep. For such a long time I had been without my old friend, the forest, that today when I lay in its arms again, I could not offend it by falling asleep without listening to its deep and melancholic voices.

These voices are all set in the minor key by the great master of creation, just as the simple songs of primitive peoples are composed in a minor key. I listened to the evening hymn of the forest – this soft, sonorous rushing which seemed to come from deeply tuned Aeolian harp strings. It surrounded me on all sides, yet, one cannot tell where it begins nor where its notes are written. Joining it with the same easy rhythm was the caressing splash and gurgle of the waves. A squirrel scrambled down the trunk of an elm, observed me with its small, curious eyes, then, calmed, returned to its nest. At times, a fish leaped in the light which the fire threw on the water, returning to its element in a loud splash. The burning branches crackled in the heat of the fire. A copperhead slithered past – he may have had its summer home near where my fire was now lit – to get to safety. A beetle, wakened from his early sleep, crawled through the leaf litter with a slight rustle. A small cloud of mosquitos did their agitated dance in the rising smoke, sounding their silvery buzz, but were occasionally interrupted by the restless hum of a fat moth crossing inconsiderately through their midst. But on one such crossing, it suffered its punishment: with singed wings it tumbled into the flames. Across from me, on the other side of the narrow cove, a frog spoke up. He had to be a giant fellow, for his croaking was literally a bellow. He seemed to be greatly insulted by my presence since he did not sound either the short, satisfied "quack!", or the long-drawn, happy "qu-aaaak!" which a frog-bariton normally uses. Instead it was an angry tone arguing – bare of all consideration and respect – a deliberate, verbal insult.

Wait – what was that?

The frog stopped suddenly and I heard it retreat into the water. It had been disturbed. But by what? By whom?

Whoever has spend time in the Wild West with its thousands of dangers, knows the need to examine even the smallest sound. A twig cracked over there, a dry, thin twig lying on the ground. I heard it clearly. And as soft as the sound had been, it told me that it had been caused by a human foot. If a small twig breaks up high, it means little. It is most likely caused by the wind or an animal. But if wood cracks on the ground, it is possible that a person is nearby. An old forest-man knows how to differentiate whether the twig was broken by the elastic foot of a slinking animal or the less flexible of a human. He even knows whether the noise was produced by the hard-soled boot of a White or the soft, yielding moccasin of an Indian.

That moment I would have wagered that an Indian was on the other side of the cove. As political conditions stood, this wasn't a calming thought.

I admit, even on the danger of giving offense that I do not condone the Whites' behavior towards the Reds. The Indian is also a human being and has human rights. It's a sin to deny him the right to exist and to take from him the means of existence. Even with the most beautiful speeches held in the American Congress and missionaries sent to the so-called savages, the impartial person will differentiate between talk and deed.

The Indian possessed the land; he was lord of the earth, lived by its products and did well. Not a single Indian account speaks of bloodshed before the coming of Whites, but as it continues nowadays. The Whites were received almost like gods and honored as such, but soon displayed inhuman characteristics. Think only of the Spanish Conquistadors carrying the holy cross on their banners, but destroying fields, cities and villages and, by ruining the irrigation system, converting the land into a great desert. Somber zealotism, feverish greed, treason and extravagant egotism annihilated millions of peaceful people and denied history the development of a particular, legitimate cultural form. Thus it happened in Peru and in Mexico. And in the United States? The Indian is to die and, thus, he will. But he ought not to be judged by reports of ten of twelve hands down the line, also not by his various driven hostilities. He ought to be visited, and one should entrust oneself to him so one can get to know him! He is frugal, just, true, faithful and brave. He has been cheated and deceived; he ought not to be judged, when he repays it likewise. If he is driven from one reservation to another, one ought not to be surprised that he will defend the small, assigned piece of land, which he once owned in its entirety. The Indian race is dying, hurt and injured a thousand fold. His parting is not peaceful, rather it is his death-struggle. The firewater, smallpox, and other similar 'gifts' of the Whites have not yet succeeded in bringing a total decline. He, the former giant, is still strong enough to choke various attackers in his death-struggle. His hard deathbed are the Rocky Mountains in whose valleys and canyons the final battles will take place. He knows that the Pueblos, Zuni, Queres, and all those who surrendered, did die the slow, honorless death of pining away, that they died by degeneration or, yet, will perish by it. But he wants to die as the hero Roland, sword in hand. All the so-called peaceful Indians will, little by little, disappear, not leaving behind their names and manly deeds. However, the Comanche and Apache of the South and the Sioux in the North, driven from the prairies, will retreat to the Rocky Mountains and will wade, step by step, in the blood of their enemies, until the last of theirs has been beaten. These battles will live on for hundreds of years in the minds of future generations. And for every skull the plow or spade uncovers from the earth, legend will spin its story, and the grandchildren of the victors, more just than their forebears, will give the beaten Indian their sympathy and, maybe, will bear the consequences of this manslaughter.

This is my viewpoint as a human being and as a German. This last word need no explanation, although it is not in the least intended to express ethical overestimation or thoughtless self-righteousness.

During my forced stay at Fort Cass a detachment of soldiers had been sent west to 'make meat'. They had come across a band of Sioux of the Teton tribe who were already engaged in the buffalo hunt. The law of the prairie states that a hunt is the right, the property of those who undertook it first. But instead of moving on the dragoons took possession of the killed animals and a fight ensued. The Indians yielded to the superior weapons of their enemies leaving behind numerous of their dead. The officers boasted to me about this victory in the midst of peace and I had been unable to impart another, more just point of view. It could be expected that the Sioux would avenge this breach of peace, which is why, when I heard the break of a twig nearby, I was on guard.

I kept my eyes seemingly closed, but peered below my lowered lids to where the noise had come from. The cove was at most twenty feet wide with the opposite edge of bushes brightly lit by my fire. One must possess very sharp senses to take proper action, but often, simple instinct does more than the sharpness of faculties. I noticed that some twigs were slowly moved aside; two darkly glowing eyes appeared, only to close again right away. The man over there was an old, experienced warrior. He knew that one could very well make out the glow of two eyes in the night, which is why he let his flash open only momentarily. I saw their shine five or six times, then the sideways-moved twigs snapped back. The man had convinced himself that I was alone.

I had seen only his eyes, not his face, and, therefore, didn't know whether he wore war paint, or whether he was here peacefully. Was he alone? Was he a spy? Might there be a band of Indians close by who had spotted my fire and had dispatched him to find out who was camped by it? I assumed that he was alone. The Indians usually send young men out to reconnoiter. But this man was old and experienced. I was convinced that he would creep around the cove to approach me unnoticed. Then, one of two cases might arise: If he came in peace, he would step from between the trees and, greeting me, would take a place next to me and tell me that I ought to be more careful. But if he came as an enemy, I would be a corpse, without becoming aware of him even for a moment. Both cases called for proving to him that I was at least as good a frontiersman as he.

I waited a while, then I opened my blanket and draped it, without rising, nor making the least noise, that it appeared from a distance as if I was still wrapped in it. Then I took my rifle and crept into the darkness.

He had to come from the left. I found an excellent hiding place under a dense growth of wild cherry bushes. Earlier, in the brief light of dusk, I saw that one could get around the little cove in about five minutes. Now, in darkness and with caution, he couldn't arrive by my fire is less than a quarter of an hour.

Time passed. I kept my eyes closed, since he might spot their shine, and relied on my good hearing. It has never forsaken me and, now too, was reliable. A very soft waft told me he was getting close. It wasn't a noise, only air pressure caused by his movement. But also my sense of smell did its job. There came a peculiar, unpleasant odor, I was familiar with: the man had killed an opossum and had eaten it. This marsupial has a bad odor and is eaten by Indians only if there's nothing else. This smell still clung to him. That he had not disdained such a roast was the surest proof that he was a scout. To save time and detours, and to avoid betraying shots, he had pulled the opossum from its tree hole to eat it.

Now he arrived, so close that I could almost touch him with my hand. He snuck past me, slowly and silently, slithering like a snake. Whoever has not tried this type of approach, will not believe the iron muscles and steely nerves it takes to creep with long-stretched-out body, touching the ground only with tips of feet and finger. If one approached on soles, the flat hand, or even the knees, repetitive noise would be unavoidable. When, earlier, the twig broke, the Indian's muscles must have become tired; consequently, for just a moment, his knee touched the ground. The spot where one places his fingertips is carefully searched for anything breakable. Precisely where fingers have briefly rested, the tips of the feet are carefully placed. Many a good shot and frontiersman remains, throughout his life, a poor encroaching spy. *La-ya-tishi*, to 'see with fingers', the Navajo very expressively, call this, for an enemy, dangerous skill.

He passed me and I took action. I left my hindering rifle in the bushes and crept after him, caught up, and lunged onto his stretched-out body. Grabbing his neck with my left hand, I hit the back of his head with my fist, knocking him unconscious. I took my lasso and tied his arms and legs. Then I carried him to the fire, after I had first retrieved my rifle. I laid him down and rekindled the fire so that I could observe him when he awoke.

It took him a long time to open his eyes. Despite the seemingly dangerous situation he found himself in, not a single move of his iron features betrayed even a trace of surprise or alarm. He closed his eyes again and remained lying as if dead. But I noticed how he softly tightened his muscles to test the firmness of his fetters. He had the bare hair bun of the common Indian and was dressed only in leather shirt, pants and moccasins. I saw a knife in his belt and a tomahawk, a medicine bag and a bullet bag. The latter told me that he had hidden his rifle, and maybe also his horse nearby, in order to approach me unhindered. I knew that, in no case, would he begin the conversation, therefore, asked him in a mixture of English and Indian dialect, in use along the Indian border:

"What did the red man want at my fire?"

"*Tcha-tlo!*" he answered gratingly.

This Navajo word means frog, big mouth, quacker, useless talker, coward, who hides right away. It, thus, was an insult, which I overlooked. Why did this man speak Navajo? He looked more like a Sioux.

"You are correct to be annoyed by the frog," I told him. He gave you away. Had I not heard him, you wouldn't be my prisoner. What do you think I'll do with you?"

"*Ni niskhi tsetsetsokhiskhan shi* – kill and scalp me!" he answered.

"No, I won't," I replied. "I'm not your enemy, but the red man's friend. I took you captive to prevent injury to me. What tribe do you belong to?"

"*Shi tenuai!*"

The word *tenuai* means 'men', which the Navajo call themselves. However I responded:

"Why do you lie? I know the Tenuai language; you aren't speaking it well. From your pronunciation you are a Teton. Speak your own language or that of the Whites. I love truthfulness and will also speak in truth!"

Following this he looked at me questioningly for the first time and said:

"The palefaces did come across the Big Water. Over there are light-haired ones, Englishmen, and dark-haired ones, the Spaniards. Who do you belong to?"

"Neither!" I told him.

"That is good! They are liars with a light scalp and liars with a dark scalp. But to which tribe do you belong?"

"I belong to the great people of Germany who are friends of the red men and have never, yet, attacked their wigwams."

"Uff!" he exclaimed surprised. "The Germans are good. They have only one god, only one tongue and only one heart."

"Do you know them?" I asked, surprised.

"No, but I did hear of a great white hunter who is from Germany. He kills grizzly with a knife; he fells every enemy with his fist; his bullet never misses, and he speaks the red man's languages. He is their friend and may stay amidst all of them, for none will harm him."

"What is his name?"

"The red men call him *Vau-va-shala*, Deathly Hand, but the white hunters call him Old Shatterhand. He knows all animals of the plains and the mountains, since Winnetou, the great Chief of the Apache, was his teacher."

"Would you smoke the calumet with him?"

"He is a great chief. I would have to wait for him to offer me the peace pipe."

"He will smoke it with you. Tell me your name!"

"I am called Pokai-po, 'Killing Fire'."

"Uff! Then you are the second chief of the Sioux, of the Teton tribe!"

"I am he," he answered proudly.

"I have heard about you. A Chief of the Sioux is not to lie fettered before me. You are free!"

I removed the lasso. He arose, looked at me surprised, and said:

"Why do you set me free? Why don't you kill the palefaces' greatest enemy?"

"Because you are a brave and just warrior. You have become the palefaces enemy because they broke their friendship with your people. But there are many great and mighty nations of palefaces, among them many who are friends of red men. You must not hate all white men, because some are deceitful and unfaithful. You thought to attack me, but I took you prisoner. Your scalp was mine, but I set you free. Let us smoke the peace pipe and then part as brothers!"

I reached for the pipe, which I carried frontiersman-like around my neck, and stuffed it. He was likely happy to have gotten away with his life. Yet, inside, he questioned whether his honor let him accept an unknown White offering him the Pipe, which is why he asked:

"Are you a chief of the Whites, and what is your name?"

"'Killing Fire' need not be ashamed to smoke the calumet with me," I responded. "I am Old Shatterhand, the brother of all red men."

Indians are used to absorb the most surprising message with greatest composure, but barely had I given my widely known name, which had been given to me by an idle trapper, when the chief leaped up and yelled:

"Old Shatterhand! Do you speak truth?"

"Can 'Killing Fire' be outwitted and overcome by a common hunter? Did I not earlier stun you with a single strike of my hand?"

"But where is Winnetou, the great Chief of the Apache?"

Winnetou and I were known as being inseparable, therefore, the question.

"He is at the source of the Tongue River, where he awaits me. I had to go to Fort Cass to heal a wound. 'Killing Fire' may sit down with me, or does enmity remain between us?"

"We shall be brothers," he said solemnly. "Your enemies are my enemies, and my brothers are your brothers. You shall be welcome in every tent of the Sioux and our life shall be like one. One will die for the other!"

From this moment on I was assured to have found a new friend who would give his life for me. I started the pipe, blew the smoke to the prescribed directions, then passed it on to him. He repeated the ceremony and, without another word, smoked the pipe to its end. The pipe had been a present of Winnetou's. The clay for its head had come from the sacred quarries in the north. Every blown puff counted as an inviolable oath to the Great Spirit to keep the concluded friendship faithfully to death. The friendship of the palefaces is often also concluded by tobacco smoke and the odor of spirits, but what is it worth? It soon ends once the smoke and alcohol have vanished!

Now, there were no secrets between us, and I learned what had brought him to the Bighorn. He was here as a scout. Without our meeting it is highly probable that the fort and its residents would have been lost.

"The warriors of the Teton came to the mountain passes to hunt buffalo which pass by there," the chief explained. "They had a good hunt, since the buffalo came in a large herd with their females and children, like we had not seen for many suns. The sons of the Teton are strong and brave, which is why the buffalo and their cows lay dead in great numbers. But, then, the palefaces came who wear colorful clothes, and demanded from us the buffalo. They had more rifles than the red men did who defended themselves, but had to give way and left three times five and three dead. Were the palefaces in their right?"

"No," I had to tell him regretfully.

"The red men think so, too. This is why they called on their medicine man and held a great council. The Great Spirit has promised them victory when they attack the treacherous palefaces. They have now come to punish the enemy. They rest here in the forest and 'Killing Fire' is on the way to Fort Cass to find out how many enemy there are and what is required to conquer the firm houses of the palefaces."

I had seen this coming! This Sioux saw me today for the first time. He knew that I was one of the fort's residents, yet he confided all this to me. Is it any wonder that I thought him more deserving my friendship than those who had so thoughtlessly provoked his revenge? But could I quietly look on for the fort to be attacked? No! And precisely for this reason I found myself now in an unenviable position.

"Will my brother Old Shatterhand come with me to the warriors of the Teton to attack the fort?" he asked when I remained pensively silent for some time.

"No," I told him honestly.

"Why not? Have you not smoked the calumet with me?"

"I am your friend, but all palefaces are also my brothers."

I admit openly that is wasn't easy for me to me say this, and right away I was to hear the consequences of it:

"You said yourself that they acted unjustly. Still, you remain the brother of these traitors and liars! I was glad to learn that you are Old Shatterhand, however, I see that it is hard to become the friend of a paleface!"

What was I to answer? I could easier tackle a herd of buffalo, than to prove to this simple savage that it would now be my duty to betray his intent to his enemies.

"You want to kill the palefaces because Manitou commanded it?" I asked.

"Yes."

"Well then! I, too, must obey my Manitou, and he says that he alone is the avenger."

"Why has this Manitou not avenged his red children? Or is your Manitou another one than mine? 'Killing Fire' has been in the cities of the palefaces and has heard the speeches of their priests. Does Old Shatterhand know these speeches? Whoever spills human blood must also die, your book tells. Why were three times five and three warriors of the Teton killed, when they had done nothing bad? You are to obey your chiefs, your book tells. If a red man kills someone, he will also be killed, since your chiefs say they have the right to do this. But when you come to us and kill ten times ten times ten men, we are not permitted to kill you, since our chiefs have no right for it, so yours say. Are then red men dogs and coyotes? There may be palefaces who do not think us to be coyotes, and you are one of them. I know that you agree with me, but that, at the same time, your belief commands you to warn the evil palefaces at the fort. Go then and do it!"

He rose, looking defiant and sad. I, too, got up and asked:

"Where are the warriors of the Teton camped?"

"Upriver."

"How many are there?"

"Ten times ten, times three, and fifteen more."

A White would never have answered both questions now. I said:

"I will not warn the palefaces, but you, yourself, must do it."

"'Killing Fire' is to warn his enemies?" he asked, totally surprised.

"Yes," I responded. "You come along in my canoe to travel to the fort with me. There you ask for reparation for your slain warriors. If you do not obtain it, then I've done my duty and you can attack the place without me saying another word."

He pondered this, looking down, then said:

"They will seize 'Killing Fire' and detain him."

"You are my brother. I promise you that you can leave whenever you wish."

"They are perfidious. They will promise it to you, but not keep their word. Can you protect 'Killing Fire'?"

"Do you think Old Shatterhand to be afraid of these palefaces? If they don't keep their word, I shall talk to them with rifle and tomahawk."

"I believe you and will come, all alone, but not in your canoe but on a stallion, as it becomes a Chief of the Sioux. *Enokh e-i anash*, farewell!"

In the blink of an eye he had disappeared in the dark forest. This was very much the Indian way, although a European would have thought that there was much more to be discussed. The savage talks less but acts more.

There could not be thought of sleep. It was necessary to reach the fort in time. The chief's quick departure could be assumed.

I put out the fire, untied the canoe, and began the return trip down-river. This went much faster than the upstream trip and morning wasn't much older than two hours, when I spotted the fort at the confluence of the two rivers. After I tied up the canoe and walked slowly up the slope, I noticed a kind of camp that had been set up in front of the fort's palisades. It consisted of simple shelters of thrown together branches, seemingly serving a bunch of trappers. I took this from the quantity of traps and other trapping instruments spread about there. These folks had arrived during my brief absence. They made a bad impression on me.

Eight or ten of them had gathered and tried each other in shooting. They had nailed a small board to the trunk of a walnut tree and, with chalk, had drawn a cross hair on it, for which they aimed. I wanted to pass them after having bid a "Good Morning", but I miscalculated. One of them blocked my way and shouted at me as if I were standing a mile away:

"Holla, mister, don't just pass by here. We have set up a shooting range where we do a little betting. The worst shot costs a drink, a full glass for each of us, and everyone outside the palisades must take part."

The fellow was extraordinarily repugnant. And where, where had I seen his physiognomy before? I had met this man somewhere, but when and where? He must have been in a bad fight, which had totally shaved off the right side of his face. He was horrible to look at, with his bearded left and the raw-colored flesh of the right side of his face.

"One must take part? Who said so?" I asked.

"I did, mister," was the reply. "Know that I am the leader of these honorable gentlemen. We've come to Fort Cass to buy ammunition and will then head out again to catch a few more beaver."

"Well, then I wish you good luck in your business, sir. Good bye!"

I was going to walk on, but he grabbed my arm.

"By the devil! You stay here and shoot for a drink with us! I told you that everyone has to!" he insisted.

"Pshaw! I'm not interested!"

I shook him off and left.

"Ah, here's a gentleman who carries a gun but can't shoot!" he called derisively, with the others joining him in laughter. "Look at him! He wears shiny boots like a dancing master and carries himself like a noble coachman. We'll force him to show us what he can do with his Sunday's rifle!"

Of course, I didn't pay any attention to this prattle and walked though the open gate into the fort. I went straight to the major, who had just risen from his night's rest and received me rather grumpily.

"Where have you been, sir?" he asked. "We were concerned. A resident of the fort mustn't stay away overnight. You know that I'm responsible for every mishap!"

This amounted to a reproof. I had given only my common name at the fort. That I was called Old Shatterhand, no one was aware of, otherwise the major wouldn't have used this address.

"Oh, please, sir," I responded, "I'm not aware that I relinquished my independence upon my arrival at Fort Cass. As a civilian I consider this place well suited to purchase a new outfit, shells, etc., and to allow myself some rest, but not to submit to some kind of discipline. Then, I may care even less for the well-being of your people."

"What is that to mean?"

"Fort Cass is to be attacked."

"What!" he shouted, becoming pale. "By whom?"

"By the Teton. The chief's not standing far from here with three hundred fifty Indians. By chance, he is my friend and has promised me, in consideration of our friendship to desist from any hostilities for the time being. He will come to Fort Cass today to demand satisfaction. If he's denied same, I'll vouch for nothing."

"Well, for that matter, you don't have to vouch for anything anyway," he answered. He had recovered from his first shock and added, "I find your manner rather peculiar!"

"I'm assuming the same of you. I met the chief in the forest and hurried back to inform you."

"You met him in the forest, sir. How come you are the friend of a Chief of the Teton? I thought you to be a lost visitor from a summer resort, who had ventured too far and had gotten away with a small bullet wound. Although you had many weapons hanging on you when you arrived, no one has as yet seen you taking a shot."

"Each to his own. I do not buy ammunition to waste it needlessly."

"Maybe," he said doubtfully. "Where and when did you meet the chief?"

"I'm not in a position to give you precise information. The Indians have been done injustice. I am a friend of the chief. I did for the fort what I could, but will not betray my friend."

"Then you don't want to tell me the whereabouts of the redskins?"

"No."

"I will force you!"

"Pshaw! I'm not afraid! I know the situation so well that I even promised the chief safe conduct."

That was too much for the officer.

"Are you out of your mind, sir!" he yelled. "Just the opposite; I shall detain the chief as a hostage!"

"Then I shall ride to him, to tell him not to come!"

"I will certainly prevent you from doing so!" he threatened.

"Try it!" I told him calmly. "First I'll gun down anyone who dares to put hand on me. Then I shall send a truthful report about the Teton situation to Washington. They will understand that one needs not be surprised if the Indian takes up weapons."

He looked rather alarmed, and when I made to leave, he called:

"Stop, sir! I can do something about this situation only after I have consulted with the officer corps."

"Fine, do that. Then let me know whether the chief will get safe conduct or not!"

I left him and went for the store where I had rented a small room. Nearby, in the stable, stood my mustang. He had had plenty of rest and neighed happily when I took him out to the yard to saddle him. I did this to be prepared for everything. I filled the saddle bags with my few belongings and acted as if I planned to leave for good. Then I went to my room to await what was to come.

After a while a corporal was sent with the message that it had been decided to offer the chief safe conduct. However, it didn't completely set me at ease.

My room lay right next to another which was used by guests and buyers. From it came the sounds of an unusual commotion, and I soon realized that it was caused by some of the strange trappers. Two had stepped out to the yard to talk there with subdued voices. They did not stand too far from the simple board wall of my abode, which is why I overheard conversation fragments.

"Magnificent mustang .... worth more than all our nags together."

"Who might he belong to?"

"One of the officers, in any case."

"Then we won't dare take it .... poor life now .... gold dust and nuggets .... all gambled away .... might we be lucky ... Oil Prince .... has millions lying about."

"Is he truly the brother-in-law of ....?"

"Certainly! .... know him very well .... since two years at Lake Shayan .... inquired precisely .... only Flowing Wells now builds big well pumps with steam power."

"It'll be a nice business ... only no one to survive, or .... the matter come to light."

Once more, a ruckus erupted in the bar and store room so I couldn't understand another word. Then the two left the yard. About who and what had they talked about? The longer I thought about what I had heard, the more suspicious I found it. Something wasn't to come to light which is why no one was to survive. Did they intend to hit an Oil Prince? Whose brother-in-law was he? What was the matter with the gold dust and nuggets? Was I dealing here with a bunch of horse thieves? Or might these characters, under the cover of trappers, be in the business of bushheaders, who loved to attack solitary farms or travelers who came from California with gold dust. While I made every effort to understand what I had overheard, I heard loud shouts coming from the yard.

"A Red, a Red, a chief's coming!"

The shout was also heard in the store and everyone hurried out to see the Indian. I did the same and saw 'Killing Fire' ride up the slope. He was by himself. But about a mile distant, stood three horsemen in a clearing, from which they could observe the fort.

The chief looked totally different. His magnificently bridled stallion had a long-flowing mane, its tail almost dragging on the ground. The horseman had his hair bound up in a helmet-like bun, in which stuck three eagle feathers, the symbol of his position as a chief. The seams of his leggings and his hunting shirt were decorated with the hair of slain enemies. On his belt hung thirteen plaited scalps, like scales next to each other, and his coat was made from precious yellow rat fur. He was armed with a knife, tomahawk, and a double-barreled rifle in addition to a bow and quiver.

When he entered through the gate, everyone hurried to see him. While he did not wear war colors, the coming of a Teton was significant.

I stepped next to his horse and offered him my hand.

"*Hos takh-shon enokh* – Good morning!" he greeted me simply. "I come alone. Has 'Killing Fire' been given safe conduct?"

"Yes," I replied. "It was promised me."

"My brother does not believe everything he is told! The Chief of the Teton will not lay down his weapons."

That's when the same corporal approached who had delivered the earlier message to me, and told the Teton that he was expected in the meeting room, but that he had to lay down his weapons first. The chief did not deign to give him a look but turned to me:

"Where is this place?"

"I'll take you there," I told him.

"Hold it!" the corporal demanded. "Except for the Chief, all others are denied access."

I did not say a word, but took my stallion's reins to lead him to the conference room, which wasn't more than an exercise room of the troops where chairs had now been placed. The chief jumped off his horse and stepped in, after which the corporal said to me:

"I have orders to take the Red's horse away!"

"It is mine!" I told him, and led the animal to the store, where I tied it to a rail.

I now got my rifles from my room and hung them over my shoulder. Now I was prepared for whatever might happen and waited.

Four men guarded the hall's entrance, and on the opposite side of the yard another six were ready to help upon a signal. This looked like a betrayal, but I determined to defend the Chief. I had a knife, two six-shooters, a loaded double-barreled rifle and my twenty five shot Henry Rifle. If I succeeded in closing the hall, I was certain of victory.

I waited for about half an hour, when I heard a whistle from the hall. The four guards hastened in, and the six others also rushed towards it from across the yard. Every one of the curious folks who, until now, had kept at a respectful distance, now pushed forward. I quickly mounted my mustang, took the Teton's stallion reins, and galloped towards the hall. I arrived there before the dragoons.

"Get away!" I shouted and drove the horses into the crowd.

As I reached the entrance, I jumped off, stepped inside, pulling the horses after me. The animals' rears filled the door so that no one could pass. A look into the interior told me what happened. The whistle had been for the four dragoons to disarm the Chief and to take him prisoner. The other six were to have come in for support, but were now prevented from doing so.

The Teton stood in a corner, his tomahawk raised, ready to kill anyone trying to lay hands on him. But all eyes were now on me. The officers were all armed, the dragoons, too, but they did not worry me.

"What's this about? What do you want here, sir?" the major shouted at me.

"To remind you of your word," I told him. "You promised me safe conduct for the Chief of the Teton."

"That he got; he was permitted free entry."

"Ah! But he's not permitted free exit?"

"No. I didn't promise that much."

"Well, sir! *Pokai-po, bite ta-ata* – 'Killing Fire', come to me!"

The Chief was just about to walk over to me when the major pulled his revolver and pointed it at me.

"Out! Or I shoot!" he ordered.

"Pshaw!" I answered. "'Killing Fire', tell these palefaces who I am!"

"Old Shatterhand!" the Indian said.

"Old Shatterhand!!" the officers repeated.

To see the perplexed faces was a real pleasure. A mere name often means more than its bearer can accomplish.

"Yes, I am Old Shatterhand, gentlemen," I confirmed to them. "Will you believe it or am I to prove it to you? I promised my red friend safe conduct and shall keep my word. But before you will allow me to participate in your discussion. 'Killing Fire' does not speak perfect English, and you do not sufficiently understand Sioux dialect. This requires a translator. Let's begin then! Whether it is with weapons or by a peaceful conversation is up to you."

Many will see a great risk in my behavior, but it wasn't. I knew my people. A German major or sergeant major would simply have had me put *ad acta*, but the good Yankees had such a respect for my trapper name that the negotiations were begun anew and, thanks to my effort, the chief waived the compensation he had asked for prior to my engagement: He had demanded the lives of eighteen Whites, one White for each fallen Teton. I got him to ask only for eighteen carbines, and these were – quite against the law – promised to him.

I now reopened the entrance. No man had been able to enter, since the horses defended their position with hind hooves. When we left the hall, there came a voice from the front-most row of the curious:

"Why don't we kill the redskin! What does he want here among gentlemen? Let's tar and feather him!"

"Yes, let's tar and feather!" screamed his companions.

Did these people act by some order, or did they intend to fish only in some mud. I don't know, but immediately ten, twenty arms reached for the Indian. As if by agreement a wedge of people pushed quickly between the two of us which separated us. I saw his tomahawk strike after which a multi-voiced scream of fury arose.

"Major, I hold you responsible!" I shouted to the officer, who stood alarmed near me.

I let go of the stallion I was still holding and jumped onto my mustang. Already, revolver shots rang. I had my horse rise up and gave it the spurs. With a long leap it rushed into the midst of the cluster of men. Then I used the butt of my rifle, as my brave animal was using its hooves.

The Indian had defended himself, but had been hemmed in by the crowd, pushed and torn down. Still on the ground he fought back with Indian cold-bloodedness. My strikes freed him. He leaped up, his rifle again in hand, its butt now striking the heads of the attackers. Everyone screamed and hollered confusedly, with knife blades flashing and revolver shots ringing. I remained unhurt and called to the chief:

"*To-ok kava* – jump on your horse!"

Despite the ruckus surrounding us he understood, rushed for his stallion, which was kicking with all fours. In one leap he was on him.

"*Usta nai* – come, follow me!"

Following these words I urged my horse to leap. He did likewise with a push of his thighs, since he had not been able to pick up the hanging reins. He yelled the triumphant scream of the Sioux. Then the two of us shot forward towards the gate. It was shut, but we aimed to its side, where the boards were lower.

"Hi ho-hi!" he shouted, and flew across, with me following.

A many-voiced shout of surprise arose. Then our animals galloped down the slope onto the plain. No one followed us, which is why we soon had the horses fall to a slower pace. Under the given circumstances it is no shame to take flight than to have oneself gunned down.

Part 2: Red Olbers

It was another evening that I sat by a campfire, but not alone. My horse was grazing nearby. It eases one's mind to have a good animal along which has sharper senses than even the most experienced hunter. A mustang smells the approach of every hostile creature and lets its owner know by fearful snorting.

I had left Fort Cass and was now at the eastern arm of the Bighorn River from where I intended to cross the Black Hills for the waters of the Tongue. There, Winnetou, the Chief of the Apache, was expecting me.

When I had ridden with 'Killing Fire' from the fort, we had not noticed any pursuit. We had come across the three outposts without being bothered. From there we rode upstream and soon met the band of Teton who were impatiently awaiting their leader's return.

Immediately, a council was called. The chief told what had happened, causing everyone to become angry and expressing their intent to avenge this new perfidy.

"Yes, it must be avenged," said 'Killing Fire', "but my brothers will see that the palefaces who carry colorful dress, are now warned and will expect us. We shall let some time pass until they have let their guard down. Nevertheless, our tomahawks must be pulled from our belts. The man with half a face said that I, the Chief of the Teton, was to be tarred and feathered. He took a hold of me and struck me. He and his men must feel the hands of the red warriors."

I was not present at this council. The chief told me about its result only later. I did not have the power to change the Indians' decision. And since I did not care to be present for their attack on the Whites, I stayed only one more day with them, then headed out to meet Winnetou.

I rode upstream, then followed the river's right arm. After a two-day ride I arrived at my present campsite. Tomorrow, I planned to turn east to cross the Black Hills.

I had finished my evening meal. Since it wasn't cold and I wasn't bothered by mosquitos, I let my fire burn down. I was tired, but right when I was going asleep, my horse snorted in the way with which it reported the presence of something suspicious. I listened, but did not notice anything, despite the mustang's repeated snorting.

I, therefore, rose and walked to him. He rubbed his well-built head on my shoulder and opened his nostrils to suck in the air coming softly from the south. I followed his silent request – and truly, there was a burnt smell in the air. Did this smell originate from an extinguished fire, or might there be another campsite south of me?

I had to assure myself and carefully advanced in this direction. I left my horse to itself, assured of it staying put. It was hobbled and would not have left its location even had it not been tied up.

The further I advanced the more noticeable was the fire's smell. The smoke became more dense, until I finally saw the fire's bright shine through the trees. I doubled my caution and, when I was standing behind a mighty oak, saw four men lying by the fire. They were Whites wearing the durable clothing of trappers.

Each had his weapons close at hand, but neither gave any dangerous impression. Inaudibly I pushed forward some more, then rose and, with three quick steps, stood next to them.

"Good evening, gentlemen!" I greeted. "Do you still have one more space by your fire?"

Upon my appearance they had immediately picked up their weapons, had jumped up and had encircled me, their rifles cocked.

"Who are you?" one asked.

"Nothing but a solitary frontiersman who's glad to have found some company."

"Oho! You don't look like a frontiersman, my boy! Everything is so clean and neat on you that you can't have seen much of the West yet. Where do you come from, he?"

"From Fort Cass."

"Ah! And where are you headed?"

"Over to the Tongue to meet a friend who's expecting me there."

"Who is this friend?"

"Winnetou, the Apache."

"By gosh! Is that true?"

"Didn't I say it clearly enough!"

"You know Winnetou? Really? Ah, that you must explain! Sit down with us, but first tell us of the company you are with!"

"I'm by myself."

"Alone? I'll be damned if that's true! You really don't look like a man who has the guts to gad about these woods!"

"Thank you, master! Then you think me to be a greenhorn?"

"Something like that. Well then, who are the people you are with?"

"Not a one. I don't mind if you are cautious, but this time you are mistaken. I am a German, and would regret if I gave the impression of a bushheader."

"Well, not quite that! So, you are German? Yes, one could expect a German to run about the woods in his best get-up to be scalped by some Indian. Where did you leave your horse?"

"Not very far by the river."

"Go get it then! I'll come along, and woe to you if I found you to have lied to us!"

I left, he following behind me. When we had reached my campsite and I picked up my rifle and blanket I had left there, he said:

"My goodness, it's true. You are alone. But, fellow, who dares to enter this area which presently swarms with Sioux?"

"Pshaw! The Sioux won't touch me!"

"No! Why not you?"

"Oh, we are the best of friends," I laughed.

"By gosh, you are a peculiar fellow. Take your horse and come along to our fire. We can talk before going to sleep."

When we returned the other three looked questioningly at their partner.

"It is as he said," he told them, nodding his head. "This gentleman is all by himself and claims to be the best of friends with the Sioux."

They looked at me unbelieving. One could see that they couldn't make heads or tails of me. The frontiersman doesn't give a hoot for his appearance; the more come down he looks, the more he has gone through. But I kept my weapons clean and had enough time to put my outfit in good order so that I appeared like a newcomer. I gave them my name.

"Never heard it," one of them said. "You can't be long in this area. But how do you get to be friends with the famous Winnetou, also with the Sioux, who are his enemies?"

"You'll learn about that, but first tell me also a bit of yourselves!"

They gave me their names. Then one continued:

"Don't take offense, sir, if we are very cautious. Because of some carelessness we have had bad luck. We are trappers. We had worked since spring and had gathered a nice store of pelts. We had filled six caches. Then a fifth man joined us whom we trusted. During a night when he stood guard his accomplices came. The next morning he had disappeared together with all our furs, even our horses."

"Oh my! Where and when did this happen?"

"Two weeks ago, up at Huntsman Fork."

"Don't you have any clue who the thieves were?"

"Enough clues, but what good is that? We could take the loss, but the crooks took even our traps. We have no money to buy new ones, but must make do with poor snares until we've caught something to trade for some dollars. We tracked the thieves, but it was of no help. Once they had reached the Yellowstone, they built a raft and took off. Who can follow then!"

"Were they many?"

"A whole bunch, at least thirty men, we figured from the tracks."

"Ah! The spot where they built a raft is upstream from Fort Cass?"

"A two days' ride."

"Why didn't you go to Fort Cass?" I asked.

"What would have been the use? I can't have been anyone else but Red Olbers with his band. For some time, he's been hanging around the upper Missouri, and what he has taken will never come back to its rightful owner."

I had only casually noticed the traps in front of the fort when I returned from my canoe trip. But the frontiersman has a sharp eye for every detail. This is why I remembered the markings on two of them; that is to say, that every trapper marks his traps with his symbol. This made me ask:

"Had you not marked your traps?"

"Oh yes!"

"I've seen traps marked W.B., also with five stars forming a standing cross on the bow."

"These are our traps! Where was it, sir?" the man asked quickly.

"Tell me first who this Red Olbers is?"

"No one knows where he comes from, but he's a Yankee, and one of the least clean. He's been seen in California, where he did some shady business at the digs. He had to disappear. He then resurfaced at Fort Benton, where he played the big man tossing lots of nuggets around. He's supposed to have gambled away thousands of dollars in gold nuggets –?"

"When was that?" I interrupted, since I remembered something.

"That was four years ago about the time of the present season. Later, he was seen down in Santa Fe, then at Bents Fort. Everywhere he popped up, large thefts occurred. He has now assembled an entire gang. But I hope that he'll be caught some time. Then he's assured a strong rope!"

"Did you see him? Can you describe him to me?"

"I just know that he has only half a face. On the right he's missing the skin with most of the flesh. He must have once met a very sharp knife."

"It's him! I saw your traps at Fort Cass."

"Holla, at Fort Cass! That's it, then. The one's marked with W.B. are mine; my name's William Brandes. We must get them back!"

"They are no longer at the fort. I lived with the storeowner there, and when I paid my rent the last day, I learned that he had bought a whole lot of furs from this Red Olbers. However, they did not sell the traps to him. But I figure the thieves are no longer at Fort Cass. By the way, no one there had any inkling that this fellow was Red Olbers."

"Don't you know where he might be headed?"

"Maybe," I responded. I remembered the conversation I had overheard at the store, which is why I asked: " Might you be known in the area of the Lake Shayan?"

"Very much so. We spent last winter there. This area belongs to the rich Wittler. Two years ago he discovered a big oil well there and ships hundreds of barrels of oil down the Missouri. If I'm not mistaken he's now using a drill rig to enlarge his business."

"Do you know his family?"

"Why shouldn't I, sir? He has a wife and three children, that is, two sons and a little daughter. A sister also lives with him whose husband perished somewhere. He was in California, from where he wrote that he would come home with a cache of gold. But he never returned. He must have left California four years ago."

"Might his name be John Helming?" I inquired tensely.

"Yes, sir, John Helming was his name. Did you know him?"

"No," I answered excitedly, "but I saw him as a corpse, murdered and robbed by this Red Olbers –"

"By God!" the four men exclaimed in unison. "Tell us, tell us about it!"

"No, there's no time for it now; we can do that on the way. Since I see now what's going on, we must leave at once. This Red Olbers gang is on the way to Lake Shayan to attack and rob Wittler's property, just like he already murdered and robbed the brother-in-law. It's likely the crooks still have your traps, which are very valuable in this remote area. You may see your property returned."

"But, sir, give us at least some idea!"

"Well. Four years ago, I visited the United States for the second time and, with Winnetou, came by Hellgate Pass. One afternoon we found the still warm bodies of several men. The murders must have taken place barely a few minutes earlier. There were five dead, all thoroughly robbed. On one of them I fond an old note book on which stood the name John Helming. We covered the bodies as well as possible, then followed the murderers' tracks, of which there were many. They had taken the loaded mules from the killed men and could advance only slowly. When we caught up with them, I counted fourteen men, yet we still tackled them. They were superior to us. I was then still a newcomer to the West. To make a long story short – we lost. They lost a few men, and their leader lost part of his face. Upon one of Winnetou's strikes with his tomahawk, the fellow moved his head sideways in time, which is why he didn't get his head split. The tomahawk's edge slid down his cheek and thus marked him for all times. We buried the dead who had been robbed, but I took the notebook along. A subsequent rain erased the murderers' tracks. I advertised the story of the notebook several times, but no one ever responded. To this day I carry it in my belt. When I came to see the prairie once again, I took it along. One never knows what one experiences or learns."

I now told them about my stay at Fort Cass. When I had finished, Brandes called:

"Sir, that is extraordinary! We must immediately get to Lake Shayan!"

"Yes, but not with me. I'm mounted, but you must walk. You can cross the mountains directly, but I must head for the Tongue to meet Winnetou. We'll split here, but will likely arrive at the Lake at the same time. Then, too, don't forget that 'Killing Fire' with his Teton is after the thieves. They'll be unable to commit their robbery nor escape us. I won't stay any longer but head out immediately."

"Us too, us too, sir. But what are we to tell the Oil Prince if we arrive before you?"

"Tell him to prepare at once for Olber's attack. He'll learn more about his brother-in-law when I arrive."

Only for very important reasons is it advisable to penetrate an unknown forest wilderness on horseback during the night. However, experience and a sense of place help to overcome much. The next morning I found myself already at the foot of the mountains and was now able to speed ahead. By late morning I had reached the watershed, and shortly after noon I saw the upper run of the Tongue.

Now I needed to find Winnetou. This may seem to be more difficult than it actually was. We had several times separated previously and yet had found each other even in rocky desert and deepest forest. We had our marks no other would notice.

I rode along the river observing the pebbles. Then, after only a quarter of an hour, I noticed two lying side by side with three thin twigs jammed between them. Two were bare with the third having small side-twigs with leaves. Its tip pointed upwards. This was one of our signs. Winnetou had set it up. The tip of the leafy twig told me where he had ridden, with the two other twigs pointing exactly to the point of the sky where the sun had stood when he set up the sign. By the leaves' freshness I could deduce the day.

I learned that the Apache chief had been here about nine o'clock this morning. Since he had no need to erase his tracks, I found those of his horse and followed them. Then I found the spot where he had rested during the hottest time of day. There was also a sign that he would return here for the night. This sign consisted of a small, thin powderwood twig stuck in the ground. Any kind of wood, such as elder, could be used, whose pith could be easily removed. This looked so accidental that the most experienced trapper or astute Indian could not identify this, to me, clearly legible writing. In that way one commands the solitary Llano, the wide prairie, the wild mountains, and the dense forest. By such means Winnetou, Old Firehand, Long Hilbers, Fred Walker and Sam Hawkens became famous. I knew them all and had learned much from them. The Wild West is like water: one must, in order to swim, jump in. One floats, and the learning time passes quickly, the more one exercises.

I hobbled my horse, let it graze, then lay down. It didn't take long to hear the report of a rifle. It was the sharp, sonorous sound caused only by Winnetou's Silver Rifle. It is almost incomprehensible to the layman that two hunters can recognize each other by the report of their rifles, but whoever has heard the 'voice' of a rifle, knows how to differentiate it from the sound of any other rifle.

Immediately I reached for my rifle and fired. I was convinced that Winnetou would also recognize its report. I was not mistaken, for only ten minutes later I heard the gallop of a horse. Then the famous Chief of the Apache stood before me.

"*Ni to, Shar-lih" Nsho-peniyil! Shi mazakan ni yaltile* – You here, Shar-lih? Welcome! I heard your rifle speak."

Shar-lih is how he pronounced my given name in English being Charles or Charlie. He said his words as if we had separated only five minutes ago and found each other at a place requiring no thought of meeting again.

He jumped off his saddle, let his horse roam, and stood before me, the paragon of Indian handsomeness.

Yet, in the eyes of a frontiersman he had the 'fault', so often also applied to me: he never neglected his appearance. The wilderness was never able to dirty his outfit and to rust his weapons. His broad shoulders and his strong, scarred chest were totally bare. A Saltillo blanket was slung around his waist, above that lay a waterproof leather belt, which, like mine, served to keep precious small items. It also held the scalping knife, the shining tomahawk, and two revolvers. Buckskin pants, tightly fitting his muscular thighs, were decorated on the sides with the scalp locks of killed enemies. The hunting shirt, open in the front, made of the finest deerskin, wore the same decoration. Leggings, woven from the hair of those killed by him, covered his calves. The moccasins he wore must have taken a diligent squaw surely months to finish. From his shoulders hung a coat made from the heavy fur of a gray bear. From his neck hung the calumet on a chain made from bear teeth. His head was not covered, his hair being arranged to a helmet-like hairdo holding the three feathers of a chief. Around his hips was slung the non-tearing lasso, while his hand held his precious, silver-studded rifle, from which a bullet, fired by him, never missed. His forehead was high, his nose could almost be called Roman, and almost unnoticeably protruding cheekbones did not diminish his manly, handsome and yet kindly expression.

This was Winnetou, the most famous chief of red men who never commanded a tribe, but ranged the prairies and mountain, alone or only in the company of his friend, to demonstrate that an Indian can also be a hero and human being.

He took a seat next to me and I offered him a cigar I had purchased at the fort. No Parisian connoisseur could have put it with greater dexterity to his mouth and to light it.

"My brother Shar-lih is well again?" he asked.

"Yes, healthy and rich. I got more than two hundred dollars for the furs. I have them in my belt."

"They are yours! Winnetou needs no dollars. He knows where gold and silver grow in the earth. In what direction is my brother going to hunt now?"

"Towards the Shayan. I want to hunt a thief and murderer. Is my brother Winnetou coming along?"

"Winnetou will be where his brother Shar-lih goes. Who is the murderer?"

"He is the murderer of the five men we buried four winters ago at Hellgate Pass."

This was also a surprise for him, but his features remained unmoved. He was Indian through and through.

"My brother Shar-lih may tell me!" he said.

I, too, was used to deal with him in monosyllables. Maybe this was why I had gained his affection. With a few words I reported what was necessary. He listened wordlessly and without any change of features, then finished his cigar most leisurely.

"Did my brother bring cartridges?" he asked.

"Enough," I told him briefly.

Having heard this he rose, tossed his rifle over his shoulder and mounted his horse. I did likewise. He directed us into the water and I noticed the ford here. Behind his saddle a round, bare-scraped deer-leather package was tied. It contained the meat the Apache had shot earlier. Thus we were equipped with everything necessary.

We understood each other without saying a word. Just now, Winnetou was headed for Lake Shayan, in answer to my report. I could rely on him. He knew the mountains, from Mexico all the way up to the Frazer River.

We rode towards the border between Wyoming and Nebraska. It was a bad way, right across the Black Hills. This was particularly so when darkness fell and the Apache did not show any inclination for night rest.

My mustang was tired, but kept up, until Winnetou finally dismounted late that evening and started a fire to prepare the meat Indian fashion. Since he did not mention night watch, I thought him to find the area safe, so I lay down next to him when he settled for the night.

The next morning we continued our ride, always through inhospitable areas. I noticed that the Apache sought out the most lonely tracts, so that no one would notice anything about our trip to Lake Shayan. He must be mightily interested to catch the man who had once escaped us, when his gang had numbers so disproportionally superior to us.

This day, too, passed. We stopped earlier for our night's camp than yesterday. The caution the Apache displayed let me know that we had arrived near our destination. Because of the supposed bushrunners' presence we had to be more cautious than earlier.

The next morning we reached a substantial river, deep and wide enough to carry larger boats.

"The Shayan!" Winnetou said.

He rode on so confidently that I was convinced the area was familiar to him. The river broadened and deepened. Its banks were covered by forest. Suddenly, Winnetou turned away from the riverbank into the forest, which consisted of such big trees that we found enough space to pass through. The terrain rose and we had to climb high until we, finally, reached a plateau where the forest changed to low brush interspersed by grassy areas.

That's when the wind carried a familiar smell towards me – the odor of petroleum. We were approaching Lake Shayan. I observed this, too, from the attention with which the Apache checked the ground for possible tracks. Then he made a sudden turn, galloped a short distance, pointed ahead, and said:

"*Tu-indchule shayan* - Lake Shayan."

With every step the stink of petroleum increased, which is why I figured to see the lake very soon. But when I stopped next to the Apache, I saw that we still had a long ride to reach the lake's shores. As it was, we had halted at the edge of a deep, egg-shaped basin with steeply rising rock walls. It looked very much as if this large depression was the remnant of a once fire-spitting volcano. Several hundred feet below us, at the crater's bottom, lay the lake. Its size looked like it would take an hour to travel around. Between its shore and the eastern cliffs I noticed active movement between several smaller and larger buildings. They included a house built of roughhewn stones, next to which stood several wooden huts. Everywhere lay barrels, staves, hoops, barrel bottoms, the barrels partly empty, partly filled with petroleum. A steam saw was busy cutting logs to staves. Everywhere stood equipment for processing petroleum. From one of the barrels, flowed evil-smelling oil. One could see that it had earlier flowed into the lake, but was now captured in several large reservoirs, so that not a drop was being lost. Further to the left operated a second steam engine moving a drill, accessing the depths to find even larger stores of hydrocarbons.

The lake had no influx except for the oil spring, but it could have several springs at its bottom, since it had a major drain on the northeastern face of the basin that cut through the rock wall. As I found out later, it entered from there into the nearby Shayan River. This drainage took place through a gap in the rocks with a width of at most twelve feet. This opening provided the only access to get to the lake from the outside, that is, to the interior of the crater. To climb down from the edge without danger seemed only possible at the western face. Individual tall and slender firs grew from the precipice; its dangerous cracks, crevices, holes, corners and edges were smoothed by luxurious creepers and thorny brush. However, the sharply cut eastern face of the basin dropped almost vertically into the depth. Although there was an occasional small landing or other irregularity a daring alpinist could use for an ascent or descent, it's attempt would require death defiance.

We now rode along the crater's lip, then down its outside slope, until we reached the outflow. This gap in the rocks allowed passage for only a single horseman, since most of its width was taken up by the lake's outflow carrying dark, oily water.

When the crater opened, we saw several narrow, long, and very shallow-built boats which seemed to bring filled oil barrels to the Shayan River, where they were loaded onto larger boats to be shipped down-river to the Missouri.

Turning to the left, we arrived at the earlier-mentioned rigs, where the workers operating there observed us with some surprise. Apparently, no Indian chief had yet be seen here, at least not as long as this 'oil colony' existed. I asked for Mister Wittler and learned that the massive stone building was his home and office. We rode towards it along the lakeshore.

The lake seemed to be very deep and did not hold any living creature in its oily waters. Towards its midst rose an island where, surrounded by various bushes a roughhewn, but beautiful pavilion rose. That this little house was used frequently was indicated by three boats tied up by its banks.

Few laborers were employed here. They were all wild-looking, sturdy fellows, who could produce. We had been seen at the house, where a man had stepped out whose face displayed more good nature and openness as is common with Yankees.

"May I speak with Mr. Wittler, sir?"

"Certainly. That's me," he responded. "You must be hunters looking for shelter? Come on in and be welcome!"

"You are mistaken, sir," I said dismounting. "Yes, we are hunters, but the frontiersman needs no shelter. We rather come to you with an important issue."

"Ah, some business matter? And this Indian has been your guide?"

"No, that neither. We only came to warn you of a major mishap threatening you."

"Really! Is that true? A mishap? Please, come in, gentlemen; I'm at your service!"

I followed his invitation. Winnetou, who had stayed in the saddle, had seemingly, not even looked at the 'Oil Prince'. He now rode on along the lakeshore.

"Why is your companion riding off?" Wittler asked. "Does he not wish to come in, too?"

"Let him be, sir! He wants to survey the lake and its shores and has a very urgent reason to do so, as you will hear right away. His intentions are beneficial."

He took me to his office and asked me to sit down. He did so, too, taking his place opposite me and said:

"Pardon me, when I'm not hospitable right away! But since you are talking of some misfortune going to happen to me, I must hear about it first, before I introduce you to my family."

"You are doing right," I told him, while I opened my belt to pull out the previously mentioned notebook. "Have four trappers arrived already who stayed with you last winter?"

"Ah, you mean Brandes with his comrades! No. Did they want to come here? What's the matter with them?"

"Also, did the Sioux of the Teton tribe show up yet?"

"No. By God! Are we to be attacked by the Sioux?"

"Not by them, but by Red Olbers."

He paled and jumped up. While he seemed to be a good fellow, he did not appear to be a hero.

"To be attacked! By Red Olbers!" he exclaimed. "What am I going to do; where do I begin?"

"Calm down, sir," I told him quietly. "It's not the time yet. Tell me first if you might know this note book?"

He took it and opened it. I noticed a scare crossing his face. He took a deep breath and called out:

"God be thanked. Finally, finally some news! The book belongs to my brother. Why does he send it to me? Why does he not come himself?"

"Because he can't come. He is dead."

I had found it unnecessary to prepare him for this news, as I would have done with a lady, he being a man. Nevertheless, some tears quickly rolled down his cheeks.

"Dead!" he said. "It's true then!"

"Yes. Please sit down again, and listen to what I have to tell you! Myself and the Indian who arrived with me, buried him and his unfortunate companions."

I told him about the events at Hellgate Pass. Then, to cut off any lament, I turned his attention to the present by telling him about my encounter with the murderer at Fort Cass, followed by the rest of the story. And, truly, he forgot about his brother's death and thought only of the danger threatening him.

"Then this Olbers is coming?" he asked terrified.

"I don't doubt it. The robbed nuggets are gone. His subsequent infamies didn't get him anything. Now he wants to pay you a visit since he thinks to find riches here."

"Then I must hide everything right away in the cellar, which is fireproof."

"First you must consider preparations to repel the attack. Do your workers have weapons?"

"All of them do!"

"Well, then there isn't much to be feared! You have been warned and can treat these bushheaders appropriately."

"But I don't understand anything about how do do this. But no fight, please! Can we not keep them away by some ruse?"

I shrugged my shoulders.

"For this I'm not cunning enough, Mister Wittler. I am prepared to help you. My companion is the famous Apache Chief Winnetou. He can take on ten of these crooks, especially in a night fight, which is to be expected. I, too, have learned to defend my skin. If you count in your workers, who don't look like cowards, then there's nothing left for you than to merely watch and wait."

"I am very grateful to you, sir, very grateful!" he said relieved. "I ask you to take command of my people. They will gladly obey you."

"We are dealing here less with command than with an energetic cooperation. We shall yet talk about it. May I ask you to introduce me now to the members of your family, although I am not wearing a topcoat."

In Mrs. Wittler and Helming I met two ladies, who appeared to possess more energy than the Oil Prince. With his abhorrence of a fight I was wondering how he had dared to settle here by Lake Shayan. The children, two boys and a girl, were mightily delighted to see a stranger. I had to answer a hundred questions, but then withdrew from their curiosity to look for Winnetou and to give Wittler the opportunity to tell the ladies what he had learned from me.

I had been occupied for more than an hour with the family, thus, the Apache had found time to gallop around the lake. Just then I saw him jump a large boulder in his way. He had not found it necessary to ride around it. When we met he suggested:

"All will die! We occupy the exit as soon as the crooked palefaces have entered. They cannot climb the cliffs in the night and will be eaten by our bullets. Howgh!"

He used this final word when he wanted to affirm an opinion. I agreed with his assessment but did not want to miss anything, which is why I took the same tour around the lake. This confirmed the opinion that the bushrunners would be lost if they dared to attack.

Winnetou now also came in the house. A meal had been prepared for us to which, however, only the children joined us. Wittler and the ladies excused themselves as being too busy to carry all valuables into the cellar. I smiled about their zeal; later, however, appreciated that it had been of great advantage.

During the meal Winnetou sat so that he could look out the window. Suddenly, he leaped up.

"Uff!" he exclaimed in surprise, pointing outside.

I turned, looked outside and recognized – Red Olbers, who was riding slowly from the crater's entrance toward the house. He seemed to be observing every detail of the terrain. I hurried to the door, tore it open and called for Wittler. He hurried up knowing my call conveyed something unusual.

"Red Olbers is coming!" I told him.

"By God!" he exclaimed, stepping back in fright.

"Don't worry! He's coming only to reconnoiter. We can let him go, only to have him the more securely with his companions. But we will capture him; the others won't escape us. Quickly, receive him in the office! Act as if you don't know anything and let him talk. I am curious how he will explain his visit. I'll wait with Winnetou till he steps out again. Then we'll catch him."

"But, sir, this murderer –"

"Quickly!" I interrupted him. "He's already getting off his horse!"

I literally had to push the man away, that fearful he was. We heard Olbers step in the hallway and ask for Mr. Wittler, who met him to take him to the office. After a few minutes we posted ourselves quietly in front of its door. I imagined his face when he stepped out again and saw me. I listened. I heard several loud words followed by a wild curse. Something hit the door. I thought that this could not mean anything good and opened it. There stood Wittler, pale from fright, his mouth open. Olbers was not to be seen.

"Where is he?" I asked him urgently.

The man pointed wordlessly to the window.

"Off?" I asked.

"Yes," he answered. "I was very courageous. I told him that he was my brother's murderer and that I had guests, who were going to catch him. That's when he tossed me against the door and jumped out the window."

I had no time to vent my anger. Only fear had caused this cowardly man trying to intimidate Olbers. From outside sounded the hoof beat of a horse. I hurried to the front of the house, Winnetou following. In a hard gallop, Olbers was rushing for the exit of the lake. Even had I shouted to the workers to stop him, it would have been for naught.

Winnetou surveyed the situation with his usual cold-bloodedness.

"I will pursue him," he said. "My brother Shar-lih may tell this 'woman' what he is to do, then follow me. You will find my tracks easily."

His horse was standing a good distance away, but came to him immediately following his whistle. He jumped up and rode off. Being a cautious man, he had grabbed his rifle when we rose from the table, thus did not need go back in the house. Using the term 'woman', he had meant Wittler.

"You can't believe the inexcusable mistake you have made," I told Wittler. "It's likely the crooks will now escape us."

"The better it is!" he replied. "In any case, they will no longer think to attack us."

"That we don't know. I will now follow the Apache. Post guards and keep your eyes open. We had intended to let the gang enter the crater to render them harmless. But now that we are gone, you will be wise to shoot anyone trying to force his way in. Whether we will return, I don't know. It may be soon, late, tomorrow or, maybe, never."

During this speech I had picked up my rifles, whistled for my horse, and mounted to follow Winnetou. The laborers looked after me in surprise, since I was now the third horseman to leave the crater in a tearing hurry. Since Olbers escaped, at most two minutes had passed. I got to the crater's opening and rushed through, following the creek, clearly seeing the tracks of Winnetou's horse. Then I noticed that the Apache had redundantly taken hold of his tomahawk to chop off branches along his trail. This way I was able to follow him faster than the escapee.

I raced over hedge and stitch, between bushes and boulders. My mustang raced like he had rarely done. After a short while I caught up with Winnetou. He was not on horseback, but rather hung on the side of his horse, one leg over the saddle, the other under its belly, and an arm at the reins of the animal. He was listening for the hoof beat ahead, while his eyes scanned the ground sharply. I, too, shoved an arm into the reins to assume the same position Winnetou had, only on the left, while he was on the right side of our horses. This way we could not miss any tracks.

This is how we chased on until, suddenly, I spotted an impression in the mossy ground. I tore my steed aside.

"*Ni sisi* – stop!" I called, while bringing my horse to a halt.

At once, Winnetou had also dismounted and stood next to me.

"*Ti teshi ni utsage* – what do you see here?"

I threw a searching look at the bushes standing to the left of us and knew what had happened here.

"Do you see the deep impressions of two heels here? He jumped off his horse while it galloped, abandoning the horse to save himself, believing we would follow it and not him. He entered the bushes over there and will likely head for the creek to have his tracks disappear in the water then, when he feels safe, to return to the bank."

The Apache bent down, investigated the tracks and confirmed my finding with a soft "Howgh!", mounted his horse once more and rode to the left directly for the creek. I followed him. Then we entered the dark water which reached not even up to our stirrups.

"*Shi ti ni, akayia* – I here, you there!" Winnetou said.

He intended to keep an eye on the right bank, while I was to watch the left. This is how we waded down the creek. We were not to miss any twig, any blade of grass, nor a grain of sand. As it happened, our attention was rewarded after about ten minutes. On my side, about two paces from the water's bank, a twig was broken still hanging from its branch, its leaves still fresh but wet.

"Stop, here!" I called, leaping back, but cautiously leaving the horse still in the water.

I checked the ground and found the grass trampled, yet artificially righted again by hand.

"He's left the water here. When he shook off the water from his leather pants he wetted these leaves. Then he tried to obscure his tracks."

Winnetou found that I was correct and walked on. His sharp eyes were not going to miss the tracks, although every attempt had been made to make them unrecognizable. For this reason we had to lead our horses so as not to lose the tracks. This was highly cumbersome and time consuming. Olbers had selected those places where tracks were least visible, which is why we advanced very slowly, while he had walked at least five times as fast.

His feet's impressions led us in a wide circle above the lake towards its eastern side. We once more reached the height where bushes grew much less densely. Here he had thought to be able to be less cautious. We, therefore, mounted our horses since his tracks were now clearly visible.

119

Thus we could catch up. About three hours might have passed since our departure from the oil basin and we were now at most two miles distant from it. We came to a rather large, open grassy area, trampled by many hooves, where his tracks ran out. Here, his men had waited for him.

A brief inspection took us into the direction to which they had left towards the east. Might they have given up their thought of attack? We had to assure ourselves. In that case we would not return to the lake, at least, not until we would have caught Olbers.

The afternoon passed and evening approached. That's when the tracks suddenly veered north and, after five minutes, turned even back to the west. I became alarmed. The deep tracks proved that the bushheaders had now picked up speed.

"Uff!" Winnetou exclaimed. "What is my brother Shar-lih thinking now?"

"They changed their mind and turned around. They will yet attack the settlement."

"Howgh!"

He only spoke this one word, but put his horse to a gallop, no longer paying the tracks any attention. The only thing counting now, was to reach the crater as quickly as possible.

It became dark and stars appeared. My mind was bothered foreseeing a coming mishap. We drove our horses to the utmost speed, but darkness and the many obstacles delayed us. Finally, we closed on the lake; already we smelled the petroleum. That's when we heard shots and screams sounded up telling us that the disaster had happened. We reached the crater's rim and looked down.

Down there we saw flames flaring high and thick smoke rose mightily. Shots cracked, screams sounded –

"They are already down there," I shouted. They have lit the petroleum stores. Down there, quickly!"

We galloped along the crater's rim, then toward the entrance. How we got down there alive, I still can't say. But the most difficult part lay ahead of us yet, the jumble of boulders we had passed by day. But now, in the night –?

"*Tkli ti sisi* – leave the horses here!" Winnetou shouted.

We jumped off, tied our horses to some trees and hurried on. Stumbling, falling, getting up again, we, at last, reached the narrow entrance gap. I was ahead getting ready to enter when a voice sounded:

"Halt!" No one is to enter!" someone called to us.

This could only be one of the enemies Red Olbers had posted here as a guard. I did not slow down. I could not see him, but I pointed the butt of my rifle in front of me and ran him down with it. A splash told me that he had tumbled into the water.

Just inside the entrance stood the crooks' horses, the murderous incinerators. The light of the high-flaring flames illuminated the terrain. We saw the attackers. They had already plundered the wooden huts and had set them on fire. Now they were trying to enter the residence from whose windows shots were fired. A few others were trying to free one of the boats to row to the island where they probably thought to find treasure.

We hurried on towards the residence, over rocks, wood piles and big barrels. Now we were coming past the drill rig. I heard the sound of the machine and thought, despite being occupied by present events, of another experience in the Couteau de Missouri, where the drill had reached the subterranean oil. Near it a lamp had burned when the escaping gas exploded after which the entire area had burned.

Of course, I did not have time now for such reminiscences. The memory passed quickly. We hurried on until we came into firing range. That's when the Apache stopped, aimed, and fired. One of the attackers fell. I, too, raised my rifle, but something prevented me from taking the life of one of these men. Behind us rose a crash as if the earth had burst. The ground beneath my feet shook that I almost fell. There followed a roar, a truly hellish hissing, groaning and moaning, and then – God help us! The same happened that I had experienced in the Couteau de Missouri!

All around terrible screams arose when I turned around. Where the drill had been operating, petroleum rose at least fifty feet in the air, its beam the girth of a human being. The drill had hit oil and the lighter, first expelled gasses, had caught fire from the adjacent fires. The oil, too, burned, forming a giant fiery sheaf, spreading far, then falling in glowing streams.

The mass of gushing oil overflowed, forming a broad burning stream that rolled on with enormous speed. The fighting had stopped. No one thought any longer of attack and defense. I realized that escape was possible only by boat; it was no longer possible to pass the sea of flames on foot. I took hold of Winnetou and pulled him along.

Just when we jumped into a boat a voice sounded from the residence:

"Oh, my wife, my children!"

It was the Oil Prince, whom fright had driven outside. He was about to run after us.

"Where are they?" I hollered.

"In the pavilion on the island!"

"Good! Hide in the cellar and don't let any of the enemy in!"

He stepped back and locked the door, but the enemies immediately assaulted the house. The word 'cellar' had told them where they could find safety from the burning inferno. Some hurried to the lake's shore to get hold of the third boat.

"They mustn't get it. We need it to get the women and children, Winnetou!" I called.

He leaped for it and pushed off, a scream following him.

121

"Put the ammunition and the rifles into the water!" I warned the Indian.

I dropped my belt, the cartridge bag, the revolvers, and my two rifles into the bilge water of the boat, for I knew what would follow. Winnetou did likewise in his boat after which we began rowing.

In such moments man seems to acquire a tenfold strength. Our two boats shot like arrows across the water. We passed by the first boat. At the moment of detonation its occupants had been so shocked that they mishandled the oars and capsized. Now the men struggled in the water.

On the shore it banged, hissed, cracked, thundered and pattered; we paid it no notice. The farther we came, the cleaner the air, but the heat followed us. Then the burning oil reached the full oil barrels. They burst with the thunder of Armstrong artillery, and immediately added their burning content into the boiling stream, which had now reached the lake's water and spread with frightening speed.

"Quickly, quickly, for God's sake, Winnetou, or the fire will get us!" I shouted.

I rowed so hard that I thought my muscles would burst. From the drill hole erupted more gas which caught up with us, but we persevered and arrived at the island. There, the two women and the three children lay on the shore half dead from fright. We pulled them in to us, I the women, Winnetou the children. Then we pushed off again to find safety on the opposite shore.

Just when we left the island we saw that the bushheaders had righted their boat again and were headed for the island. They appeared to have lost one of their oars which is why they advanced only slowly.

I cannot describe the next fifteen minutes. Across the lake the entire shoreline was in flames. From this sea of flames the fire flowed on the water, following us. Sometimes, when the flames parted, one could see people trying to climb the crater wall. Their escape was doubtful.

The air became ever worse, possessing the fire and sharpness like the reflex of a mirror hit by a sun's ray. Whole balls of fiery oil flew through the air and crashed down into the water around us where they instantly formed burning circles. I felt as if I was breathing glowing iron. My heart raced, my head glowed, my tongue lay like a hundredweight of flesh in my mouth. My senses seemed to leave me. I began to fantasize: I was a steam engine and had to bring my craft to shore. The boat flew forward and the shore towards us. A few more hearty strokes, then I rose. The boat ran ashore with me tumbling into the water. This brought me to my senses again.

I took hold of the women and dropped them off on land. Winnetou had also arrived. What to do now and where to? We, too, seemed to be lost. The burning oil came ever closer. Back, at the Couteau de Missouri, the speed of my horse had saved me, but now –

"Hi, ho, hi!" it sounded above us from the rim.

We looked up and saw many brown figures climbing down in a zigzag line. Was it possible? Was there a way?

"*Pokai-po pa-e* – 'Killing Fire' is coming!" we now heard.

Yes, the killing fire was following us to destroy us, but 'Killing Fire', the Chief of the Teton, came from above to save us. There was more than daylight and I could see every step the Indians took. I looked up to them; whatever else was going on was of no concern to me. The women whimpered and the children cried. I pressed the little ones to me, but their looks did not turn from the Indians.

Finally, the first had reached bottom. It was the chief himself.

"'Killing Fire' is coming," he said, to show Old Shatterhand and the Chief of the Apache a trail leading up these rocks. The Chief of the Teton knows it for a long time already. His men joined him to carry the squaws and children up."

There was no time for an introduction of the two chiefs; death was behind us.

'Killing Fire' went ahead followed by myself and Winnetou. Behind us were the Indians with the two women and children. How I got up there, I do not recall any more. I only know that flames flared around me, that I 'drank' fire, and that my head seemed to be larger than the biggest balloon. I'm only sure that I slept long and deeply.

When I woke up, it was already the evening of the following day. I lay in the tent of the Sioux chief, next to me lay Winnetou still asleep. My hands hurt. I checked them in the light of the camp fires: I had rowed the flesh off my hands. But the pain disappeared right away when I saw all my weapons lying beside me. The good Teton had rescued them from the boat. Had I not put them into the bilge water, all the cartridges would have exploded.

I tried to get up. While I succeeded, it seemed that the poisonous gases had eaten my intestines. My outfit hung down in tatters. Beard, hair, eyebrows and eyelashes had disappeared. The same had happened to Winnetou.

Stepping from the tent I was greeted with joy by the so-called 'Savages'. Then I saw that the tent stood right next to the crater's rim. Down below the burning petroleum was still rising high, but almost two hundred Teton were busy damming the fatal stream little by little. The crater looked like hell, and the Indians looked like devils dancing around the giant column of flames.

There stood a second tent for the women and children who, also singed like myself, were alive. The place where the stone house, the residence, had stood, was nothing but a sooty rubble pile of stones. From it the Sioux had pulled the unconscious owner together with some of his people and, with much effort, had returned them to consciousness. It seemed not a single one of the Olbers gang had escaped. Even the guard I had pushed into the water with the butt of my rifle, was found outside, drowned in the creek, which carried the unconscious man to his death.

That the Sioux of the Teton tribe had come, and that at the right time, is easily explained. They had been following the gang of Red Olbers to avenge the insult to their chief. In them, I found serious, true friends. In the company of Winnetou we recovered with them from the effects of the oil fire. We had been more successful than I had thought.

9. The First Elk

Penned in 1890, this narrative was published only in 1893 in 'Über Land und Meer. Deutsche Illustrierte Zeitung' – 'Across Land and Ocean. German Illustrated Newspaper'. The content of this story was, with few changes, incorporated in the first chapter of the first volume of the Old Surehand trilogy, written in 1894, for the book series 'Karl May's collected Travelogues'.

Did I know him? What a question! Under his tutelage I experienced my first adventure in the Far West, an adventure which – well, I will tell it to you, although you will then heartily laugh about me.

His real name was Fred Cutter, but because of his wobbly gait and because his outfit hung so loosely from his lean body, he was always called Old Wabble. In earlier times he had been a cowboy down in Texas and had become so used to how people dressed there that up here in the north no one could get him to drop his outfit and trade it for another.

I still see him standing before me, tall and overly lean, in totally indescribable footgear with his legs stuck in age-old leggings. Over his shirt, whose color I'd rather not mention, he wore a jacket, whose singular advantage was its openness. Chest and neck remained free. Under his battered hat he wore a piece of cloth wound around his forehead, whose corners hung down to his shoulder. In his belt stuck the long Bowie knife. From his earlobes hung heavy silver rings, and in his large, brown, bony hand he held the inevitable burning cigar. Rarely would another person have seen him differently. Most precious was his old, weather-beaten, creased, but always smoothly shaved face with its full, Negroid lips. There was his pointy nose and sharp gray eyes, which never missed anything, although their lids were always half-closed. Whether his face was quiet or engaged, it always carried an expression of superiority, never to be tipped out of balance. And this superiority was fully warranted, for Old Wabble, despite his shaky appearance, was not only a master in riding but also in the use of rifle and lariat. Furthermore, he possessed one of the other characteristics no real frontiersmen fall short of: 'That's clear' was his constant idiom, usually proving that even the difficult was easy to him, just being a matter of course.

As to myself, I had been something like a bookkeeper down in Ogden at the railroad, and had earned enough to equip myself to follow my original plan to venture off as a gold digger to Idaho. I was a greenhorn, a complete newcomer, and took, so as not to have to share the hoped-for riches with too many others, only one companion along, Ben Needler, who knew the West as little as I did. When we left the railroad carriage at Eagle Rock, we were equipped like dandies and loaded like pack mules with lots of nice, good and shiny things which, unfortunately, had the characteristic of being of no use. And when, after a week, we arrived at Payette Fork, we looked like true vagabonds. We were close to starving and, on the way, had thrown away all superfluous items of our equipment, that is, except our weapons and ammunition. I would honestly say that I would even have handed over my entire armament for a good sandwich, and Ben Needler was surely thinking the same.

Sitting by the edge of some bushes and hanging our sore feet into a river, we spoke of various delicacies we would not have mentioned had we had them; of venison leg, buffalo loin, bear paws, and elk roasts.

"Yes, there's supposed to be elk in this area, almost as big as bison," Ben suggested, while he smacked his tongue. "Good luck it would be! If such a fellow came close now, I would happily fire both my bullets between his horns, and then –"

"And then it would be your end!" a laughing voice sounded from behind the bushes. "The elk would make porridge of you with his horns. One doesn't shoot such an animal between the horns, which it doesn't have, but antlers. You must be students from New York who were kicked out and fell out of the sky here, gentlemen."

We jumped up and looked over at the speaker who was working his way out from the bushes from where he had listened to us. And now he stood before us, as I described him earlier, Old Wabble, with an expression which, in no way, was respectful to us, and an indulgent, superior look from his half-closed eyes. I want to pass over the following conversation. He examined us like a teacher does his boys, then requested us to come along with him.

About a mile from the river stood a log house on a small prairie surrounded by forest, which he called his rancho. Behind it stood some open stables for the horses, mules and cattle, now grazing in the open. From once being a cowboy, Old Wabble had become an independent rancher. His employees were Will Litton, the white foreman, and several Snake Indians, he called vaqueros, who were very loyal and devoted to him. We saw these men loading a light wagon with a tent canvas and other objects.

"That's for you," the old one suggested. "You want to shoot elk. They are getting ready for a hunting party over there. Let's see what you can do. You are to go along. Should you be useful, boys, you can stay with me. But before, come with me in the house, that's clear. A hungry hunter will shoot into the air."

Well, that was just the right thing for us. We ate and drank. Then we departed, since Old Wabble wouldn't think to delay his excursion. We got some horses and came along, first to the river where there was a ford we had to cross. The old one took the lead, and had asked me to stay by his side. He was leading a pack mule. When the two of us had crossed, the others followed, Ben Needler on his brown and Will Litton on his white horse. They were followed by the wagon drawn by four horses, which were guided by an Indian. His name was Paq-muh,

Bloody Hand, but, in his civilized outfit did not look bloodthirsty at all as his name implied. His tribesmen stayed on the rancho since the old one could rely on them.

On the other side of the ford we briefly passed through an open woods, then entered a green, treeless valley which opened on a prairie. After several hours, we reached the opposite side of the prairie, where the terrain began to rise. There we stopped to set up camp. The wagon was unloaded and the tent put up. While the animals were tied to the wagon's back, a fire was lit up front. The intention was to stay here for a day to stalk pronghorn antelopes or, possibly, to come across some buffalo that, at times, passed through here, as we saw from a few skeletons lying about. A sun-bleached skull lay close to our tent, which was to remain standing here under Bloody Hand's supervision. We Whites were to head for a high fen, a somewhat soggy meadow, were lots of elk were supposed to be, Old Wabble claimed.

Unfortunately, neither the first nor the second day an antelope was to be seen, which made the old one quite furious. It was all right with me though, since I feared his crass judgment with regards to my shooting ability. At the time, I was confident to be able to hit a church steeple from thirty paces. However, I figured to shoot a big hole into nature for sure if I were asked to kill a fast-footed antelope over sixty paces away.

That's when Old Wabble hit upon the unfortunate idea to test our shooting ability by asking us to aim for a vulture. Some of these birds had settled on a buffalo carcass about seventy paces from us. I was the first to demonstrate my ability. Well, I tell you: the vultures were happy with me. It happened exactly as I had thought. I shot four times without hitting one. None of them even thought of taking off. Of course, these creatures know very well that no reasonable fellow will shoot at them. A shot rather attracts them instead of scaring them away. They know that at least the innards of killed game will be left to them. Ben' shots missed twice. Only his third shot killed one of the vultures and scared the others away.

"Absolutely incomparable!" Old Wabble laughed, his wobbly limbs shaking wildly. "Gentlemen, that's clear, you've been created smack-dab for the Wild West. Have no fear! You've made it, fellows! What you can become, you have accomplished already, and you'll never make it any further!"

Ben took this judgment in stride. I, though, erupted angrily which had however no other effect than that the old one answered:

"Be quiet, sir! Your friend hit on his third try at least. There's hope for him. But you are a man lost for the West. I have no use for you and give you the good advice to get lost as soon as possible."

This vexed me mightily. It's a truth that no master falls from the heavens, and the powder I had wasted surely didn't weigh a full pound. I decided to force the old one to extend me at least some respect.

127

The following morning we left for the high fen in the Salmon River Mountains. Provisions, cooking gear, blankets, and other required things were loaded onto the mule. The wagon, which couldn't be used in the impassable mountains and the tent stayed behind. Well, you know this land, and I, therefore, don't want to describe our ride. It was often downright life threatening, particularly were the Snake Canyon makes a sharp turn, that is, where the trail leads steeply into its depth to reach the clear Wihinasht Trail on the opposite side. To the right were heavenward-reaching rocks, to the left the black abyss. Between the two led the barely two foot wide riding trail. It was fortunate that our horses were used to such pathways and that I had never tended to bouts of acrophobia! We crossed it happily. But soon another danger threatened which, only I, did not consider being one.

That is to say, that when we rode up the Wihinasht Trail, we crossed with a group of eight Indians on horseback. Four of the men were adorned with chiefs' feathers. They didn't seem startled in the least by our sudden appearance and observed us during our silent passage with that melancholic-idle expression so characteristic of the Indian people. One of the first, riding an Appaloosa, carried in his left arm a peculiar, longish item, decorated with feather tassels. I was oddly touched by the silent, melancholic meeting with these former masters of this area. They did not appear dangerous at all to me, the less so, since they did not wear any war paint and seemed to be unarmed. But barely had we passed the next rise and lost them from sight, when Old Wabble stopped and said, throwing a grim look back:

"Damn them! What do these rascals want here? They are Panasht who live in discord with the Snake Indians the tribe my vaqueros belong to. Where are they headed? Their way will pass by my rancho. That's dangerous with me not being home!"

"But they were not armed!" I objected.

From his half-closed eyes Old Wabble flashed a disdainful look at me, did not honor we with a single word, and continued:

"We are done with our elk hunt, at least for today and tomorrow and must get back down to our tent, maybe even to the rancho. We must forestall them. Fortunately, I know a trail leading down not far from here. It's no good for a horseman, only for good mountain climbers. Let's go, boys! We've got to get them into our rifles sights, that's clear!"

We took off in a gallop, five minutes long, to the left into the rocks. Then we arrived at a small high valley with a floor of bog and meadow. At its rocky sides grew tall hemlocks. A creek was crossing its midst. Old Wabble jumped off his horse to tell us:

"There, at the end of the valley is the trail leading down. If we hurry, we'll be at the tent before the Reds get there. One of us must stay here with the animals, the one we can miss the easiest. Of course, it's this good Sam, who missed four times. He would rather hit us than one of the Reds."

Well, this good Sam was, of course myself, Samuel Parker, former bookkeeper with the railroad at Ogden City! I angrily objected to this decision, but in the end had to resign myself to it. The other three took their weapons and ran off, after the old one had ordered me to take good care of the animals and not to leave the valley until his return.

I was furious. Did I have to put up with this? These poor Indians were to be killed, yet had looked so harmless! Was I going to permit this? No! They were human just like us. Then there was – revenge for his insult! I did not know the Wild West and followed my lack of judgment. I tied the mule and the three horses to the next trees and, in a gallop, rode back up the trail we had just come down. I wanted to carry out the duty assigned to me, but warn the Indians first. I rode down the Wihinasht Trail as fast as possible into the Snake Canyon. Then I saw the Reds ahead of me. They heard me coming, looked back and stopped. Here, the canyon was still wide enough. I pulled up my horse and asked whether one of them understood English. The one on the Appaloosa, who carried the longish item, answered:

"I am *To-ok-uh*, Fast Arrow, Chief of the Panasht-Shoshone. My white brother returned to deliver a message from the old man whose herds down there arc guardcd by Snakc Indians?"

"You know him then?" I asked. "He thinks you to be enemies and is trying to head you off to kill you. I am a Christian and took it as my duty to warn you."

His dark eyes literally drilled into my face when he inquired:

"Where are your animals?"

"They stand in a green valley beyond the Wihinasht Trail."

"For a brief time he quietly spoke with the others, then asked me with a friendly face:

"My white brother is in this area only for a brief time?"

"Only since yesterday."

"What do the palefaces want up there in the mountains?"

"We were going to hunt for elk."

"Is my brother a famous hunter?"

"No. I still miss everything."

Smiling, he continued on with his questions until he had learned what he wanted to know. I even had to tell him my name, after which he said:

"Samuel Parker is a difficult name for a red man to remember. We shall call you *At-qui*, Good Heart. Should you stay longer here, you will become more cautious. Your kindness could become your downfall. Be glad that we are not on the war path! Look! This *wampum* – with that he showed me the tasseled longish item in his left hand – holds a peaceful message to the chiefs of the Shoshone. We come without weapons to carry it to the old man's rancho, whose Indians are to carry it on. We therefore need not fear anything. But our gratefulness is just as great as if you had saved us from death. Should you need friends, then come to us. *At-qui*, Good Heart, will always be welcome with us. Howgh. I have spoken."

After he had offered me his hand, he and his men continued their ride. I called after him not to give me away to the old one, then turned, contend with my success, but not about the wisdom I had totally lacked. On the opposite, I had been most careless.

Arriving at the high valley, I took off the mule's load and untied the animals to let them graze. Then I used my leisure time for shooting exercise. I had a full powder horn and our gear held another full container. When my horn was empty I could claim to my satisfaction that I was now able to hit a church steeple from two hundred paces.

By evening Old Wabble returned with Ben and Will. They had met the Reds down by the tent and told me something totally new: That the Reds had come with peaceful intentions, had given the wampum to Bloody Hand to carry to his tribal leaders, then had immediately headed back. Of course, I kept silent about my action. For the night we stayed in the little valley. The following morning, we rode out to the not too distant high fen.

This was located in a much larger valley than our previous one. In its midst lay a small lake with soggy banks. There was also brush and forest growing on the somewhat soggy ground. Surrounding us were the high, bare, and much fissured, broken rock walls, which enclosed the valley. The valley was surely an hour's ride long and of similar width.

After the mule had been unloaded, a fireplace and campsite was set up. I was to remain there to guard the horses. Afterwards, the others headed out on a search. It remained quiet until noon, when I heard a few shots. Later, Ben Needler returned alone. He had shot too early at an elk cow and had thus been chased off by the furious Wabble.

He and Litton returned only at dusk, quite angry about the misfortune.

"There were enough tracks," he argued, "not just of elk, but also of Reds, who must've been there before us to drive away the game, that's clear! We came upon a single elk cow. Needler banged away too early with both barrels, causing her to run off. That's what you get dealing with greenhorns. But I don't want to have come up here for nothing and will stay another day or two or as long as it takes to fell a heavy old elk."

He didn't speak another word with the two of us and maintained this air also the following morning, when he declared that he was going to hunt only with Litton. The two greenhorns were to stay in camp where they could not wreck anything. Well, he had the right to do as he pleased. We, however, silently took the same right for us. When both had left we did what we had agreed upon the previous night. If the elk had been driven off, then they were no longer to be found in the valley but outside it. That's where one had to look. Since our stalk could take until evening, we took the mule along for our required gear and, possibly, even some game.

We walked out the valley and into an adjacent one. There was neither a lake nor bog, but certainly no elk. But there were people, people who had a mule with them. Although we did not see the people, we saw the mule, which, without saddle and headgear, was well hidden in the grass at some distance to our right. Where were the people? I had to find them. While Ben marched leisurely over to the strange mule, I kept walking straight ahead with ours. The apparent mule kept grazing until Ben had approached him to a hundred paces. That's when the animal picked up his scent, raised its head, turned lightning-fast and, with great leaps, fled straight towards me, likely from sympathy for its relative at whose side I stood. But what was that? This wasn't a mule! It was game! That much I saw, even being a greenhorn. I quickly knelt behind my mule, leveled my rifle, aimed, and fired. The strange creature took still two, three leaps, then collapsed. I ran to it, Ben coming too. The shot had hit right on. The two of us agreed that I had bagged an elk cow. It was tied to the packsaddle of the mule and we went on, but not far, for the valley came to an end. To the right and left were unscalable walls. Ahead was a rather steep height, which seemed to lead to a kind of saddle, behind which likely lay another valley. Our mule was a good climber, which is why we decided to head up the incline.

With some effort we gained the saddle and saw that we had not been mistaken. Ahead of us the terrain dropped off again. But there, in the distance, arose a peculiar noise, seemingly produced by human voices. We needed to know what it was about and searched for a good lookout. On both sides of the narrow saddle were rather high but sloping rises one could easily climb. We, therefore, made our way up the left one to gain a good lookout into the opposite valley. For the moment we left our mule where it was. Once on top, Ben Needler was going to creep farther out to see better. But since he was easier to spot because of his light colored outfit, I pulled him back, being clad in a darker outfit and looked down.

I could not see what was going on right below us, since my position wasn't high enough. But, in the distance I saw seven Indian horsemen who, in a broad line and screaming at the top of their lungs, were advancing slowly. This screaming was, therefore, coming closer and became so strong that our mule, standing below us on the saddle, began to twist its ears and tail critically. Hence I sent Ben to calm it down.

That's when my eyes fell onto the forty-foot distant slope opposite mine. To my surprise an Indian sat there across from me. It was To-ok-uh, Fast Arrow, who nodded significantly to me while putting his right hand over his mouth to keep quiet. How had he gotten here? Why was I to keep quiet? The day before yesterday he had been unarmed, now he had a rifle lying across his knees. While I contemplated this, noise had come closer. Below me I heard rocks tumble and looked down. Heavens! What a monster I saw there! With loud, angry panting it was climbing up from the valley ahead of me towards the saddle. Over six and one half feet tall at its withers, with a short plumb body on long legs, broadly overhanging upper lip and a bristly chin beard and glittering eyes, it struggled up to the height of the saddle. Arriving there, it saw Ben Needler and the mule hard ahead. It threw its ugly head with the mighty, broad, palmed antlers backwards and broke towards my side. Needler, when he saw the behemoth appear, seemingly rising out of the ground only six paces away, let go a shout of terror, threw away his rifle, turned and ran, no, tumbled head over heels from the saddle into our previous valley. Our mule didn't display any more valor than its master. It took a like leap backwards and, fortunately, using all its four legs, sledded down in the same direction.

I had no time to watch if they arrived safely at the bottom. After all, the behemoth had turned in my direction and had not noticed that the path ahead of it was now open. In mighty leaps it came straight towards me. I was no less terrified than Ben Needler. My rifle dropped from my hand. Escape, only escape was on my mind! I leaped from boulder to boulder along the rocky slope, the monster following me. A large hole gaped before me and I crept in, faster than I had ever disappeared in a hole in my entire life. Then its opening darkened. The monster stuck its head in as far as that was possible limited only by the width of its antlers. It panted like a devil. I felt its hot breath on my face. But the fear of the chased animal was greater than its anger. It pulled back its head to flee on. Doing this, it offered the coldbloodely waiting chief its flank. He aimed and fired. The elk dropped from the shot.

At once, To-ok-uh climbed down over there and came leaping up to my side. While I showed my head very carefully from the hole, he looked over the mighty animal, then asked me with a smile:

"My brother may come out! This *peere*, elk, in the Shoshone language, has been felled by your bullet and is, therefore, your property."

"From my bullet?" I asked surprised while climbing from my hiding place.

"Yes, he nodded craftily. "You are *At-qui*, Good Heart, who wanted to save us. For it you are to gain your people's glory. The warriors of the Panasht did deliver their wampum and arrived before you in the valley of elks where they had cached their weapons. You will not have found any game there, only the young child of an elk, which I saw on the back of your mule. You were so honest as to tell me that your shots are still missing. But you must keep it a secret, for I wish that your companions will respect you, just as I love you. I positioned myself on the rocks over there to have this rare, strong animal driven towards me. Then I saw you and, right away, decided to make it a gift to you. It is to be hit by your bullet, so that you may gain glory until your bullet will truly hit home. Your brother did not see me. I will leave now so that he will not get to see me. My eyes wish to see you again. I have spoken. Howgh!"

He shook my hand and hurried off to disappear in the opposite valley. This was the gratitude of a so-called savage man. He left the glory to me, when it was actually his. Was I to reject this gift? No. I was too weak for it – too young. Old Wabble had derided me. Sure, it would be a mistake, a lie, to dress myself up with someone else's accomplishment. But the old frontiersman was to envy me, the greenhorn!

I walked down into our old valley. Far, far from the saddle stood Ben Needler with the unhurt mule. I waved to him to lead him up to where the elk lay. Of course, I had picked up my rifle again. He had not seen the Indian. No one was even aware that I knew the man. Therefore, Ben had to believe that I had killed the animal. One can imagine his surprise, his amazement and – his envy!

I felt sorry for him. Honestly, I admit, that to relieve my conscience, I suggested to tell Old Wabble that he had shot the 'young child of the elk'. He was so happy for this that he hugged me. I had to stay with our bag as a guard against predators. Needler took off with the mule to return to the high fen to fetch Old Wabble and Litton. It was late afternoon when they arrived. The two hadn't seen even a hair of an elk. The old one stood silently before my bag. Finally, he admitted to never before seeing such a mighty example of an elk. Envy shook his lanky figure so that his limbs 'wobbled' pell-mell. Then he measured me with an almost threatening look from his half-closed eyes and said:

"Well, I know where I am at with you, sir. When you holed nature four times the day before yesterday, you pulled a joke on me, that's clear. But I hope, that this won't happen again if we are to remain friends!"

Well, we became friends, stayed friends, and have done many a good shot together. It was, as if the chief's present had given me, suddenly, a sharp eye and a sure hand. Right from this day my bullets hit home. Happily, the old one never doubted that I might have fibbed with that elk. I often kept meeting Fast Arrow and am still called *At-qui*, Good Heart, by his people. He has faithfully kept the secret. Today is the first time that it is given away. Yes, gentlemen, I confess with hunter's honesty that my first elk wasn't even my first one, but, also not by far, my last elk. I have spoken. Howgh!"

10. The Stakeman

The Stakeman (Der Pfahlmann) was first published as the second part of the volume 'Die Rose von Kairwan' (The Rose of Kairwan), whose first and third part are 'Ein Kaper' (A Caper) and 'Eine Befreiung' (A Liberation). All three narratives are older works and were more (the first two) or less (the latter) rewritten by Karl May. The first version of 'Der Pfahlmann', 'The Stakeman', being shorter by a chapter, carries the title 'Ein Dichter' (A Poet). Here now follows the story of 'The Stakeman'.

Part I

Between Texas, New Mexico, the Indian Territory, and the Ozark Mountains stretching north, lies an area where nature does not provide more rain than it does for the Asian Gobi or the African Sahara, to make it fertile for human beings. No tree, not a solitary bush provides a welcome point of reference to the burning eyes. No hillock, not a single worthwhile rise breaks the deathly quiet, monotonous plain. No spring refreshes the thirsty tongue, brings rescue from death to anyone who has lost direction or missed his way, to lead him back to mountains or one of the green prairies. There's only sand, sand, and sand again, nothing but sand is to be seen. Only here and there, the bold hunter, daring to enter this wasteland, comes across an area where a passing rain has brought forth a sharp-pointed, prickly cactus vegetation. The passing foot must avoid it to prevent injury, just as it injures animals. It holds barely a drop of juice to cool the hot tongue for a moment.

And yet, a few roads cross this terrible land. Man is master of creation and subdues even the hardest and resisting areas. These roads lead to Santa Fe, to the creeks, springs and gold fields of the Rocky Mountains and down to the Rio Grande and rich Mexico. But these are no roads like civilization provides for traffic. No, what is called such consists of nothing but thin poles that have been pushed into the sand to point the traveler in the right direction. They may be followed by the slowly advancing oxcart train or by the fast trapper and scout. Woe to those who miss these signposts from which this part of the Southwest received its name, Llano Estacado, the Staked Plain, or if posts have been removed by wild Indian bands or rapacious gangs of robbers to lead travelers astray. He is lost!

Far, like the infinite, endless ocean this desert spreads. The sun burned fierily, and above the hot sand flickered a light, which hurt and blinded the roving eye. Five living creatures could be seen in this wretched desert, a rider with his horse and three vultures, following them high up, as if waiting only for the moment when man and horse would succumb to exhaustion and become their welcome prey.

The traveler was a young man of maybe twenty-six years of age. He wore the common outfit of the prairie hunter, a tasseled leather hunting shirt, like leggings and moccasins. His felt hat's color and shape told that its owner had not come in touch with civilization for some time. The man's pale, exhausted features which, earlier, might have been spirited and lively, his dim, glassy eyes, his blond, disheveled-hanging hair, and the convulsively held rifle let one guess that he would not be able for much longer to resist the privations and exertions of the ride.

Just as fatigued was his horse. It was, one could see immediately, a mustang captured from a herd, a few days ago still full of spirit, strength and endurance. Now, however, it was broken and driven to the last of its strength. Its tongue hung dry from between its gaping teeth, the eyes looked bloodshot, and it dragged itself only mechanically, step by step, through the deep sand.

Thus it had gone for days already. He had left Santa Fe in the company of frontiersmen to ride to Arkansas, crossing the Ozarks. However, they had been attacked by a band of Comanche and he could thank only the excellence of his horse that he had been the only one to escape. They had pursued him into this area, otherwise he would surely not have dared to enter it without company. He knew its dangers and had never entered it before. Only certain death threatening him from behind had been sufficient reason to dare this desperate ride.

Already, since early yesterday, the poles had ended. He had no other guide but his compass and the heavenly stars. For three days not a drop of water had crossed his burning lips. His disconsolate look rose to the vultures which descended lower and lower the slower and more stumbling the movements of his exhausted horse became.

Finally, it came to a stop and could no longer be urged on. Its limbs trembled and it threatened to collapse upon another forced effort.

"Then, to here – and no further!" mumbled the stranger in German, a rarity at this location. "Is there then no rescue for me and you, my good animal?"

In vain did he search the horizon for a delivering appearance and was just about to dismount, when his horse's behavior caught his attention. Its slack nostrils had suddenly opened and firmed. It also raised its formerly drooping head and, with that characteristic snort of the true prairie horse, indicated the nearness of a hostile being.

The wanderer pulled out his binoculars to search the visual field more closely and noticed that the vultures had disappeared and were now hovering above a slowly moving point to the west. It had to be a human being.

"God be thanked!" he sighed. "This may mean some help. Come, my good animal, come! Gather your strength for a few more minutes until we reach this man over there!"

He dismounted, took the reins, and dragged himself and the horse forward. He did this in such a way that his direction had to meet the other man's at an acute angle. When he came closer, he recognized to his surprise that the other was on foot. This surprise was justified, for every frontiersman knows that a man without horse is lost in the Llano Estacado.

The other now spied him too and halted to let him come closer. He was unarmed and carried a gourd on a strap. When they had come close enough, he shouted to the horseman:

"Hello! That's a surprise and joy to see a living human being here in this wasteland! But tell me, sir, are you an honest man, or do you belong to these fellows one must avoid hereabouts even more than elsewhere?"

"The former, the former! You need not be concerned. I got lost and am close to dying. Might you have some water in your gourd?"

"Only a single sip."

"Give it to me, give it, or I will collapse!"

"Hmm! I'm in the same spot, yet you will get this sip. You've got an honest face. Here, take it!"

He handed him the gourd and the other greedily sucked the pitifully bit to the last drop.

"Thank you!" the horseman said. "But now you don't have anything to drink."

"We'll soon get some, from something that's extraordinarily rare here." With that he pointed to a small cloud that had appeared above the horizon. "But tell me, sir. Who are you and how did you get into the dangerous Llano Estacado?"

"I come from Santa Fe and wanted to get up to the mountains to travel via the Red River to Arkansas. I escaped a Comanche band. My name's Richard Forster, and my home is in Frankfort, Kentucky."

"Richard Forster? Frankfort, Kentucky? By God, sir, then I thank you a hundredfold for this meeting! You are the famous man who writes the songs, which are printed and read far beyond the States?"

The other nodded smilingly.

"You guessed right! I am the man who wanted to compose 'Savannah Images' and went out onto the prairie to almost have myself eaten by coyotes."

He now stood straight, his arms propped against his hips – a right and true Kentucky man. His long, blond curls, a long time not taken care of, hung long onto his broad shoulders. His deep-blue eyes shone full of life once more, and the first so pale, handsome features had taken on color again.

"Or to have yourself gored by Comanche and put to the stake. I, too, came recently across them a bit, sir. I was pursued by them to this damned sand ocean from which they turned back. They may have been the same band which also took you before its arrows."

"Possibly! But let me ask you now the same question, you asked me earlier, sir."

"Mind the sir, please. I'm neither president nor governor and need not hear it. What's my name? Tim Summerland, that's it, as long as I've lived. And it will remain that until I lose my scalp or will be devoured by a grizzly with skin and hair. Might you have heard of Bill Summerland, the attorney?"

"Do you mean the famous advocate Bill Summerland from Stanton, Arkansas?"

"That's the one. He's my brother I was on my way to. I would have brought him a nice load of gold dust and nuggets, I had fetched myself up there at the Canadian River, but the stakemen took it all from me."

"The stakemen?"

"Yes, the stakemen. Or do you not yet know the name given to these criminals? There's all kinds of rabble, which must leave the States for certain reasons and seems to be safe here from the law. They rove about in groups, plunder, murder, and cause all kinds of trouble. They are especially out for the travelers and wagon trains forced to cut across this deadly desert. To lead them astray they pull out the stakes and remove them, or they insert them in a wrong direction. When the traveler is half-dead, they fall upon him and – well, now you know why they are called 'stakemen'. When we left the Spanish Peaks and the Canadian we were more than twenty well-armed frontiersmen. They all fell under the tomahawks and arrows of the Comanche, except for myself and two others. We could save ourselves only by entering the Llano Estacado and had traveled already the greatest part when the poles suddenly stopped. This warned us to be on guard but, despite all caution and attention we were surprised. It happened in the middle of night. I escaped the scuffle in the dark, but just as you see me here without horse and weapons. I was only able to save the gourd with some water. But old Tim Summerland will yet get a rifle and horse again."

He stopped. The nomad of the West is usually a taciturn fellow, and Tim Summerland had just held the longest speech of his life. The good fellow didn't look very gentleman-like either. The toil had not spared his body and even less of his outfit. However, his face displayed that frequent trapper physiognomy, in which is paired an expression of extraordinary cunning and craftiness with those of honesty and faithfulness.

"About the rifle, there's help right away," Forster suggested. "In addition to my double-barreled rifle I have a fine carbine hanging on the saddle which you can have, Tim. There's enough ammunition, only water, water, that's what's needed, not just for us, but much more so for my animal without which we will be lost. But – God be thanked – you are correct. That cloud over there is growing visibly. It almost takes in half the sky now. I believe we will be saved dying of thirst!"

"That's as sure as my hat! In five minutes we'll get a downpour, believe me. Not for nothing has Tim Summerland entered this deadly desert and knows its moods like his bullet pouch. Hurry up to stake down your horse and protect your powder, or both will be gone."

He took off his hat. It was a piece of headgear which one could not easily find a like. Many years ago he had fashioned it himself from a piece of bear skin sewn together with deer sinew. It likely had had already an exceptional shape when it was given birth. Then, in the course of time, its hair was lost, except for a few scattered strands. Those now hung long and dirty-brown from the bare skin like attached leeches. A thousand times drenched by rain and just as often dried again by the sun, this beauty had, by now, assumed an almost indescribable form. It rested on his head like a dried-up jellyfish or a piece of soaked and fried roofing felt, which heat had pulled into a semicircular shape. Such pieces of equipment are no rarity on the prairie. Like this one, they served their owner well, are sacred to him, and will also not be discarded when he briefly returns to civilization.

Although the air was now even stickier than before, the two men felt strengthened already by the hoped-for rain. The horse, too, raised its head high with a snort. Its instinct let it sense the approaching rescue. It was now firmly staked down. Forster took care that his provisions and ammunition could not become wet. Barely had this been accomplished, when things broke loose. Not gradually like in other areas, but suddenly in a torrent, it fell from the sky as if it wanted to slam everything into the earth. Upon the terrible downpour's beginning the two hunters literally dove down. But then Summerland held his hat upside down towards the falling element. In the blink of an eye it was full.

"Cheer up, take your hat and do like myself! To your health and that of old Tim Summerland!"

He poured the water, despite it having found a few different ingredients in his hat, into his wide-open mouth, smacked his tongue, as if he had emptied a pint of real New Hampshire whiskey and, once more, held the bear skin up to repeat the refreshing drink.

Forster followed the invitation. The wetness penetrating the man's tight but desiccated outfit, acted on his body like balsam on an open wound. All the fullness of his former strength and joy returned. His horse, too, neighed loudly and kicked front and back, to show the return of its almost faded life.

For more than an hour the heavenly gates poured forth. Then the flood stopped just as suddenly as it had begun. "For goodness sake, that was a deluge!" Summerland suggested. "I wish the entire gang of stakemen and Comanche had drowned in it, like king Belzasar in the Red Sea, when he wanted to kill the Egyptians. How are you doing?"

"As well and comfortable as if I were sitting in a sweet dive in St. Louis or Cincinnati," Forster replied, smiling happily about the historic mistake his companion had just been guilty of. "I feel so totally refreshed and alive that I would love to mount my horse and ride off."

"That's likely the best! The air is now cool and refreshing. We ought to put it to good use. Come on, jump up, and lets get out of this devilish desert to a land, where there's a bit of grass and a few trees!"

"Don't you want to have a piece of meat first? I have enough of it."

"Give me some! But I can do that while I'm walking."

"You, walking? No. You ride the horse. I'm better on foot than you."

"Do you think, Tim Summerland, old trapper and gold digger, will sit like St. Mary, on the donkey and let you limp along till we get to the district of Mesopotamia? There you are mightily mistaken. I did get a good portion of water and shall run like a Cheyenne chief. This is your animal, which is why you must ride it!"

"Well, but let's alternate then. But we must agree on the direction yet, Tim!"

"I know north and south very well and you surely too, but that's not enough. The main thing's to know in which direction we will most quickly reach green country."

"Then, what's your opinion. You know the Estacado better than I."

"Hmm, if the stakes were not missing, it would be easier to decide. But now one must really pay attention not to get any deeper into this desert."

"I suggest we head north to northeast. Earlier, I saw a coyote running in this direction. No predator can be long without water, which lets me guess that some can be found there, also fodder for the horse."

"You are a poet. One cannot trust such gentlemen to be very practical, since they are usually someplace else with their minds than common folk, who don't compose rhymes. I'd have almost thought that of you. But I must apologize now, for I realize that your eyes are where they belong. Ahead, then, north to northeast!"

"Take my carbine and the Bowie knife first; I'll keep the rifle and the tomahawk for myself. I must also load it again. One never knows what one will come across."

"All right! Hand it to me. I won't disgrace myself handling your shooting gear."

After a brief stop for loading they left the place which could have become so fatal for them. The horse was totally well and alive again and carried its rider with its earlier ease. However, one had to keep in mind that this might be only a temporary result of the rain shower. It had not had any grass for quite some time, and the refound strength could only be maintained by some soon-to-be-found fodder.

Nevertheless, it performed well until evening, when it showed signs that its strength was waning again.

Summerland halted to sniff the air. A peculiar smell had caught his attention. Forster, too, inhaled.

"Cactus," Forster suggested, "we must avoid it."

"Avoid it? Tim Summerland wouldn't think of it. On the opposite, we must head straight for it. That's as sure as my hat."

"Why so?"

"Because it's become juicy from the rain –"

"You're right, Tim," Forster injected, to avoid admitting to his oversight. "With the spines off the leaves, the horse might eat them even."

"If it's the right kind. Then let's head straight on!"

Shortly, they arrived at the cactus oasis. The plants were mostly of ball-type. After some skinning the horse ate them greedily, which, at another time, would have disdained. When it was sated, they resumed the ride until late into the night. Then, men and animal were so tired that rest was called for. But right after daybreak they continued and by noon, to the immense delight of the two men, individual, dried-up tufts of the short, curly buffalo grass appeared in the sand. The further they traveled, the denser the vegetation became. At last, the desert was left behind to be replaced by green prairie.

They were saved. The horse literally reveled in the juicy grass. The two hunters lay down in the fresh, cool greenery, lustily stretching themselves in it. Then they decided, if at all possible, to still reach a blue-gray line on the northern horizon before nightfall. It had to be brush, maybe even some early woods, possible, despite the desert's proximity, as long as there was some kind of watercourse.

The sun stood already rather low when they reached their destination. It was a very light stand of wild cherry, interspersed by many grassy areas, but becoming ever more dense, until individual trees could be made out in the distance.

"Fare well, hunger, thirst, heat, and misery!" Summerland said. "Up there forest begins – and do you see the contours above it? These are mountains. This is – by God, now I know where we are. I know these hills. And over there flows the Bee Fork, going into the Red River, that's as sure as my hat!"

"Then let's ride as far as the forest. There's still enough light to find a good place to camp."

The suggestion accepted, they continued in a straight line through the brush. Summerland was on horseback. Forster walked ahead, alternately looking at the ground and into the distance. He suddenly stopped and bent down to check the grass thoroughly. Summerland, too, dismounted and looked at the broken and bent blades.

"Tracks! One, two – five – eight, nine horsemen with one, two – four, five pack animals. Am I counting right?"

"Yes. There are nine individual tracks and five of strung-together animals. These were no Indians, but Whites, since they did not ride behind each other, but rather carelessly hither and yon. Shall we follow them or not?"

"Why not? We must follow them for our own safety!"

"But slowly then. They must have passed here barely a quarter of an hour ago. If it were longer, the blades would have righted themselves again."

Now leading the horse by its reins and keeping a sharp eye on the tracks, they turned to the right and maintaining good cover, they kept the terrain ahead of them under close observation. The group might have halted already and noticed the pursuers earlier than it was advisable.

Then the tracks crossed a place which, due to its sandy condition, showed the hoof prints most clearly. These men must have felt totally safe, or they would have surely avoided these signs of their presence.

"God bless my soul!" came Summerland's utterance in an undertone. "These are the stakemen who took my nuggets. They were fourteen. Five we put away, which leaves nine. That's as sure as my hat!"

"How can you know so precisely that they are the ones, Tim?"

"How? Well, don't you see these tracks in the sand, which – ah, well, you can't know that! Look at this right rear foot impression. Isn't it a bit shorter on the left side than the other?"

"That's true."

"This impression was made by my old sorrel mare. If that's not so, I'll be gored right through! It once stepped into a thorn, which began to fester. The foot healed completely, but one side of the hoof bent up a little, so that the sand never gets a full imprint. Even now, when the poor animal is burdened beyond its capacity, it's still the case as you can see from the depth and frontal sharpness of its tracks. I must get my sorrel back, even if it costs me my life! Are you with me?"

"Of course! These scoundrels removed the stakes and brought us close to death. That's not even counting that you were attacked and robbed by them. They must get a good lecture, although I don't like to take a man's life without dire need."

"By the devil! Didn't they also go for our lives? Tim Summerland is an old, good fellow, you can believe that. He's never chewed an elephant or a whale to death, but with such rabble he knows no mercy. I want my mare back, also my nuggets, my rifle, knife and tomahawk, then some ammunition and so on. Maybe, also a drop of scoundrel blood, if it's not otherwise possible. But, pardon my question. They are nine; we are only two – and I don't know you that long yet?"

"Not to worry, Tim," Forster laughed, while he raised his well-build, tall, and unusually strong figure. "I am a Kentucky-man and while you don't know me yet, you must have come across others who are at home between the Ohio and the Cumberlands!"

"Well, sir! No hares run about there, but rather two-pawed bears. I think you know also how to use your paws. Forward then! We'll fall over them like Samson over the Pharisees, Saddzaer and Colosser. Maybe, he slew even the Epheser and Philipper, because once one gets going, a people more or less won't matter."

They kept following the tracks. Individual trees grew among the bushes. Little by little they became more numerous, until they finally stood closer to form a moderately dense forest under whose canopy the tracks continued in a straight line.

Suddenly, they noticed a burnt smell.

"Stop!" Summerland whispered. "They set up camp and lit a fire. Wait a bit; I'll be back right away!"

He led their horse back to the forest's edge and staked it down in a little meadow between several bushes, so that it could neither be seen nor escape. Then he returned and said:

"Now we must get close to them unnoticed. Come along!"

He scurried from tree to tree, always looking for cover and, lightning-fast, crossed open spaces, all totally inaudible. Forster followed him likewise. In a little while they noticed some light smoke seeking an exit through the foliage, then also the fire, around which all nine were camped. Summerland leaned against a spruce whose big trunk offered both of them cover. He waved to his companion to join him.

"They haven't taken the harnesses off the animals and did not post any guard. What terrible incautiousness!" he whispered.

"Where are the horses?"

"I heard them pant over there. I need weapons. If there are some, not a drop of blood needs to be spilled. Come!"

They scurried on until they came in close proximity to the horses, which did not make any suspicious noise, since they were as yet not free to move about.

"Do you see my sorrel over there? It really has the bags of nuggets still hanging from its back. And the stallion over there has a complete hunting outfit on the pack saddle. I'll take both. You take also one or two, the others we cut loose. Go on, quickly now!"

He slipped forward, in the process cut several loose and gave the animals a slap making them storm off neighing loudly. He then leaped on the sorrel, took the stallion by its reins, and only now looked for Forster. He was done so fast that almost all horses had disappeared. Forster sat on a bay, ready to leave, when loud screams arose with the stakemen bounding from between the trees.

The foremost of them was a broad-shouldered, black-bearded fellow, who launched himself right away onto Forster.

"That's their leader, Mister poet," Summerland shouted, firing his carbine at two others. "Give him some!"

Forster's tomahawk rushed through the air and the blackbeard collapsed, hit to the midst of his forehead.

"Right on. Well done. Off now!"

They turned tails. Shots rang from behind them and loud curses could be heard. The forest slowed them down, however they reached the bushes without being hurt, where Summerland had left their horse.

"Let's get him out quickly and hurry on! Before they get their horses back it will be night and they won't be able to follow our tracks until tomorrow morning. But they won't catch Tim Summerland and his sorrel, that's as sure as his hat!"

Part II

In the State of Arkansas and by the like-named river, a few hours upstream from Little Rock, lies the city of Stanton. Although, its origin does not date back more than a few decades, it constitutes nevertheless, lying at the confluence of two smaller tributaries, the junction for an extraordinary land and water traffic. With true American speed, it grew house by house and street by street. And where only recently the wild son of the prairie watered his horse at the river's edge, his 'white brother' now beds in white down and delights in the blessing – maybe also in the curse of civilization, which mercilessly wipes a human people from this Earth, counting in the millions.

Where several miles before the city the mountains lower to the plain, a cavalcade of young gents and ladies worked their courageous horses in the springy grass, shot through by yellow *Helianthus* flowers. An older man of the company was distinguished from the others by his appearance. Being exceedingly heavyset, he rode a white horse, which was certainly its equal in physical circumference. The movements of the two so alike beings had something of a pachyderm-like quality to it, drolly accentuated by the flashy colors in which the rider was dressed. He wore yellow trousers, a red-checkered vest, a light-blue coat, and a broad-brimmed, black and white plaited horse hair hat. Below the wide, stiffly starched shirt collar a green and lilac striped cloth had been tied into an imposing knot, which sent its well-folded corners down to the precious jewelry dangling with a tinkle from the heavy watch chain. His face, reddened from the ride and covered with pearls of sweat, had a most good-natured expression, yet the peculiarly sharp feature around his mouth could also indicate a bitter tinge, and the short, thick neck could be a sign of obstinate endurance.

He and his horse made a panting effort to follow one of the ladies, who, as the most adroit of all, was chasing about in wild capers and zigzag movements, while her long, blue veil flew high through the air. Anyone calling her an attractive person would have said too little. Such a wonderful beauty was not to be observed during her daring ride, she ought to be written into the heart at a moment of peace and contemplation.

"Hold on, hold on, Marga," the colorful man groaned. His horse had made a terrible effort and had made a leap which had got its rider totally out of balance. "You will break your neck, and I, I break – brrr, stop, ohohoho, you hellish beast!"

One of the gentlemen hurried over to help him get properly back into the saddle again.

"Your horse is getting too much care, Master Olbers. Let him get a few less oats, then he won't leap so excessively about."

"It's not the oats' fault, but the bad example which corrupts even the best of manners. The old jade can stand his portion of oats without becoming excited just as easily, as I do my bottle of Madeira, I won't have it taken from me. But with your jumping and chasing, even the most reliable creature can't remain quiet. May I urge you to ride over to my daughter and tell her that I will faint immediately if she risks even a single ventre-à-terre again!"

"Let her have her fun, Master. It lifts the spirit, strengthens health, makes you dexterous and, just between us, puts Miss Marga into a light no real gentleman can withstand."

"Light here or there! I prefer the safety of healthy limbs, Master Wilson. Have a look for the man who's coming over there. His horse walks step by step, as if it were counting the flowers it is trampling down. Truly, it even picks up a mouthful occasionally. He patiently allows it, all the while hanging in the saddle as if he's trying to bite his nag's mane. He doesn't seem to mind whether he arrives in Stanton today or tomorrow. No, he isn't a daredevil like you and Marga. For the first rib he breaks, I'll confidently promise you fifty thousand dollars in cash!"

"You think so?" the other wondered, giving the still distant strange horseman a questioning look. "I'm quite convinced that you might soon lose your fifty thousand dollars. It looks like the man has broken more than one rib already."

"Hoh! He doesn't really look it."

"That's what you think, since you've never been on the prairie. I bet the same amount that he is a real frontiersman, who has done already more rides than you have seen and has looked death daily in the eye. I know these people. My properties in Texas border the prairie, which often gives me the opportunity to observe these folks, even to participate a bit in what they are up to. Precisely his bent-over position marks the hunter. That's how they all sit on horseback, otherwise the continuous ride couldn't be endured."

"A prairie hunter! Half wild? We must talk to him. A conversation with him should please our ladies very much."

"I think so too. Let me take care of it!"

Wilson was still a rather young and handsome man whose dark, sparkling eyes matched his black, well-groomed full beard splendidly. He was dressed in an almost excessive elegance and sat on his horse with great ease. His broad Panama hat had slid a bit from his forehead to his neck and thus showed a dark red scar stretching from the base of his nose into his head hair. A few loud calls of his drew their group together.

"Ladies and gents, we can expect some fun. There comes a beaver skin haggler, we want to have a word with. It's likely the man has never seen a real lady and will get into horrible embarrassment by our demand to talk with us."

The suggestion was picked up with delight by the frolicsome gathering. Only the daughter of the 'colorful man' protested it.

"Let him pass in peace, gentlemen! The man hasn't done you anything and could feel insulted!"

"Insulted?" Wilson laughed. "He ought to think it an honor to be addressed by such fine people. I shall make him understand that!"

He turned his steed towards the horseman. The others followed, forcing Marga to come along, but keeping to the rear. The intention of the rich farm owner was contradictory to her way of thinking and feeling.

The stranger had by now come within hearing distance. Someone not familiar with the life and people of the prairie might have thought that he had not even noticed the group, such as his looks were focused onto his horse's neck.

"Good morning, man," Wilson called. "Are you asleep and dreaming, or have you lost your last two senses?"

While he was dressed in a dirty and much tattered leather outfit, the accosted man righted himself lightning-fast. It was peculiar how the looks of the two met. The deep-blue eyes of the hunter literally drilled into the face of his opposite. His eyes lit up like in sudden recognition and threw a destructive look from below his battered hat brim.

"Good morning, ladies and gentlemen," he replied in a full, sonorous voice. "I was dreaming of the Llano Estacado and of missing stakes and stolen nuggets. Good bye!"

He made to continue his ride, Wilson, however, blocked his way.

"Hold it. You don't continue until you've explained what this answer is to mean!"

He had paled, but his eyes sparkled, with the scar on his forehead swelling to twice its size.

"Hold it?" the other asked with a superior smile. "Who dares to demand a free man under open skies to stop? Who thinks he can demand his explanation, which he will provide only of his own free will?"

"I do, fellow! What's this talk to mean? Speak right away or –"

He raised his riding whip threateningly. His intention to make this plain man the target of wanton fun had thus quickly led to a threat, which none of those present found the time to divert.

"Or –?" the hunter thundered, shaking his long, tangled, blond curls, like a lion does his mane. With his left hand he raised the reins and, instantaneously, something like a threefold life seemed to rise in his horse, seemingly not able to any fast move. "Away with the whip!"

"Out with the answer!" he got back.

"Here it is."

A soft pressure of his thighs and the mustang leaped close to Wilson. A moment later, he dropped from his saddle to the grass, struck by a terrible blow from the hunter's fist. The powerful frontiersman, suddenly displayed spirit and fire, tore his horse around, his looks flashing from one to the other, his eyes dark with anger.

"Do any of the other gentlemen want an answer still?"

No one moved, for every single one of the gents had to recognize that the man's answer would once more be instantaneous and likewise.

"None? Well, then we are actually done. But let me warn you to ever again dare to think a good frontiersman to be a fitting object of some antics. His little finger is worth more than all of you. He notices already from afar what you are up to, and knows exactly who's going to laugh."

Already going to ride on, he reined in his animal to approach Marga. His face assumed a totally different expression. He lifted his hat deferentially, his looks passing over the lovely, bright appearance of the girl. Softly and in an undertone he said:

"Thank you, Milady! You were the only one not intent on derision and are worth better company. Good bye!"

With the manner of a real gentleman, he covered his head again, pulled the strap of his rifle tighter, and rode off in a brief, elegant gallop.

Not a single time did he look back, although he would have dearly loved to do so. For the first time, he had gazed at a girl's face, where he had to admit to himself that he would never forget again. When he reached the city, he stopped at an inn whose sign was the first he spotted. He turned his horse over to the stable boy and entered the bar. There he drew general attention by the hurry with which he reached for the kept newspapers. A trapper, knowing to read, can almost be seen as being a miracle. After a while he waved for the bar keeper.

"Who is Mother Smolly?"

"You don't know Mother Smolly, Master? Then you must have never come here before! She was the most beautiful mulatto girl far and wide. Set free she married a wealthy Mississippi merchant, whose widow she now is. She's the most respectable woman in the entire town and is known everywhere as the angel to those in need. That's why she's called by everyone nothing but Mother Smolly."

He thanked the man for the information, then read the advertisement once more, which had initiated his question: 'A real gentleman can find fine lodging and good fare, together with a library, at Mother Smolly.'

The advertisement, maybe because of its peculiar wording, had an odd attraction for him. He inquired for the address, which was not shown in the advertisement, then decided to look her up.

The house indicated to him, lay in a most beautiful and quiet street of Stanton. He rang the door bell, after which, from a gap in the door a very sweet, dark face peered at him.

"Is Mother Smolly home, my child?"

"Yes. I shall call her."

"No, please announce me." He smiled about the suspicion his outfit must have caused. "I need to speak with her for some time."

"Then I ask you to wait, please!"

It took a while, most likely because the servant had to describe the visitor in great detail. Then he was asked in, however, only to the entry hall. A buxom, extremely well-dressed woman received him there, who might have been perhaps forty years old. The color of her face told of her descent from a very beautiful colored lady.

"Pardon me, Milady, if –"

"Mother Smolly, nothing else, if you please!" she quickly interrupted him.

"Well then, Mother Smolly it is. I read your advertisement in which you offer fine lodging and good fare."

"That is so. But did you also read to whom?"

"To a real gentleman."

"Therefore, not to one of these many who call themselves that, without being it, but only to one I can call rightly so."

"This kind is rather rare here in the Southwest, Mother Smolly."

"Then my place remains not rented. Into my house I take only people who I can be, aside from a strict hostess, also a good Mother Smolly. Did someone send you?"

"No, I decided myself to lodge with you, provided your facilities please me and I you."

She was unable to suppress a small laugh.

"My place would surely please you. But tell me first, Master, who and what you are! I take it you are a hunter or trapper."

"From my present outfit, yes. I've come from the Rocky Mountains and have since then been unable to change my clothing. I wanted to do this only once I had found a home here.

"Why here in Stanton?"

"Because there's a printing shop here, where I would like to have something printed to publish it."

"Then you are actually a scholar, maybe even a poet?"

"Maybe. I undertake my travels only for knowledge. My name is Richard Forster."

"Richard – Forster –, please, please, sir, come in here!"

She flung a door open and, rather than he walking, pushed him into a very nicely furnished room. There she pulled a velvet-covered book from among others off a shelf, showing him its front page.

"'Heart Sounds', sir. Did you compose these songs?"

"They are mine."

"Is it possible! My husband was German. He left behind a precious library and yours were his most dear books. I cannot read them, only know their titles, but have kept them as something sacred here in my room. You are to get a room with me, you must take it. Come, I will show it to you."

All at once an extraordinary vivacity had come to her. She leaped ahead up some stairs and opened three rooms to him, which all very much would satisfy the requirements of an educated man.

"Here's the bedroom, here the living room with a balcony, and here is the library, where you can work. I entrust the books to no one better than to you."

"Fine, I shall live here. What is the cost?"

"Let's not talk about it now – later. First have a look around if you truly like it! I won't let you leave again. What you need, I shall get for you."

"Concerning my clothing and the like, yes, there I must ask for your help, my good Mother Smolly, but some other things I need to take care of myself. My horse, still standing at the inn, requires my presence."

"We will have it fetched. I have a good stable in the back building, which will likely satisfy you."

By evening, with the aid of the clothier, the outfitter, and the barber, Forster had become a totally different man. His hostess clapped her hands in wonder when he came downstairs to introduce himself in his new outfit.

He then walked to the bookstore, which was also a printing shop, and, simultaneously the publisher of the local morning and evening newspaper, where he was received with honors. He inquired there for the private address of the advocate Summerland. In Preston, by the Red River, he had separated from good Tim to make one more excursion into Indian Territory. He was now not going to see the first day pass without paying him a visit. Unfortunately, he wasn't home. As the girl told him, he had been invited for the evening, together with her master and mistress by the banker Olbers.

He returned home to occupy himself with the library of the deceased Mississippi merchant. In the course of his task he noticed that the third floor of the adjacent big house was brightly lit. From there, it was easily possible to look into his rooms, which is why he closed the curtains.

Over there a big group of people was gathered at a dinner table over which Marga presided. Among those present were also, except Wilson, all participants of today's riding excursion, including Bill Summerland with his wife and his brother Tim, who, in consideration of his relatives, had today dispensed with his customary trapper outfit and dressed appropriately for a parlor. However, one could see that he felt quite uncomfortable in it. He wasn't the man to move correctly in a setting like this. Not that he minded it for an evening. He was well aware that all these dressed-up gentlemen and ladies would be decidedly more helpless on the prairie, than he was in this fine setting of the rich money man, a place he had never set foot in. Actually, he was the principal person of the group, whose members did not grow tired to be entertained by his adventures.

He had just come to the events on the Desert of Death.

"Yes, gentlemen, there's a small difference between here and there. And do you know who I met there? A poet, yes, don't look so surprised, a poet, but not one who hangs helplessly between heaven and Earth, but a real man who, wherever he's put, could deal with the best."

"What's his name?" the heavy-set banker asked. Being a friend of literature, he did not care to miss the opportunity to make his extensive reading known.

"Forster, Richard Forster, it is. His rhymes are soft as butter, but his fists are hard as steel. He's a giant of a man, but with the heart of a child. I can swear by it like on my hat!"

"Forster, the German philologist! Over there sits his greatest admirer," Olbers said, pointing to his daughter. "She learned of his poems at Mother Smolly. He is very important in his genre, but could become really important only if he were writing in English."

"In English?" Tim Summerland asked. "I don't know whether he struck in German or in English, but his blows were good in any case, you can believe that. I saw it when we got my nuggets back. I will tell you that story yet!"

He continued with his report, which he closed with the comment:

"And if you wish to meet him, this could, perhaps, happen quite soon. When we parted at the Red River, he promised that he would come to Stanton. He had ventured onto the prairie only to write a book of rhymes on it, which he wants to have printed here. Rhymes about this old, great desert. A devilishly odd thought! The first time I entered it, I was a greenhorn only eighteen years old. Now I'm an old boy and have never really left it. But as long as I live, I promise to eat nothing but turkey and buffalo steaks, if I'll ever be able to put together a single rhyme, let alone an entire book! With that you say, Master Olbers, that he isn't great? Look at him first, then tell me if you'll find anything small about him!"

The party rose from the dinner table and spread out into various rooms. Marga had followed the account of the frontiersman attentively. When he had talked about the disappeared stakes and the nuggets, she had involuntarily connected these with the reply of the hunter, who had given the wanton Wilson that severe lecture. Because of this blow, Wilson had been unable to attend this evening's party. What had been the meaning of the surprised looks with which the opponents had measured each other? She could not get the tall, proud figure of the stranger out of her mind. How hard had his voice hit upon the enemy, but how soft and warm had it sounded then to her! She tried to catch Tim Summerland for a moment without being overheard.

"Did you not say that Forster intended to come to Stanton?"

"Yes, I said that, Miss."

"Could you describe him to me?"

"Very well. He's tall, broad and strong, has long blond hair, a like beard and blue eyes. His mouth is small and his teeth are good. His hunting coat is frayed and tattered, the leggings too. His moccasins – frayed and cracked, the hat is a piece of felt without form and color. His horse is a bay with a white star. Weapons – a double-barreled rifle, a carbine, knife, tomahawk and lariat. Distinguishing marks: Composes songs and slugs stakemen. So, now you can put out a warrant for him, that's how accurate my description is."

She knew enough now. The description given exactly fit the strange hunter.

"Will you introduce us to him when he has arrived, Master Summerland?"

"If you wish, Miss, I'll bring him, as sure as my hat."

"I hold you to your word!"

He turned back to the party while she stepped to a window where her father stood.

"Mother Smolly must have rented out," he said.

"Really? It can only have been today. When I visited her yesterday, the apartment was still empty."

"Then she must have found a 'real gentleman' after all, as she'd specified in the morning paper. The windows are lit and a male shadow is moving behind the curtains."

The 'shadow' had found many a worthwhile book in the library and it was late when he thought of going to sleep. When he entered the dark living room, he noticed that the lights on the third floor of the adjacent building had been extinguished. Now, a few windows on the second floor were lit and their curtains had been withdrawn. The balcony door stood open through which shone the light from a large, bright lamp from the sofa side table. A female figure in a white, airy dress seemed to glide through the room. Stepping to a table the blindingly bright light fell on her tall, lovely figure, but since she was turned away from him, he could not see her face. Unable to move, he kept looking at her, hoping that she would turn a bit sideways. Now she picked up a book, opened it, held it closer to the light, and whiter than the paper, like a luminous object, her hand shone over to him.

He quickly fetched an opera glass he had seen lying on the writing desk, then hurried onto the balcony, where he could not be noticed in the darkness, and put the glass to his eyes. Now the unknown figure appeared clearly before him, as if he were standing right next to her. Her hand once more caught his look. He had seen many a beautiful hand already, maybe even sung about one, but how far did all his poetry fall behind the reality he saw here! How gracefully did her long, pointed fingers touch the paper, how light and well-bent moved her wrist, and how charming looked her arm from her transparent lace covering! It appeared to him as if he needed only to bend over to press his lips onto this lily hand, so close, so clearly did he see it before him. And still, her owner would not turn, still he was unable to look at her face! Would the beauty of her features match those of her hand? Her head was small and nobly shaped, and from between her rich, brown curls peeked a more dainty ear than he had ever seen in his life.

He was taken by a totally strange feeling. It appeared to him as if he was waiting for some bliss, withheld from him minute by minute, and his impatience grew more and more, when – she turned halfway, and he looked at the same wonderful, beautiful face, which had made such a deep impression on him earlier that day.

"It is her, I suspected it!"

A heat wave pressed to his heart. Was it from the strains of looking through the glass? Giddiness, a condition like drunkenness, was taking hold of him. He knew of the power of female beauty, but had as yet not experienced it himself. Now its influence made him tremble most deeply. Not for all the world would he have surrendered the fullness of presentiments and subconscious desires wafting through his breast.

Then she took the lamp and stepped into the adjoining room. The white curtains which covered the windows there, let him see only her shadow which soon also disappeared when she extinguished the light.

Long did he still stand there, whether thoughtful or without thought, he could not have said himself. Not her beauty alone had fascinated him, no, he had been captivated by her superior stance, her nobility, and the purity that surrounded her like the light of the sun.

"Sleep well, you magnificent, incomparable being!" he whispered from the bottom of his heart when he stepped back into the library. Driven to the writing desk, his hand picked up the quill, and soon glowing stanzas flowed onto the paper, so bell-like and colorful, as only the first, everything earthly surpassing love can dictate. He picked up the sheet and read it repeatedly.

"My best work, maybe the single good and flawless one of all. Not I have written it, but the heavenly power, which today revealed itself to me for the first time. What am I to do? May I or may I not? The editor's office is still in the process putting the morning paper together – yes, I shall dare it!"

He reached for his hat and, despite the late hour, left the building to walk to the printing shop. His contribution was welcome after which he returned pleased with himself. In the door recess, not illuminated by the moon's light stood two people, who he bumped into not too softly because of his hurry. It was a tall male and a dainty female person.

"Who is it?" he asked.

"It's me."

"Who's me?"

"Sarah."

"Which Sarah?"

"Mother Smolly's girl."

"Oh, it's you. Good night!"

The little, cute pistol had an admirer then. Forster thought to recognize something familiar in the indistinct outlines of the beau, but did not want to disturb the two folks any further. He walked up to his apartment and, for the first time for many months, slept between swelling feathers again. His sleep was so deep and firm that the god of dreams was unable to weave even happier images than had enticed him while he fell asleep.

Part III.

Despite his firm sleep Forster awoke early next morning. His toilet was quickly finished after which he stepped to the window to search for his beautiful vis-à-vis. He found all windows closed, while the door to the balcony was still open like last night. He now dropped his drapes so that he could still observe without being seen himself.

He did not have to wait long for the curtains to move with the unmistakable, charming hand which retracted them and opened the window.

For just a few moments the observer was permitted to admire the appearance of the girl, yet it was sufficient to commit every attractive detail to memory. Would he never see her again, this image of ideal womanly beauty would have accompanied him beyond his grave. Slim and tall was her figure. From her perfect breasts rose a snowy soft neck and her small, wonderfully shaped head, whose shiny, dark-brown hair framed the noble oval of her face, and fell in heavy, unconstrained curls onto her lovely shoulders. Her features were cut so very finely, her beautiful nose was delicately shaped, her coral lips were splendidly formed, and from below her graceful dark eyebrows peeked two light brown, soulful antelope eyes. Her entire appearance was nobly unaffected and her movements showed self-confident quiet and appealing lightness.

After she had moved the drapes and had thrown a look onto the street, she stepped back into her room and disappeared from Forster's eyes. His heartbeat had doubled and a desire, a yearning had taken hold of him like never before in his life.

He was already going to step back from the window when, like a cloud of mist, she appeared once more through the salon to the glass door and, in a white-blossomed, airy morning dress stepped out on the balcony. Looking down on the street, she put her batiste cloth onto the iron grating of the balcony and lowered her beautifully rounded arm to support it, then let her charming hands hang crosswise from the railing.

As if in a spell he stood before the wonderful, enchanting image. She was more beautiful than anyone he had seen before. She was lovelier and more graceful than anything his fantasies had taunted him with. She was a fairy, a goddess, surrounded by clouds.

After breakfast she appeared again and settled into a red-velvet easy chair a neatly white-dressed Negro boy had set up for her, right across from her father. The latter then unfolded the morning papers the two now began to read. Forster once more stood observing by the window. He could have remained standing like this, absorbed by love and bliss until all eternity.

The heavyset gentleman seemed to be her father. He looked up in surprise, seemingly having found something of interest in the journal. He smiled and handed her the paper. Could it be my poem? When she reads it, she will know right away that it can only be addressed to her!

He looked through the binoculars. They were his stanzas. While he could not distinguish individual words, he saw from the set's position that there was nothing else but his poem where she was looking. A deep blush spread from her face down her neck.

"She read it!" Forster whispered, his voice trembling from joy. "She's reading it again. Oh, if she only knew how ardently the poet holds her dear to his soul. If she only knew how happily his heart beats this very moment!"

Immovable, enchanted, his look clung on her and searched to read the words in her wonderful eyes and from her fresh lips that she spoke to her father. She called a brief command to the salon after which the Negro boy brought a pair of scissors. She took them, cut the poem out, and handed the newspaper back to her father. But the cutout she folded up to hide on her bosom.

Seeing this, it felt as if fire was shooting through Forster's veins. Every nerve trembled in blissful delight. His hand, holding the binoculars, trembled from the blissful shiver wafting through his heavy-breathing chest.

There was a knock on the door. When he opened it, there stood the pretty, Little Pistol of his hostess, presenting to him a listing from which he was to put this week's menu together. She was one of those quietly glowing beauties who had to thank the mix of the black and white races for their pleasure-seeking existence. He was annoyed by the disturbance, but did not let on to it, and promised to put the list together right away. She withdrew to the door but hesitated to leave the room.

"Do you want something still?"

"A request, Milord Forster," she replied blushing.

"Then speak!"

"You met me last night at the door with a gentleman . . ."

He remembered that the man seemed to be somehow known to him and decided to inquire further.

"A gentleman? What kind of gentleman will stand with a servant at nighttime at the door?"

"He is, Milord. He is a gentleman. I know him very well. He is, he is . . ."

"Your lover?"

"Yes," she replied quietly, while a deep glow shone from her dark complexion. "But my mistress is not to learn about it. That's why I – I wanted to ask you to keep it quiet, that you saw me with him!"

"Well! Who is this gentleman who infatuates your little heart?"

"I call him Tom, Milord!"

"And what's his other name?"

"I am to keep it quiet, but will tell you. His name is Tom Wilson. He is a very rich plantation owner from Texas. He often visits with the banker Olbers across from here. He saw me through the window and came to love me very much."

"Olbers? Is that the heavyset gentleman sitting on the balcony over there?"

"Yes. And the lady is Miss Margaret, his daughter. She often comes to my mistress. She's called Marga."

Forster now knew whom his lively interest belonged to. A thought flashed through his mind.

"Does your lover have a scar on his forehead?"

"Yes. Then you know him, Milord! He got it from an Indian."

"How do you know that he is rich?"

"He took me once to his home where he showed me a lot of nuggets and gold dust. He will shortly travel somewhere."

The girl had become communicative. Forster had to use the opportunity. What he learned now could be of use to him.

"Where is he going?"

"To Mexico to see his brother."

"Ah! Why so far?"

"His brother, the Alcalde in Morelia, wrote him that he has some big business to conduct with him. I read the letter."

"What's the name of the Alcalde? Also Wilson, of course!"

"No, because he is only a step brother. His name is Antonio Molez."

"What kind of business is this to be?"

"That wasn't said. Will you honor my request, Milord?"

"Yes. But only under one condition: that you will not tell your lover about our conversation either!"

"Be thanked. I shall be silent."

She left. Forster hurried back to the window. Marga and her father had left the balcony by now. He sat at the writing desk and completed the kitchen notes. Then he dressed to leave. He wanted to visit good Tim Summerland. While he was occupied, he had not noticed that his secretly beloved had left her home. Dressed in black, wafting silk she had crossed the street and had entered Mother Smolly's house. Smolly had been friends with her deceased mother. She entertained a great affection for the beautiful girl but, this time, received her with a friendly reproach.

"But, my child, what do you think? Yesterday, you didn't visit with me for the entire day! Did you totally forget your good, old aunt Smolly?"

"Yes, auntie, you are terribly old! But I did not forget you after all. Just the opposite, I very much longed for you. Already in the morning I had to make never-ending preparations for the evening party. And imagine, after breakfast I had to come along for a ride with this nasty Wilson, father patronizes so incomprehensibly. Could I come then? Then there was this boring soiree, which would have been unbearable, had not Wilson been absent and Tim Summerland hadn't spoken so interestingly."

"You don't seem to like this Wilson at all?"

"No, auntie, even much less than that. Can you imagine why?"

"How could I!"

"He indicated to papa that he stays in Stanton only because of me. Then, father asked me to be as friendly as possible to him since he was planning to conduct some important business with him. He wants to tie him to us through closer bonds. Is that not to annoy me?"

"Certainly! Something like this is quite annoying if one isn't at all interested in the person concerned. But you just wait, Marga. The time will come when . . ."

"You will rent your apartment. Right, Aunt Smolly, that's what you were going to say?"

"Actually not, you little rogue. But since you raised the subject, you should know that I finally rented out yesterday."

"To a true gentleman?"

"Yes. Shall I tell you his name?"

"Of course. I must know who lives in your house!"

The mulatto opened the poetry volume triumphantly showing her the title.

"There's his name. Read it, and right loudly!"

"Richard Forster! Auntie, is it possible? He lives with you?"

"With me!" she nodded importantly.

"But how did this happen?" the girl asked, clapping her hands in happy astonishment.

"Totally unexpected, so that I committed a downright inexcusable mistake, my child. Imagine, Aunt Smolly was impolite and inconsiderate, impolite and inconsiderate for the first time in her life, impolite and inconsiderate to the truest gentleman there can be, against your favorite poet and that of my blessed husband!"

"That's unimaginable!"

"One should think so, and yet it happened. I would give a lot for it not to have happened! It happened like this: Sarah comes in and tells me that a man wants to see me, who looked very torn and tattered, and gave the appearance of a dangerous hobo. Of course, I did not receive him in the parlor, but the entry hall. Seeing him, I found the girl's description totally justified and was much surprised to hear him ask for lodging. I thought to reject him quickly, but did not get to it, for, in the course of the conversation, I learned who he was. Imagine my shock. To see such a man as a scamp and to receive him in such an insulting way. Obviously, I thought to quickly make up for my offense, but it is almost too great for him to forgive me for it."

That very moment the bell rang and her girl entered.

"Master Forster is bringing the menu, Ma'am. Should he come in?"

"Of course, right away, always, whenever he comes. Always remember this, Sarah!"

Marga looked around as if looking for a hiding place, but it was too late. The gentleman stood already in the door. A flash of delight crossed his face when he saw her, but he quickly recovered.

"Good morning, Miladies," he greeted them with that elegance of look, tone and motion as is owned only by those experienced in the ways of the world. "Excuse me, if I permit myself to enter!"

"Not an excuse, but thankfulness we owe you, sir. You find me in dear company," Mother Smolly continued, introducing her young friend. "This is Miss Margaret Olbers, a very special friend of Germanic poetry."

"I'm happy then to meet you in such a magnificent subject, Miss," he replied with an adroit bow towards Marga and a look expressing, aside from total respect, honest admiration.

"An encounter more peaceful than yesterday's," she breathed in sweet embarrassment.

"Shall we make peace?" he asked, involuntarily offering her his hand.

"Gladly!"

She put her lovely little hand into his right one which he then drew to his lips. Upon this touch a dark carmine blush crossed her face and both felt as if a magic force streamed through the clasped hands, putting their hearts into blissful rapport.

157

"You already met yesterday?" the mulatto asked surprised.

"Riding past each other, Mother Smolly," he replied. This more than modest frontiersman could not expect that such lips would remember him still. My heartfelt thank you for it, Miss!"

"Oh," Marga smiled, "a certain Tim Summerland would have made every effort to keep this memory alive!"

"Tim Summerland? You know him?"

"He had joined us last night and entertained us talking about his adventures in which a brave, circumspect hunter assumes the same position like the poet Forster in the Germanic literature of the United States."

She had totally regained her composure and spoke with an assurance and honest civility appropriate to her royal figure and noble bearing. It excluded any thought that her words were designed to express a common compliment or even cheap flattery.

He raised his hands in polite defense.

"The hunter did what the simplest trapper would have done. And the poet, you were so kind to mention, knows only too well the weaknesses of his work, since his poor life is not warmed and lighted by a single ray of love and fortune. His father died before he was born, and the moment that gave birth to him, robbed his mother of her life. No eyes of a sister guarded his steps, no girlfriend came close, and yet, only a tender, heartfelt womanly being can soften a man's hardness. Especially the poet has need for a heart that beats in unison with his and whose inspiration encompasses his heart without which no masterwork can be accomplished."

He wasn't sure how these words had come to him. The very moment had drawn them from his innermost conviction, just as, according to myth, the sun's greeting causes the column to ring.

"Who, as a poet, causes so many hearts to beat higher, may be assured that even the best would not refuse to partake in his fortune," Marga replied.

But barely had she finished when her soft, long eyelashes lowered and a heavy glow crossed her cheeks. With indescribable embarrassment she became aware of what she had just said. What must he, who surely knew to weigh every single word, think of her!

"As we will do, for instance," Mother Smolly made the situation worse with this comment. "That my husband was German, I have mentioned already. Marga's mother, too, was from Germany. The two deceased were related in spirit, in their views and inclinations. We are their faithful heirs."

"Then you speak German?" Forster asked the girl.

"I prefer it to English. With Mama I spoke almost never otherwise. Unfortunately, this enjoyment is rarely permitted me these days. My father does not maintain any private contacts with Germans and speaks only English himself."

"Then I may have to drop the thought to introduce myself to him. I am in possession of several securities I intended to ask him about. He has been recommended to me as being the most obliging businessman in Stanton."

"May I say that I spoke of his private contacts. And the exclusion of Germans is not the consequence of principle but mere accident."

"Then I may make this introduction after all?"

Again, she found herself in renewed embarrassment for, behind this question was hidden another she could neither confirm nor deny. It was self understood that an invitation would be the necessary result of such an introduction.

"It will surely be no problem," came the reply, while her look turned to the floor.

He saw that he had been understood. The entirely not captious assent filled him with great delight. He would have loved to continue the conversation, but knew not to be immodest. He handed in his menu and took his leave. Mother Smolly accompanied him out to the hallway. When she returned she put her arms to her sides in comic indignation and exclaimed:

"Now, what was that to mean? You meet him without me hearing a word about it! That is subject to punishment and smells poorly!"

"Forgive me, my good auntie. I haven't had the time yet to report this interesting intermezzo to you. But that was my intention for seeing you!"

"Good, then confess, but nicely detailed, I advise you. Come, sit with me on the divan here! You told him: A meeting, which would be more peaceful than yesterday's. Then your encounter must have been a hostile one!"

Marga now told about the event. From the way she did this one could hear that she enjoyed doing it. The event still stood vividly before her eyes and she described it in colors which, unconsciously, surfaced from her heart. When she had finished the mulatto remarked:

"He seems to be an extraordinary man! But that's how these Germans are: mild, compliant and tolerant, more than any others, but only to a point. Once that is passed, there will be an explosion no one can resist. Wilson will remember this lecture."

"And avenge himself. He always met me extremely honorably, nevertheless, I suspect his character to call for caution. He could never win my confidence."

Meanwhile Forster walked the streets to the Summerlands' house. There he learned that the brothers had left for the reading club. It was the hour when its members submerged themselves in the morning papers. Because of his affection for his advocate brother Tim had accompanied him, although he would have found it easier to kill a bear than to decipher a line of print. Forster went after them. He slowly passed by the small, enclosed spaces where the individual readers had retired to from the large room where disturbing noises could not be avoided.

In one of these rooms hung the regulations of the club. He stepped before the framed writing to look for an item telling him whether entry was permitted to strangers. The heavy runner covering the floor had made his steps inaudible. Thus his presence remained unknown in a side room from where the voices of two men came in an undertone through the thin partition. Without intending to he understood every word of their conversation.

"Well, sir, you convinced me completely that an exceptionally high and secure profit can be made by this transaction. Several times already Texas tried forcefully to secede from Mexico, but was always stymied by the superiority of her troops. Now, Washington has decided to extend strong assistance. The consequence will be that the magnificent, rich and fertile land will eventually swear allegiance to the Union. A flood of immigrants will pour in and the cost of land will increase twenty-fold and more in a short time. Whoever has the means to obtain a few grants of sufficient dimension will make millions. Although yours are substantial, your profit can only become greater, if you permit me, Master Wilson, to add a sum I have presently available, "

"How much would that be?"

"Forty, maybe fifty or sixty thousand dollars, which I can have you take along to Galveston in good promissory notes. Although your circumstances were, until now, unknown to me, the recommendation you presented from Harris and Thomson in Jefferson City were entirely sufficient to gain my full confidence. When will you leave?"

"As soon as possible. There's no time to lose. We know the situation is public, and I wouldn't be surprised if not also others are entertaining the same speculation."

"That thought is, of course, obvious. Come with me to my home where we can right away conclude the business."

"And your daughter, Mister Olbers?"

"She's too dear to me that I could give her more than an intimation. Rest assured, she is a free person. And you are a gentleman who should not have any difficulty to gain the affection of a girl. You have my consent, all else is your concern."

They got up and left their space without noticing Forster standing hard against the wall. It was the corpulent banker and the man who had received the fist strike yesterday. That was Wilson then. Forster thought of the figure in the door recess.

"Tom Wilson, Sarah's lover. It is him, no doubt about that! Could I be really mistaken thinking that he's one of those scoundrels who led the stakemen? He carries himself differently here, but this face can't be mistaken and the scar increases the certainty. But how did he get the recommendation from Harris and Thomson? It's impossible for him to have been in Jefferson in the meantime. Even if I am completely mistaken, he is a rogue as is proved by his yesterday's behavior and the love affair he maintains with the Little Pistol, all while he is after Marga's hand. I shall expose him!"

He wandered past the other rooms and soon found the two he was looking for. Tim Summerland sat at a table turned away from him leafing through pictures in an illustrated journal. Yesterday's formal dress had been much too uncomfortable, which is why he had exchanged it for a new trapper outfit, as it appeared. But on his head, true as ever, sat the old hat, looking for its equal. He had not been able to let go of it.

Forster stepped up to him and slapped his shoulder. The hit man jumped up lightning-fast and assumed a boxer's position.

"Why did you hit me, Master? Would you like to get a few good punches?"

Due to the change of his comrade's exterior he was unable to recognize him right away.

"I know your punches, Tim Summerland. Keep 'em to yourself, old boy!"

The trapper's eyes opened wide. Then he jumped up and took him in his arms as if he wanted to make flour of him.

"The poet, by God, the poet. It's him, that's as sure as my hat. Amazing how the fellow has dressed up, enough for the eyes to start tearing. Here, Bill, catch him, and squeeze him some in your paws. He's the best friend I have!"

He pushed him over to his brother, who greeted him with similar cordiality. The advocate was one of these self-made men, who, by their own strength and by overcoming the greatest difficulties, succeeded to rise to a respected position. He had become one of the most famous advocates of the United States, and was certainly handling every large suit in Arkansas and the surrounding territories. He, too, knew Forster from the reading of his works.

"Had you not shown up soon, sir," Tim told him, "I would have taken off again. Here, between the houses and palaces wafts an air I can't tolerate. I had to endure it for some time already."

There was no longer any thought of perusing the newspapers. The advocate kindly offered Forster every hospitality. However, Forster declined, asking only for permission to visit his comrade at his heart's desire. He was unable, though, to refuse the subsequent invitation for dinner.

They left the club and parted company. Forster walked to the banker's house and had himself announced by a clerk. He was led to the room where Olbers and Wilson were still discussing their speculation. Both were unable to hide their surprise when they saw the young man, but each showed it differently. Wilson's eyes flared high. He then turned quickly and walked to the window to prevent the newcomer from studying his expression. Olbers, once more, looked at the business card he held by which the announcement had been made.

"Your name is Richard Forster, sir?"

"Yes. I have come with a request. Would you be kind enough to verify these papers?"

The banker took them and gave them a quick look.

"They are fine."

"I wish to cash in part of the amount. The balance I want to deposit with you, to have it later, upon my departure, issued into promissory notes."

"I am at your service, sir! Do you know Master Summerland?"

"You mean Tim Summerland? I met him in Llano Estacado and just now visited with him here."

"Then my assumption must be correct that you are the author of the poetic work signed with the same name as the one on your business card?"

Forster nodded in agreement.

"Then it will be my pleasure to meet you also aside from business matters. Please, consider my home yours! My daughter will be very pleased to get to know you."

"I had already the honor to be introduced to the Miss by Mother Smolly, my hostess."

"Ah! You are lodging with Mother Smolly? I'm pleased. This makes us neighbors and we can enjoy each other without any difficulties. Might you be engaged already otherwise tonight?"

"No."

"Then I would ask for your presence. We shall be entirely among ourselves: I, Marga, and this gentleman, I take permission to introduce to you – Master Tom Wilson, plantation owner in Texas."

He had avoided any mention of yesterday's event. Wilson turned halfway around and responded with a cold, superior bow. Forster responded in the chilliest way he was able to.

"I shall come, sir, if I succeed to separate from good Tim, who tries seriously to monopolize me."

"Bring him along. He was introduced already to me yesterday and will be very welcome again."

This is what Forster had wished for. Accompanied by Olbers he was taken to the cashier, received his cash and deposit papers and left the comptoir.

"That was a devilish blunder you committed yesterday, Master Wilson," the banker said, when he returned to the room Wilson was waiting in. "This man is no other than the hunter you attacked. He must have obtained a quite miserable opinion of us!"

"I don't mind! I've never had the need to curry favor for the friendship of a rhymester and, thus, won't do it here either. That you invited him for tonight is less than pleasant to me. I thought to have Marga for myself to come clean with her. Now, these two people will spoil this opportunity."

"Your concern is unnecessary. I will monopolize them so that you will be totally at liberty to settle your affair. But let's return to our speculation!"

It was decided that Wilson was to leave already by tomorrow. After the contract had been drawn up and signed, Wilson received the papers and left. He had traversed already several streets when he saw Sarah step from a store. With a few more paces he stood next to her.

"I must speak to you very urgently. Will you keep the door to your room open again today?"

"When?"

"As soon as it is dark. I'll come only for a moment, but shall return later."

"I will leave the key in the lock."

He nodded and walked on. Having arrived at home, he pulled the papers from his satchel and tossed them with a triumphant expression on the table.

"The dice have been cast successfully. Fifty thousand dollars in my pocket. Together with the nuggets of the poor devils we sent to hell in the desert, I'm now supplied with the necessary means to play the gentleman. If this Olbers only knew that the recommendation from Harris and Thomson did come from my own pen! But, should I gain Marga, he will not lose this sum and receive his honest share of the profit. I shall be his only heir then. But if this would-be-poet plays a joke on me I'll disappear never to be seen again. Marga is like Venus, a goddess, who can make a man crazy who's even colder than myself. But Sarah, this girl, is a most lovely toy, full of trust and ready to make sacrifices. She's pretty too, so that one can make up with her, for some time at least, for the loss of the banker's daughter. In any case, I will permit her to accompany me. She must disguise herself as a boy and pass for my servant."

He paced the room with large steps and reveled in the thought of the pleasures awaiting him.

"Without doubt this Forster is the scoundrel I have to thank for my scar. And he recognized me just as well as I did him. This can be deduced from his yesterday's allusion to the Llano Estacado and the nuggets. He will make every effort to do me harm. But he's not going to succeed! Before I leave I shall settle with him and pay him back for the two blows.

"And this Tim Summerland who's also coming today," he continued after a while, "is obviously the other fellow who robbed us a while ago of the animals and part of the gold. I'm anxious to know if he will also recognize me. In any case, I'm secure as it is. No notice against me has yet been posted. Should I be forced to disappear, I will be looked for only down in Texas, where I shall shine by my absence. Then, when I succeed with the help of my brother to acquire the grants, I'll sell them again on the spot and go to Brazil with Sarah. There she can stay with me until another one pleases me better!"

He packed several items to make the necessary purchases for his trip. As soon as it was dark he walked, clad in a wide travel coat below which he carried a parcel, to Mother Smolly's house. He walked in right away, climbed two stairs and opened the door leading to the small room assigned Sarah as her sleeping

163

quarters, which also held all her belongings. It was totally dark in there, but he found his way around very well.

A little while later the girl entered.

"Are you here?" she whispered.

"Yes, my sweetheart," he replied embracing her. "I have come to bring you a joyful message."

"What kind?" she asked, returning his caresses impetuously.

"I will leave. Do you want to come along?"

"Oh, how very much! I go with you wherever you lead me. When do you leave?"

"Today already."

"That's too fast. I need time to get ready and must talk with my mistress."

"You need not make any preparations. I've arranged for everything. And you must not tell the mistress anything or she'll not let you leave."

"But she's so good. I can't be so ungrateful as to leave her secretly."

"Then she's dearer to you than myself?" he asked reproachingly.

"How can you think that! You are more dear than anything else I know. And for you, I will do anything you demand of me. I will come along, even today already!"

"I didn't expect anything else, Sarah. You will not regret it. Only now will you begin to live and get to know the pleasures you were denied so far. But you can't accompany me as a girl. This would prevent us from being always close and to enjoy our fortune to the hilt."

"Not as a girl! How else?"

"As a boy. Here in the parcel is everything necessary. The suit will fit you magnificently."

"As a boy?!" she said flattered and delighted, while she nestled ever more fervently against him. Oh, how wonderful this will be. I will be your servant and not leave you for a moment."

"But you will have to make big sacrifices, my dear child."

"You just tell me! None will be too great."

"You hair, your magnificent hair, I will have to cut off. Otherwise, it would give away that you are not a boy, but the most beautiful girl of the United States."

"Go ahead and cut it off. I gladly give it for the fortune to be so ardently loved by you."

"For how long must you be with Mother Smolly today?"

"Until ten o'clock, then I'm free."

"Take care from then on that I find the house open. Make sure to also dress carefully and be ready that I need not wait. Isn't there's a Master Forster living at your place?"

"Yes, a very handsome and very dear gentleman."

"Ah, I notice it is time to get you away from here. You must also serve him?"

"Yes. His rooms have been turned over to me by the mistress. I carry a separate key to them, so that I can do my work while he is away."

"Make sure you have this key when I come."

"Why? Must you get into these rooms?" she asked unsuspectingly.

"Yes. One can look from them over to the Olbers. I need to observe something before I leave the house. Bye now, Sarah, and carry everything out exactly as I told you!"

After a hearty embrace and leaving his coat, he walked down the stairs, and, a few moments later stood once more in the banker's salon.

He was the first of the invited and found Marga alone.

"Good evening, Miss. Master Olbers allowed me to spend my last evening in Stanton with you. May I be so conceited to think that my presence is not unpleasant to you?"

"Conceit is a widespread and sorry habit, sir. My conscience will never permit me to support it!"

He pulled the tips of his mustache through his teeth and replied:

"No person lives by anything else but what he imagines. All life is play behind the scenes to which delusion contributes its lights. Wealth and beauty, intellect, power and honor come and go. Only he is happy who exploits the moment. The present one is one of the nicest of my life, and I cannot let it pass without admitting this to you."

Marga was going to reply, but was relieved from it by her father's entry. With him appeared Forster and Summerland. With no word had Forster told his friend about Wilson. His comrade's reaction was to tell him, whether his suspicion was not erroneous.

The trapper hurried to the girl and took her hand with simple cordiality.

"Now you've got me again, Miss. And if I'm not welcome to you, you may chase me away without me becoming angry for it!"

"Stay on, my dear Mr. Summerland. I do like to see you very much!"

She also offered Forster her hand.

"A German welcome without compliment and windiness, sir!"

Just when he was going to bend to her hand, he jerked up. Next to him a word had been uttered inappropriate for the environment they were in.

"Damnation! Who is that?" Tim Summerland had turned away from Marga towards Wilson and thrust out this word. "Master Forster, be so kind and have a look at this physiognomy! Do you recognize him?"

"Who is it, Tim?"

"I'll have myself chopped and pickled on the spot, if that isn't the stakeman who attacked us, and whom you later drew your tomahawk across the skull! What is this person doing here with you, Master Olbers?"

The banker didn't get to reply, as Wilson forestalled him.

"Is this man crazy?" he thundered. "One more such word and I'll take care to have him put in a straightjacket!"

"Or you in shackles!" the trapper replied in the same voice. "Had I found you, boy, at another place, within the next five minutes you would be in the hands of the sheriff."

"Don't trouble yourself! Although Master Olbers invited you, I'll get you some sheriff. Here, take it!"

Marga emitted a cry of fear and the banker moved to a corner of the salon. Wilson had raised his fist. He carried already his traveling arms on him. A Bowie knife flashed in his right hand, while his left reached into his breast pocket to pull out a revolver. Right away, though, Forster stood behind him, grabbed him by the hips, and tossed him with such force against the winged door that it flew open with Wilson tumbling into the corridor. Before anyone could get to him, he had risen again and was leaping down the stairs.

No one made an effort to follow him. Marga lay on the sofa with Forster kneeling next to her. The banker trembled all over, holding himself up by the back of a chair. Tim Summerland had jumped for a bottle of water standing on a table. His anxiety for the endearing miss was greater than the wish to get his enemy into his fingers. He was sure that he would not escape him. Once the frontiersman has found the tracks of his opponent, or has seen him even, as happened here, he is never concerned of catching him eventually.

"Master Summerland, what did you do!" Olbers complained! "Such an accusation was really nothing but insanity!"

He did not get a reply. Both men were too occupied with Marga to have paid attention to his words. She opened her eyes again. What had caused the girl to faint, being otherwise not affected by any weakness? Without intending to do so, her initial words answered this question. Her first look fell on Forster.

"You are alive. Did he injure you?" she whispered.

Hearing these words a sweet shiver trickled through him. Had she only fainted from fear for him? He couldn't help himself; he took both her hands and, for a moment, bent his forehead over them.

"No one is injured, Miss. We are only concerned for you!"

"Oh, now all is fine! I saw the flash of the knife and was terribly afraid."

"Which was most likely caused for no reason," her father broke in.

"Without reason, sir?" Summerland called offended. "Do you think I can't differentiate between a mirage, a prairie reflection, from reality? I do not know how the fellow calls himself to you and has insinuated himself. But it's as sure as my hat, that he isn't just a stakeman, but even their leader, of whom I told you yesterday. Just ask the poet here. He must have recognized him just as I did. Maybe you trust him more than me!"

Olbers looked questioningly at Forster.

166

"Tim told you the truth, sir," he confirmed.

"Proof, give me proof, gentlemen!"

"I believe, sir, our best proof lies in our testimony. I'm not used to tell an untruth. But I'm also ready for other things!"

"Pardon me, if I insulted you from ignorance! I have reason to grant Wilson my full confidence. Your accusation is so terrible that I can't comprehend it. What else do you know?"

"You concluded a business with him today which covers the acquisition of Texan properties?"

"How do you know?"

"And gave him permission to assure himself of Miss Marga's affection?"

"Are you all-knowing?"

"At least to the extend that I am certain of this man's personality. He courts your daughter while, simultaneously, maintaining a delicate relationship with Sarah, my hostess's servant. Now, tell me whether he's worth your trust?"

"Can it be possible!"

"I have seen them myself last evening, and right this morning she asked me for discretion. Is my word good enough for you?"

"Of course. My God, if you aren't mistaken, I'm threatened with a very substantial loss! I contracted with him today and transferred fifty thousand dollars to him."

"Maybe our warning isn't too late. Are you certain that the recommendation from Harris and Thomson in Jefferson City was genuine?"

"You are informed about this too? It is genuine. I checked it closely."

"But you did not send out for verification? A man like him doesn't shrink even from forgery. We must have him arrested!"

"Are you absolutely certain of the matter?"

"Yes. For an opportunity to ascertain yourself, I'm prepared to wait a few hours. Send a telegram. The reply will be here soon and convince you."

"You are correct, sir! But I will not send someone but go myself and wait for the reply. With a significant sum like this I must be cautious after all."

"Then I will go and watch his place. He's decided to escape, but mustn't get away."

"Stop, Master Forster," Summerland interrupted. "For that I'm the right man; you as well, but . . . Stay here! Or would you leave the dear Miss alone, since her father will go too?"

"Yes, stay!" Olbers asked. "Marga must not be without protection under these circumstances!"

They left, the banker for the telegraph office and Summerland for Wilson's home, whose location was described to him by Olbers.

When he had rushed from the house, the escapee had run down the street, but had then crossed it, returning on the other side. It was still too early for him to meet Sarah in her room, however, he walked up and waited for her to come. He then assisted in her transformation to a boy and with the packing of the items she was going to take along.

"Is Mother Smolly still awake?" he asked.

"No."

"And the front door?"

"It's open. Here's also the key to it."

"Do you have also the one to Forster's room?"

"Yes."

He took both, then ordered her:

"Go now, Sarah. We are not to be seen together. Wait for me above the ferry house by the willows!"

"I will, but, please, come soon!"

She had a light on in her room and in it she truly looked most lovely in her suit. He took her into his arms and kissed her lips repeatedly.

"I'll come soon, but go now!"

When she was gone he extinguished the light, locked the room, and sneaked down to the second floor. Once there, he unlocked Forster's anteroom, locked it again from inside and began to search the rooms. Even without a lamp this was rather easy, since the light from gas lanterns fell through the windows as well as that from the candelabra in Olbers' salon.

Right at the beginning his search was in luck. He had begun in the library, noticed the writing desk with its unlocked drawers and opened them. In one of them lay a wallet on top of several rolls of money. Stepping to the window he opened the wallet.

"Found it!" There was the deposit slip aside from several unexpected letters of credit, and there was the money he had received from Olbers. "But I have enough and only need to settle with him still!"

He locked everything, then stepped behind the curtains to observe his vis-à-vis. The lights had been extinguished in the salon, in their stead a lamp now burned in the balcony room of the lower floor. The people in there must be sitting behind the light, since he did not notice any kind of shadow.

"Might he still be over there?"

His question was answered right away. Marga with Forster behind her appeared in the shine of the light. They stepped onto the balcony where they rested their arms on its railing, seemingly looking for someone.

"By the devil! How comfortable they are with each other. There, by God, he puts his arm around her waist, only softly, but nevertheless. And she permits it! Is that how it's meant? Just you come home. If you have too much fire in your veins, I'll help you. I shall fleece you a bit! – Who's the fat fellow who comes running there? Oh, it's Olbers! Where has he been? At the police? And where is the miserable Tim Summerland, nowhere to be seen? Now they are stepping back in!"

A lively conversation must be taking place in the balcony room, the shadows showing uncommon liveliness. Then, Olbers and Forster left the house, one of them walking downtown, the other in the direction of Wilson's home.

"What do they want there? They must think of pursuing me, but they will be mistaken!"

Some time passed until one of the two showed up again. Then a hackney-coach arrived and stopped in front of the opposite house. Forster got off. He disappeared in the banker's house, but soon left it again to cross the street.

"He's coming. Now's the time!"

He bent down and crept under the desk, after he had unlocked the outside door again. Forster entered and lit a lamp. He pulled out clothing, opened the dresser and prepared to pack. --

Olbers and Summerland's absence had availed him a few blissful moments. Marga had risen from the divan and walked over to him to ask:

"Is there really no mistake possible, sir?

"No. By his behavior he has given proof that we are not in error. Whoever does not know a different defense in such a situation than by knife and revolver is aware of his guilt. His escape was the final proof."

"What a person! And we kept ourselves in such dangerous presence for so long without any presentiment what was threatening us! This knife. It was terrible!"

Her memory of the flashing knife had almost the same effect as the terrible moment itself. She staggered, her hand searching for a support and did not find any. He stepped closer and held her upright. Her head sank to his shoulder, her eyes closing. He put his arm firmer around her and bent down to her ashen face. His heart, every fiber in his body knocked and quivered.

"Miss Marga!"

The sound of these two words was a wonderfully blissful tone. Her full, soft figure twitched softly. Her lids opened, and with an indescribable expression her look met his close, happily beaming eyes.

"This is how I would love to hold and support you, now and forever, as long as thoughts will carry me and a breath of life dwells in me!"

He did not dare to embrace this noble, pure woman much more. He thought that such a move would mean the unforgivable betrayal of the trust with which she leaned against him. Once more she had closed her eyes. The pallor of her face disappeared, changing from the faintest tint to the deepest purple. The faintness was gone. She no longer had need for his support, yet she remained motionless in her position. A delighted smile fought with an expression of sweet bashfulness descending from her delicate temples. That's when he took both her hands and guided her back to the divan. There, he let her slide gently onto the

169

velvety cushion and sat next to her. Her head still rested on his shoulder. His hand caressed the shiny, soft fullness of her locks and did not become tired to embrace with his eyes her noble figure with her enchanting features.

They sat like this for a long time. Neither spoke a word, which would have sounded like a desecration of this sacred silence of the heart. But both knew that their souls were united from now on and for all time.

Finally, in sweet confusion, her look struggled up from the slowly rising eyelashes and timidly the words came:

"Papa must come soon!"

"Pardon me, Marga! Bliss never looks at the moment, I had forgotten about him."

"Could you only also forget yesterday!"

"Never. I will never be able to, for yesterday a star arose in me, whose rays opened up the richness of a hotly longed-for world. May it shine also for me in the future?"

"Stars shine for the poet, no other can know. A beam of earthly heaven must not go astray on its way to him."

"And yet he would gladly pay for such straying with a thousand lives, had he those at his disposal. Marga, be my ray, my light, my star. I only want you, only you, and will renounce all suns circling next and about you!"

She sprung up as if to escape him.

"Marga, forgive me! I shall leave!"

He, too, rose. Already distant from him, his words drew her back. She turned, hurried to him, and took both his hands.

"I am too poor for you, too small, too inferior. I am merely allowed to read the rhymes you write, to be elevated by their spirit, to be enchanted by their beauty. But any right to their creation, your fame, which love provides, is denied me."

She felt his hands turn cold.

"Then it may go, this fame! I toss it from me and renounce everything except the memory of the beautiful dream from which I am awaking now. Fare well, hope, luck and star. The poet dies. However, the hunter disappears to the West like the light which is followed by the darkest night!"

He pulled his hands away from hers and walked to the door. She stood motionless until he had disappeared. But then her life returned.

"Richard!"

It was impossible for him to hear her shout of fear. She hurried after him and caught him at the lowermost stairs.

"Not so, not so!" she exclaimed. Her hand, holding the corridor lamp, was trembling so that its cylinder rang. "You must not leave your post Papa put you to until he returns. Come, let us wait for him!"

He noticed her excitement, her anxiety, and could not help but follow her. She stepped into the balcony room after she had given orders to extinguish the lights in the salon.

"Why did you want to leave, sir! I have to ask you for so much yet."

"Speak, Miss!"

"You ought not give up on life, but must hold on to fame, even increase what you have already accomplished!"

"Fame is cold. No laurel warms when the heart grows stiff. If it is to live, it needs love, nothing but love!"

She folded her hands over her chest and gazed at the floor.

"Love! I never knew it. It is not child's love you mean. A woman's heart is soft and knows no other feeling. But can she also make a man's heart subject to it in such a brief time?"

"God is love, Miss, and both are almighty! It comes, it is there and, at a moment's notice takes command of the most hidden thoughts and peoples' deeds. Whoever tears it from the heart, destroys this heart and with it himself."

She put her hands imploringly onto his arm.

"Oh, don't do this. I would have to be forever angry with myself!"

Before he could answer she had left the room and had stepped onto the balcony. He followed her and stood next to her, without being aware that the escaped stakeman was standing in his own room watching them.

"To be angry only, Miss? Would anger be the sole thing you would feel?"

"No, much, much more!" she breathed.

"What else? Please, do tell me!"

Bent over the railing, she felt the touch of his arm and made a move to distance herself.

"Such terrible things that I don't find a name for them."

"Marga, am I allowed to love and hope?"

"There comes Papa!" She stepped back into the room. Her eyes were shining with her cheeks glowing. "Am I worth this love, this hope?"

"Marga, my life, my bliss! Were I the greatest of Earth's great, I would nevertheless beg in all humility for the littlest word that I would hear of love!"

The banker entered. He was so excited that he did not notice the unusual bearing of the two.

"You were right, sir!" he panted, almost out of breath. "The recommendation was forged. We must catch the scoundrel!"

"We shall capture him, even if he succeeded in escaping us now. But if he went to his home, which he surely did, if he wasn't prepared for what happened, then Tim Summerland won't lose him from his sight. In any case, have you been with the police already?"

"No, not yet! In my anger and hurry I didn't even think of it!"

"Then you must quickly make up for the omission. Meanwhile I will go see Tim and expect you there. We are dealing with a cunning and audacious man and must not lose any time!"

They left, leaving Marga alone. She sat down on the sofa and opened her album. In there she had hidden the poem she had cut from the newspaper. She read it again and again.

"Ungrateful fool that I am! To almost forfeit such fortune, such happiness! Yes, he is right. When love arrives, when she's here she rules. This is how it was with me, also with him, and every shrinking from it is a sin. Oh mother, could you only be alive to see how happy, how infinitely happy your child's heart is!"

She leaned into the soft backrest, closed her eyes and dreamt sweet, lovely images, rising from her blissfully anticipating heart. Long did she lie like this. Then steps came from outside. Someone knocked, but before she could rise, her beloved stood before her. He saw the newspaper clipping in the open album and now knew that she had occupied herself only with him.

"I come as a messenger. Wilson has not been to his home yet. The police are looking for him at all the places he usually frequented. Since he is unknown to them, your Papa must participate in the search. He asks you not to be concerned for him. I, too, together with Summerland will look for him, but I assume that he has left Stanton already. In that case I know exactly where he is headed and I shall follow him still this night. May I ask you to be so kind to excuse me with Mother Smolly, I can, by no means, say my farewell."

"You are leaving to pursue him, and will be getting into danger, with him – no, no, that I cannot permit, I cannot possibly allow! Stay, sir, stay, and leave the pursuit of the criminal to the police!"

A happy but knowing smile crossed his face.

"Against a known enemy, which he now is, I know no danger. Then, my departure is still open. It's quite possible that he hasn't left town yet. In that case he will fall into our hands and I shall remain here."

"In any case, promise me to stop by here once more! I will stay up until Papa comes back and I have more precise news."

"I shall come back. Until then – Good Night!"

He offered her his hand. She saw his begging, questioning look and felt his tender wish to pull her close. By her own impulse she now embraced him.

"Richard, keep yourself for me. Protect yourself when you meet up with him!"

Their lips met in a quick, soft kiss, then she escaped into an adjoining room.

There she changed from her salon dress into a comfortable negligé. Just when she had finished, she noticed that he must have gone to his rooms, since the windows were now illuminated. It was obvious that he would leave there again soon. She wanted to see him and stepped out onto the balcony.

After some time the door to the balcony across the street opened, too, and Forster stepped outside to look for Summerland who was to pick him up. He waved his hand in greeting. She lifted hers to respond, but stopped in the midst of her move. A shadow slipped past the two windows of the study and, immediately thereafter she saw Wilson's face appear in the door to the balcony.

A sudden scare flashed through her, but in a moment she had recovered, lifted her arm and shouted:

"Wilson behind you!"

He turned, not an instant too late, for the criminal was standing behind him, his knife raised for the stab.

"Help, help!" Marga screamed deathly afraid. She only saw the two men struggling with each other on the balcony. She ran back into her room, down the stairs, across the street, there to fly breathlessly up to his rooms, where she arrived the very moment Forster left the balcony.

"Richard, where is he? He was going to kill you!"

Upon Wilson's initial attack she had fainted, but now, she showed herself courageous and quick-witted. The single kiss had obligated her to dare everything for her lover, even her life.

"He's gone. I had to let go of him to remove the knife. His leap from the balcony saved him."

"You are bleeding! He injured you! By God, let me have a look quickly!"

"It's nothing, Marga, only two small flesh wounds. Let me go. I must follow him!"

"Not in the whole world!"

He wanted to get away, although being with her filled him with nameless pleasure. But she hung with such strength on him that he would have had to apply force to get free.

"Please, Marga, he will get away!"

"Let him, let him! I would die from worry, if I would let you go like this. Come, remove your coat and let me have a look at the wounds."

Aware that resistance would be in vain he followed her request. Wilson had inflicted a cut in his left arm and a stab into his right. Both were not dangerous, but were causing some heavy bleeding. He looked at her with a smile while she attempted to still the bleeding to then apply a professional dressing.

"So," she said when she had finished, "now there's no further concern necessary, you bad, dear man. But without your Marga you would have run after him and might have bled to death on the way."

Heartfelt, he pulled her close.

"So that you'll always hold me as dear as now!" she whispered nestling fondly to him.

She was so very attractive in her filmy dress that, for a moment, he forgot the fugitive and drank only love and bliss from her lips. But not for long. Steps sounded outside and Summerland entered. He was not a little surprised to see the girl. Then, in a few words, everything was explained to him.

"He was here? Damn! Did he steal from you, sir?"

"I don't know, Tim, and I had no time to look for it. If he did, I'll find out. But now we must go after him."

"Of course. But take a revolver along or something like it. The fellow is not to be dealt with gently!"

They left the house. Forster accompanied Marga to her home, then joined his waiting comrade.

"Where to now?" Tim asked.

"Nowhere else but back to my apartment. I'll have a look for the girl-servant, I just remembered. Without Sarah he would have been unable to get into my rooms. She must give us information. All else will fall into place then!"

"All right! That's not a bad idea. Master Wilson may run for a while, I don't care if it's all the way to Babylon, to where the willows stand, the seven fat cows of the pharaoh ate up. We'll catch up with him eventually and help him to a good rope, that's as sure as my hat!"

Part IV

A stiff Northeaster blew, swelling the sails of the United States brig 'Union', so that she flew across the waves before the wind, gracefully canting sideways, her sharp bow splashing up great flocks of spin drift.

Headed for Vera Cruz, carrying wood from Galveston, she carried only two passengers, who were, just then, standing by the railing to watch a *tintorera* which was following the ship at the moment. This most rapacious and dangerous of all sharks loves the proximity of the coast and was thus a sure sign that the ship's destination was close.

One of the passengers was clad in comfortable gray and wore a Panama hat, common for these latitudes. The other wore a tattered buffalo skin outfit and a hat which had caught the happy attention of the crew. Both were registered in the passenger list as Mr. Richard Forster and Mr. Tim Summerland and seemed to be in an exceptional hurry to get to Vera Cruz.

"What a monster this was, sir. What a jaw and those large eyes it has. Whoever gets between such teeth, will not be as lucky as the prophet Elias, who spent three months and six days in the belly of a whale until the animal spit him out onto Lebanon! And you really believe there are people who, armed with only a knife, will jump into this devilish water to fight such a monster? I thank you for such passion. I'd rather find myself within a herd of wounded buffalo, than to be swallowed by such a creature and to drown on top of it! Water is quite fine, as we found out in Llano Estacado, but to have it in such a mass as here is a dangerous invention. I'll be glad once I've a square foot of firm ground under me again!"

"That will be the case before evening, Tim, the captain told me. And if the mail carriage connection works out, we'll be in Mexico City by tomorrow."

"That would be fine with me! But it would be extremely annoying, if we were following the wrong tracks and had swum across this rotten puddle for nothing."

"We can't exclude that possibility. But if I figure correctly, then we will find this rich plantation owner from Texas with his brother, the honorable Alcalde Don Antonio Molez."

"If that's the case then, at the very first opportunity, I'll jab my knife into his belly for the theft he committed."

"I'm quite sure that Olbers and myself, will get back what's ours. Sarah said that she saw a lot of gold dust and nuggets he had. This ought to have been more than enough to cover the cost of his trip. Of course, he must have exchanged the banker's papers for others."

The captain now joined them. To his delight, Forster had found in him a friend of like interests. In the course of the journey he had conveyed to him the reason and purpose of their travel.

"How much longer will it be, Williams?"

"In two hours we will be in port. Here's the telescope. Yesterday, we crossed the Tropic of Cancer, then passed Tampico. The shadow ahead of us is the coast of Vera Cruz."

And yes, Forster recognized the dark strip on the horizon.

"Do you know the postal carriage's schedule?"

"No. In any case, you won't need to wait long. You really believe to find the fellow in Morelia?"

"Most likely. But I can't be sure."

"I rather think he's in Texas. He must know his way around there, or would not have talked so much about the country. It's so large that, despite his concern for a possible pursuit, he can easily pursue his speculations there. Just remember that it isn't a territory of the United States, but a Mexican province. His extradition would require lengthy negotiations during which he could escape more than ten times."

"With all respect to your opinion, but I don't follow it. His appearance indicates Spanish background, and Mexico must be better known to him than Texas. His brother lives there, whom I don't figure to be his stepbrother at all. Most likely Master Wilson was originally a Señor Molez. However, like you, I don't think he will give up on the execution of his speculations. But the grants are in Texas, where they can be obtained only with difficulty and protracted mediation, while in Mexico they can be had firsthand and much cheaper. He may have connections with someone engaged in the administration of state lands, or may hope to find one through the Alcalde. If he succeeds he will not come to

Texas at all, but will try to sell the grants right away for a profit, then disappear never to be seen again."

"Well, sir, that's not unlikely," Summerland agreed, "but we will take care that he'll be visible to a few more honorable folks, that is, five yards high on a rope, if my knife didn't tickle him already before!"

"How long will the 'Union' stay in port?"

"That's open," Captain Williams responded. "It depends how easy it will be for me to gather cargo. Do you intend to return with me?"

"With no one more gladly than with you."

"Then hurry up to catch your man. And bring him along that I can make his interesting acquaintance!"

"If I only could! Although I have police authority, it's only the authorities of the United States that might be of service to me. It is worth nothing in Mexico."

The captain's promise came true. In not much more than two hours the Union anchored between the wave-tossed rocky fort of San Juan de Ullao and the old town of Vera Cruz. The two passengers took their leave from the captain, had themselves rowed over to the broad harbor stairs, and walked up and across the plaza, filled with people, to the customs building.

After they had there completed their entry obligations, they learned that the postal carriage was to leave very soon. Quickly they left the unhealthy, treeless sandy plain of the coast to head for the old emperor's residence of Mexico City. The next day already did they get their first look at the beautiful city from the mountains, which enclosed magnificent Lake Tenochtitlan. Rolling from the mountains, they were taken by the carriage man to one of the best hotels. Although its host seemed to marvel at Summerland's exquisite head cover, he received the gentlemen with the greatest courtesy.

They had to stay for the day to recover from the uncomfortable ride and to wait for the opportunity to carry on to Morelia. Dusk closed in, the time when the capital's population indulged in strolling about Mexico City's most favorite location. It was quite likely that Wilson was in the City. He had a head start of only a day. One could assume that he would also visit this location, the Alameda. They decided, therefore, to walk there separately to search for him.

Summerland went first. Forster knew that he would encounter the fashionable and beautiful world of the city and paid great attention to his appearance. It wasn't far from his hotel to the gate of this public promenade of parks, fountains, and resting-places. Immediately upon entering there, he was surprised by the magnificent spectacle presenting itself.

The great and the rich of Mexico City strolled the clean pathways of the Alameda, with the rich, gleaming garments of the ladies demonstrating the luxury the descendants of the Spanish conquerors had become used to. Wafting in silk, enveloped by airy lace dresses, dressed in the attractive, picturesque Basquina and adorned with diamonds and pearls, the beautiful women and girls promenaded along. Some had covered themselves, according to ancient custom. Others walked about openly, the thrown-back Mantillas revealing the magic of their rich finery and their sparkling black eyes. In a swinging, easy gait they ambled along on their dainty feet. Every move of their bodies was supple. The play of fans, which these ladies knew to use with such virtuosity displayed great eloquence. Like a bouquet of flowers of this sun-drenched tropical land did this stream of enchanting New Spaniards sweep through the park. Showing off among them were the rich uniforms of the military and the no less gleaming outfits of the nonmilitary classes. The further the sun declined towards the westerly mountains, the more fiery the icy peaks of the two volcanos in the south glowed, the more numerous became the crowd strolling about or was taking seats on the benches. They are beautiful and enchanting, these Mexican females, plotting and unfaithful in marriage, wild and unruly, be it in love, be it in hate, and woe to him who responds to their heat with cold calmness or commits to a breach of faith. Then their small, white hands will not shy away from a dagger, and they know how to guide it so accurately that it almost never misses its target.

Forster walked slowly among them and observed everyone he encountered, for an inner voice was telling him that he had not made this journey for naught. He noticed the attention his magnificent, in distinguished nonchalance walking figure caused. Hundreds of eyes followed him and just as many fans tried to speak to him. He had to think of the pure, sacred being he had left in Stanton and passed over this attention with indifference.

An exceptionally rich and fashionably dressed lady passed him on the arm of a much older gentleman who must be a member of the upper classes. She was a beauty as one rarely sees and, in passing, gave him a long and much telling look. A minute later he turned at the end of his path and when he had not yet covered a major part of the promenade, he saw her again. She, too, had made a turnabout. When she had come close to him she held her fan with a kiss to her lips, unnoticed by her companion and, as if coming from a great depth, threw to him a full glowing look from her large gleaming eyes.

As if by accident her fan dropped from her hand. Forster picked it up, handing it back to her. It was of an exceptionally fine work studded richly with precious stones. When she accepted it her little finger touched his hand.

"Thank you, Señor! Are you a foreigner that you promenade all by yourself?"

He bowed in agreement to her and her companion, who returned this gesture with aristocratic reservation.

"So it is, Doña," he replied in his best Spanish.

"And how do you find Mexico?"

"It is the home of fairies, the land of bliss of which poets tell, from which none return and will be lost once they overstep their boundaries."

"Then you, too, are lost?"

"I am protected by a mighty sorceress!" he smiled, bowing deeply and stepping back.

An indescribable look struck him, a mix of struggled admiration and anger at the faux pas, he had committed by breaking off the conversation she had so craftily initiated. Then she flowed away.

He did not leave the place until it had nearly emptied and he was certain that the one he was looking for had not been here. In order to see some of the streets in the evening light, he did not return to the hotel, but took a detour that led him to the interior of the sea of houses. He had already passed several streets, observing the truly beautiful, however frequently also bizarre architecture, when his look passed a narrow building and was held by one of the upper windows. It was open and the uncovered head of a woman peered down. He retreated into a doorway he was just going to pass. His eyes did not leave her face, which he recognized very clearly.

"What a coincidence! Sarah, the Little Pistol! Where she is Wilson must also be!"

He waited until her head had disappeared then stepped into the house. Judging from its exterior, it could only house ordinary people. This did not require much in the way of consideration, which is why he walked straight into the room at the ground floor. It was furnished rather poorly but cleanly. An old woman rose from an easy chair she had been dozing in.

"Forgive me, Madrina, if I disturb you. Isn't it that Don Carlo Piscaldo lives above you, who I'm trying to find?"

He had picked the first best name he could think of.

"Don Carlo Piscaldo, Señor? No. He does not live here and has never lodged with me. My rooms belong to Don Tomasio, who arrived only yesterday with his little woman and, for a few days, left Mexico City again right away."

"That's correct. It must only be a mistake in the name. Thank you, Madrina. I need to speak to the Doña!"

He left the room and climbed the narrow stairs to knock on the door. A soft call answered after which he entered.

It was her! Looking at the door, she recognized him immediately, as shown by the fright which paled her face, despite its dark complexion.

"Milord Forster!" she exclaimed, with both hands reaching for the table she stood next to.

"It is me, Sarah! Why are you scared?"

"I – I – am not scared. It – it was only the joy of seeing you!"

"Really? Then permit me to sit down. Where is Master Wilson, who calls himself Tomasio here?"

"He went to Morelia to his brother."

"When does he come back?"

Uncertain, her looks attempted to read his face.

"Sarah, the truth!" he demanded sternly.

"In four or five days."

"What is he doing there?"

"I don't know."

"Where are his effects?"

"Here."

"Letters and other writings?"

"Also here."

"Show them to me!"

"I'm not allowed to do that, sir. He has locked them up, because, I too, am not to see them."

"Where are they?"

"Here in this chest of drawers."

"Fine, then I will help myself!"

He took the fireplace stoke, propped it into a joint and sprung the lock. She did not dare offer resistance and came no longer with any word of objection. Deep underneath the clothing he found a wallet and a tied-up package with various letters. He opened the first and a triumphant smile crossed his face. It contained the depository note, the stolen bills of exchange and all of Olbers' drafts for the value of fifty thousand dollars. Wilson must not have felt safe enough and had left cashing the papers until later. He took the wallet, then opened the parcel.

It contained samples of his writing tests and a small monogram and stamp sample, the surest proof that their owner had done forgeries before. There were also several letters. He opened them and scanned their content. The last one, with the latest date, caught Forster's total attention.

When he was finished reading it, he returned the other papers to their place and asked while pocketing the letter:

"Did he talk to you about Count Hernano?"

"Not with a single word."

"You told me in Stanton that he had lots of gold dust and nuggets?"

"He sold some of it in New Orleans. The rest is in the bottom drawer."

It, too, was broken open. It contained several heavy bags representing a substantial value.

"All of it stolen. He will not keep a single grain!"

"Stolen?" she asked frightened. "No, Tom did not do this!"

"He did, Sarah! He stole fifty thousand dollars from Master Olbers, several thousand from me, and this gold here he did rob from gold prospectors he murdered."

"Murdered? My God, sir, do I hear right?"

"You do. He is a murderer, robber and forger and fled Stanton in the night because the police was after him. His scar is not from an Indian, but from me. I met him on the wild prairie amidst murderers and struck the blow which caused the scar."

"No, no, that's impossible, Milord Forster!"

She threw herself on the sofa and covered her face with her hands. He decided to deal out the most assured trump.

"Not only that, even more. He also cheated you."

"Me? Never!"

"He did, while he saw you, he also asked for Miss Marga's hand. I stood next to them. It was on the day of his flight."

She leaped up, her eyes flashing.

"Is that true, sir? Can you swear by it?"

"Yes, Sarah! He only took you along to leave you later faithlessly."

"This scoundrel!"

Her southern nature now manifested itself in anger.

"He has no plantation, not a foot of land in Texas. He only lives from crimes and will lead you also into ruin."

"Me, Milord Forster? No, that he will not!" She balled her little fists. "I loved him like my own life, but I believe you. He wanted Miss Marga. Now my love is gone. As soon as he returns I will . . ."

"He will not return to you Sarah, for you will right away leave this house with me."

"I may not. He has ordered me sternly to stay here until his return."

Forster smiled.

"You don't seem to comprehend your situation! I won't judge your leaving Mother Smolly without her permission. It was ingratitude, but no crime. But, Sarah, you fled with a murderer and robber and supported him in his actions. You are his accomplice before the law – do you understand now why you must come with me? As my captive!"

"As captive?" she screamed. "I didn't do the least thing!"

"And the money he stole from me before leaving Stanton? I came across him in my room. He intended to kill me with his knife, but only afflicted two wounds before escaping."

"Is that true? He asked for your key, because he wanted to observe something in Olbers' house from your room."

"The key had been entrusted to you and was not to be given to anyone. He robbed and injured me." He brushed up the sleeve of his coat. "Do you see here the cut and stab wound? You are an accomplice in the robbery and the attempt at murder."

She paled as deeply as was possible with her skin's complexion and stared at him absentmindedly. A long time later only was she able to find words.

"This is terrible, sir, utterly terrible! Oh God, if I had only never believed him, that I had never left Mother Smolly! Is there no help for me, sir?

"Maybe, provided you tell me everything truthfully!"

"I will do it, Milord Forster. Ask me; I will tell you everything."

He now interrogated her in detail and learned everything necessary. He felt deep compassion for the seduced girl, who carried no guilt except for her love.

"If you obey me, Sarah, then all may yet turn out well!"

"You tell me, sir! You shall find that I will do even the most difficult."

"Then pack your belongings. You will come with me."

With trembling haste she put her few belongings together. He took all of Wilson's valuables, then quietly left the house with her, so that the hostess was unable to provide any information about it. They soon arrived at his hotel. There, the previously returned Summerland was not a little surprised when he saw the girl. Forster told him everything after he had arranged for a room to which Sarah had to retire.

"By the devil, that was an excellent catch. And the letter: What's in it?"

"I'll explain it to you. Already at the earliest times of Spanish rule in Mexico, its government distributed large tracts of land to private individuals. It was either with the stipulation to settle a given number of people on it within a specific number of years, or it was sold to individuals for a very small amount, with no relationship to the land's value and which, usually, ended up in the pocket of a higher official. In Mexico such land tracts are called *Empresarios*, with us, in the North, Grants. It is not uncommon that even nowadays, *Empresarios* are given away cheaply due to scarcity of money. A *Legua* of four thousand five hundred acres may be handed over for the price of less than a thousand dollars, thus a single man will cheaply acquire from the government often ten to fifteen *Leguas* in this way. The sale of these grants rests presently in the hands of Count Don Ventura Hernano. In the letter, the good Alcalde proposes a trick to his brother. Although its language isn't too clear, it is sufficient to understand the allusions, which are to cause the Count to willingly assign a larger tract of land. He travels weekly, as it says here, to one of his estates in the vicinity of Morelia. The Countess usually accompanies him. Upon such an occasion they are to be attacked and captured. Then, Wilson is to appear as the savior to free the Count, while the Countess is to be kept for ransom, this becoming the share of the accomplices."

"A devilishly neat plan, one can only expect from such a Spanish knave. But why did Wilson not destroy this letter?"

"I wonder too. For every evil deed there's a mistake which will bring it to light. We are safe now. We got back what was robbed and even some more. I couldn't have acted any other way under the conditions. We could actually return home right away, but I must put a stop to Wilson's practices. Early tomorrow morning I shall go see the Count to present the situation to him."

"All right! We shall accompany him and take the rascals together with the rescuer by their scalps. That's as sure as my hat! But what about the girl?"

"She stays here until we return. I am convinced we can trust her from now on."

"Then go to sleep now, so that we may not miss the fun tomorrow!"

They went to bed with the happy knowledge to have accomplished more within the first hours than they could have ever imagined.

The next morning Forster inquired for the Count's palace. Having arrived there, he learned that he and the Countess had left already an hour ago. Immediately, he went to a horse trader and arranged for three good horses with staying power and a guide. Only a little later he was back at the hotel. Tim Summerland was ready. There was no time to be lost, since the Alcalde's plot could happen already today. Sarah swore to stay put and not to step even to the window until their return. Then they left.

Their guide was a young and, as it seemed, reliable fellow. He also appeared to ride well.

"I'll serve you to Morelia, Señor!" he mentioned, once they had the city behind them, "but I would not have come along to Querétaro and Guanajuato."

"Why so?"

"For some time now this area is ill-reputed because of the Braveros who hang about there and will not let anyone pass unmolested. Only eight days ago they attacked an entire Mula[3] and killed the travelers. Santa Maria, what did it help to send horsemen against them! They retreated and will shortly do even worse than before."

Forster became thoughtful. Quite involuntarily, he connected these Braveros[4] with Wilson's enterprise. He gave his animal the spurs.

They soon reached the foaming waters of St. Jago, crossed by an old, halfway collapsed bridge. The area became more desolate, the trail was less traveled, and finally lost itself in sandy rubble. In the midst of his chase Forster kept his eyes on the ground, where one could see the tracks of three horses. These must be the tracks of the Count with his lady and servant.

Little by little bushes appeared again and, finally, evergreen trees. Then a forest received them under whose far apart growing giant trees they did not need to slow down. That's when Forster thought to have heard the cry for help of a female voice. Summerland, too, had heard it.

"Go on," he shouted. "They've got the Count and we got them. Forward, Richard!"

The horses got the spurs and now flew like arrows across the soft ground, making their hoof beats almost inaudible. After barely a minute they saw a lady in the hands of several men with blackened faces, while two men fought valiantly against a substantial superiority. Forster pulled his revolver. Arriving at the

---

3 A mule caravan

4 Robbers

location of the fight, he jumped off his horse, leaped to the side of the lady and fired. Two of the men dropped, a third ran away. He now turned against the others while he pulled out his knife. Summerland was already well at work amongst them. Their guide, too, did his part. Forster's and Summerland's courage had fired up his own. The bandits were so surprised by the energetic attack that their resistance quickly faltered. They fled into the protection of the forest leaving their dead and wounded behind.

Only now did Forster have a closer look at the rescued people and recognized in surprise the gentleman and the lady he had talked with yesterday at the Alameda. The Count had been slightly wounded, the Countess was already well enough.

"It is you, Señor," she asked. "Then your mighty sorceress must have led you here!"

The count, too, stepped closer and did not show the least of his yesterday's aristocratic reserve.

"Accept my heartfelt gratitude, Señores, for your timely help! Without you we would have been lost for sure."

"We must reject the gratitude, Don Hernano, for there was no threat to your life. They were only out for ransom," Forster replied.

"How do you know this, and how do you know my name you being a stranger?"

"Permit me to explain this later! First of all, we must get away from this place. Where are your horses?"

The two animals of the Count and Countess lay shot on the ground. The servant's horse, like the other three, had decamped. Summerland, together with the servant and the guide took off to retrieve them, while the Countess looked after her husband's wound.

Forster occupied himself with the removal of the dead horses' saddles. The injury turned out not to be serious. With some effort the runaway horses were caught. One of them was given the lady's saddle, then they left the place, the servant and guide on foot.

The Count's estate was not very far away. They reached it after half an hour and now could discuss the events in peace.

Forster and Summerland sat with the couple in the most elegant salon there could be. The Countess, who must be of a strong, fearless nature, did the honeurs, as if she had just returned from visiting a friend. However, the Count, whose age must have made him more susceptible to the kind of violent experience he had experienced, had not fully recovered yet, and recalled with a shudder the danger he had been in.

"First of all, Señores, let me learn your names," he asked.

"Mine is Forster, Richard Forster, from Frankfort, Kentucky, in the United States, and this gentleman is my hunting and traveling companion, Tim Summerland – – of the prairies of the United States," he added with a smile.

"And what do you do, Don Forster?"

"I – write books, Señor, an occupation which frequently requires me to travel to find the necessary material."

"Then you intend to write about Mexico?"

"No. This time I had other intentions, which are closely connected with today's event. Permit me to convey them to you!"

Briefly, he told the Count what he needed to know, then closed with the remark:

"With that I gave you proof that you were not in danger for your life and that we followed you only in our interest. Hence, we must absolutely reject any rights or any obligation on your part."

"No, Señores," the Count vividly protested, "you may not! I was in danger for my life. My injury is proof to that. And you could have easily returned and considered your task completed, had you not learned the danger threatening me."

"My husband is absolutely right," the Countess added. "What might I have suffered in captivity, not counting all the incalculable circumstances endangering my life. I feel very much obligated to you, Señor Forster, like no other yet, and shall not have such a sacred obligation taken from me! We urgently request that you do not reject our hospitality during your stay in Mexico!"

"That is self understood, Señores, and I hope not to fail in my request," the Count added.

"And, yet, we must decline! Our path must take us straight to Morelia, where we will assuredly meet our man who was prevented today from playing his savior's trick. Most likely, he intended to execute the rescue from behind some bushes and, after the failed attack, was informed by the fleeing Braveros. He will quickly head for the Alcalde where we must settle our account."

"Pardon me, Señor Forster! He has committed an attack in the country here and, therefore, falls under our laws. In such a case they are very strict, but with what they leave, you may very well settle. In this way, I assure myself two guests whose rare characteristics I acknowledge from the depth of my heart."

"But," Forster objected, "he will escape if no immediate action is taken!"

"This is all taken care of. Right upon our arrival I sent a reliable messenger to Morelia and shall now, after I understand the connection better, have a second one ride there, who will take care of everything, as if we, ourselves, would be there. Also, a number of workers has been sent to the forest to retrieve the fallen. I have every reason to believe that we were dealing with the same men who inflicted misery on the area of Querétaro."

He rose and left. Summerland could positively no longer stand the superbly furnished room and stepped out onto the verandah. A short while later the Count returned and reported:

"The messenger is off. You can rest assured that the police has alarmed the entire surroundings and will do its duty. Now you can confidently remain here."

"For myself, Don Hernano, I may accept, but my companion must, by all means, return to Mexico City."

"Is there a reason for it?"

"A very valid one. The apartment Wilson occupied must be guarded by someone who knows him personally. Wilson will return there if we will not catch him hereabouts."

"Indeed, then I must agree. Señor Summerland will receive from me a letter for the police who will then be very much at his service. But now, let us show you to your rooms that you may rest."

Forster smiled about the thought that he would have need for rest after the short ride. The Countess rose.

"Follow me, Señor. Permit me to take you there myself!"

"Allow me a moment, please!"

He walked to the door to the verandah.

"Tim, you must get back to Mexico City right away!"

"Well, that's very welcome to me. I'm devilishly little engrossed in the Counts' ways!"

"Our guide will accompany you. You will receive a letter from Don Hernano to present to the police. Then you will guard the house where Wilson rented. I do not know the street's name, but you can find that out from Sarah. I can't tell you when I will follow. Should you see him, don't leave him out of your eyes!"

"All right, Master Forster. Don't worry. I shall watch out like the spies in the land of Canaan, until they found the large grape and dragged it over to Mesopotamia."

Forster then turned and had the Countess take him to his room which was truly princely furnished and led to an adjoining sleeping room.

"I hope it will suffice, sir?"

"Entirely, Señora. It isn't my intention to cause you any trouble or unusual effort!"

She left. He stepped to the window to look out onto the magnificent garden where a rich, southern vegetation was most colorfully displayed.

He almost felt like Tim Summerland, not being comfortable in this place. Shortly thereafter he left the room to go to the garden. From there he noticed the Braveros being brought in from the forest. He hurried towards the group surrounding the black-faced bodies and learned that only the dead had been found while the wounded had disappeared.

The Count, too, joined them:

"Wash their faces! Maybe we find a known one among them."

They followed his order, and barely had the features of the first five resumed their original color, when one of the workers called:

"Por Dios, the Alcalde of Morelia!"

"Yes, it's him. I know him," the Count confirmed. "How does an administrator like him get to be among bandits?"

Forster bent down to check the man's clothing. His chest had been penetrated by a bullet. While he opened the buttons, he noticed that life had not entirely passed from him.

"Did you not notice that he's still breathing! Get some water."

The chest wound was deadly. It appeared the bullet had penetrated in the immediate vicinity of the heart. When he checked the wound's small hole, the injured man jerked from the pain. Forster was not disturbed by it. This pain, exactly, was most helpful to return consciousness, if only for a brief moment. And, truly, the closed lids opened, drooped again, to then open once more for a broader look to take in the environment.

The Count bent down to say:

"Antonio Molez, death is close to you. Do you want to die without confession?"

The Alcalde remained silent. He first had to remember what had been said. Then he whispered:

"Forgive me!"

Forster pulled the letter from his pocket and held it before the dying man's eyes.

"Did you write this?"

"Yes."

"Where is your brother?"

"In the forest. He – was – going to free the Count."

"You hear, Don Hernano, that I told you the truth."

Turning back to the dying he asked:

"Where did he go from the forest?"

"I – do not know. Santa Madonna – pray for me – I am dying. I wanted – to – get rich. My – position protected me – I am the leader of –"

His chest heaved in a convulsive move, a stream of blood spilled from his mouth, then he sank back, dead.

"God have mercy on his soul! He was the leader of the Braveros and had a terrible plan against me. I forgive him!" the Count said.

The other four were no longer alive. For the time being, the five corpses were locked up for safekeeping.

During dinner, which united the three people in the dining room the attack was, of course, the main subject of their conversation. Don Hernano contemplated long as to how he could express his gratitude without being obtrusive. Finally, he hit upon an idea, following which he wondered why he had not arrived at it right away. The purpose of the attack had been to acquire the favor of the Count and to gain possession of cheap lands through him. Could this not be a means to reward the man who had rescued them? He did not appear to be a rich man, and the gift of a few *Leguas* of good land would not cause the Count the least difficulty. He decided to carry out this idea and to execute the respective documents immediately upon his arrival in Mexico City.

That's when hurried hoof beats sounded from the gate. The two messengers who had been sent to Morelia had returned and were now coming to the dining room.

"Well?" the Count asked, reading important news from their faces.

"We've got him."

"Ah! That went fast against all expectations."

"He just arrived after the police had occupied the Alcalde's house."

"Did he offer resistance?"

"Very much so. He was well armed and injured several people."

"And where is he now?"

"In the prison, from where he will be transported to Mexico City tomorrow after the initial interrogation."

"Very well, you may leave again!"

He then turned to the Countess and Forster:

"I must have a look at this fellow and shall ride to Morelia after our meal. Do you want to come along, Don Forster?"

"Absolutely."

"We will be welcome there. The captive isn't personally known and you could identify him. We are also very much involved in the investigation, so that our presence would greatly facilitate the work of the official."

"Am I to be excluded from this ride?" the Countess asked.

"I think you might better stay here, than to expose yourself to the presence of such a person!"

She realized that her husband was right and decided to stay home, while the Count and Forster, in the company of a servant, rode off. After arriving in Morelia, they went to the Alcalde's deputy. This official knew already what had happened to Wilson, but was told that they had to deal with him now, since his superior, as the leader of the bandits, had been caught and killed. This caused him no little surprise. When he had recovered, he took them to the prison to subject him to an initial interrogation. Once there, the Count told Forster:

"Remain outside the door, Señor, and let me enter first alone!"

"Why?"

"To surprise him and convict him."

"Will that be expedient, Don Hernano?"

187

"Certainly! He has no idea that you are here and, most likely, will disavow his involvement and pretend to be someone else. Once I call you in, then the shock of seeing you may very well overcome him and I expect to hear a complete admission."

"Will the shock not be quite the same if I enter together with you?"

"No. I understand this. Let me go ahead as I wish!"

Forster did not like this proposal, but had to comply with the Count's wish. The deputy unlocked the cell and the two men stepped in. The door was shut again behind them.

Forster listened. At first he heard quiet voices then, suddenly, a cry for help, followed by a second. He hurried to the door and yanked it open. The deputy lay bleeding on the floor and, just then, Wilson, a knife raised in his hand, was pressing in on the Count to stab him. Immediately, Forster was next to him, tore the knife from his fist, grabbed him with both hands by his hips, lifted him high and tossed him with such force against a wall that all his limbs cracked and he remained unconscious lying on the floor.

"Are you injured?" the poet asked the Count, looking at him quite concerned.

Due to the shock the Count had lost his composure and it took a while before he was able to answer:

"No, but our man here is injured."

Saying this he pointed to the official, who was just then rising from the floor. He had received a stab that had been aimed at his heart but, due to a quick, defensive movement had penetrated only an arm and was, fortunately, not dangerous. The force of the stab had dropped the struck man to the floor.

"How was that possible?" Forster asked the injured man.

"He feigned," the deputy replied. "At first he showed himself being very peaceful, then he suddenly tore my knife away."

"Was he not tied up?"

"No."

"A dangerous man like him!"

"Is that my fault, Señor?"

"It was absolutely necessary to have him tied up, after he defended himself so exceptionally upon his capture!"

"I wasn't present and am not at fault. But, we shall now deal with the scoundrel more strictly."

"Yes," the Count agreed. "He must be tied up so that he can't move. For today I don't want to have anything to do with him any more and decline to interrogate him. He ought to be tied up right away to then be sent still today to the capital under a large and secure guard. There he shall be judged. Already the fact that he is a stakeman will cost him his life. Added to it is that he intended to murder us. He is certainly lost. Of course, I resume that you recognize him, Señor Forster."

"That I do," he confirmed.

"Then he is truly the Tom Wilson you followed to Mexico City?"

"Yes."

"Fine. Then his days are counted and he shall surely never again find the opportunity to lay hands on his fellow men and their property."

He issued the necessary orders after which they returned to Don Hernano's estate.

The Count did not talk about anything else but his never-ending gratitude for Forster who, once more, had saved his life. Once they had reached their destination and he talked to the Countess, he flowed over with praise for his guest. The lady now seemed to appreciate that her earlier, liberal behavior towards Forster had not been correct and presented herself with greater reserve. Since she displayed to him now such honest respect, he totally forgot her previous manners.

The next day the princely couple and Forster returned to Mexico City. There the necessary steps were taken to bring Wilson towards his well-deserved punishment. Forster, Tim Summerland, the Count and Countess bore witness against him, even Sarah, the Little Pistol, had to give her deposition. This so completed his charge that he was sentenced to death. The high position and influence of the Count had the consequence that procedures were kept short and the murderer was executed the day after the judgment.

Of course, the process kept Forster in the capital. During this time he had been the guest of the Count, while Tim Summerland, who would have found the princely palais too refined, stayed with Sarah at the hotel.

During this entire period, not a word of gratitude had been dropped, but when the hour of departure arose and Forster and his faithful companion said their farewell to the princely couple, Don Hernano handed each of them a closed envelope and said:

"What we have to thank you for, Señores, you know as well as we do. We need not tell you or remind you of it. We will never forget it. Should you return to Mexico City – and I certainly hope this to happen – make sure to see us again. You will be most heartily welcome to us. So that you may remember us at times until then, I give you a small souvenir, we think, will please you a little. But we tie a condition to it. Do you promise to keep it?"

"If we can, most certainly," Forster replied with Tim agreeing.

"You can. We ask you not to open these envelopes until you are on the high seas. Do you promise?"

"Yes, although we will miss the opportunity to thank you for this, most likely, valuable gift."

"To give thanks is not your, but our duty. Travel then, in God's name! In my mind I shall take good care that you will reach port safely and without accident."

He shook hands with them most heartily. The Countess, too, bid farewell in a way of total proof of her gratitude and respect. Here she showed herself totally different than days earlier upon their first encounter at the Alameda. Forster's character, for which he had to thank his German extraction, had impressed her.

A few days on the two comrades and Sarah crossed the waters of the Mexican Gulf on their way to the Mississippi. They had boarded the ship by evening and had been tired out by the ride to the coast that they had gone to sleep right away not thinking about anything else, even the envelopes. The next morning Forster walked the deck. That's when Tim Summerland came literally leaping up to him from his cabin. He held a piece of paper in his hand and shouted already from afar, his face literally beaming with pleasure, asking:

"Did you open your envelope already?"

"No," Forster replied.

"Do it quickly then. Quickly! You will read about a miracle!"

"What kind?"

"I'll keep this a secret, since I want to see your eyes when you read it. Hurry, do it!"

He took him by the arm and pulled him along to his cabin. There, Forster opened the envelope, pulled out the sheet, unfolded it and – – for the first moment stood there totally frozen and speechless.

"Isn't that a present!" Tim rejoiced. "You, too, received a grant?"

At first, Forster could only nod.

"I, too, got such a thing, an entire *Legua*, that is over four thousand acres of land," exclaimed Tim. "That makes me a rich, an immensely rich fellow. That's as sure as my hat!"

Forster was provided even richer, for the documents he held made him the owner of ten – ten *leguas*. This was truly royal gratitude, which, to be sure, had not cost the Count anything.

The two so gifted could almost not settle to their sudden riches. Although Forster felt very happy for his new possession, he was even more delighted to the fact, that he could now, without appearing selfish, think of the union with his loved one. With what joy, what yearning did he look towards his destination!

There was one other person who felt almost the same longing, that is Sarah, the Little Pistol. She comprehended the mistake she had made and regretted it honestly. Mother Smolly had always been a good and lenient mistress, yes, had been more mother than mistress, while she had paid her with such ingratitude. How gladly did she return to her! Of course, it was questionable whether she would find acceptance again. She asked Forster to be her intercessor for which he promised to do his best.

Finally, the long ocean and river travel came to an end. They had reached their destination and left the steamer. In front of the advocate's house, where Tim Summerland was, of course, rooming again with his brother, he asked Forster:

"What now? You'll come in, too?"

"Not today, Tim. I'll come tomorrow to visit you. Keep my things with you for the time being. I will pick them up tomorrow."

He continued on with Sarah. On their way, the printing shop's lights were still illuminated. He had prepared a surprise for Marga and walked in to leave a poem for the morning issue. It was immediately accepted.

Everyone had gone to rest at the banker's house, as one could see from the dark windows. But there was still a light on with Mother Smolly.

"I won't go in, sir. I am afraid!" Sarah said.

"Then wait in the hallway until you are called."

He rang the bell. The hostess herself appeared at the door.

"Who – by heaven, sir. Is it possible!" she exclaimed.

She had almost dropped the light from the pleasant surprise.

"It is true and also possible, my good Mother Smolly. "Might you have my rooms rented to someone else?"

"Rented to someone else? How can you think that! I would have kept them reserved for you for the next ten years. But come in, quickly. You must be terribly tired from your long journey!"

She invited him to the salon where, expectantly, she took a seat across from him.

"How did it go, sir? Did you find him? Did you see Sarah? I have had several girls in the meantime, but had to let them all go again."

"I did find him."

"Really? And your money?"

"I've got again, also the fifty thousand dollars of Master Olbers."

She clapped her hands in astonishment.

"That is absolutely exceptional. I must hear this. Please, tell me, sir!"

He followed her request with all possible brevity. When he remarked at the end that the Little Pistol was standing outside, she jumped up and hurried outside.

"Sarah!"

"Ma'am!"

"Will you leave me again?"

"Never!" the girl cried.

"Then stay, and remember that you'll never have it as good as with Mother Smolly!"

Returning to Forster she told him about Marga, that she had come to see her every day and had spoken only of him.

He listened with a happy smile and asked her to keep his arrival secret until tomorrow morning, then went to his apartment where he soon fell into well-earned sleep.

When he awoke the sun stood already high in the sky. Across the street the windows and the balcony door stood open. Marga sat, occupied with some work, on the balcony. He noticed how frequently her eyes went to his window.

Then the banker came to bring the newspapers. They shared them and began reading.

"How beautiful she is, how pure and good!" Forster thought.

He dressed as quickly as possible, took the binoculars and posted himself behind the curtains. Then he saw her twitch. A deep red crossed her beautiful face and her hand reached for her heart. Then her eyes flew across to him. Immediately, he stepped onto the balcony and greeted her.

"Papa!" she called so loudly that he heard it and pointed up to him.

"Sir – ah, come very quickly, quickly!"

Forster nodded agreeably and left the balcony. Arriving over there, father and daughter greeted him already in the hallway.

"Welcome, Master Forster! Come in quickly! How did it go?"

He stepped in, pulled out his wallet, and opened it.

"Would you care to look at these papers, Master Olbers?"

"Yes. Ah – my promissory notes and letters of credit. Is it possible? Marga, nothing has been lost, not a penny, not a single one!"

"I, too, got my money back. And here, please, read this!"

The banker threw a look at the sheet, took it from his hand and stepped to the window.

"Grants, *Empresarios* – ten entire *LEGUAS*!" he exclaimed in surprise. "Master Forster, this is unbelievable. This is a whole territory, an entire country!"

"And yet, it is true! The land doesn't cost me a dollar. I received it as a gift."

"A present? A value of millions? Tell us, if I am to believe it!"

He had to give his report, doing so with great detail. He was listened to in great suspense. When he was finished, Olbers rose and took his hand.

"Master Forster, you are not only a poet, but a real man. Marga, who would have thought when we met him the first time! You are rich, ten times richer than myself, sir! How can I thank you? Not with money!"

At that she rose from her seat. Fully conscious of her fortune his return was giving her, she overcame her female shyness and stepped to Forster's side.

"Papa, I know how we can thank him," she said with a deep reddening. "May I show you?"

"Do so, my child!"

Now she heartily embraced her loved one and offered him her beautiful, rich lips for a kiss.

"So, Papa! May it be like this and remain so?"

The banker was so surprised that he forgot to reply. In that moment the door opened and Summerland walked in.

"Who was going to visit me, but didn't come?" he asked. "He isn't at home and there – by God, they've got each other by their heads! That makes this old trapper superfluous!"

He wanted to disappear quickly, but in time Olbers, who had by now recovered, took him by his arm.

"Stay on, Master Summerland. We've here an engagement. Right now only among ourselves, but the affair will yet be arranged in a more festive way!"

"Engagement?" the trapper laughed. "Well, to that I'll give my blessing right away. Because, Master Olbers, these two are such a good match, maybe even a better one than Jacob and Judith, he was courting a full fourteen years, not counting the months and days. That's as sure as my hat!"

Karl May – translated by Herbert Windolf

11. An Adventure on Ceylon

In 1878 Karl May's financial situation improved, having found new employment as an editor with Bruno Radelli, a Dresden Publisher. He took care of Radelli's entertainment publication 'Frohe Stunden' (Happy Hours) in which he published twelve narratives, among which were eight exotic stories and his first novel 'Auf der See gefangen' (Captured at Sea). The following story, one of the eight, is 'Ein Abenteuer auf Ceylon', An Adventure on Ceylon.

I stood atop the lighthouse of Point de Galle, immersed in the enjoyment of the magnificent panorama spread below my feet. Numerous ships lay at anchor in the harbor and the ones entering and leaving kept the scenery alive. Among them were a variety of sizes and types, from the largest and most magnificent European steamer down to the miserable Chinese junk. Small rocky islands covered with coconut palms and pandanus (Screw Pine) rose from the glimmering waters. Between the islands stretched coral gardens through which swam red and blue fish. Sharks tore at the cadaver of a dead dog, and many-legged crabs crawled over the shore's rocks. The houses and huts of the town lay teasingly hidden under the crowns of the palm trees. Where the clean streets opened to a view, a multitude of life became visible: grazing Zebu oxen, black-clad guards, promenading ladies, clean-cut white English children with brown Singhalese nurses, tobacco-smoking native children, portly, proud-walking Muslims, haggling Jews, pigtailed Malays, betel-chewing Rajputs, Buddhist priests in long, safron-yellow dresses with head and face shorn clean, English midshipmen in red jackets carrying heavy swords, and picturesque Hindu girls, their nose, ears, forehead, arms and legs hung with gold and precious stones. Suspended over all this hung the enchanting spicy scent of the South. The sun was sinking into the ocean's waves and threw reflections from the deepest purple to the most shiny flaming gold across the restlessly moving surface of the ocean. It was a view that one could immerse oneself for hours without becoming tired of it.

Next to me leaned Sir John Emery Walpole. Of all that I observed, he did not notice anything. The magnificent tints off the glowing sky, the crystalline light flashing from the sea, the refreshing balsam of the cooling air, the colorful, lively movements on this little piece of Earth spread out before us. Yet it was lost to him; it was of no interest, all of this could not claim the attention of his senses even for a moment.

And why that? What a question! Actually what is this Ceylon? An island with a few people, some animals and a number of plants surrounded by water. What is it really? Surely it's not something wonderful or even remarkable! What is Point de Galle compared to London? What is Colombo's governor versus Queen Victoria? What is Ceylon versus Old England? What is the entire world versus Walpole-Castle, where Sir John Emery was born?!

The good, honorable Sir John was a superlative Englishmen. Possessing great wealth, he had, however, never considered marriage. He was one of these taciturn, buttoned-up Englishmen, rummaging across every corner of the Earth, who showed up in the most distant lands and endured the greatest dangers and adventures with infinite equanimity. Then, finally, tired and sated, they sought home once more. There, as members of some famous travel club, they made monosyllabic remarks about their experiences. Sir John was possessed by this to such a degree that his tall, lean, yet extraordinary powerful personality only rarely displayed a small touch of enjoyment. Nevertheless, he had a very good heart and was always ready to make up for his peculiarities in which he delighted. After he had visited a wide variety of countries, he had come at last to India, whose Governor General was a close relative of his. He had crossed it in various directions and had already been on Ceylon a few times. Once again, he was here in the service of the Governor to deliver some important messages to the local government. I had joined him, since his experience and connections could be of great service to me. He had become such a good friend that he, despite his apparent lack of approachability, had shown me a truly brotherly affection.

He now rested next to me, totally untouched by the surrounding natural attractions, and squinted with such perseverance through the golden *pince-nez* resting on the very tip of his nose, as if he intended to make some important world-historical discovery through this viewing instrument. That's when I noticed a group of native soldiers heading towards a long, rocky peninsula. In the lead walked a carefully guarded man, bound by his hands. By his clothing he seemed to be Singhalese. In any case, this must mean an execution. Since I knew the vivid interest my companion had for something like this, I made an attempt to rouse him from his world-shaking contemplations.

"Would you care to have a look over there, Sir Walpole? I believe someone is going to be tossed into the water."

"Well. Let him drown in peace, Charlie!"

He had not moved his attention from his *pince-nez* and kept studying it with unchanged zeal.

"What do you think the poor devil did? Both his arms have been tied back."

"He's tied up?" Sir John asked, whose interest had been stirred by my last remark. "Shame! That is cowardly and miserable! This would never be done in Old England!"

"You are correct. The Briton is noble in every respect! If he hangs someone, he, at least, lets him die with his limbs free. But barbarism does not know such human considerations. Look how many guards are accompanying the poor chap!"

He threw a look over his eye glass to the place my outstretched hand was pointing. I expected to hear one of his indifferent remarks, but this time was mistaken. His right hand came up to put his *pince-nez* closer to his eye, and when his sight did not acquire the desired acuteness, he opened the carrying case hanging from his chest, pulled out the telescope and pointed it at the delinquent. Something about him must have caught his interest.

"Shall we bet, Charlie?" he asked some time later, while his face became ever more interested. Englishmen love to wager and Sir John was passionate about it. Uncountable times he had already attempted to get me to bet. Unfortunately, it was always in vain.

"What about?"

"That this man is not going to be drowned."

"Ah!"

"Isn't that so; it sounds impossible? I wager a hundred sovereigns!"

"You know, sir, that I don't wager."

"Yes, that's true! You are a fine chap, Charlie, but you'll never become a perfect gentleman. Otherwise you wouldn't refuse to accept a good stake. However, I will prove to you that I would win this bet!"

The group had now arrived at the rocky point of the peninsula. The Englishman put two fingers to his mouth and produced a sharp, penetrating, far off audible whistle. The condemned man heard it too. With a quick move he raised his deeply lowered head and looked up to the lighthouse. Walpole tore the white shawl from his shoulder, waved it through the air and thrust out a second whistle.

Its effect was instantaneous and surprising. The man, condemned to die by drowning, leaped through the soldiers surrounding him to the edge of the cliffs and jumped into the sea.

"You see, Charlie, that I would have won? This is Walawi, a former servant of mine, the best diver and swimmer on this boring island. But this, the good *Mudellier* (Judge), who condemned him, does not seem to know. By the way, he must have committed something devilishly bad, for these district judges let every native slip through if at all possible, being themselves Singhalese. Look, now he's surfacing. His tied-up arms don't bother him. He's swimming on his back and heads straight for the lighthouse."

The otherwise so taciturn man had suddenly become very much alive. He followed every move of the swimmer with close attention, waving his hands back and forth, as if that would be of help to the man. Meanwhile, he provided the necessary explanations.

"See how he pushes, how fast he advances! He's being pursued. But long before the soldiers will make the detour from the peninsula to the lighthouse, he will have arrived here. I know him. The two of us swam across the *Kalina-Ganga*, the *Kalu-Ganga*, and even the rushing rapids of the *Mehavella-Ganga*. He is a former pearl diver from the *Negombo Banks* and followed me into the island's interior only because of his love for me. There, he's reached the shore! It's fortunate that no shark was close by, or the tied-up poor chap would have had difficulty. Come, Charlie, let's go meet him! He has recognized me and is coming up."

Walawi had climbed on land and, in a run, headed for the platform from which the slender column of the ironwork tower rose. We quickly walked down the stairs and met him at the door.

"*Vishnu* may bless you, *Sidhi*," he greeted breathlessly. "I was close to death. They were going to tie up my legs and cover my eyes. But you are a *Raja*, a Lord, a great Lord, and will rescue Walawi, your faithful servant!"

"Yes, I shall do that!" Walpole replied. At that he pulled out his knife to cut the bast ropes the Singhalese had been tied up with. "What was your offense?"

"Oh, nothing, nothing, Milord, almost nothing. My kris was very sharp and pointy and entered someone's heart, because he was going to rob me of my wife, the flower and fortune of my life."

"By the devil, man, that's a bit more than nothing! Did you kill him?"

"Yes."

"Who was he?"

"His name was *Hong Tshe*. He was Chinese."

"A Chinese only? That's good! Did he want your wife for himself?"

"No, for his captain, who had seen her at the beach. He lay in port with his junk. I don't see it any longer; it must have sailed away."

"I've learned enough! You know the Hotel Madras?"

"How could I not? You, yourself lived there twice!"

"I live there again. Hide now; your pursuers are coming. But look for me in an hour."

"Oh, *Sidhi*, Lord, how can I thank you? I have my life once more and can embrace my wife. *Vishnu*, the kind, may reward you!"

He took the Englishman's hands and pressed them to his forehead. Then he leaped away with the agility of a cat.

The soldiers had come close and a large crowd, who had noticed the escape, came running up. I was rather concerned about the course this affair would take. Walpole, however, met the pursuers, whose leader had now reached us, with his usual equanimity.

"What do you want here?"

The man was taken aback by the gruff, commanding tone of the question.

"We are looking for the man who escaped from us. The Great Judge condemned him to death, but you helped him in his escape. I must arrest you!"

Our good Sir John Emery just laughed until tears ran down his cheeks. "Arrest me? Me, a gentleman from Old England! Here on Ceylon? Man, you are crazy! The chap you are looking for is my servant. He's mine, and no one may hurt a single hair on his head!"

"Why did the man not remain with you, if he is your servant?" the soldiers' leader asked the Englishman.

"I sent him off, because I chose to. But you shall hurry quickly to the High Judge and tell him that I shall visit him to have a talk with him!"

"You shall talk with him, because I will arrest you and take you to him. The one you call your servant I shall pursue and catch again!"

"Try and see if you'll succeed!" Walpole answered amused while he pulled out two giant revolvers.

Of course, I followed his example. The Ceylonese soldier became terribly embarrassed. His duty fought with his fear that our weapons inspired. The latter seemed to win.

"Can you prove to me that you are truly from Anglistan?" he asked concerned, "and will you truthfully go see the High Judge?"

Walpole smilingly caressed his sideburns. His *pince-nez* had once again slipped down to the tip of his nose. His look across it sparkled with pleasure.

"I am a *Maharajah* from *Anglistan* and this *Sidhi* here is an even greater one from *Germanistan*. I shall prove it to you."

He reached into his pocket and pulled out the menu he had pocketed at the Hotel Madras.

"Here. Read it!"

The good man took the sheet, put it respectfully to his forehead, looked at it with expert eyes while moving his lips as if he were reading it. Then he carefully folded it up again, pressed it to his chest, and handed it back.

"You spoke the truth. It is written here. You will go see the High Judge which is why I may let you go!"

He turned while greeting us and, together with his men, walked back to town.

Less than an hour had passed and we were sitting in one of our hotel rooms waiting for Walawi. Our visit with the High Judge had been brief. The high official, adorned with pigtail and comb, had received us with a sinister look. However, once Walpole had presented his official papers and had informed him of his relationship with the Governor General of the Indian colonies, he had become almost fawningly friendly. Close to our departure, he addressed the actual reason for our visit. Walawi did not need to fear anything anymore. Lord Walpole, the great *Maharajah* from *Anglistan*, had received his former servant's freedom as a gift.

Walawi finally arrived. He did not yet know anything of the happy end his escape had taken and had, therefore, come only by secret ways and with the greatest caution. The information that he was now totally free did not produce the joyous result I had expected. We were to learn the reason right away.

"*Sidhi*, you are a great lord, and I knew you would rescue me. But what am I to do with the life whose flower has been taken from me!"

"Robbed?" Sir John Emery asked in surprise. "I thought the robbery had failed since you stabbed the robber!"

"My kris did kill him, yes, but while I was incarcerated, a second came and took her away in the night. I was at my hut and learned it there. The junk sailed today, and Koloma, the most beautiful of the women of the *Vayisa* will die in the embraces of a Chinese rat eater. But your servant, *Sidhi*, will dive into the sea where it teems with sharks to have himself devoured!"

Walpole sat quietly contemplating for some time. He finally asked:

"Do you truly love her that much, Walawi?"

"As much as the tree loves light and the grass the dew. I cannot live without her!"

"Shall we bet, Charlie?"

"What about?"

"That Walawi will get his Koloma back. I put up a thousand guineas!"

"You know, sir, that I don't bet."

"Yes, that's true! You are a splendid fellow, Charlie, but you'll never become a perfect gentleman if you continue to refuse a good wager. But I shall prove to you, that I would have won the thousand guineas after all!"

He rose and rang the bell.

"Two *palanquins* (sedan chairs) to the harbor!" he commanded when the hotel employee appeared. Then he turned back to the Singhalese.

"Do you know the junk?"

"Yes. It is the *Jao-dse*. I would recognize it immediately by its patched sails."

"The *Jao-dse*. Fine! Where is it headed?"

"Earlier, I dared enter the harbor and inquired. It is going to cross the Indian Ocean for Canton."

"Ah! You know this for sure?" he asked surprised.

"Very sure!"

"Then its skipper must have a special reason for his hurry. The Passat blows against him and the journey is wrought with great danger, if it's made now instead of the forthcoming season. The junk can't be far yet; we shall steam after it!"

This decision was received with true southern jubilation by the servant. I wished him every joy for the renewed hope that had arisen in him and, at the same time, had to smile how Walpole, as a matter of course, had expected my company.

The rich son of Albion owned one of these wonderful steam yachts, built on the Scottish docks of Clyde. They are famed for their extraordinary speed and are mostly purchased by well-off individuals for their fast ocean travels. He had traveled around the Cape to India and had used it also to circumnavigate Ceylon faster than by any other means possible. After our bills were paid, we entered the *palanquins* to be carried to the harbor.

Our arrival got all hands on the yacht, engaged in whatever celebration, into high activity. The departure from Point de Galle had been set for the following day, which is why no preparations had been made. But it did not take long for water to hiss in the boiler. The anchor winch creaked, the propeller drilled into the resisting waters, and the trim vehicle passed in graceful moves past the other craft lying in the harbor towards its exit. Then we headed out to sea.

Night had fallen, but a brightness lay on the water like the stars of the north were unable to provide. I stood next to Walpole on the raised quarter deck. He had once more become the taciturn man, here and there calling only one of his brief, sharp commands across the deck. When we had acquired full steam he addressed the man at the wheel.

"Keep the present course, hard east by south. As soon as we pass Cape Thunderhead have me awakened!"

"Very well, sir! May I ask where we are headed?"

"Don't know it myself yet. We are on a hunt."

"A hunt," the old skipper asked delightedly. "Who are we after, if I may ask?"

"For the junk *Jao-dse*, headed for Canton."

"Ah – – !" the man stretched. "After that fat bath tub? I had a look at it and didn't find it very attractive. It must be carrying a peculiar freight, a very peculiar one! They loaded during the night and were exceptionally quiet and cautious at it. It's unlikely that it was cinnamon, coffee or sugar!"

"We shall find out soon enough! It seems we are putting at least four more knots behind us than the Chinese, and by morning we will be on the same longitude as they are. Then we steer north by east, then north by north, after which, I think, we will surely cut across his sails."

"All right. I think so too, sir! Is it going to be an adventurous hunt?"

"It might come to it. Have grapeshot and bullets at the ready. Good night."

"It will be taken care of. Good night, gentlemen."

We went to our cabins to sleep. There was nothing to be done for the moment. To sacrifice sleep for mere conversation was never the style of the good Sir John Emery.

When we were awakened, bright morning had long since come. Cape Thunderhead with its famous temple ruins already lay far behind us, so that all around us only sky and water could be seen. Numerous sails enlivened the horizon. They belonged to craft, which either hailed from Trinkomalo and

Batticalao or from India, China and Japan, heading west before the favorable Passat. We did not pay attention to them; the *Jao-dse* could not be among them. Our good yacht cut the waters, leaning slightly at a partial side wind, always north by east and around noon turned to north by north. Walpole, who himself functioned as captain, had all sails set, and it was surprising at what speed we now followed exactly this geographic longitude despite the adverse Passat.

The time had come now to send a man up the mast to be on the lookout for the craft whose course we would cross. Walawi asked to take over this post and Walpole gave him permission. He could be sure that the Singhalese would make his utmost efforts to discover the junk.

Among the sailing ships it would be the only one headed east. It was impossible for it to slip away from us. Still, the afternoon passed, and we had gone beyond Cape Palmyra without the Chinese junk having come into our sight. I went to see Walpole who was impatiently pacing along the railing.

"I think the *Jao-dse* has given the harbor master a wrong destination and does some secret business along the coast. You might want to turn, Sir Emery!"

He tossed a finished cigarette over board and squinted ironically at me across his slipped-down *pince-nez*.

"What a good admiral you are, my dear Charlie! You are a mighty fine chap, but you'll never become a perfect gentleman, and you are still far off from being a seaman. Whether the Chinese has landed somewhere along the coast or not, is of no consequence to us. We can only catch him on the open sea. Since we don't know where he has dropped anchor, we would have to laboriously check every bay along the shore. In the meantime he would get away from us, without us being able to say good-bye to him. Nevertheless, I'll turn, but only to cruise between south and north."

"Keep at least a bit closer to land and watch more towards lee. I don't think that a girl robber, conducting his raids in a big way, would dare to enter the busy waters around Batticaloa. He will be found between Batticaloa and the latitude of Dowandara."

"Charlie, you aren't quite as wrong as I thought. Your suggestion has something to it. I shall follow it and put a few more knots to the yacht!"

He picked up the speaking trumpet and ordered his men into the braces, after which the ship turned from north by west to now head southwest. Now the Passat lay fully in the sails, the machine operated at full steam, and we flew before the wind back to Cape Thunderhead, which we had passed earlier this morning.

Walawi still sat up in the lookout. He didn't want to be relieved and remained the firmer at his post when we, shortly after midnight, reached coastal waters south of Batticaloa. Today, none of the yacht's crew rested. The perseverance paid off, for a shout came from the lookout:

"Fire straight ahead in the west!"

"Quickly, reef in!" Walpole ordered immediately, and the yacht headed straight and noiselessly for the coast. The closer we came, the more the fire became visible to those on deck. The sky reddened even more, and finally the flames flaring up from the ground were clearly visible.

"There's a ship, straight ahead of our bow!" Walawi called from up top.

"Is it moving or lying fast?" Walpole asked.

"It was stopped but it's now setting sail."

"Go straight for it, steersman, straight ahead, then turn to its windward side!"

When we came closer to the craft we saw that it was the Chinese junk.

"First mate, get grapeshot ready!" commanded Walpole, which meant he had no intention to let it lower its flag by firing the customary shot across its bow. The steersman concluded this from the command and put the yacht so close to the junk that it could be hailed by voice.

"Machinist, stop the engine; men, ready weapons!"

A peculiar sensation gripped me. We were only eleven men on board the yacht. The junk's crew had to be far superior to us. Walawi had climbed down to us, the flashing kris in his fist.

"Do you want to board it, *Sidhi*?" he asked. "There are only a few men on board presently; the others are just now pushing off from shore."

"Let's see first! Do you understand Chinese?"

"Whatever a skipper needs to know."

"Hail the junk then!"

The Singhalese did. Instead of a reply a shining rocket flew up.

"They gave us a warning signal. They are robbers, burners and murderers. Hoiho! Lay hard alongside for boarding, then push off again!"

The yacht crew followed these orders and went alongside the junk. Only the helmsman and machinist remained on board. The other nine of us jumped across. The Chinese had not dropped anchor, but had only heaved to, and had no more men on board as were necessary to prevent its drift. They were quickly overcome and tied up. Indeed, the ship was the *Jao-dse* we had been looking for.

In the meantime the boats coming from shore had come closer. Their crews had noticed the signal as well as the yacht, which, despite its small size, was not completely hidden by the junk. Since it had drifted away from the junk, they thought this unknown vessel might have had only a talk with their people and did not expect that, instead of their crew, it was us to receive them.

When they reached the *Jao-dse*, we dropped the ladders and ropes. They tied their boats to the ropes and quickly climbed up on deck, leaving their cargo in the boats until they learned the reason for the yacht's presence. They were received with the necessary force. A fight developed which, although costing us a few wounds, ended with our victory. We had to thank the fortunate circumstance that the boats did not arrive all at once, but one after the other, which gave us time to overcome the enemies one by one.

Like the previous captives, they were bound, and taken to the yacht. While this was done Walpole and I climbed down into the boats. They were full of bound women and girls, who told us that their village had been attacked by the Chinese. The frightened men had simply run off, after which the women, as many as could be caught, had been bound and loaded into the boats. Thereafter, the primitive huts of the village had been set on fire.

We inspected the *Jao-dse's* cargo. It consisted of cinnamon, rice, tobacco, ebony, coffee and – kidnapped women. The latter had all been picked up in and around Point de Galle. Among them was Kaloma, 'the most beautiful among the women of Vayisa', as she had been called by her tenderhearted husband. The two people's happiness was immeasurable and just as indescribable were the expressions with which they showed their gratitude to the great *Maharajah* from *Anglistan*.

By dawn all necessary tasks had been completed. A few sails were raised on the junk and it was taken in tow by the yacht. We passed Cape Thunderhead for the second time, but now in the opposite direction. By evening we had reached Point de Galle once more, where our appearance caused quite a stir. It was unprecedented that a small private yacht had dared to tackle a well-crewed 'girl robber'. These junks, coming from China, infested the local waters and, at times, engaged in kidnapping women. However, the *Mudellier* was the most surprised, when we turned the captives from the *Jao-dse* over to him for punishment. He had thought the ship to be a harmless trading vessel and its captain to be an honest man. For this reason and – most likely following a considerable gift – he had our poor Walawi sentenced to death by drowning, for stabbing a crew member of the Chinese junk.

The *Mudellier* conducted himself very amicably towards us and asked Walpole to tell the mighty Queen of *Anglistan* of his wisdom and justice. Walpole promised to do this, while, at the same time, across his mighty *pince-nez* expressed something entirely different than the acknowledgment of that famed wisdom and justice.

We returned to the Hotel Madras, where we received the same rooms we had previously occupied. When we sat down on the divan to, once more, relive our adventure in our minds, the good Sir John Emery suggested:

"Do you realize now that I would have justly won both my wagers?"

"I'm aware of it, but precisely because of it, I do not bet."

"That's no reason. You might once become lucky and win. You are a fine chap, Charlie, but if you are so afraid of losing, you'll never become a perfect gentleman. I'm very fond of you, but must pity you from the bottom of my heart. Make some effort to finally improve yourself!"

12. The Revenge of the Mormon

A Story by D. Jam, a Karl May pseudonym.

Mormons may have been *bête noires* for Karl May, perceived as culprits when their exploits were still fresh and closer to his time. He portrayed them as such as in Herbert V. Steiner's translation of, 'Die Felsenburg', The Rock Castle, and here, in this short story, penned in 1889, then published in 1890/91 in 'Illustrierte Romane aller Nationen. Unterhaltungsblätter für Jedermann' (Illustrated Novel of all Nations. Entertainment Pages for Everybody).

The Rio San Carlos has two sources. One arm springs from the Sierra Blanca, the other from the Mogollon Mountains. Climbing the latter, step by step, ascending from deep canyons, on whose barren ridges grows no tree, no bush, and no blade of grass, one reaches the Montaña de la Fuente, and the spot where water trickles from the rocks. Three Macolla spruce reach skyward there. Behind them the plateau, which in earlier times was grown over with trees of the same kind, drops almost vertically into a narrow, deep canyon. It once had a different name but is nowadays called Cañon de los Cotchisos.

If one hops across the boulders rising above the creek's surface to the edge of the canyon, a view presents itself, which evokes a thought that a terrifying catastrophe once took place there. A square plateau, totally cut off by this canyon and, to the left and right, by similar, precipitous side canyons is seen. Behind it, on its fourth side, sits a giant, sheer rock wall rising to the heavens, from which several small clear streams of water descend. In the Apache language its name is *Selki-tse*, however, the Spanish speaking residents of Arizona know it as Peña del Asesinato. Both mean the same, that is, Murder Rock.

With this small, square high plateau, totally cut off from the rest of the world, one might think that a living being had never reached it, that no one had ever lived there. Yet one can find traces proving that, not too long ago, more than a few people, had lived there. Nourished by the small streams, a forest once stood there, which had burned down. Charred tree stumps prove it. Among them lies the blackened wreckage of simple adobe huts and the remains of half-burned animal and human bones.

What did happen there? What events turned this once so lively locality into a place of death?

Not too long ago two men stood by the three Macolla spruce and looked across the canyon to the forest under whose sun-dried crowns spread the busy life of an Indian *Ko-uah-clar* (village of huts).

205

They were still young, but their faces had a severe expression of affected piety. Befitting it were the tight and long black coats they wore.

"Well then," said one of them. "Do you really believe, Brother Jeremiah, that Brigham Young would marry me to this Indian woman?"

"Most certainly!" the other nodded. "We were sent out to convert these red heathen, who have the same right as we do, to become Latter Day Saints. The equality of right assures you of the consent of our leader."

"Intah-tikila (Black Eyes) is a great beauty and need not hide from the fifty-eight women of our twelve apostles. But her father, the chief, wants to give her only to a brave Apache warrior."

"Did you talk with him yet? Well! Force him and he will ask you to take her."

"Force him? By what means?"

"Kiss her! An Indian woman must become the wife of the one who kisses her in public. Only this can reestablish her blemished honor."

"But you know also that . . ."

"No buts!" Brother Jeremiah exclaimed. "Are we to return as unheard preachers? It would be a shame and no apostle would give us a second look thereafter. You love the Indian woman. Make her your wife. Then she will become a Mormon and be your greatest support in the conversion of her own people – or are you afraid?"

"Afraid?" the other laughed disdainfully. "Before I became a Saint I carried rifle and Bowie knife and caused many a Red and even White to bite the grass. Young didn't give me the name Gideon, the name of Israel's greatest hero, for no reason. Let's go to the village! I shall show you that I do not know fear."

They walked to the canyon's edge which, at the time, was crossed by a bridge made of braided ropes of untanned, smoked buffalo hide, its ends anchored on both sides to the rocks, on which woody cactus plants grew.

This swaying bridge offered the only means to get to the plateau, which the chief of the Cotchiso Apache inhabited together with the greater part of his tribe. Only a single guard was required at the bridge to keep the settlement safe from enemy attack.

A young warrior stood there now letting the two Mormons pass without a word. But his look followed Brother Gideon with a scowl. An expression of fierce hate contorted his bronze face.

The village held several hundred warriors with their families, horses and dogs. The squaws, kneeling or sitting, were busily at work below the trees. They were weaving blankets, kneading clay for vessels, or were pounding maize and barley to flour. Girls and boys either played or trained in the use of weapons. The men, however, lay in front of their huts and looked idly upon the activity of their folks. A warrior would be disgraced by working.

The best adobe hut stood in the village center. Outside its door sat Pesh-itshi (Iron Heart), the chief, speaking with an uncommon friendliness for a redskin with his daughter.

Her slender yet pleasant figure was wrapped in a light, colorful Navajo blanket. Her hair hung in long, heavy braids far down her back, her face having an almost Egyptian cut. But the most beautiful were her eyes, those large, long-lashed, black, velvety eyes with their melancholically serious, dreamy Indian look.

Because of these unfathomable eyes, the girl had been given the name Intah-tikila (Black or Dark Eyes).

When the two Mormons approached, the chief's daughter fled from Gideon into the hut. She knew his intention and hated him for it. She heard the two Mormon missionaries talk of Joe Smith and the Book of Mormon, of New Jerusalem and Brigham Young, of the joys of bliss that Latter Day Saints anticipated after death.

The chief listened quietly like someone who did not put much stock in those words, but would not say so out of courtesy.

Ill-humored, 'Black Eyes' stepped to the window-like opening in the hut's back wall to look out. She saw the bridge guard approach. He had just been relieved and had to pass by the window. Her face brightened and her eyes took on a fervent shine when she stuck her pretty head out of the opening.

He saw her and whispered to her in passing: *"Ti-tshi kenoana!"* (Tonight!)

"Ha-au, shi hahr!" (Yes, my love!) the girl replied.

The Apache daughters have a heart just like other girls. They, too, love and meet with their chosen in places where they need not fear eavesdroppers.

Intah-tikila had given her small, yet, oh, so proud heart away. She felt the urge to look after her lover. Since she could not do this from the window, she quickly stepped to the front of the hut.

"Ah, 'Black Eyes', why do you flee me?" called Brother Gideon. "You are to become my squaw, to be the happiest of the Given!"

Saying his, he embraced her and pressed his narrow, colorless lips onto her full mouth.

Seeing this, the chief jumped up lightning-fast, tore his daughter away from him and shouted:

"You mangy dog, how dare you to soil the pure daughter of the Apache! Onto the ground with you to beg for mercy!"

With that he struck the face of the man dropping him to the earth.

However, Brother Gideon scrambled up at once. Anger made him thoughtless to what he was doing. He forced himself onto the chief and returned the blow.

The effect of this strike was unexpected. Pesh-itshi stood very still, yet his eyes were measuring the audacious man with a scathing look. Then he emitted a shrill scream, which carried across the entire village.

At once his warriors hurried up. A word of the chief sufficed. The Mormons were pulled down, bound and gagged, then thrown into the hut. The gags prevented them from talking with each other.

Two long, long hours passed, then the two were dragged outside into the circle of the assembled warriors, sitting serious and silently around Iron Heart.

The chief turned contemptuously away from Brother Gideon and said to Jeremiah:

"A blow is an insult calling for death and can only be wiped off by the perpetrators blood. The warriors of the Apache have sat in council and decided that the Mormon is to die. They also wanted to kill you, but I spoke for you. You are to witness the punishment, but then be allowed to return to your saints."

The two Whites could not defend themselves. Gideon was tied to a tree and shot without first being put to the stake.

The chief stepped to the corpse, wetted his hand with the flowing blood and wiped it across his face. With that done his honor had been reestablished.

Jeremiah's pockets were filled with provisions. Then he was carried across the bridge, relieved of his gag and ties and let go.

He left without saying a word or looking back. Then he waded down the gorge through the spring's water, following its course down to the second canyon.

Only then did he stop, balled his fists and exclaimed gratingly:

"Revenge, revenge! The blood of this Saint is to come over you! You have taken his body, but I shall send all your souls to follow his, that they will serve him and crawl before him for all eternity!"

He felt his pockets and noticed with satisfaction that they had not taken his knife, which had been kept under his coat. Then he hid in a rock crevice so as not to be noticed by possible pursuers.

He left there at dusk to return to the spring of the Montaña de la Fuente. He stole past the three Macolla spruce until he saw the guard standing by the bridge. He now crept behind a boulder, which hid him entirely. This is where he stayed until the Apache were asleep. Then he would creep up to the guard and stab him. Only by this means would he be able to enter the plateau.

On the other side fires burned in front of the huts and lit the terrain right to the canyon's lip and the bridge. In its light the Mormon noticed that the guard was just being relieved. Its place was now taken by the young warrior 'Black Eyes' had asked to join her that evening.

Time passed. One fire after another was extinguished and the noises of life fell more and more silent. Finally, the last flames died down and deep darkness ruled all around.

The time had come. Jeremiah crept from behind his boulder towards the canyon. Silently like a snake he slithered along its edge towards the bridge which was, at most, twenty paces long.

Just when he had reached it, he heard whispering coming ever closer from across. That meant there were people on the bridge, above the yawning chasm, in the deepest night. He gave way and waited.

Intah-tikila had come to her lover.

However, since they could be surprised by someone from the village, destroying the good name of the chief's daughter, the two used to cross the bridge when her man stood guard and go past the spring. Beyond it was a snug little spot. Although the village was not visible from there, they could talk without worry of being surprised.

While this was a lapse of the guard's duty, it was not a dangerous one. Why guard the bridge? At this time the Cotchiso Apache lived in peace with everybody and, had there been an enemy to creep up, he would have had to pass by the lovers and would have certainly been spotted by them.

Thus the two crossed the bridge tonight and walked to the spring talking with each other.

The Mormon turned and crept after them to assure himself of their whereabouts. After they sat down, he stole back, very satisfied by his observation. Now he did not need to kill the guard. He would recognize the deed Jeremiah was to commit only at the time when it would be too late to prevent it.

On all fours Brother Jeremiah crept across the bridge. He halted once to reconsider his action. He wanted the Apache to perish in flames. There was enough nourishment for a fire. The trees' crowns were dry. Everywhere, dead creepers hung about and the tall, broad Espada grass stood in sapless tufts. If the fire spread quickly, the Indians would be lost.

He pulled his lighter from his pocket and knelt down. A spark glowed and a small flame sprung into the grass to eagerly eat forward. Quickly, the Mormon crept back across the bridge and pulled his knife to cut the ropes holding it. They were extremely tough. He needed all his strength, but eventually succeeded.

When the last strand was cut the suspension bridge slid off and hit the opposite canyon wall with a crash. The only way of escape for the Apache had been cut.

Now Brother Jeremiah's attention returned to the fire.

The small spark leapt into flames that bordered the canyon's side. To the right and left the flames ate their way along the drop-offs and now fiery tongues licked up the first trees.

And all of the Apache slept, relying on the guard at the bridge! But there were other guards, the horses and dogs. The first began to snort and neigh, the second barked and howled. The Reds had to wake up.

Jeremiah ducked close to the rocks to observe his work with devilish joy.

The two lovers could not look over to the plateau, they heard, however, the neighing and barking. They jumped up and hurried past the spring. Across the open gorge they saw the sea of flames already reddening the sky.

Screaming from dismay they ran forward to the bridge, he ahead, she following, looking only at the sea of flames. He arrived at the spot where the bridge had been anchored. In a leap already, he noticed too late that it was no longer there. A terrible, bone-chilling scream and he dropped into the horrible depth.

'Black Eyes' was close behind him, but his scream and fall had warned her. She was able to stop her forward rush and looked, unbelievingly, into the black, yawning abyss.

That's when next to her the Mormon's dark figure rose asking:

"He's down there, your fiancé! And you must follow him! Your entire tribe is going to burn to death and I shall marry you also to death!"

Now her Indian blood manifested itself which, even at this most scary time, did stop her only for a single moment. Jeremiah had not quite finished yet when Intah-tikila stepped back a pace shouting:

"It is you, you monster! Go down yourself!"

Before he could react she leaped against him – a strong push, followed by an indescribable roar from him – and he dropped after his shattered victim.

'Black Eyes' collapsed. She looked across wringing her hands.

The flames were now a single weaving mass. Through it, dark spots ran back and forth – animals and people. The latter stormed screaming from their huts. There was only safety across the bridge, but after only a few paces did they drop, blinded, singed, and burned. Just a few reached the spot where the bridge had been. The fire drove them down into the canyon's depth.

The neighing and barking, the howling, screaming and shouting became less and less and finally fell silent. Only a single voice could be heard, that of the flames: a deep, dull roar like that of a distant, surging ocean.

The crowns of the trees had been consumed. Now the fire attacked the trunks, eating deeper and deeper into them. Brightly glowing smoke swirled skyward to form a mighty black cloud hovering above the conflagration through which occasional sparks rocketed. This cloud appeared to suppress the flames while coming lower and lower. The trunks no longer burned, they only glowed becoming carbonized.

The heat died down too, only here and there did sparks erupt any longer. Then it became night, a terrible night of death, wrapped in thick, suffocating smoke.

When, in the morning, the sun shone on the place of ruin, 'Black Eyes' still sat in the same place. She had no tear, no sigh, no sob, no word for her pain.

The hoarse cry of a vulture woke her from her soul's numbness. She rose and staggered off, down the spring's gorge, down, down, ever farther, until she reached the canyon's bottom after many hours, where the Mormon lay with his victims. There she sat the entire day and the following night by the shattered remains of her beloved.

The next day she showed up, a shadow of her former self, at the Estancia del Trigo. Monotonously and without emotion she recounted what had happened.

She was offered food and drink, but only shook her head. She wanted neither and rejected every comfort offered. Then she left, never to be seen again.

From this day on this rocky abyss is called Cañon de los Cotchisos, the Canyon of the Cotchiso Apache, and the rocky plateau rising from it, the Peña del Asesinato, the Murder Rock.

Karl May – translated by Herbert Windolf

13. The Fire in the Oil Valley

An Adventure in the United States.

The following story appeared in 1894 in 'Der Karawanenwürger und andere Erzaehlungen. Erlebnisse und Abenteuer zu Wasser und zu Land." (The Caravan Strangler and other Stories. Experiences and Adventures on Water and Land), by H. Liebau, Publishers, in Berlin.

Karl May seems to have had a fascination with enclosed, steep-walled basins, which appear in many of his stories and in all three of his 'Oil Fire' narratives, the one at Vanango, in Old Firehand, and in The Oil Fire, the #8 of this collection.

And, while his alter ego, Old Shatterhand, is named Bill Harry in the story below, there are certain similarities with the Great Hunter, and, in every story he rescues young girls.

"By the devil, don't you also notice the perfume, Bill, that's infiltrating my nose as if a three-yard long *stune*[5] had splashed me? I truly don't know what to make of this 'odor of violets'. Might you be familiar with it?"

The speaker of these words was Sam Hawkens, one of the most weathered trappers between the Mississippi and the Pacific Ocean. His companion, a young man by the name of Bill Harry, was very much aware of the smell that was saturating the air for some time now. The frontiersman's question was just a test for him.

"It's possible, Sam, that I know it, but as a greenhorn I'm not interested in educating an old woodsman like you. Open your nose a bit wider. To be sure, it's large and robust enough to deal with this incomparable atmosphere!"

"You're right, sir!" he replied, while he caressingly touched his fabulous sniffing organ. "The nose, which grew onto my mother's son's face, is truly magnificent. But I must confess openly that I'm not at all familiar in this quarter of the heavens. There's this smell of oil, but I see nothing but prairie, which must come to an end for the petroleum to show itself."

He straightened up as far as he could on the back of his camel-legged mare and, with his small, intelligent eyes carefully searched the area ahead of the two horsemen.

"May the devil get your Young-Kanahwa, or whatever you call the creek you want to get to. I don't see a trace of it."

---

5 Stune is a old English word referring to lamb's cress, Cardamine hirsuta, which exudes a strong, sometimes overpowering scent. Three yards long, it would certainly be overpowering.

"It's not possible from here, Sam Hawkens. The river runs through a bluff and I bet my Arrow for your Mary, we will suddenly halt in front of the valley before we are aware of it."

"That would be very desirable. A bit of water would do us good as well as the horses. But forget about your bet. Your Arrow is the best horse ever to carry a true and right frontiersman, which must be said. But my Mary also has her twenty-five characteristics. Although she's lost her hair and, of the figure of this good animal, one might find fault here and there, she's carried me honestly for almost twenty winters. Except for your mustang, one can hardly find an animal, which, despite such an age, can still throw its legs like her. I wouldn't give her away for all the beaver pelts and Indian skins I've pulled of their bodies."

He tenderly patted the long, skinny neck of his *Rosinante*[6], and then sank back to the indescribable position he normally assumed on her sharp-ridged back. Bill knew the old, at times quite obstinate, but otherwise truly excellent animal and therefore approved of Sam's attachment. Anyone who knows what a good horse means to a prairie hunter is not surprised about the uncommon affection both have for each other.

Carrying on in a short trot, they soon saw that Bill's assumption had been correct. They halted before one of those gorges, which cut like a trough through the otherwise very flat terrain. These depressions usually serve as the bed of a little river and are called bluffs. The abruptly and steeply dropping valley ahead formed a narrow pan through which the deep, black Young-Kanahwa flowed. Rushing and foaming, it found farther downstream a dangerous exit between the narrowing rock faces. The entire bottom of the depression was covered by equipment for the production of petroleum. Upstream, very close to the water, a drilling rig was operating. At the center of the valley, a little in front of the production facilities, stood some handsome living quarters. And wherever the eyes roved lay staves, bottoms, rings, and finished barrels, some empty, but most of them filled with the much-desired fuel.

"Great, sir," Sam said. "That's all we can ask for. Isn't that a store there by the river?"

"Indeed, it's something like it. A store, restaurant, distillery, inn and all kinds of other things together. Dismount, Sam. If we don't want to risk our necks, we must descend this steep path leading down there on foot."

"My opinion too, sir. At times the neck is the best thing my mother's son has to take care of."

He followed Bill's example and got off his horse. Only now the figure of the man could be seen in the right light. A stranger would never have seen the daring rifleman in him. From below the melancholically drooping brim of a felt hat, whose age, color and shape would have caused even the sharpest mind some

---

6 Rosinante: Don Quixote's steed, by Miguel de Cervantes.

headache, peered the giant nose from a dense forest of a tangled black-gray beard. It could have served any kind of sundial to throw the shadow. Due to the mighty beard growth and the so lavishly endowed scent organ, only the two little eyes were visible. Yet, they showed an extraordinary mobility and flitted back and forth with an expression of roguish cunning. The small body stuck in an old leather hunting coat, which had evidently been made for a substantially bigger person. It gave the honest Hawkens entirely the appearance of a child, which had, just for the fun of it, slipped into grandfather's dressing gown. From this 'wrapping' looked two thin, sickle-shaped legs. The tasseled leggings enclosing them, the little man must have surely outgrown some twenty years ago. They allowed a look at two Indian boots wherein their owner could have found room and protection during a downpour.

As he slowly and carefully climbed down the narrow canyon trail, leading his Mary by the reins, he resembled more a caricature than what he truly was. However, Bill knew there was rarely a trapper before whom Sam would have cast down his eyes. Once arrived in the valley, he remounted his horse and pointed to the store.

"Let's hurry up, sir. I'm so hungry that I could devour a buffalo, and my thirst is no less. Whom do these oil works actually belong to?"

"They belong to rich Josias Alberts, if I'm not mistaken. He came here from Oil Creek in Venango County and is counted among the first Oil Princes of the Union. We may get to see him."

"I have no longing for a look at him. A juicy piece of buffalo loin is more dear now to my mother's son than ten of these money bags who may stay forever scrawny in their oil broth."

A few moments later, they halted in front of a small house on whose shutters were written in chalk the words, 'Store & Boarding House'. They had not yet dismounted when several men stepped outside. One of them one could immediately identify as being the innkeeper and an Irishman, too. His wooly features let one guess that he was used to exposing the content of his bottles to diligent sampling.

"Good day," Hawkens greeted. "Are you the landlord of this palais, man?"

"I'd think so," nodded the other.

"Might you have something a hungry man can take between his teeth and a sip to happily wash it down with?"

"I'd think so," came in a repeat.

"Well, then keep your legs apart to catch me dismounting, or you'll simply collapse!"

"Hmm, your heap doesn't look to be oversize!" the innkeeper answered, examining the two friends with a half-disparaging, half-suspicious look. "Have you got any money on hand?"

"That's not yours but our business! Or do you think us to be miserable Yambowikos?" Hawkens asked, his eyes flashing.

"Ho ho ho, little man. Don't act so important here," one of the other men cut in, who had stepped next to Bill and was inspecting Arrow with expert eyes. "It's no prairie country here and who ever forgets courtesy will be taught it!"

Hawkens turned around and, with one of his unique looks, took the measure of the speaker. "Hell's bells! That means you, too, are here to study it?"

"Man, watch your tongue, or we'll blue your leather."

"Never mind, man! My hide has seen blue often enough. But why don't you tell me your name, you big fellow you?"

"Everyone can hear it. It's Josias Alberts, and whoever knows it, respects it."

"Well, then we are cut from the same wood. I'm Sam Hawkens, and whoever knows me, respects me. But I think there's a small difference. Anyone can find oil that stumbles into it with his nose. Mine would be long enough for it, but I don't care at all to put it into your sauce. Get lost, Master Petroleum, and don't involve yourself with things which concern only the innkeeper and myself!"

Alberts pale Yankee physiognomy turned blood red upon these words of the fearless small man. Anger raised his figure and with balled fists, he stepped several paces closer to the speaker.

"Lift this dwarf off his horse!" he ordered the others standing around. "Let's rub his nose a bit in pit oil."

Right away, the men set out to follow the request but miscalculated in Sam. A few leaps of his old Mary cleared his back. She was wagging her long ears and lifted her hairless tail stump joyfully in anticipation of the forthcoming brawl. Then he quickly pulled his rifle from the saddle holster. The enigmatic shooting implement looked as if it originated from the previous century and Bill dared touch it only with the greatest caution. But every shot Sam took from its rusty, crooked barrel was sure to be a master shot. He aimed.

"Hold it, men, or you'll get holes in your skin! Sure, it's not prairie land here and your rules may govern in this valley. But I haven't dismounted yet and shall act according to the woodland laws: Whoever comes closer than ten paces will get to taste a bullet."

Indeed, Bill's companion was right, and two experienced prairie men had no reason to be afraid of a small bunch of oil workers. But what use would be a fight? The months of roving the Wild West had taken their toll, which is why their appearance resembled very much that of people who would visit a store or inn without paying their tab. That's why Bill pushed between the quarrelers trying to settle the dispute peacefully.

"Would a gentleman like Master Josias Alberts truly deny two tired hunters to turn in here, who haven't done him any harm?" he asked. "Please, call your men back, sir! We have come to buy ammunition and some provisions and will pay for everything to the penny."

"That doesn't matter to me!" came his reply with a glowering look. "The little one insulted me and must pay for it. But for once I'll make an allowance if you'll fulfill a wish of mine."

"What kind?" Bill asked curiously.

"I saw your horse already from a distance and like it. Sell it to me!"

"I can't let you have your wish. The animal isn't for sale."

"I give you one hundred fifty dollars."

"I won't sell it."

"Two hundred!"

"Not for many thousands! It was a present, which is why it isn't for sale. I said so already!"

"But I want it, and if you don't sell it, you'll have to make it a gift to me."

"Good luck, sir! That sounds rather odd," Bill said with a laugh. "Do you really think to be able to force a frontiersman to give his horse away without which he would be lost?"

"I give you another one."

"Keep what you have. I don't have the least desire for any of your hinnies!"

Bill now saw clearly through Alberts' behavior. His excellent mustang, not having its equal, had caught the man's eye. He had decided already upon their approach to gain possession of it. That's why he had started the row with Sam and was now out to put the prestige he carried here to use for his purpose. An Oil Prince would not – particularly in the Far West – see himself denied a wish. Bill was to see this right away.

"Hinnies! Is that to be an insult?"

"Are your horses such gentlemen, sir, that one can insult them? Why don't you leave? We've got nothing to do with you!"

Turning to the innkeeper, Bill continued, "We need powder, lead, tobacco ..."

"Hold it!" Alberts quickly interrupted. "Don't try. Without my permission, you won't get any of the things you want! I alone am master at the Young-Kanahwa. Dismount and come along with me. If I can deal with you, you'll also be satisfied with me."

"Don't be ridiculous and head off! Landlord, do we get what we need? Yes or no?"

"No!" the innkeeper replied fearfully, seeing himself threatened by Albert's' sharp look.

"Fine! You can have your will and learn what it means to deny a frontiersman the necessities of life he's prepared to pay for. A store is an open place. You are refusing us service and have thus lost your rights. Your place will be closed until we receive what we wish to buy!"

217

"Oho!"Alberts exclaimed. "I'd like to see how you are going to do this?"

"You'll see it in a moment, sir. We simply block the house!"

A wink to Sam Hawkens sufficed. In a moment, the little man had disappeared behind the building to guard the rear entrance. Bill took his Henry carbine from its holster and readied his two six-shot revolvers. The Irishman became frightened. He might have heard before what it means when a rejected frontiersman 'blocks a house'.

"You'll fare badly with that!" the Oil Prince replied.

"Just you wait, sir! Now hear what I've got to tell you: Whoever approaches this door or hasn't withdrawn within two minutes from the house to a hundred paces will simply be wiped out. Now do as you like!"

His weapon in one hand, Bill pulled out his watch with another. He was able to assume this threatening position since his opponents were few and none of them were armed with knife and rifle. The result was just as Bill had foreseen. The men knew that one could fire twenty-five shots from a Henry carbine without reloading. Added to those were twelve revolver shots. At least for the moment, Bill was a man one could not tackle. And barely had the two minutes passed, when he and Sam were in sole possession of the terrain. They did not know if anyone else was still in the house. If that was the case, they could only be people they would not need to worry about, like the wife and children of the Irishman. In any case, they likely witnessed the hostile encounter, but did not show themselves from fear. Of course, the two frontiersmen refrained from entering the house, which would have been an illegal act. They rather confined themselves to observe from outside what might be undertaken against them.

Presently, this was little to nothing. A Son of the West never jokes with a threat once he reaches for his weapon. Alberts knew this. Even if he were able to assemble sufficient manpower to overcome the two hunters, he had to foresee a rather high casualty rate so long as daylight provided a sure aim. He had disappeared with his men and the hunters guessed that he would pay them a visit by evening. This wouldn't take much longer. The sun had sunk already past the bluff's rim and the shadows of dusk were spreading gradually across the deep valley. Hunger and tiredness made themselves ever more felt with the two hunters, but they decided to persevere and teach the inhospitable residents of Young-Kanahwa a lesson.

It became darker and darker. Here and there a flickering light appeared. That is when they heard steps approaching from the direction from which they had originally come. It could not be one of their opponents, who would have made an effort to conceal every noise. Sam had come over to Bill for a moment and, with rifle in position, attempted to penetrate the darkness. His little eyes had some attributes of cat's eyes; even in the night, he was able to see for a decent distance.

"Hold it. It's not a man but a female. I can't make out yet if she's young or old. She has gathered up her dress and wants to get past us. Shall I gun her down? This woman-folk is no good for anything anyway!"

"Let her pass, Sam! Who knows who she is? In any case, she's not one of those out to do us harm."

"Pah, Bill. All women want to do us ill, and the son of my mother could ..."

He was interrupted, for, at this very moment, a mighty thunderclap sounded and, to the hunters, it seemed as if the earth below them had burst apart. The ground trembled and when Bill looked frightened to one side, he saw at the upper valley a glowing stream rise about fifty feet into the air where the drill rig had been in operation. At its top, it spread, flickering wildly, sinking back to Earth, and flooding the sloping terrain with immense speed. Simultaneously, a sharp, stinging gas smell penetrated the lungs and the air seemed to be filled with liquid, etheric fire.

Bill knew this terrible phenomenon. He had experienced it with all its horror in the Venango area, where an oil drill had hit oil. And since, incautiously, some light had been kept burning nearby, the rising petroleum beam, together with the light gases suffusing the nearby air, had caught fire.

"The valley's on fire!" Sam shouted, rushing for his horse. "Let's hurry, Bill, or we'll be fried!"

He spoke the truth. The lights burning at various workstations provided the oil ever more ignition points. The flood of the high-spouting fuel spread with enormous speed across the entire upper valley and had now reached the river.

They no longer thought of 'blocking the house', What counted now was only to save their bare lives. Bill had already one foot in the stirrup, when he heard a plaintive call. Where they had last seen her when the thunderclap had sounded, the female was on her knees. Fright had caused her to fall down and now terror paralyzed her every move.

With a quick leap, Bill was next to her, pulled her up and carrying her, rushed back to Arrow to swing himself into the saddle. Just then, Sam on his Mary galloped down the valley into the night illuminated by the terrible glow. Bill's mustang followed quickly. Its instinct made the use of reins and spurs superfluous. The mountain trail they had come down was closed to them since the glowing stream had already flowed past it. They had to gain height and could find rescue only downstream. But by day, Bill had seen nothing resembling a path, on the opposite, the rock walls came ever closer so that the river had to force itself a foaming exit.

Old, long-legged Mary ran admirably. Bill's stallion could pass her by only a few lengths. The good animals sensed that the danger was increasing by the second. The glowing stream had reached the storage sheds, where the barrels exploded in canon-like shots, immediately spilling and adding their brightly burning content to the ever growing and faster advancing conflagration. The hot air was suffocating. The horsemen felt as if they were being cooked in a pot of boiling water, yet heat and dryness grew at such speed that they eventually thought they were burning inside. Bill thought of loosing his senses, but not only his life was at stake, but also that of the lifeless being lying unconscious before him across the saddle.

The flames illuminated the rock walls sufficiently to see that no path led upwards on the river's other bank. But they had to cross the river nevertheless. Then Bill felt renewed strength, new life pulsing through his veins. But then his horse disappeared underneath him. It did not matter. Across, over there, was all that mattered! He swam like he had never before in his entire life, dragging his load along, an indescribable fear driving him. Hawkens had followed. He heard his groaning behind him.

When Bill reached the opposite bank something panted next to him. "Arrow, you faithful, brave friend – is it you?" Bill swung himself up again, along with his burden. Almost crazed from excitement and exertion, they stormed on. Bill no longer knew what he was doing. He left his horse to itself and felt only that it shot forward mightily, jumping gullies in long leaps. Then, gasping and panting, it climbed from rocky ledge to ledge, finally to stand still, neighing happily.

It took a long time before Bill had recovered sufficiently to be able to evaluate his situation. The sky shone blood red, and the exhalation of the unchained element lay in dense, black cloud balls over the seat of destruction. How the horse had been able to climb the steep wall with twice its normal load, where no trail led up, was incomprehensible. It had also served as guide for the good Hawkens, for he lay, although unmoving, quite close to Bill, but, in any case, was alive.

Of course, now Bill first paid attention to the person his faithful Arrow had saved together with him from the heat. It was a girl. She lay before him, cold, ashen and stiff. Had she suffocated in the terrible heat or, later, drowned while they crossed the river? Her light dress was completely soaked, and on her motionless face played gloomy reflections of the fiery rays sparking over the bluff's ledge onto the plain. Bill was greatly embarrassed, since he did not know how he could help. That's when a deep and heavy breath sounded next to him and Hawkens voice asked:

"My God! Have I been roasted or boiled? What's happened to my mother's son?"

Rising slowly, he noticed Bill.

"There you are, Bill! Ah, now I know what happened. The valley's burning and my Mary – by the devil! Where's Mary? I lost her in the water and only ran and climbed after your Arrow. Mary! Mary!! Mary!!!"

A brief neighing answered him some distance away.

"Mary, you old critter, come to your Sam!" the little hunter called joyously. When his camel-legged mare slowly came limping to him, he slung both his arms round her scrawny neck, almost crying. "She's lame, she hurt herself. I think she was driven by the rapids through the terrible narrows down there, and then climbed up below them. Look here, Bill, she's flayed a knee. I will cut a piece off my coat to put a good clean bandage on. Had I only hurt myself instead of her!"

It still took a long time for the blaze to retreat to the upper part of the valley, where the rising beam of oil provided continued nourishment. The girl had recovered, but had not yet overcome her fright and was unable to speak in coherent sentences.

When morning came and the sun rose above the plain, the shine of the flames paled in its golden rays. When they stepped to the edge of the bluff to look over the devastation the terrible conflagration had caused, they were overtaken by a feeling of great dismay and, simultaneously, of gratefulness for their happy and miraculous escape. Everything had been destroyed, everything! What was left of the buildings lay in ruin. The ground looked black and incinerated. There was no trace of life and no human being could be spotted. Those, who had yesterday still been alive and breathed happily, had they all found their end? All of them? But didn't something move over there by the rim? Was it human or animal?

"I'm hungry, terribly hungry," said Hawkens. "I'll have a look if I can shoot something. It may not be anything better than a miserable coyote, which has been lured here from the prairie. But if one can't get some buffalo loin, one is also satisfied with a piece of jackal. Meanwhile, stay with the horses."

He took his shooting implement and cautiously approached the area where they had seen the solitary being. Today, good Sam looked even funnier than he had yesterday. Just like Bill, the heat had also singed all his head and beard hair. His coat, leggings and boots, all made of leather, had, in the change from heat to water, lost their cohesion and, piece by piece, were crumbling from his body. His old felt hat had shrunk so bad that it sat like a burned pancake on his bare head and made the incomparable nose visible in its entire length.

A bit later, he returned in the company of a man Bill immediately recognized as being Alberts.

"I was out of luck!" Sam complained. "There's neither buffalo loin nor a miserable coyote quarter. The animal I was going to shoot was this noble master here, who's searching for his daughter and wails about having lost her. Have him take a look at your miss."

The change that had happened to the proud man was touching, just like the scene that now developed. The girl was his daughter! Yesterday, she had taken a small outing and, on her way home, was saved by Bill's Arrow from otherwise inescapable death. The Oil Prince had lost everything in the terrible catastrophe. Of all living beings only six, four people and two horses, standing together here,

221

had escaped from ruin, and Alberts only because of the circumstance that he had been at a place upstream from the bore hole at the moment of detonation, while the river of fire had taken its destructive route down the valley, down where he had gathered the men who were to attack the two hunters. The unfortunate men had not even reached the river, but on their way had been caught by the flames and been killed.

"You see, Master Petroleum," the still angry Sam told him, "it's always dangerous wanting to rub a certain Sam Hawkens with pit oil. None has succeeded at it yet and you would have done better to put your own nose into that oil. You might have then smelled in time that it wanted to spill from the hole. But that's over now. Let's not think about it any more. You have been punished enough. Let's see that we can get something to eat. Then we'll see if we can be of some service to you."

Alberts sadly shook his head. "There's nothing here, nothing, not a sip, not a single bite. It's far to the next settlement, and we will starve if you don't take pity on us."

Hawkens looked questioningly at Bill, who knew that, despite his peculiar ways, the little man had a good heart and would not abandon anyone in need.

Hence he replied, "That's bad, sir, very bad. The water in the river down there is undrinkable with the oil flowing into it and, for the same reason, there will be no fish any more in the valley. We must therefore walk upstream to catch anything. Let's see about it. What do you think, Sam?"

"That's most likely the best! The miss my ride my Mary. You trade places on your Arrow, and my mother's son will accompany you on foot. By the water, we may find some fodder for the horses. For that matter, we'll also get a course of fish into the thing, hanging presently in my body like an empty tobacco bag. It would be ridiculous if we don't get somewhere, hale and sound, where we find people and a juicy piece of buffalo loin, too."

Said and done! The small group began to move. When they parted from the place where 'blocking the house' had come to such a horrible end, Alberts stayed briefly behind. He was taking a silent farewell from the grave of what was likely the greater part of his wealth. It would certainly require immense sacrifice and a powerful effort to capture the mighty beam of oil, and to cover the losses a single night had wrought. Sam Hawkens was right to make himself the equal of the rich Oil Prince. The two rejected frontiersmen were now respectable people, on whose endurance and experience the fate of the millionaire and his child depended. The Ghost of the Savannah does not suffer the might of the glittering metal, and on the 'dark and bloody grounds', everyone weighs in just as much as the danger he is prepared to face boldly.

14. The Hamaïl

The following story appeared in 1887 in issue #19 of 'Der Gute Kamerad' (The Good Comrade), 'Spemanns Illustrierte Knaben-Zeitung' (Spemann's Illustrated Boys' Periodical).

Karl May certainly knew some Arabic and transcribed the Arabic terms he used into German. Since this story, as well as the subsequent one #15, Ibn al-'Amm, has been translated to English, some terms have been re-transcribed to conform to English language spelling.

May appears to have used a number of Arabic dialect words as spoken in North Africa, which were retained here in their original form, whereas all classical Arabic terms have been updated to those used by contemporary Arabic scholars.

Between *Bir al-Aswad* and *Ain Tajib* hovered, high up in the sky, one of those *Saqr* (falcons) Beduins like to train for hunting. It was not difficult for its acute eyes to spot two groups of horsemen, who, while traveling about several hours of riding time apart, seemed to be headed for the same destination.

The group in the east, moving south, appeared to be a *Qafila* (a trading caravan). It consisted of, maybe, twenty pack camels and ten mounted *Hajjan* (camel riders). Eight of the men were armed the Oriental way and two in the European one. The former carried, in addition to their light-stocked guns, long lances, whose broad and sharp steel points were shining in the light of the setting sun. *Shaykh al-Jamali*, their guide, riding in the lead, was the most dark-skinned of them with almost Negroid and, by no means, confidence-inducing features. The latter two one could have thought to be Europeans. If they were not, then they must be coming from the *Gharb*, that is, one of the North African coastal countries.

High up in the air the falcon emitted a loud, shrill cry. When the leader below heard it, a satisfied smile crossed his, until then, immobile features.

"*Khabir* – Guide, did you hear the bird?" one of the two 'foreigners' called.

"*Na'm, Siddi* – yes, Master," he replied.

"If the falcon were a tame one, there would be people nearby. I think him to be a wild one."

"*Haqq* – so it is!" the guide briefly replied, while something like malicious joy played over his protruding lips.

"When will we arrive at our resting place?"

"*An qarib* – soon."

"And shall we be safe there?"

"*S'lon bi al-Aman*[7] – as in Allah's lap."

The group traveling almost parallel to the other in the west was, in all events, a *Qafila at-Tayyara*, a 'Flying Caravan'. It consisted of fourteen well-armed, dark-skinned men, all of whom were riding very good camels. One of them was a precious gray *Bisharin Hajjin*[8]. Its rider seemed to be the group's leader. He had flung the hood of his white *Ha'ik*[9] back. Like his companions, he was a *Tedetu* of the *Kra'an* tribe. However, his short, wooly hair indicated that Negroid blood flowed in his veins, a fact no one among the *Tibbu* needed to be ashamed of.

He, too, heard the falcon's scream.

"*Ikh, ikh!*" he called, an order causing his *Hajjin* to stop. The others gathered around him. "Al-*Hamdu L'illah* – Allah be thanked!" he said. "Al-*Asward* does guide them into our hands. He succeeded to deceive them. If we now turn straight east, we shall acquire their *Darb* (tracks) and can follow them. I shall call the *Saqr*."

He put a finger to his mouth emitting a penetrating whistle. The falcon heard it despite the great distance and, a few minutes later, hovered above the men.

"*Ta'ahl* – Come here!" the leader commanded.

Obediently, the bird settled on the high saddle knob. It was tied there by a chain and had a leather hood attached. Then the men turned at a right angle from their previous direction to head slowly straight east, their leader always ahead of the group.

When they had traveled for about half an hour, he halted to indicate some distant point and said only a single word:

"*Hunak* – There!"

In the direction he pointed one could see the glitter of lance points. The fourteen men cautiously retreated behind some sand dunes, waited there, and only after some time continued their ride. They soon reached the tracks of the other caravan. The leader had his animal kneel down and dismounted to check them.

"Thirty *Hayawan* (animals)," he said. "They are the ones we are pursuing. At *Bir Fitna* Allah will deliver them into our hands. Then we shall share the plunder and will be richer than ever before. Let us follow them slowly that *Al-Aswad* need not look too long for us!"

---

7 This is an example of North African dialect. In classical Arabic this would be 'Fi aman Allah', (in the peace / security of God)

8 Hajjin is a North African term for camel.

9 Ha'ik is an outer garment of white woolen worn by desert people.

It was obvious that the fourteen riders were a *Gum*[10], a Robber Caravan, and *Al-Aswad*, the guide of the trading caravan was their secret ally. He was to deliver those that had entrusted themselves to him into the hands of the desert robbers. For this purpose he engaged as *Khabir* with the unsuspecting travelers. That the robbers spoke Arabic, not their *Tedaga* dialect, was a sign that they undertook their sinister exploits far beyond the borders of their tribe.

While they followed the tracks the sun had reached the horizon. However, the riders did not halt for the evening prayer. Darkness fell quickly. Then the Southern Cross rose, and by the stars' shine the ride continued until the camels increased their pace on their own. This was an indication that an oasis and water was close. The leader ordered a stop. His men dismounted and lay down to rest in the sand. In that way they waited for several hours until, quite close, they heard the subdued bark of a *Fennec*, a desert fox. The leader responded, and soon the guide of the other caravan appeared out of the darkness. He was greeted with the words:

"Since one week I did not hear your voice, although we were always nearby. Today, we have arrived at *Bir al-Amwat* (Well of the Dead), where we let many drink death already. Now we will finally learn who are the masters of your *Qafila*."

"They are two rich *Tujjar* (traders) from *Tarablus al-Gharb* (Tripoli), who are carrying weapons, silk and other precious items to *Bornu*. They are accompanied by seven *Bani Riyah,* we need not kill, since they will not defend themselves. I led them from *Temissa* by ways of *Wau* straight into the desert and sent you a message to the *Duar* (camp). They are now sleeping at *Bir Fitna* (Well of Acacias). I will take you to them."

"What are their names?"

"One of them is called just *Abu al-Hamaïl*, because he has two *Qurans* hanging from his neck. The other's name is *Halif Bin Jubar*."

Hamaïl is a *Quran* one purchases in Mecca. To show that one is a *Hajji*, it is carried visibly by one's neck.

"Two *Hamaïls*? Then he has been twice in the city of the prophet and is a very pious man. Nevertheless, he must die today, for we need his goods. Allah will bestow eternal life on him, and I shall dedicate an *Ihram* to him once I get to Mecca myself. My father has also been there twice. He had two *Hamaïls*. One of them he made a present to someone who had saved his life when the *Tuareg-Kel-Tinalkuhm* threatened to kill him. Allah bless him for it in Seventh Heaven. Get ready now, men! *Al-Aswad* will guide us."

Not just once had these men made such an attack. They knew what needed to be done. They took off their white *Ha'iks* whose glaring color would have

---

10 Gum is apparently another North African Arabic expression which, in classical Arabic, would written as 'Qawm'. May's original spelling has been retained since he used it as the title of one of his other stories called, The Gum.

made their covert approach difficult. Also their guns were left behind. Only their broad, sharp, dagger-like *Sakikin* accompanied them. Then they followed their guide to the close-by oasis.

Where the well sprung from the ground, it was surrounded by shrubbery of Egyptian acacia, which is why it had been given the name *Bir Fitna*. The travelers had built a kind of wall from their packages within which they slept. The fire, nourished by dried camel dung, was almost dead. All of them slept solidly after their strenuous ride. Even the guard, crouched in some corner, two lances in hand, had fallen asleep from being overtired. The full moon rising just now from behind the sand dunes illuminated the scenery with southern intensity from which the stars' shine paled. It was to shine the last time for the two traders.

The men of the robber caravan laid down on the ground from which their half-naked, dark bodies were barely distinguishable and crept inaudibly closer. They reached the wall. Lifting their heads, they peered cautiously across. Their leader picked the spot where the two traders had bedded down. One of them lay snoring on his back covered by his *Ha'ik*. The other lay to the left and, even fast asleep, kept his rifle firmly in his hand. Then the leader bent over the wall lifting his dagger for his deadly thrust. His companions were waiting for his stab to conclude the attack with a terrible howl.

But what was that? The Tedetu kept his hand stiffly raised, not stabbing down. His look had fallen on a package by the trader's head. On this well-tied package lay two books – two *Hamaïls*, the sleeper had taken off his neck to sleep more comfortably. They lay side-by-side, the one on the right provided with a strong metal lock on its opening side. The lock's peculiar work was clearly recognizable in the bright moonlight.

"*Assuwal 'an ehsh* – What's the matter?" asked one of the two men crouched behind their hesitating leader. "Stab him!"

"*Allahu akbar* – God is great!" he replied, while his arm dropped. "This is my father's *Hamaïl*. Allah wanted to prevent me from killing my father's rescuer."

"*Waih*! Are you going to let go of this great booty? Is he truly the rescuer?"

"I will learn it right away. If it is truly him, then woe to any of you who dares to hurt a hair on these people's heads or to rob them of the smallest dust grain of their property!"

He now shouted:

"*Hajji Umar Bin Kuwwad Ibn Hanssari!*"

Instantaneously the sleeper was on his feet.

"Who's calling me?"

"Are you the one I named?"

Only now did the trader realize that his camp was surrounded by strange figures. He quickly raised his rifle, but also answered:

"It is me, but who are you?"

"Did you get this *Hamaïl* as a present?"

"Yes, from a *Shaykh* of the *Tibbu* by name of *Arun as-Saleta*."

"That was my father. I am *Nuwad Bin Arun as-Saleta*. The angel of death had reached for you already with his hand when . . ."

"*Allah karim* – God is merciful!" the trader exclaimed fearfully.

"Yes, Allah is merciful. He saved you. We are the *Gum* and you are camped at the Well of Death. My knife was raised already over you when I saw the *Hamaïl*. But now you are as safe with us as if you were in the Tents of the Blessed, you, your companions and your property. And we shall accompany you across the mountains and the *Hammada* beyond. Speak only the words, you must say!"

The attackers stood outside with the frightened members of the trading caravan standing inside the wall. The trader realized the danger from which only these words would save him. And he said it:

"*Dakilah ya Shaykh* – I am the protected one, oh Chief!"

"*Dakilah ya Shaykh!*" his companions also shouted.

"Yes, you are the protected!" replied the robber. "You are our brothers. The *Hamaïl* saved you from death. Now we present you our greeting: *Allah wa sahla wa marhaba* – you are all welcome to us!"

15. Ibn al-'Amm

by P. van der Loewen (a pseudonym of Karl May)

Ibn al-'Amm appeared in 1887 in 'Der Gute Kamerad' (The Good Comrade), 'Spemanns Illustrierte Knaben-Zeitung' (Spemann's Illustrated Boys' Journal).

It is set in the Sudan at the time of the Mahdi uprising, which was eventually eliminated by the British, at the time holding sway over these lands.

Karl May played a bit tongue-in-cheek here with his pseudonym. The German 'Loewe' translates to 'Lion' in English and, to a large extent, this story is about lions.

It was a rather long drawn-out group of *Habaniyya* Arabs and *Fahri* Negroes that moved through *Wadi*[11] *Salamat* towards the *Jabal Marra* Mountains. All of these black or dark-brown men rode donkeys, for in the Sudan the 'Ship of the Desert', the camel, is not at home.

Ahead rode the brave *Rakab al-Saraf,* in English, Giraffe Neck, a name he had received because of the unusual length of his neck. He was a recruiter for the *Mahdi*[12] and was taking this group to the *Mahdi's* brother-in-law, the well-known *Shayk Al Ubayd.*

Using the night's coolness, the caravan had gotten under way before sunrise and, since day had not broken, the faithful had not yet spoken their morning prayer.

This is when *Al-Saghir*, the Little One, drove his animal to the leader's side. He owed his name to his dwarfish figure but was known to be a brave man. He was the only one of the caravan to ride a horse, one of those famous *Garbani*, brought east from Lake Chad.

"Look!" he said, pointing ahead, where, between parting rocky hills, a strip of light could be seen at the horizon, "dawn nears, the time when *Saba Bey* is most hungry. Shall we not be careful and rather camp until he has bedded down again?"

---

11 Wadi - wash, a dry river bed.

12 Mahdi = full name is Muhammad Ahmad ibn As-Sayyid abd Allah. He created a vast Islamic state stretching from the Red Sea to Central Africa and became a great threat to British dominance. He was eventually defeated by a British/Egyptian army under General, later Lord Kitchener, at Omdurman, Sudan, in 1885. Muhamand Ahmad, claiming to be The Mahdi, meaning the Rightly Guided One, in Islamic eschatology a messianic deliverer, styled himself as being The One to gain a large following.

Saba Bey is the Lion. The residents of these lands shy from speaking the lion's name aloud. They believe that the animal will hear it and will thus come closer. This is why *Rakab al-Saraf* immediately made a warning move with his hand and answered softly:

"*Dakhil Allah* – for God's sake! Don't speak so loudly, or the 'Lord of Tremblers' will come running and will tear us both from our saddles! He is said to have his lair nearby, which is why we must pass it in secrecy. Tell the men that they are not to make any noise and should pray the first words of the forty-eight's *Sura!*"

Al-Saghir delivered the command and soon every mouth whispered:

"Truly, a great victory has been granted you, so that God may forgive your sins and will extend his mercy to you, and guide you on the right way, and stand by you with his mighty protection."

Thus the caravan moved on as silently as possible. The banks of the *Wadi* now narrowed. They rose precipitously and, due to a sharp bend, obscured the riders' view ahead.

That's when, suddenly, that deep-throated roar sounded, beginning with a rattle, quickly rising to a terrible strength, then to lose itself in a thunderous roll – the roar of the lion. The Arabs call it *Rad*, that is Thunder, which is why they call the lion the 'Lord of Tremblers'.

Everyone, humans and animals trembled.

"*Allahu Akbar, Allah Karim* – God is great, God is merciful," calls sounded confusedly. "*Kawahm, kawahm* – quickly, quickly, gallop away!"

Instantly, the men took off in a gallop that their loaded pack animals were barely able to follow. The lion's voice had caused multiple echoes, so that it was impossible to know exactly where it had come from. Had it come from up front, from behind, or from either side of the banks?

When the fleeing men came around the bend, the *Wadi* opened, and ahead, where the left bank was lower, one could see the first rays of dawn. This is the time of *Fatiha*, the first prayer, which no true believer may miss or speak at a later time. Therefore, despite their fear, *Rakab al-Saraf* halted his donkey and called in a loud voice:

"*Hayy 'ala al-Sallah* – to the prayer! *Al-Shams*, the light of day, begins to rise. Honor Allah, who has given this light to us!"

He jumped off his mount, the others following his example. Kneeling down, he faced Mecca and, with his hands, made the motions of washing. He loudly prayed the *Quran's* first *Sura*, the others falling in.

The animals stood there panting, with the pack donkeys waiting near a prickly mimosa brush, at the foot of the left bank, from where a narrow side gorge entered the rocks. They seemed to be very uneasy and trembled under their loads, to which the pious, eagerly praying men did not pay attention, however.

The prayer rose in a multi-voiced chorus:

"In the name of the all-merciful God! Praise be there to God, the Lord of the World, the All-merciful, who shall rule to the day of judgment. You, we want to serve, and you we will entreat so that you may lead us on the right path, the path of those who rejoice in your mercy, and not the path of those you are angry about, and not . . ."

The kneeling men did not get any further with their prayer. Already upon their arrival, there had been some soft movement in the mimosa bushes. And now, at this very moment, the terrible roar rose once more in the immediate neighborhood, and not just from one throat, but from several.

For a moment deep silence ruled. The men were frozen in fright. Then the Negro *Al-Rih* was the first to leap up and to scream:

"Help, help! Run away! Run away!"

He ran off. But *Rakab al-Saraf*, the leader's thunderous voice kept intoning:

". . . and not the path of those going astray!"

As a true Muslim, believing in Kismet, that is fate, he completed his prayer despite the monstrous danger. His example had the effect that all the others repeated the words after him. Of course, this did not happen in devout quiet. The men had all jumped up and were fearfully running helter skelter.

Their fear was totally warranted, for an enormous lion had thrown itself onto one of the pack donkeys, had torn it down and, with a single bite, had crushed its neck. A lioness, not much less strong in build, just then threw itself onto another donkey, which attempted to get away with a fearful leap. Another, almost mature male lion appeared that very moment from the bushes and proudly posing, with a deep, challenging roar selected its own victim. In the background a young, but already strong lioness, crept up to another pack animal which, fearfully, had run right towards the danger into the bushes.

The fearful Negro *Al-Rih* experienced the same fate. He had run like mad right towards the old lion and, in the process, had received a mighty kick in the chest from a donkey trying to get rid of its load, that he tumbled to the ground. In an instant the lion was upon him.

The wild scene presenting itself baffled all description. Men and animals ran hither and yon, with the men being pushed over and trampled by the hooves of the animals. Everyone shouted, screamed, called, moaned and clamored at the top of their voices.

The residents of the South are not as cold-blooded and quick-witted as those of the North. That a single man, with sure aim, would courageously and self-confidently face the King of Beasts like the famous lion hunters Jules Gérard and Gordon Cumming, is, to the Southerner, something unheard of and incomprehensible. But then, the men of this caravan were only equipped with old slow-match and flintlock guns, insufficient against such animals.

Only two had not lost their senses – the brave Giraffe's Neck and *Al-Saghir*, the Little One. The latter jumped on his horse, so that he could be seen by the men, and shouted for everyone to hear:

"Don't flee, you men, you heroes! Stay put, you scoundrels, you cowards, you dogs! Take up your weapons, you courageous, you miserable ones! Shoot *Ibn al-'Amm*! He has come with his wife and his two children to devour us and our donkeys. *Allah jenahrl hatha Shaytan* – Allah may damn this devil!"

Ibn al-'Amm means 'Paternal Cousin', which is another name for lion, if one shies from speaking its proper name.

The Little One galloped towards the king lion, jumped off his horse, held his gun's muzzle directly against an eye and fired, just when the lion was crushing the Negro's head. But right away he jumped far aside. The mighty animal jerked and, for a moment, did not move. Then it fell to one side, its limbs sprawling – it was dead.

An indescribable jubilation ensued. The example of the Little One had its effect. The fleeing men gathered and prepared to attack.

"*Ibn al-'Amm* is dead! *Al-Hamdu L'illah* – Allah be praised!" the men hollered. "Kill his wife and his children! Shoot the entire clan!"

One pushed the other forward. The matchlocks started to smoke, shots rang out and bullets whistled about. Of course, of twenty shots only one hit home. But the fever of battle had taken hold of the men and all of them were of the belief that Allah had listed their fates in his Book of Life anyway. Thus they fought bravely.

Obviously, it was a grisly battle. Several men were killed by the animals, many were lightly or seriously injured. But, at last, the lions lay dead on the battle field with badly punctured hides. None of the attackers, except *Al-Saghir*, the Little One, could claim to have fired a deadly shot. The wife and children of the 'Paternal Cousin' expired from loss of blood, the consequence of the numerous bullet wounds.

Now the victors fell upon the vanquished, pulling their hides, kicking them with their feet, spitting on them, and giving them all kinds of abusive names, with which the Arabic language is so richly endowed.

First, the injured were taken care of. Then the dead were covered with rocks so that *Al-Büj*, the mighty bearded vulture, would not devour them. The hides of three lions were cut into many pieces, so that each victor received one as a memento. However, *Al-Saghir* received the skin of *Ibn al-'Amm,* since he had killed him all by himself. This trophy became a heavy burden for his pack animal. The others carried a lighter load.

When the caravan arrived at last at its destination the men's adventure was, of course, trumpeted loudly.

When the *Mahdi, Muhammed Ahmad,* heard of it, he said:

232

"This Negro *Al-Rih* was like the air, cowardly and quick to escape. He had to die, because he did not finish his prayer. Upon the Final Judgment he will tumble from the Bridge of Trial into hell. But *Rakab al-Seraf* is a brave leader. I shall make him *Mulasim* – Lieutenant. And, while the hero, *Al-Saghir*, is of small stature, he is mighty in courage. He is to join my personal guard and receive the honorable name *Abu al-Bunduqiyya*, Father of the Rifle, until Allah calls him from us. *Fi Aman Allah* – God bless him!"

ABOUT THE AUTHOR

Karl May (1842 - 1912) is today hailed a German literary genius. His unequaled imagination gave birth to a whole collection of characters that lived through exiting and realistic adventure tales that captivated generations of German readers both young and old. Yet his writings were never available to English readers.

ABOUT THE TRANSLATOR

Herbert Windolf was born in Wiesbaden, Germany, in 1936. In 1964 he emigrated to Canada with his family to provide his German employer with technical services for North America. In 1970 he was transferred to the United States and eventually became Managing Director of the US affiliate. He has translated several literary works from German into English, among which is Karl May's, "The Oil Prince", published by Washington State University Press and "The Treasure of Silver Lake", and other works published recently by Nemsi Books. In addition he has taught a number of science courses at a local adult education center, and has written several science essays and travelogues.

Other Karl May Translations:

Title	Author	Publisher
The Oil Prince	by Herbert Windolf	Washington State Univ. Press
The Treasure of Silver Lake	by Herbert Windolf	Nemsi Books
The Ghost of Llano Estacado*	by Herbert Windolf	Nemsi Books
The Son of the Bear Hunter	by Herbert Windolf	Nemsi Books
Black Mustang	by Herbert Windolf and Marlies Bugmann	BookSurge
Thoughts of Heaven	by Herbert Windolf	Nemsi Books
Winnetou I	by Victor Epp	Nemsi Books
Winnetou II	by Victor Epp	Nemsi Books
Winnetou III	by Michael Michalak	Nemsi Books
Winnetou IV	by Herbert Windolf	Nemsi Books
Holy Night	by Marlies Bugmann	BookSurge
Oriental Odyssey I Through the Desert	by Michael Michalak	Nemsi Books
Oriental Odyssey II The Devil Worshippers	by Michael Michalak	Nemsi Books
Oriental Odyssey III Through Wild Kurdistan	by Michael Michalak	Nemsi Books
Oriental Odyssey IV The Caravan of the Dead	by Michael Michalak	Nemsi Books
Oriental Odyssey V From Baghdad to Stambul	by Michael Michalak	Nemsi Books
My Life and My Mission	by Michael Michalak	Nemsi Books
The Rock Castle	by Herbert V. Steiner	Nemsi Books
Krüger Bei	by Herbert V. Steiner	Nemsi Books
Along Unfamiliar Trails	by Kince October	Nemsi Books
Old Surehand I	by Juergen Nett	Nemsi Books

* abridged